PIERS ANTHONY

KNOT
GNEISS

TOR®
fantasy

A TOM DOHERTY ASSOCIATES BOOK
NEW YORK

KNOT GNEISS

A Tor Book
Published by Tom Doherty Associates, LLC
175 Fifth Avenue
New York, NY 10010

www.tor-forge.com

Tor® is a registered trademark of Tom Doherty Associates, LLC.

ISBN 978-0-7653-6337-4

First Edition: October 2010
First Mass Market Edition: October 2011

Printed in the United States of America

0 9 8 7 6 5 4 3

What was an angel doing here? The place beside the angel was vacant, so Wenda went there. "May I join you?"

"You may," the angel said. "I would like someone to talk with. I am not accustomed to this land."

Wenda sat beside her, Dipper perched on her shoulder. "I am Wenda Wouldwife, and this is my Companion, Dipper."

"I am Angela Angel."

"You are not a Xanth native," Wenda said. It wasn't a difficult guess, as she had never heard of an angel in Xanth.

"I am from Heaven," the angel agreed. "It is one of the Worlds of Ida."

Wenda considered, and decided it was premature to mention that Ida was here, complete with the first moon orbiting her head. Her masquerade concealed that.

"Why are you here?" Dipper asked.

Angela glanced at him, surprised. "A talking bird!"

"I was given the gift of tongues so I could join with Wenda and be useful. I am searching for meaning in my life."

"So am I, in effect," Angela agreed.

"But you're an angel!" Wenda said. "You already have the meaning the rest of us are searching for."

"By no means," Angela said. "Heaven is perfect. There is no challenge there. It is possible to find meaning only when there is something to achieve."

"So you came to imperfect Xanth," Wenda said. "That's so noble."

"Right now it's mostly confusing. I have no idea what to do. I wish someone could tell me or show me."

Wenda was developing a certain feel for the intricacies of the human condition. The angel's story did not quite align. "Please, I don't quite understand. You said you are searching for meaning, in effect. How can you qualify meaning? This makes it seem that this is not precisely what you seek."

Angela looked at her. "I did not want to bore you with my dull story. Heaven already is boring enough."

TOR BOOKS BY PIERS ANTHONY

THE XANTH SERIES
Vale of the Vole
Heaven Cent
Man from Mundania
Demons Don't Dream
Harpy Thyme
Geis of the Gargoyle
Roc and a Hard Place
Yon Ill Wind
Faun & Games
Zombie Lover
Xone of Contention
The Dastard
Swell Foop
Up in a Heaval
Cube Route
Currant Events
Pet Peeve
Stork Naked
Air Apparent
Two to the Fifth
Jumper Cable
Knot Gneiss
Well-Tempered Clavicle

THE GEODYSSEY SERIES
Isle of Woman
Shame of Man
Hope of Earth
Muse of Art
Climate of Change

ANTHOLOGIES
Alien Plot
Anthonology

NONFICTION
How Precious Was That While
Letters to Jenny

But What of Earth?
Ghost

Hasan
Prostho Plus
Race Against Time
Shade of the Tree
Steppe
Triple Detente

WITH ROBERT E. MARGROFF
The Dragon's Gold Series

Dragon's Gold
Serpent's Silver
Chimaera's Copper
Orc's Opal
Mouvar's Magic

The E.S.P. Worm
The Ring

WITH FRANCIS HALL
Prentender

WITH RICHARD GILLIAM
Tales from the Great Turtle
  (Anthology)

WITH ALFRED TELLA
The Willing Spring

WITH CLIFFORD A. PICKOVER
Spider Legs

**WITH JAMES RICHEY AND
ALAN RIGGS**
Quest for the Fallen Star

WITH JULIE BRADY
Dream a Little Dream

WITH JO ANNE TAEUSCH
The Secret of Spring

WITH RON LEMING
The Gutbucket Quest

Contents

KNOT
GNEISS

1

MOOD SWING

Wenda Woodwife Charming was horribly distressed. She knew that a good part of the reason Prince Charming had gone on a royal business trip far, far away was to get away from her. Oh, he still loved her; she knew that. She still loved him, too, and longed to be with him. But lately her moods had become violently changeable, making her unfit to live with. She knew it, but somehow couldn't stop it.

Distressed, she went to the private courtyard and sat on the swing there. It had become her place to think about things, because none of the servants ever went to this particular alcove; she could be alone. The swing was next to a round court called the Social Circle, where people became highly social. Unfortunately this too was isolated; no one visited it.

She pushed her legs forward and leaned back, getting it started. Then she leaned forward, tucking her feet below her, reversing the motion. Soon she was swinging back and forth across the court, so high that she could almost peek over the top of the wall into the next yard. It was exhilarating.

But it didn't solve her problem. What was she to do to save her marriage from her own difficult nature? She had thought that once she found true love, and married, and became a real woman instead of the half woman she had been, everything would be perfect. And for a while it had seemed so. She and the prince had shared so much delight that sometimes she had feared the stones would melt around them. They had surely given the storks a headache from overlapping signals.

Then she had started suffering the moods. One day she would be utterly sweet. Then unutterably sad. Then so cheerful she couldn't stop smiling and laughing, even when there were serious matters afoot. Then unreasonably angry. Or impossibly analytical. She was constantly changing, seemingly at random. Why? She couldn't say. That was frustrating.

In fact it made her angry. So angry she could hardly see straight. "Bleep!" she screamed at the top of the swing and her voice. The dread word bounced off the wall and fragmented, leaving acrid smoke and dropping cinders.

That appalled her. She had never been a person to swear. She liked to think of herself as a nice person, in all the ways feasible.

That was it. She definitely had to do something about it. But what?

What else? She would go ask the Good Magician Humfrey. He would know how to fix it. True, it would cost her a year's service or the equivalent. But if it fixed the problem, it would be worth it. After all, she had been to the Good Magician's Castle before, and knew the way.

She stopped the swing, got off, and hurried to the bedroom, where she quickly penned a note for the prince and left it on the pillow where he would be sure to find it when he sought to kiss her.

Dearest beloved bold handsome prince husband—I have gone to see the Good Magician about my moods. I'll bee back when I can. Dinner is in the kitchen; dew knot go hungry. I wood knot dew that to yew. Hugs, kisses, & unmentionable passion. I love yew, Wenda.

She hesitated, concerned that she was making it too cold and distant. She wanted him to be sure that her feeling for him had not changed. Well, it would have to do. Still, she felt almost unbearable nostalgia and pity for the prince when he returned. He did so like his passion! Sometimes she feared his enthusiasm would break the bed. How would he ever cope with her absence? Tears of regret coursed down her face. But of course this was yet another mood, in her ever-shifting kaleidoscope of emotions. She simply *had* to deal with it.

She left the castle, crossed the moat, and hesitated again. Something had bothered her about the moat ever since she came here, and suddenly she realized what it was: there was no moat monster. A castle just wasn't authentic without a decently horrendous moat monster. She would have to look for one. But now was not the time; she had moods to nullify.

She followed the winding path into the forest. Trees were her second love, after the prince. After all, she had until reasonably recently been crafted of wood herself. As a woodwife she had been in effect an animated carving resembling a shapely nymph—that was a pleonasm, because *shapely* and *nymph* pretty well defined each other—from the front, while she had no back. In fact she had been hollow from behind, showing the outlines of her shapeliness in reverse, inverted. So that when a man clasped her, he felt everything against his front, but his questing hands found nothing behind. That was said to be disconcerting.

Prince Charming had especially delighted in taking handfuls of her rear aspect, when she turned real. Just to be sure it was truly there, he said. She might have thought that after a year he would have developed some confidence about it, but he still insisted on those handfuls. It surely showed how much he valued her, needing constantly to be certain that none of her was missing. Maybe he thought that it could not be lost as long as he kept a firm hold on it. He was certainly conscientious in that respect. He was just so devoted!

She came to the key tree. The forest all around her was perfectly manicured, every tree being large, tall, and without blemish. That was because Prince Charming's castle was the setting for more than one fairy tale, and artists could come at any time to paint scenes from it. It would be humiliating to have it be weedy or otherwise imperfect, ruining the pictures.

The tree marked the boundary between fairyland and Xanth, though the perfect forest extended well beyond it. The path passed by it without pausing, so that strangers would not know. But Wenda knew.

She looked around, just to be sure that no painter was in the area at the moment. Because she was about to climb, and if a painter happened to glance up under her skirt and see her panties he would freak out. That would be embarrassing, because the prince was the only one allowed to freak out on *her* panties. If a painter painted a painting in that condition, the picture might freak out all male viewers—and a few females too. That would never do for a children's story.

She put her small hands on the bark and drew herself up. She could climb very well, because of her wooden legacy. She related perfectly to trees, and they knew it. She shinnied up the trunk until she reached the first major branch. Then she circled the tree to the opposite branch, and shinnied back down the trunk until she touched the ground.

She turned away from the trunk and looked around. The forest had become a jungle that entirely surrounded the tree. There was a palmetto hand, which was a giant palm of a hand with splayed fingers. There were milk-weed plants with bottles of milk. She was now in the Land of Xanth, where things tended to be literal, and puns abounded. Her native country.

She saw something and paused. There was a stray goblin frozen in place like a statue, his eyeballs crystallized. Oops! She had forgotten to look around before she descended, and he had seen her panties and freaked out. Fortunately goblins hardly counted; the males were normally ugly and crude to the point of disgust, while the females were pretty, sweet, and nice. There was no risk of him painting a picture.

She walked behind the goblin, snapped her fingers, and faded instantly into the anonymous brush. The goblin came back to life, bits of crystal flaking off his eyes. He didn't even know what had happened. Had he caught on that there was a nymph in the vicinity, he would be chasing after her with lascivious intent.

Meanwhile Wenda was making her way to the nearest enchanted path. It wasn't that she needed it for safety, because she was a natural creature of the forest who had no fear of its aspects. It was that the path was the quickest and surest route to the Good Magician's Castle, and she was in a hurry. If she was lucky, she might even find a bicycle.

Yes! There was a Playing Card stand with several bicycles for travelers to use. A bicycle magically tripled a person's traveling efficiency. She selected a nice wooden one with balloon tires, flowery petals, and a banana seat. The balloons were bulky, but they made the bike lighter.

The banana could be peeled and eaten if it got too battered. Bicycles were supremely practical.

There was another woman there Wenda hadn't noticed in her focus on the bicycle. She was dressed conservatively, but there was something odd about her. Wenda couldn't quite place it.

"Oh, hello," the woman said, startled. "I was just trying to make sense of these devices. Do you happen to know what they are for?"

"Yes. They are bicycles. They triple yewr walking efficiency."

"Oh, good! I need to go see the Good Magician, and this will help." She paused. "I should introduce myself. I am Freja, often nicknamed Freka."

"I am Wenda Woodwife. I am going to see the Good Magician too, because I have such violent moods." She hesitated. "If I may ask—"

"My talent—my curse—is to freak out men when I dress normally. That's why the nickname. I have to show my underwear to snap them out of it. I hate that. I am a modest person."

"I wonder whether a chip of reverse wood wood fix that," Wenda said.

"No it wouldn't. I tried a chip to change my hair color, but it didn't work."

Wenda got an idea. "What did yew dew with the chip?"

"I left it in my hair. It's been there for years. I am still hoping it will work."

"That may bee yewr problem," Wenda said. "Yew never can tell how reverse wood will reverse. It may bee affecting yewr clothes instead of yewr hair."

"Oh!" Freja put her hand to her hair and removed the chip, dropping it to the ground. "That never occurred to me."

"We can test it," Wenda said. "A man is approaching." Actually it wasn't a man so much as a male gnome, but the principle would apply. "Hello, gnome!" Wenda called.

The squat little man paused. "What do you want, woodwife?"

"Please take a good look at Freja here. Is there anything about her?"

"I am Gene Gnome," the gnome said. "My talent is to change living things as they are. But this woman looks perfectly ordinary. She doesn't need any change."

"Pick up the chip," Wenda whispered.

Freja stooped to pick up the chip.

Gene glanced at her, and froze, his eyes fixed on her flexed skirt where it was tightest. He had freaked out.

"Oh, bleep!" Freja swore. She quickly lifted her skirt to show her panties. The gnome returned to animation.

"Drop the chip," Wenda whispered.

Freja did, along with her skirt.

"If that is all, I will be moving on," Gene said, evidently bored. He did so without delay.

"You have solved my problem," Freja said. "How can I ever thank you enough?"

"No need," Wenda said. "I like helping people."

"Now I can go home. It's such a relief!"

"I am glad." And she was.

Freja departed, and Wenda focused on the bicycle. She mounted, put her feet on the petals, and pushed down. There was a burst of flowery scent and the bike moved forward. She was on her way.

After that it was routine. She rode rapidly, and by nightfall was near the castle. She pulled into a weigh station, weighed in, and foraged for a dietary pie. The prince might love her flesh, but she knew better than to get too much of it.

In the morning she weighed out and resumed her journey. Soon she saw the highest turrets of the Good

Magician's Castle. She hoped she would be able to navigate the challenges soon so as to get her Answer. Of course then there would be the nuisance of the year's service. She hoped there would be an alternative service that would take less time, because she wasn't sure how the prince would react to a year's separation. He might even run out of food.

She parked the bike beside the path and walked the last bit of distance to the castle. The Good Magician would be expecting her, of course. Somehow he always saw querents coming, and prepared three relevant Challenges to discourage those who weren't really serious.

Sure enough, there was a robot barring her way. On his chest was printed the word DENT.

She sought to pass by him, but he grabbed her and enfolded her in a metal embrace, seeking to kiss her with his faceplate. What was this? A robot getting fresh with a live girl? That did not compute. Then she caught on. "Robot Dent," she said. "R Dent for short. Yew're ardent."

"Oh, clang!" he swore. "You calculated the pun."

"Well, one learns to dew that, in Xanth," she said. "It's a matter of survival."

He let her go, but still barred her way. Behind him was a pattern of pictures. Now his chest panel said CADE.

"That wood bee Robot Cade," she said. "Arcade. Does that relate to my challenge?"

But already it was changing. Now it said TILLERY, and there was the sound of big guns firing in the background.

"Artillery," she said. "But I'm knot sure what relevance this has."

It changed again. Now it said SENIC, and the robot was looking sickly.

"Arsenic," she said. "Look, we can dew this indefinitely. R ME, R RAY, R REST, R SON, R TERY, R TICKLE, R TIST—what's the point?"

The robot did not reply, except to put another word on: DOR. He advanced on her with ardor.

"I think yew have a screw loose," Wenda said, retreating. "But I dew knot see a gremlin to fix it." In fact all she saw was a bale of old hay. What good would that do her?

Then a bulb flashed over her head. She stepped to the bale, pulled out a wisp of hay, whirled, and jammed it into the robot's front grille. "How hot does that make yew, lover?"

It worked. The robot heated. A wisp of smoke issued from his grille. Then he started running crazily in a circle.

Wenda moved on by. She had used the hay to convert the machine's hay fever and make it go haywire. That was the solution to the Challenge, rather than guessing endless pun identities. Sometimes it was necessary to get out of a particular rut of puns, and find new ones that worked better.

She walked on down the path toward the castle. One down; two to go.

The path led to a playground filled with children. There were swings and slides and seesaws, but the children weren't using them. Instead they were taunting one another. That made Wenda wince. She loved children, but she preferred them to be well behaved.

"I think, I think, you stink, you stink!" a girl cried at a boy.

"You stink worse!" the boy retorted.

Wenda tried to pass through the playground, but the crowded children blocked her. She realized that this was not accidental; it was a Challenge. She had to get past without making a child cry—which was surely not possible without finding a way to get them to stand aside. She had no experience with children, and was sure she would not be good with them. Not until she had some of her own, and learned the ropes. Which made this a nasty Challenge for her.

Not that these were normal children. Wenda saw that the boys were actually composites, formed of masses of slugs, snails, and puppy dogs' tails, while the girls were all sugar and spice and all things nice. No wonder they weren't getting along!

She gazed around the playground. Could she get them interested in the normal diversions? If only to make the children jealous of them?

She went to the nearest swing and sat on it. It was standard hemp for the ropes and beechwood for the seat, sandy like a beach. She pumped her legs and started swinging.

No child noticed.

She worked her way higher. This swing was subtly different from the one at the castle. It did not involve her emotionally in the same way. It was just a swing, with no magic. No wonder the children weren't interested.

Totally ignored, she gave up on that. She let the swing subside, got off, and tried a slide. It was nice and tall. "Wheee!" she exclaimed with a full three E's as she slid down. But she wasn't persuading even herself, let alone the busy children.

She gave it one more try. There was a sidewalk with a hopscotch diagram chalked on it. She sniffed a scotch, verifying that it was fake; they would not really let children use such an adult drink. But the diagram was authentic.

She hopped on it, following the pattern. No girl seemed to notice. They were all still too busy exchanging insults with the boys. Of course that was because boys and girls interested one another, but didn't know how to relate, so they argued instead. That way they could safely interact.

There had to be some other way. Wenda looked around, but saw nothing but the children, the vacant equipment, and a few spaced trees. They lacked leaves;

this was evidently winter, here, if not in the rest of Xanth. One tree had a mass of green in its branches.

Green. That would be mistletoe. That was a forest plant, and she understood it well. And it just might be the key to resolving this Challenge—if the dreaded Adult Conspiracy to Keep Interesting Things from Children didn't intervene. She wasn't sure whether it applied; she would just have to proceed and hope for the best.

She walked to the mistletoe tree and shinnied up its trunk. She wasn't concerned about any children looking up her skirt; they wouldn't think to do it, even if they were paying attention, which they weren't.

She climbed to the mistletoe, which consisted of clusters of toes on green stalks. She grabbed a handful, then shinnied back down the tree.

Back on the ground she set the stalks carefully in the ground, the toes pointed at the children. "Three, two, one, ignition," she said.

The stalks jetted fire, rocketing upward at an angle. They arced to the crowded children, then exploded. Toes went flying like shrapnel, bouncing off the children.

There were screams of surprise, then of horror. Caught by the magic, the boys and girls came together, hugged, and kissed. "Ooo, ugh!" they exclaimed, disgusted. It was clear that of all the things they might ever want to do, this was bouncing at the bottom of the list, or below.

During their distraction, Wenda quietly made her way past them and out the far gate. She had found her way past the second Challenge. But she was sorry she had not been able to interact more positively with the children.

"Two down," she murmured with satisfaction.

The path entered a kind of corral with an unpleasant smell. Wenda recognized it immediately, because it was of a forest creature: skunk. But she didn't see any such creature there. There was only a central pole. How did that relate?

Then she caught on. It was another pun. "Pole Cat!"

Sure enough, the pole shortened and thickened into an odoriferous creature. But it was a lovely cat. This was surely a Challenge, but of what nature?

She stopped before the cat. "Hello," she said in mew talk. She knew all the forest dialects, of course. "Are yew my next Challenge?"

"No," the cat replied in the same language. "*I* am the Challenge, not a forest tree."

Wenda took stock. The cat had evidently mistaken her word. It was best simply to explain. "I am a forest creature, or I was before I married Prince Charming. I speak the forest way; I can knot help it, regardless of the dialect. I said Why Oh Yew, yew. Yew heard a tree. I wood speak the other way if I could, but I can knot."

The cat considered. "Now I understand. I apologize for my confusion. Let's introduce ourselves. I am Pollyanna Polecat, Polly for short, and my talent is making others stink. That's why I'm not popular."

"I am Wenda Woodwife. Or at least I was before I married and got real."

"Ah, that's why you have a backside."

"Yes. I filled out behind when I won the love of a real man, Prince Charming. I dew knot have a talent, being of magical origin myself."

"I beg to differ," Polly mewed. "You surely have a talent, or are developing one, from the time you got real. That's how it works."

"Oh, I dew knot think so. I wood have noticed."

"Not necessarily. You must have a good one, at least potentially. The Good Magician has serious plans for you. He wants you to win through and ask your Question."

"He does?" Wenda asked, amazed. "I am just a regular girl now, with a simple question. I will probably have to serve as a scullery maid for a year."

Polly shook her head. "I doubt it. But you will surely find out for yourself."

"I suppose so," Wenda agreed. "But yew say yew are the Challenge. How is that?"

"My talent. I hate it. It ruins my social life. I came to ask the Good Magician how to fix it, but he wouldn't answer."

"He wood knot answer?" Wenda asked, surprised.

"He said he couldn't use a smelly cat. Instead he made me a deal: serve for a single Challenge, where I might get my Answer without having to serve any more time. So naturally I agreed. And here I am."

"I dew knot understand."

"Just as your special words are inherent, so is my talent. The moment I get frightened or upset, I stink my companion. It's a reflex. It makes it impossible to keep companions. Find me a way to nullify it, so I can maybe find me a tomcat who can stand me, and yowl happily ever after. That is your Challenge."

"That wood bee easy. Yew can use reverse wood to convert the stink to perfume."

Polly glanced at her. "There is something odd about the way you said that."

Wenda smiled. "Sometimes when I say 'wood' it really is wood. I always say 'wood.'"

"Oh. Yes. That's it. But I tried reverse wood. It doesn't work."

"It does knot work? But it reverses anything."

"It reverses in different ways. If I'm in cat form, it reverses me to pole form. If I'm in pole form, it makes me be cat form. In fact it keeps switching me back and forth. So I can't use it."

"Oh, I see. I never had that problem. Let me think." Wenda pondered. How could she get reverse wood to reverse the way it was needed? "There are different varieties of reverse wood. Maybee yew need to try others, until yew find one that reverses the right way."

"I've tried them all. None were right."

Wenda looked around. There in the corner of the corral was a little pile of wood chips. Reverse wood—she could instantly identify any kind of wood. The only reason for it to be here was because it was the answer. She just had to discover *how* it was the answer.

She went to pick up a chip. She had no concern about doing so because it was, after all, wood, and she could handle wood of any type. It simply didn't affect her.

She sorted through the pile, sensing the nature of the chips. Each was from a different tree, with its own flavor. One was subtly dissimilar. "I think yew missed this one," she said. "Try it now."

"It won't work," Polly said dispiritedly. But she took the chip in her mouth, holding it in her cheek.

"Now stink me."

"But you won't like that. It will take hours for it to wear off."

"Dew it anyway."

So Polly let fly with a stink. It wasn't a physical thing, but a feeling. She was supposed to feel stinky.

She didn't. She felt perfumed.

Polly sniffed. "You smell good!"

"Yes. Yew are reversed."

"But how—?"

"I found the different chip. That's all it took."

"But I tried all of them! None worked."

Wenda shrugged. "This one works. Now yew can go court a bold tom."

"Yes, I can!" Polly exclaimed. "Thank you, thank you! You have saved me and won the Challenge."

"Yew are welcome." Wenda was pleased, though she did not think she had done much. Wood was her medium; sorting chips had been almost too easy. Maybe the Good

Magician really did want her to win through. But why? What possible mission could he have in mind for her, that someone else couldn't do better?

She exited the corral. Three down.

She had reached the moat, and the drawbridge leading to the castle. There stood Wira, the Good Magician's favored daughter-in-law. "Welcome back, Wenda," she said. "I'm so glad to see you." That was literal, because though Wira had been blind most of her life, now she could see.

"Yew just like girls with W names," Wenda said, smiling.

"That must be it," Wira agreed. "This way, please; the Good Magician is expecting you."

Obviously true. "May I ask a question?" Wenda asked as they walked across the bridge.

"About the relevance of the Challenges? Of course."

"That robot with the printed pun names—"

"For this mission you need to be inventive. The Good Magician wasn't sure how well you could think outside the box, because for most of your existence you lacked a brain."

"My head was hollow," Wenda agreed without annoyance.

"So it seemed that you just had to guess the puns in the names, but actually you needed to see beyond that. To change the rules, as it were. You did."

"I did," Wenda agreed. She had been half afraid she had cheated. "And the quarreling children?"

"More outside-box thinking. But also, the swing."

"The swing? It was dull. No wonder the children did knot bother with it."

"The swing at your castle is different."

"It does feel different. But how does that relate?"

"It's a Mood Swing. It changes your moods every time you swing on it. That's why you became so changeable."

Wenda's pretty mouth dropped open. "That's why! I never suspected!"

"You hadn't had experience with regular swings before, so you didn't know the difference."

"But that means all I have to dew is knot swing on it. Here I've come for an Answer that will cost me a year's service, when I could have figured it out myself."

"Yes."

"But I have knot even asked my Question of the Good Magician yet. I could just go home now, and avoid the service."

"Yes."

Wenda looked at her, realizing that something more complicated was afoot. "Yew would never make a mistake like that, Wira. Yew told me deliberately. Why?"

"Because it's a truly challenging and dangerous mission that only you can accomplish, and it would take you away from your husband for a long time. It seems unfair to inflict it on you, for such a simple Answer."

"So yew are messing up the Good Magician's plan? I dew knot believe that either."

"He told me to tell you," Wira confessed.

"*Why?*"

"Because this mission has to be voluntary. You have to want to do it, and nobody with any sense would want to. So you are free to go home now."

That was too much for Wenda to assimilate at the moment, so she reverted to the subject. "And the third Challenge?"

"That relates to your developing talent, which makes you uniquely qualified for this particular mission."

"*What* talent?"

"The talent of working with reverse wood."

"But all I did was sort through the chips and find the one the Pole Cat needed. I understand wood, having derived from wood myself."

"No."

Surprised, Wenda looked at her. "I dew knot think I've ever heard you say that word before."

Wira laughed. "You do understand wood, and that's important. But you did not merely sort the chips. Every chip of reverse wood has the capacity to reverse several ways. You fixed that selection, locking that chip into the manner you desired. That's your magic: to guide reverse wood. When you did that, we knew you qualified."

"Qualified for what?"

"The Good Magician will tell you. Remember, you have the right to decline. I recommend that you do."

Wenda shook her head. "I dew knot think that would bee fair. Yew gave me my Answer."

"Well, listen to what he says, then decide."

"I will dew that," Wenda agreed.

They entered the Castle Proper and came to a central courtyard. There was a lovely woman in overalls and gloves, with a bandanna on her hair. She wore a necklace of Rose quartz, with the quartz-sized beads alternating with pintz-sized beads. She was evidently the Magician's Designated Wife of the month. He had five and a half wives, but wasn't allowed to have more than one with him at a time, so they took monthly turns. "Rose of Roogna, this is Wenda Woodwife Charming," Wira said.

"Oh, I'm delighted to meet you," Rose said. "You surely understand plants."

"I understand wood, anyway," Wenda agreed cautiously. "And many of the plants of the forest." She had heard of Rose, who had lived for centuries in Castle Roogna, until marrying the Good Magician. She grew magic roses.

"That should be close enough. My world is roses, but I have encountered one I do not understand. Maybe you can help."

"I doubt I could tell yew anything about roses."

"Oh, I simply love the way you speak! It's so woodsy. Here is the rose." She showed a lovely plant with a single large red rose with blue polka dots. "I received it from a goblin who found it deep underground. I can't make it grow, and fear it will die before I can clone it."

Wenda saw the problem instantly. "That's knot a rose," she said. "It's carved wood, magically animated to resemble a rose."

"Oh!" Rose exclaimed, amazed. "It certainly fooled me."

"I think there's an acceptance spell on it, so that people are dissuaded from questioning it. But I can knot be fooled by wood. That's cut wood, so it will never grow. That goblin is playing an unkind joke on yew."

Rose considered. "Goblins do malicious things. I should have realized. Thank you, dear. I hope my husband can help you as much as you have helped me."

Wira reappeared, which was mildly startling because Wenda had not realized she had departed. "The Good Magician will see you now."

Wenda followed Wira up the dark winding stone stairway to the Good Magician's dingy office. "Good Magician, here is Princess Wenda Woodwife Charming."

The gnomelike figure looked grudgingly up from his huge tome. "Thank you, Wira." Then he focused on Wenda. "What, back again, wood nymph?"

Wenda smiled. He was having his little joke. "Yew saw me coming, Magician. Yew even gave me my Answer in advance, so I could escape the year's service. Yew surely have a reason, unless yew are becoming forgetful in yewr dotage."

He did something astonishing. He laughed. Then he got serious. "The service is to fetch an object and bring it here. Unfortunately it is a difficult object that others can't readily handle. You will find it a challenge too. It is too bad we don't have the man with the talent of Ease."

"Ease?"

"Anything he tried became easy. But we had nothing for him, and let him go. Then we learned of this difficult chore. I do not like to admit mistakes, but that was a bad one. He could have fetched the object without difficulty. It will not be easy for you, but it will be possible."

Wenda was cautious, having been forewarned. "What kind of object?"

"It is a knot of petrified reverse wood, buried for centuries, that was exposed when a new crack opened from the Gap Chasm. It terrifies anyone who approaches it. It must be taken to safekeeping before it falls into the wrong hands."

Naturally petrified wood would frighten people. "But if no one dares approach it, how can wrong hands get it? And what could they dew with it?"

"Goblins could rope it from a distance, or drop stones on it to chip flakes away, which they could carry at the ends of long poles, and fling into neighboring villages to terrify the inhabitants, making them easy to rob, rape, or kill."

"How could I approach it, to carry it? I am knot brave. I wood bee as frightened as anyone."

"Not so. I remind you that this is petrified reverse wood. It has changed its nature, and now frightens rather than reverses, but you would relate to its fundamental nature. It will not affect you."

"Oh. Then I could carry it quickly here, before the goblins learn of it."

"No."

"I dew knot understand. Why woodn't I carry it?"

"Because it weighs, in Mundane terms, about a hundred and fifty pounds. You could not lift it, let alone carry it. You will have to use a wagon."

She was beginning to get a notion of the challenge of it. "Still, if I had a wagon—"

"The intervening terrain is rough. You would have to navigate the wagon through the Gap Chasm, bring it to ground level, then haul it through trackless jungle. Goblins and others would catch on long before you completed the mission."

Wenda made a sudden decision. "I'll dew it. Give me the wagon and the address."

"You are aware that you don't actually have to do it? You haven't asked your Question, and I have not Answered."

"It needs to bee done."

"Then we shall have to do something about your accent, so you can be anonymous. Wira will delve in the cellar and give you a potion to eliminate it."

"A potion will dew that?"

"Yes. It will cause you to say 'do' instead of 'dew,' for example. We got it from a couple who needed a favor, GenEric and GenErica."

"Who?"

"A boy and girl who had the talent of substituting things that would still do the job. In this case, it will make you substitute other words that will suffice, even though they are not the original ones."

"Substitutions will make me anonymous?"

"Yes, essentially. Your forest accent is a giveaway to your nature. Then no one need know your identity, unless you tell them."

"But why wood I need to bee anonymous? I am already thoroughly unknown."

"Less so than you might think. For one thing, you're a princess, ever since you married Prince Charming. People notice princesses. For another, you were part of the party that repaired the gravity cable from Mundania. There are those who remember. For this purpose, you must become an anonymous protagonist."

"A what?"

"A person at the center of a narrative. A viewpoint character. One who sees what is happening, without necessarily governing it."

That was still too complicated for her to comprehend. But at that point Wira reappeared. "Here is the potion."

Wenda didn't wait. She took it and drank it. It tasted like thickened water, and had no apparent effect. "I do not think it's working," she said. Then paused, startled. Then tried again, using more of her words. "I would not do that to you. It would not be fair."

The Good Magician nodded. She was ready for the mission. At least in this respect.

2

COMPANIONS

Wenda petaled her bike along the enchanted path toward the dread Gap Chasm. She had a compass the Good Magician had lent her that pointed toward the Knot. She planned to go find it, then decide how to move it. The Good Magician said the wagon would be there when she needed it, and she trusted that.

Several people came running toward her, along the path. She drew the bicycle aside to let them pass. They looked distressed, as if fleeing something. But what would they have to flee, on an enchanted path? It was guaranteed safe.

So she asked a woman as she ran by. "What are you running from?" It still surprised her to hear herself say "you" instead of "yew."

"The flees!" the woman gasped as she fled onward.

This did not seem to make a lot of sense. "What are you running to?" she asked the next man.

"The Isle of Cats and Dogs," he puffed as he went by. This still did not clarify it much.

"What's at the Isle of Cats and Dogs?" she asked the next person.

"Flee bags!" she responded in the breeze of her passage.

Wenda finally put it together. Flees must be bugs that made people run away, even if there was no life-threatening danger, and they could be stopped by flee bags. It was another of the dreadful puns Xanth was made of.

She resumed progress. Soon she came to a sign saying BEWARE OF BARES. Surely that should be spelled BEARS?

She rode on. The path led to a village where everyone seemed to be bare. It was a nudist colony! No wonder there was a warning. The Adult Conspiracy prevented children from seeing unclothed people, so the sign was there to warn them. It wasn't a physical danger, so the path's enchantment did not bar it. Wenda wasn't sure exactly what was wrong with a child seeing a bare person, but of course the Adult Conspiracy did not consult with ignorant nymphs like her.

In due course she reached the brink of the Gap Chasm. It was every bit as impressive and intimidating as she remembered. The path went up to the very verge of the brink and stopped. She knew there was an invisible bridge continuing on across the gulf, but she couldn't see it. In any event, she didn't want the bridge; she needed to go down inside the chasm to find and fetch the Knot.

And suddenly it struck her, not physically—she was after all still on the enchanted path—but emotionally. What had she gotten herself into? How could she ever tote a boulder of virtual stone that weighed more than she did up out of the awesome gulf? Without anyone else knowing? It was impossible! Whatever had she been thinking of, when she volunteered to do this? She was plainly incompetent. She knew she would mess it up badly if she even tried.

There was only one thing to do: go back and tell the Good Magician she had changed her mind. Or at least realized her limitation. He would have to get someone else to do it, someone with the necessary guts and muscle.

She turned the bike around and started back. Only at this point did she see the dark floating blob of fog that had surely been following her. Fracto! Cumulo Fracto Nimbus, the worst of clouds, always looking to rain on someone's parade. He must have thought to catch her just as she climbed laboriously down into the Gap Chasm, so he could drench her when she was helpless. She had run afoul of him before.

The moment Fracto saw that she saw him, he puffed up hugely and intensified. He sent a cold wet draft of wind down at her. He was angry that she had spied him before he could spring his trap, so now he was going to really soak her. She had to get under cover in a hurry.

She rode the bike as fast as she possibly could, zooming down the path right toward the cloud. There was a campground not far along; she had passed it not long ago.

The storm moved to intercept her, gusting low. This was going to be close. She ducked her head and forged through the early winds, trying to win through before the rain came.

She almost made it. She saw the camp, and its covered shelter, and zoomed right at it without slowing. But the rain caught her just before she got there. In a quarter of a moment she was drenched, her clothing plastered to her body.

She reached the shelter and jammed on the brakes, but they were wet and slipped, and a mean gust of wind whipped her skirt up almost over her head, exposing her panties, and pushed her forward. She veered away before she crashed, lost control, and skidded into the side of the shelter. "Oh!" she cried as she landed. The bicycle slid on past, dumping her unceremoniously by the shelter. She couldn't even see, because there was splash in her eyes.

Then hands were on her, helping her get under cover. Who was it? She hadn't seen anyone. Suppose it was a man, seeing her in such soaking dishabille? What mortification!

"You're safe now," a dulcet voice said. "But I fear you have some scratches."

It was a woman! Wenda was so relieved. "Thank you."

"That's all right. I saw you racing to beat the storm. I was lucky; I flew down here before it caught me."

Flew? Wenda wiped the wet from her eyes, blinked two and a half times, and looked.

It was a winged mermaid. "Oh!" she repeated, startled.

"I'm sorry. I didn't mean to disgruntle you. I do surprise people who first meet me."

"That's all right," Wenda said. "I'm a magical creature myself, or I was until recently. I have met more than one mermaid. But never a winged one."

"We're rather rare," the maid agreed. "I am Meryl Winged Mermaid. But let's get those sopping clothes off you before you shiver to death."

Wenda realized that she was indeed shivering; the rain was icy cold, and her clothing was clinging frigidly. Fracto had scored on her. "I am Wenda Wouldwife," she said, just before remembering that she was supposed to be anonymous. Well, maybe it didn't matter; she wasn't going to fetch the Knot anyway. "Thank you."

"You're a woodwife?" Meryl asked as she efficiently helped Wenda strip. "You don't seem hollow."

"Not anymore," Wenda agreed. "I turned real when I found love and married Prince Charming."

"You married a prince? Then you're a princess!"

Oops, again. Any chance at anonymity had been banished. Wenda was turning out to be not much at secrets. "It's a long story," she said ruefully.

"Tell me!" Meryl said. "I'm sure it's more interesting than my story."

Wenda took her first really good look at her companion. Meryl's wings were like those of a butterfly, shifting colors iridescently as they moved. She had dark red eyes and bright red hair flowing down to her waist. Her tail was the most splendid of all: it seemed to change color with her moods, shimmering pearly white to deep green and blues, wine reds to dark blacks. Overall, she was an astonishingly lovely creature. "Oh, I do not believe that," Wenda said, surprising herself yet again with her accent. She would have to have that spell nullified, as she no longer needed it.

Meryl wrapped a warm blanket around her. "Believe it. Mine is simply told: my father, Foremost Fairy, was negotiating with goblins when they attacked him. He escaped, but was badly injured, so he flew to a healing spring and plunged in. Only it turned out to be a love spring. Unhealed, he lost consciousness and floated down the stream, where he was rescued by Meriel Mermaid. She not only nursed him back to health, she became my mother. Now I'm questing across the countryside, looking for something, though I don't know what."

"A winged merman?" Wenda asked.

"That too," Meryl agreed with a third of a smile. "Now what's your story?"

"I was a wouldwife, hollow behind, about to be raped by a village lout when a giant spider appeared and rescued me. I helped him learn to talk the human dialect. We became friends. By the time our adventure was over, I had found Prince Charming, who—"

"Prince Charming! He was saved by a mermaid, just like my father."

Wenda realized that this was a story a mermaid naturally would know. "Yes. But she decided not to marry him, so I did. That made me real." She felt herself blushing. "He likes my hind side."

"I can imagine," Meryl agreed. "Father still likes Mother's. It's the way men are."

Wenda was feeling a certain camaraderie. "Yes."

"So why aren't you with him now?"

"I had these violent mood changes he had trouble handling. So I went to the Good Magician, and learned it was the Mood Swing. That's a swing in the castle. Now I know to be wary of it. But I still have a service to perform. Or I did."

"Oh? What is it?"

"I don't think I should say. It's supposed to be secret."

"Oh, of course," Meryl said, hurt.

That twisted Wenda's gizzard. She liked the woman, and wanted to be her friend. "I suppose I could tell you, if you promise to keep the secret."

"I do, I do!" the winged mermaid said eagerly.

"It's to fetch a big not of petrified would and bring it to the Good Magician, who can take care of it."

"A big what?"

"A big not of would." Then Wenda realized what she had said. "The spell—it stops me from using the forest dialect. I can't say not. I mean, a bolus, a mass of would. I mean the stuff from a tree."

"You can't say knot or wood?"

"That's what I can't say," Wenda agreed. "Or a buzzing be, or morning do, or a you tree."

"You poor thing!"

"No, it's necessary, because I would give myself away if I said those words my way. It just didn't occur to me that I would need them."

Meryl nodded. "Spells can have unanticipated consequences. You can get your dialect back after your mission is done."

"But I don't think I can do it."

"Because you're petrified!" Meryl said.

"Actually, no. I can handle would. But the thing weighs almost as much as the two of us together, and it's down in the Gap Chasm. I just do not see how I could ever get it out."

Meryl nodded. "I see the problem. It's funny that he gave you that mission."

"I'm just not the woman he thought I was," Wenda said sadly. "I'm sorry to disappoint him, but its better just to confess it and let him find a better person."

"He must have had a reason. I've heard he always knows what he's doing."

"Well, he blundered this time."

Fracto had given up the chase, being unable to get into the shelter. The sky was clear, but evening was approaching. They foraged for pies and boot rear for supper. Wenda liked boot rear, because its mild effect reminded her of her husband. He liked to spank her gently.

"I wonder whether the Good Magician could tell me what I'm looking for," Meryl said as they ate.

"Suppose he blundered?"

"You've got a point. I'll stay away from him."

They slept side by side in the shelter. Wenda realized how much she had missed the companionship of the people she had traveled with the year before. Certainly she loved Prince Charming, and there were servants galore; she was seldom alone. But they weren't friends. It wasn't the same.

In the morning they got up, swam in the small lake, and washed. Meryl was a good swimmer. She folded her wings back tightly and used her hands and tail. Instead of wading back out, she spread her wings and flew. Walking was not for her, obviously.

They dried and dressed. Wenda's clothing was dry and not much the worse for wear, to her relief. Meryl's clothing was a sort of vest that covered her nice bosom, and a skirt that covered her tail. When she propped herself on her tail, the skirt settled to the ground all around, making her look human. The same thing happened when she sat on a chair.

"But I feel best when I'm bare," Meryl said.

"You're prettiest bare," Wenda agreed.

"Yes. But human men tend to stare."

"At least you don't freak them out with panties."

"But my front sometimes freaks them. So I can go bare only when I'm alone, or with women. I was so relieved when you turned out to be female; it would have been awkward with a boy."

"Yes. They have eyes."

"And hands," Meryl agreed. They both laughed, understanding each other perfectly.

They shared a greenberry pie and milkweed pods for breakfast, chatting, getting to know each other. They had things in common, being rare creatures.

"I think I know what I want in life," Meryl said. "I want to accomplish something significant and beneficial to Xanth. Then I could settle down with my winged merman, if I can find him."

"What significant thing?"

"That's the problem: I have no idea. Just something. Maybe like your mission to fetch the Knot, though I don't know how I could help."

"I don't know either," Wenda said. "If I thought I could do it, I'd be happy to have you along. But it's beyond me."

"Well, if you should change your mind, summon me, and I'll come and help any way I can."

"Summon you?"

"Father gave me a bag of tokens I could invoke to summon him when I got lost or tired," Meryl explained. "Now that I'm grown, they can be used similarly to summon me. Here's one." She gave Wenda a small green disk. "Just bite it, and I will feel it and know where you are. It may take me a little while to fly there, but I'll come."

"Thank you," Wenda said, touched. But she feared she would never have occasion to use it.

They hugged, kissed, and separated, stifling tears. Their friendship was new and brief, but it filled a gap in Wenda's outlook and she valued it. Wenda rode her bike south, while Meryl flew east across the forest. It was sweet sorrow.

"You *what*?" Rose and Wira demanded, aghast.

"I can't do the mission," Wenda repeated. "It's too hard for me. I need an easier one."

"But no querent has ever done that before," Wira said. "They always muddle through."

"Maybe that's why the Good Magician arranged it so I wasn't fully committed. He knew I was inadequate."

"Nonsense," Rose said. "He says you're the only one who can do it."

"I don't think I could even move that big would not," Wenda said. "Let alone haul it up the side of the Gap Chasm."

"Oh, my dear!" Wira exclaimed. "We thought you understood. You don't have to do it alone. Nobody does a fantasy quest alone. They have Companions."

"Companions?" Wenda asked blankly.

"Companions. The protagonist travels around, gathering a suitable number, generally five or six. Then they do most of the work while the protagonist gets most of the credit."

"I do not think I would care to do that," Wenda said, still wincing internally to hear her unforestly dialect. "The one who does the work should get the credit."

"Then give it freely," Rose said. "It's not a rule, just common practice."

"But I don't know who would want to join me on so dangerous a mission. Finding five or six seems impossible."

Wira smiled. "The Good Magician anticipated that problem. He provided a name for you to start with: Princess Ida."

"Princess Ida!" Wenda exclaimed, astonished. "I would not have the temerity to even think of asking her! She's an important elder citizen."

"Then decide on one for yourself," Rose said. "Once you have one or two, others will join you on their own. That's the way it works."

"But—"

"Remember how it was with Prince Jumper Spider," Wira said. "You were one of his Companions, for his quest, and you did it on your own."

"Jumper!" Wenda exclaimed gladly. "My best friend. I can ask him!" The thought of traveling again with Jumper buoyed her. The challenge of the mission seemed to become more manageable.

"So there you are," Rose said. "He can surely help move the Knot."

"Yes! When he is big he is very strong." Then she paused. "But he's married now. The Demoness Eris may not let him."

Wira smiled wisely. "She has had a year of him. She may be willing to spare him for a few days while she relaxes."

"Relaxes?"

"He's male. You know how males are with women."

Wenda found herself blushing. "Oh. Yes." Of course she would never say so openly, but there were times when she wished she could go to bed with Charming and just sleep. It wasn't that she didn't love him, just that his love tended to be more repetitively physical than hers. It was surely much the same with Jumper and Eris.

"Of course he may not be easy to find," Rose said. "The Demoness has him hidden away."

"I know how to find him," Wenda said. "There's a secret access he told me about."

"Then you're all right," Wira said.

Before she knew it, Wenda found herself cycling along the enchanted path to the nearest camp. There she parked the bike, then stepped into the surrounding forest, questing for a hypno gourd. She was of course expert in plants of the forest, and quickly found one. She took the gourd, not looking into its peephole, turned it about, and looked at the opposite side, where the stem connected. There, under the stem, was a tiny window. She looked into that—

—and was at the splendid frozen underground realm that had once been the prison of the Demoness Eris, but was now her private estate. The palace was made of glittering ice, with stately columns, snowy roofs, and flat panes of ice for the walls. Yet somehow it wasn't cold. That was part of the impressive magic of it.

Jumper appeared, in his giant spider form. "Wenda!" he exclaimed.

"Jumper!" she cried, embracing his two front legs.

"I'm so glad to have you visit," he said. "I miss you and the other Companions."

"It is not an innocent visit," she said. "I would not deceive you about that. I—"

"Wenda, are you ill?"

"No, of course not. Why would you think that?"

"Your dialect. You're not saying wood, or knot, or yew. It's startling."

Oh. "No, the Good Magician gave me a potion to reverse my accent, so as not to give myself away. You see, I'm on a secret mission."

"But aren't you married to Prince Charming?"

"Yes. That's how it started. But I swung on this Mood Swing, and my moods kept swinging, so I went to see the Good Magician, and he gave me a Quest to fetch a very special not of would, and now I need Companions. It may be dangerous. So will you be my first Companion?"

"I'd love to," Jumper said. "I miss those old days of our association. But I'm not sure Eris will agree to let me go."

"Ask her," Wenda said wisely.

"Well, all right then," he said dubiously. "Eris—"

"It's a lovely mission," the Demoness said, appearing in beautiful human-woman form. "I can spare you for a few days."

"Good enough," he said, surprised. "But will you be all right without me?"

"I will manage," Eris said fondly. "In any event, I'll visit you nightly to tuck you in."

Wenda didn't think she had seen a spider blush before. It must be a rather intimate tucking. That, oddly, bothered her. "I'm jealous," she said.

Eris looked at her. "You miss the prince."

Now Wenda blushed. She wouldn't care to confess it openly, but she did miss that constant attention. It normally didn't take Charming long to satisfy his initial passion, and then he fell right to sleep. So she did usually get to sleep beside him, after that first rush, and she liked that. The thought of sleeping alone did not offer much appeal.

"I will bring him along when I visit Jumper," Eris said, understanding perfectly.

"But won't he be surprised?"

"Not unpleasantly. In seven minutes, when he falls asleep, I'll conjure him back to his own bed without waking him. He'll be satisfied."

That seemed likely. The Demoness understood almost too perfectly. "Thank you."

Eris turned to Jumper. "For this excursion, you'll need some abilities. I'll give you form and size changing, and of course you'll be invulnerable to injury. It's a secret mission, so you should normally travel small."

"But I won't be able to keep her pace in my natural size," Jumper protested.

"You'll ride in her hair, and bite the head off any bugs there," Eris said with half a smile. "No one will notice."

"My hair?" Wenda asked, alarmed.

"Don't worry; he won't poop in it," the Demoness reassured her. "In fact, he'll keep it in order for you. Just make sure he gets off before he assumes large size, whether spider or human."

Wenda realized that the Demoness was being humorous, in her fashion. "Thank you," she said weakly.

Then she was back by the gourd, alone. Eris had conjured them there. Demons were not limited to single talents; they could do anything they chose. But they tried not to interfere with the internal affairs of other Demons, so Eris was staying out of Xanth proper.

Where was Jumper? She looked around.

I am here, in your hair. It was Jumper's voice, sounding in her head. *She gave me telepathy, too, so we could communicate privately.*

"It must be nice having such a partner," Wenda said,

somewhat disgruntled. She had encountered more than one Demon in her day, but they tended to unnerve her. They had such absolute, overwhelming power, and so little conscience.

Actually she's wonderful. She has dedicated her present life to making me happy. That's why she let me go on your Quest. She knew I wanted to travel with you again. Without her, I would have died of old age six months ago. Now I'm virtually immortal. She doesn't want it to get dull.

"Do Demons get bored?" she asked as she returned to the campsite and fetched the bicycle. She didn't get on it, because she hadn't yet decided where to go.

Definitely. That's why they spend so much effort making bets for status with each other. It lends a little meaning to their dull existence.

She was curious, so she asked. "Do you really wear her out with constant physical attention?"

I don't think so. She devotes only about one percent of her attention to me. If I demand too much, such as two percent, she becomes restive.

"Restive? What does she do?"

She turns into a literal cold fish, in the midst of whatever.

Wenda couldn't help laughing. The mental image of him in handsome human-male form intimately embracing a giant cold fish was too much. She almost regretted that she couldn't do that when Charming wanted to have at her when she was sound asleep at midnight. What a surprise!

What next? Jumper asked.

"I have to find other Companions, until I have five or six. They told me I should ask Princess Ida, but I don't think I have the nerve."

There must be someone else, he agreed. *Such as some friend you meet along the way.*

"Meryl!" she exclaimed.

Who?

"Meryl Winged Mermaid. She even said she'd like to be in just such a mission. I'll summon her now."

I don't think I know her.

"I met her during a storm. She's nice. She gave me a token to summon her." She brought it out, put it to her mouth, and bit on it.

The token quivered, and grew warm. It had evidently been activated. *I sense someone's mind orienting on this spot,* Jumper thought.

"Yes. That will be her, flying here. Oh, I'm so glad I remembered. She will be good company."

You will have to introduce her to me carefully. She may not be at ease with spiders.

Wenda hadn't thought of that. "Maybe you should assume normal-sized human-male form for that."

Coming up. She felt him jump from her head. It was a fine long jump, as befitted a jumping spider. He landed on the ground before her, and became a full-sized handsome man.

"Oh!" Wenda said, embarrassed. Because he was nude. Naturally he lacked clothing in his spider form.

Jumper looked down at himself. "Oops. I'll have to find a shoe tree, pants tree, and shirt tree." He was speaking with sound now, no longer needing the telepathy.

"I can find them," she said. She parked the bike and returned to the forest. In two and a half moments she found exactly those trees and blushingly helped fit him with a suitable outfit.

"This reminds me of the first time I assumed manform," he said. "And those naughty twins, Princesses Dawn and Eve, took turns teasing me with their panties."

"I remember. They made you . . . react."

"Yes. Embarrassingly. You never teased me like that."

"I did not find it funny."

"I liked you for that. You were only half a woman, but a whole friend."

"You were a spider, and a friend."

"We are still friends."

"Yes," she agreed simply. It was so good to be with him again, sharing understandings.

They returned to the camp. "There's something flying in," Jumper said, squinting.

"That must be Meryl."

So it was. The mermaid fluttered to a neat landing beside the bicycle. "You summoned me," she said breathlessly.

"Yes," Wenda agreed. "I decided to attempt the Quest after all. This is my friend, Jumper Spider."

"All I see is a freaked-out man."

Wenda looked. Jumper was standing there, frozen.

"Oh, you're bare!" she exclaimed, realizing.

"I can't fly well in clothing. I didn't realize you would not be alone."

"Let me fetch you some clothing," Wenda said.

"Oh, I have my outfit in my purse." The purse appeared, and disgorged a surprising volume of clothing. Soon Meryl was demurely clothed. She leaned against the fence to maintain an upright posture.

Wenda snapped her fingers by Jumper's ear. He blinked, not aware of the passage of time. "This is my friend Meryl Winged Mermaid," she said.

"Hello, Meryl," he responded automatically.

"And this is my friend Jumper, the Prince of Spiders," Wenda continued.

"Hello, Prince Jumper," Meryl said.

"Oh, I'm not really a prince," he protested.

"Yes he is," Wenda said. "We elected him prince, so he could marry the Demoness Eris and free her from confinement. I understand they are very happy together."

Meryl was amazed. "Did I hear a capital D?"

"Yes," Wenda said. "She's a Dwarf Demon, parallel to Demon Pluto. It's a long story."

"It must be," Meryl agreed, seriously impressed.

Wenda took a deep breath. "Now I have to see if I can recruit the Princess Ida as a Companion. I really don't see why she would bother, but Wira said the Good Magician had recommended her. I suppose at worst she can say no."

"A princess!" Meryl repeated, awed. "That Knot must be really important!"

"It is, because it's dangerous," Wenda agreed. "If bad folk get it, they could use chips of it to terrify others into submission. So we have to get it to the Good Magician's Castle before that can happen."

"Maybe Princess Ida knows something about it," Meryl said.

"I suppose so," Wenda agreed. "The Good Magician surely had a reason for recommending her."

"So we need to go to Castle Roogna," Jumper said. "Maybe Princess Dawn or Eve will be there."

"You like them," Wenda said teasingly.

"Yes. Dawn was the one who got the idea to make me a prince, and Eve . . ."

"I heard that ellipsis," Meryl said. "That's always significant and usually interesting. What's in it? Something sexy?"

"There's really no need to go into that," Jumper said uncomfortably.

"And such a demurral means it's really interesting," Meryl said. "And probably romantic. I'm a fan of romance. You have to tell us."

Now Wenda was curious. As far as she knew, the twin Princesses had delighted in teasing Jumper, and they really were his friends, but it had never gone further than that. "What is it?" she asked.

"She seduced me," he said, blushing.

This was news. "Eve did that?"

"It was when we feared the mission was lost. She faced the prospect of becoming the plaything of the Demon Pluto."

"How was she?" Meryl asked mischievously.

"She was every man's desire. I'm really a spider, but in manform . . ." He shook his head. "I know she's a Princess, and a Sorceress, but she's most of all a woman, to me."

"What of Eris?" Wenda asked sharply, suppressing a touch of illicit jealousy. She always liked Jumper, and half wished that she had been the one to seduce him.

"She's everything else. She understands."

Wenda realized that they had gone too far. It was not their business. So she changed the subject. "We must be on our way."

"I'll change," Jumper said. He disappeared, his clothing collapsing in a heap.

"Oh!" Meryl said.

"His natural form is a small jumping spider," Wenda explained, as she felt Jumper land on her hair. "He's riding with me." She mounted the bicycle.

"I'll fly, of course," Meryl said. "Is it all right to strip?"

"It's all right," Wenda said. "He doesn't freak out when he's a spider."

I freaked out? Jumper's thought came.

"Yes," she murmured subvocally, so as not to confuse Meryl as she picked up and folded Jumper's new clothes. She packed them in her knapsack for future use. "When she flew in she was bare-breasted."

That would do it, he agreed. *I have gotten used to Eris in bare human form, but new breasts would catch me unprepared. I thought she appeared rather suddenly.*

Meanwhile Meryl was disrobing and packing her

clothing. She spread her wings and lifted from the ground. "I will track you," she called as she sailed up into the sky.

"Agreed," Wenda called back as she put her feet on the petals. The bike moved smoothly forward.

Actually I do admire her form, Jumper thought.

"But it doesn't freak you out."

Correct. My natural form provides me some objectivity about human things.

Castle Roogna was a reasonable distance away, but Wenda was sure they would make good progress. She loved traveling like this: swiftly and smoothly, and with compatible company. If only she didn't have these foolish notions. Like resenting what a princess did with a friend.

You could have seduced me too, if you had tried, Jumper thought. *But I'm glad you didn't try. I'd rather just be your friend.*

And just like that, her trace of jealousy dissipated. She had forgotten that his new telepathy meant that he was reading her thoughts. "Thank you," she murmured.

Welcome.

They did make good progress, but did not quite reach Castle Roogna before the day expired. Wenda consulted with her Companions, and they agreed to camp for the night.

Wenda pulled her bike into the camp. Meryl dropped down from the sky. Jumper jumped out of Wenda's hair, becoming giant-spider sized.

"Eeeeek!!" Meryl screamed, managing five E's and two exclamation points. She was evidently upset. "A big hairy spider!"

"It's just Jumper," Wenda told her. "In giant-spider form. So we can see him, and not step on him."

"I'm afraid he'll eat me!"

It seemed it would take a while for Meryl to get used

to Jumper in this form. "Maybe you'd better assume manform," Wenda suggested.

Jumper became a man. And promptly freaked out.

"Maybe you'd better put your clothing on," Wenda suggested to Meryl.

"What about him?" the mermaid demanded. "Now he's a big hairy bare man."

"I will dress him," Wenda said, quickly unpacking Jumper's clothing.

Soon both Companions were clothed and able to relate to each other. Form and clothing made all the difference.

They went to the shelter. There were two human beds and a pile of hay. But there were three of them.

"I don't need a bed," Jumper said. "I can resume spider form."

But Meryl was already trying to stifle a burgeoning eeek. She wasn't ready to share lodging with a giant spider.

"I still don't need a bed," Jumper said. "I'll sleep on the hay in human form."

That seemed to be a reasonable compromise. Already Wenda was coming to appreciate the complications of having Companions.

They washed in the local lake, taking turns so that neither Jumper nor Meryl would freak out. They harvested pies and milkweed pods for supper.

Then there was a whirring as a small bird flew in and landed. "Cheep!" he exclaimed, seeing them.

"We were here first," Meryl informed the bird. "Go perch on a branch."

But the bird refused to settle. He stood on the ground and continued cheeping at them. What did he want?

"The gift of tongues," Jumper said. "You gave it to me, Wenda, and it made all the difference. Can you get some for him, so he can tell us what's on his mind?"

Wenda hurried into the forest. She quickly found a clump of the tonguelike plants, and harvested a small one. She brought it back and offered it to the bird.

The bird took it into his beak. "Thank you, wood-wife," he said. "That's what I need."

"Who are you, and what is your business here?" she asked.

"I am Dipper Swimming Bird. I fly, run, and swim. The Good Magician sent me to join your party."

"He sent you!" Wenda exclaimed, surprised. "Why?"

"I asked him how I could get meaning in my life. He told me to become one of your Companions, at least for a while. So I came."

"How can you help us?" Meryl asked.

"I don't know. But I'll try."

That seemed to be it. They had another Companion, if not exactly by mutual choice. At least Dipper would not need a bed; he was satisfied to perch on a convenient rung.

They were about to settle down for the night, when two more people appeared. "Charming!" Wenda cried joyfully.

"Eris!" Jumper cried similarly.

The Demoness had promised to visit and bring Charming too; that had slipped Wenda's mind for the moment. She was about to try to explain to Meryl, but then she found herself alone with Charming in a curtained room sectioned around a bed. He kissed her and caught hold of her backside. First things first, of course.

In seven minutes he was asleep beside her. Then the curtains faded and he was gone. She saw that Jumper was similarly asleep on the other bed. Eris was gone too.

"Fascinating," Meryl said. "What happened?"

"I think we blinked," Dipper said. "Suddenly they were asleep on the beds."

Wenda realized that the Demoness had frozen time

for the remaining two. They did not know the whole or even the half or quarter what had happened. Maybe that was just as well. "I think they are just trying out the beds," she said. "I will tell Jumper to move."

She went and touched Jumper's shoulder, waking him. "You said you'd use the hay," she reminded him.

"Oh. Yes," he agreed, catching on. Then he smiled. "There was a time when you would have said 'Yew said yew'd yews the hay.' I miss that accent."

"So do I. I'll be sure to take it back when the mission is done."

"Something happened," Meryl said suspiciously.

It seemed better to explain. "Jumper and I are married. Our spouses made conjugal visits. You and Dipper were suspended for the duration."

"Conjugal visits!"

"Spouses get restive if neglected," Jumper said.

"I wish I had an ardent spouse," Meryl said.

"Quests can be good for meeting potential spouses. Wenda and I met ours last year during my Quest."

"Just what was your Quest?"

"I had to splice together the cable that brings the magic of gravity from Mundania. Wenda and the Princesses Dawn and Eve helped. It was quite a challenge."

"And you met the Demoness on the way?"

"Yes. It was a convoluted adventure."

Meryl shrugged. "Maybe there'll be a convolution for me along the way."

"It's certainly possible," Wenda said. "Now we need to get to sleep. We may have a big day tomorrow."

They did that without further ceremony.

3

PRINCESS IDA

In the morning, after a bit of maneuvering so that neither Jumper nor Meryl saw the other bare, they washed, breakfasted, and resumed travel.

Jumper turned back to a small spider and jumped to Wenda's hair. Wenda packed his fallen clothes and got on her bicycle. Meryl and Dipper flew into the sky. They were on their way.

But still Wenda wondered: How could Princess Ida, a mature woman of forty-one and a Sorceress, possibly be interested in joining such a motley crew? A woodwife, a spider, a flying mermaid, and a swimming bird. None of them were fully human, while Ida was completely human, and the twin sister of King Ivy. It seemed impossible.

Yet the Good Magician had said to ask her. He had to know something Wenda did not.

The high turrets of Castle Roogna came into view. Wenda quailed, but kept cycling. All she could do was ask.

They came to the orchard surrounding the castle. Meryl and Dipper flew down to join them. Meryl caught

hold of Wenda's bike for support, and Dipper perched
on her shoulder. Evidently the two had gotten to know
each other during the flight, and were getting along
well.

"I'm not sure I should go in," Meryl said. "I'd have
to fly, and that means bare. They might not approve."

Wenda saw her point. Still, she preferred to have her
Companions with her, if only for moral support. What
to do?

"Can Jumper assume other forms than spider or man?"
Dipper asked.

Certainly, Jumper thought to them all, startling bird
and mermaid. *What would you like?*

"Maybe if I could ride, clothed," Meryl said.

"Like a horse?" Wenda asked, intrigued.

Wenda felt Jumper jump off her hair. Then he mani-
fested as a huge four-footed animal.

"A unicorn!" Meryl exclaimed, delighted.

"Solves the problem of clothing for them both," Dipper remarked.

That was true. A unicorn didn't need clothing, and
the mermaid could don her outfit and ride.

Meryl promptly did. In a moment and a half she was
perched sidesaddle on Jumper, fluttering her wings to
maintain her balance since there wasn't actually a sad-
dle. She brought out a comb and fixed her hair, then used
it to clear a small tangle from his mane. It seemed that
mermaid and spider were becoming comfortable with
each other too. It was all a matter of form.

They moved through the orchard in style, Wenda on
her bike, Dipper on Meryl's shoulder, Meryl on Jumper.
It remained an odd party, but now it was a proud one.

Three girls appeared, about fourteen years old. "Hi,
Jumper," the first one said. Evidently they recognized
him in any form.

"Who's your friends?" the second asked.

"And what's your Quest?" the third concluded.

I'm not the Quester, Jumper thought. *I'm a Companion. Wenda's the Quester. You know her.*

The three put their hands to their mouths, covering triple O's. "So we do," the first said. "I'm Princess Melody."

"I'm Princess Harmony," the second added. "We apologize, Wenda. We didn't recognize you, whole."

"I'm Princess Rhythm. Welcome to Castle Roogna," the third finished.

"Thank you, Princesses," Wenda said, half taken aback.

That set them off again. "You didn't say yew," Melody began.

"The Good Magician gave me a spell. Now I can't even say would."

The three burst out laughing. "You sure sound funny," Harmony continued. "Now you're a wouldwife."

"You're lucky Prince Charming didn't notice," Rhythm concluded. "He would have stayed awake longer than seven minutes."

Wenda looked sharply at her. What did this child know of that sort of thing? The princess met her gaze, and the answer was clear: too much. She wasn't nearly the child she looked.

"Princess Ida is expecting you," Melody said, starting a new round. The three always talked in turns.

"She's all packed and ready to go," Harmony added.

"She's hot for adventure," Rhythm wound up.

That seemed unlikely, but Wenda was not about to argue. "Then we shall go see her now."

They approached the castle. The drawbridge was down across the moat. As they started across, a huge serpentine head rose out of the water and eyed them.

"It's okay, Soufflé," Melody said brightly.

"It's Wenda, Jumper, Meryl, and Dipper," Harmony added.

"They're on a Quest," Rhythm finished.

Soufflé nodded and sank back under the water. Wenda was relieved; as a forest creature she was not completely comfortable with sea monsters. But she still did want one for her own castle moat.

The three little princesses showed the way to Ida's room. No one challenged the presence of a mermaid riding a unicorn in the castle; it almost seemed this sort of thing was routine. Jumper navigated the broad stairway with dispatch, his hooves finding secure footing. He knew how to handle multiple legs, regardless of the body.

Ida was indeed expecting them; she stood outside her room, her little moon orbiting her head. She was a matronly woman looking fully as old as she was, with a substantial handbag. "Shall we go?" she inquired.

"But—but we haven't even been introduced," Wenda protested, severely out of sorts.

"Princess Aunt Ida," Melody said. "Meet Princess Wenda Woodwife Charming."

"And her friend Prince Jumper Spider, in unicorn mode," Harmony continued.

"And her Companions Meryl Winged Mermaid and Dipper Swimming Bird," Rhythm finished. "They have a Quest."

"I am so glad to meet you," Ida said graciously. "You seem like a fine group, including the handsome and talented bird."

"We'll get along famously," Dipper said, preening.

"I am sure that will be the case," Ida agreed.

And that, Wenda realized, meant that it was true, or had become true when she said it. Because Princess Ida's magic talent was the Idea. Any idea she approved was true, as long as it was suggested by someone who did not know her talent. Dipper evidently did not know it; the subject had not come up in their dialogue. Could that be why the Good Magician had sent him to join the party?

"But there are one or two details to attend to first," Ida said. "I need to notify my sister, King Ivy, so she doesn't worry about my absence. And I will need to obtain transport, as I'm sure my elderly legs could not keep the pace of a unicorn or bicycle."

She had a point. "Could you use a bicycle?" Wenda asked.

"I fear not. My long skirt would interfere."

Another point. Wenda wore a short skirt, and it stretched tight on occasion. A long one would be a disaster.

They walked toward the throne room. "I haven't been able to speak Human very long," Dipper said. "I know very little about Human affairs. But I thought the King was male."

"The King is an office," Ida answered. "Any qualified person can hold it. The qualifications are being human or close to it, and having a talent of Magician or Sorceress caliber. So when King Dor decided to retire, his elder child, the Sorceress Ivy, assumed the throne. She is thus King."

This intrigued Wenda. "I don't know much about Human affairs either. But isn't she married to Magician Grey Murphy? The father of the three little Princesses? Why isn't he King now?"

"He wasn't interested," Ida explained. "He would rather take over the Good Magician's practice at such time as he retires. Besides, he is foreign born. He's the Man from Mundania. That could complicate it. So that left Ivy."

They had arrived at the throne room. There was King Ivy sitting at a table buried in papers. She looked just like Ida. Her crown was being used as a paperweight. "Whoever thought there would be so much bleeping paperwork!" she exclaimed. Then she saw the visitors, and blanched. "Ooops."

"I'm sure I didn't hear anything," Meryl said, blushing.

Ida cut straight to business. "Ivy, I am joining a Quest, because the Good Magician feels I can help. I wanted to let you know before I departed."

Ivy sighed. "Are you sure you wouldn't rather be King?"

"Quite sure. Here are Wenda Woodwife, Jumper Spider, Meryl Mermaid, and Dipper Bird. I fear I will not be able to maintain their pace on the trail."

"Take a carpet," Ivy said.

"Thank you. I will hope to return it in good condition when the Quest is done."

Ivy stood, and the sisters embraced. For that instant the little moon orbited both of their heads. "Don't lose your moon," Ivy said with a smile.

"I will keep an eye on it."

That was it. Wenda suspected that the parting was more emotional than either sister cared to show.

They repaired to the supply closet. There was a pile of ordinary-looking carpets. Ida took the smallest one. She set it on the floor, then sat on it with her handbag between her knees. In a moment the carpet lifted to about waist height, carrying her with it, and hovered there. She neither moved nor spoke. Wenda realized that an experienced magic-carpet rider could communicate directives without any outside indication.

"We seem to be ready to go," Wenda said, impressed. She realized another thing: the princess would have no difficulty getting down into the Gap Chasm, because she could simply float there. That would surely help.

They moved out of the castle. As they crossed the moat, another huge monster head lifted out of the water.

"Hi, Sesame," Melody called.

"Our visitors are leaving," Harmony continued.

"They're going on a Quest," Rhythm concluded.

The monster head eyed Princess Ida questioningly.

"I'm going too," the princess said. She floated out and petted the head. "Thank you for your concern."

The head sank down out of sight. Obviously the castle was well-guarded. But how was it that the monster had changed?

"Soufflé's shift ended," Ida explained. "So Sesame took over. They wouldn't want to leave the castle unprotected."

"That makes sense," Meryl said. "I'm a sea creature as well as a winged monster. I'll make sure to introduce myself, if I ever have to come here alone."

"Now I trust you know where we are going, Wenda," Ida said gently.

"Yes. The Good Magician gave me a compass that points to it. But it doesn't ensure that the way is clear or easy, so there may have to be detours. And we're not supposed to let outsiders know about the Quest. Only folk we know and trust."

"Naturally," Ida agreed. "This is why I am traveling incognito."

"Um, I don't want to seem critical," Meryl said, "but you don't look very incognito to me. Your crown, the moon orbiting your head, and that magic carpet sort of give things away. Folk are bound to guess that if Princess Ida is along, it's important."

Ida smiled. "Do you have a mirror?"

"I'm female," Meryl said. "Of course I have a mirror." She dug a small one out of her purse.

"Look at my reflection."

Meryl did, and dropped the mirror. "Oh!"

"What's the matter?" Wenda asked, alarmed, stooping to pick up the mirror, which was by the unicorn's hind foot.

"Look at her reflection," Meryl said.

Wenda did. There in place of the princess was an ancient old ugly crone with wispy white hair, gap teeth, and rags. Her tattered skirt fell to the ground; there was no sign of the floating carpet.

Wenda held the mirror up before Jumper's face so he could see too, and finally held it for Dipper. All were amazed.

"I apologize," Meryl said weakly as Wenda returned her mirror. "I forget you are a Sorceress."

"No need," Ida said. "You made a good point. It's a masquerade spell my sister let me borrow from the closet. The four of you see me as I am, but strangers see only the illusion, as does the mirror. Similarly you hear my name, Ida, as it is, but others will hear it as Haggai, or Hag for short. The rest of you are already anonymous, not being well known."

But when we speak your name as Ida, won't that give it away? Jumper asked.

"It will still be heard by others as Hag. It's a competent spell."

"Then let's be on our way," Wenda said, mounting her bicycle, which she had been walking in the castle.

"No need to carry me farther," Meryl told Jumper. "I can fly." Then she paused, reconsidering. "Of course I have to do it bare."

No problem, Jumper thought. *I'll ride with Wenda.*

But Meryl didn't get off immediately. "Jumper, I'm sorry your big spider and man forms freaked me out. I think that won't happen again, now that I'm getting to know you. You carried me; would you like me to carry you? You could get quite a view of things, from the sky."

That would be interesting. If you don't mind having a spider in your hair.

"Not anymore." Meryl spread her wings, lifted off him, and hovered.

The unicorn vanished. Meryl put her head down low. Wenda couldn't see anything, but then came Jumper's thought. *I'm on.*

Meryl flew upward. Dipper joined her. In two and a half moments they were high in the sky.

That left Wenda on her bike and Ida on her magic carpet. "Perhaps this is just as well," Ida said.

"Just as well?" Wenda asked uncertainly.

"We need to talk. I couldn't do it while Dipper was with us."

"Dipper's all right," Wenda said.

"Of course he is. I mean, he doesn't know my talent. So he is free to suggest things I can make come true. That's valuable, and I don't want him to find out any sooner than is needful. As you know, only a person who does not know my talent can make a suggestion I can use."

"Oh. Of course. But he is sure to figure it out before long."

"Yes. Then there will be no one in our little party who can effectively suggest things. We will be limited."

"I suppose so," Wenda agreed.

"But there's another matter," Ida continued inexorably. "I am concerned that someone knows our mission."

"We haven't told anyone," Wenda protested.

"Neither has anyone at Castle Roogna. But I have an intuition that news has leaked."

"Prince Charming wouldn't tell. And neither would Demoness Eris."

"It may be that the number of folk who know it exceeds the critical number, so that a leak is inevitable. It's a rule of magic the Good Magician espouses. It does not mean that anyone is telling, just that the secret cannot be contained."

"I suppose so," Wenda agreed uneasily.

"That means we must accomplish the mission as rapidly as possible, and be prepared for opposition."

"I wouldn't know how to handle opposition," Wenda said.

"We shall simply have to avoid it. I merely wanted you to know it is to be expected."

"This is already more complicated than I expected!"

"There is more. I have been provided with special magic that should help. But it may be awkward to apply."

"I don't understand."

"It is the humidor."

"The what?"

Ida got off her carpet, rolled it up, put it in her handbag, brought out a small box and opened it. Inside were a vial of clear liquid and a glass tube with a sponge in it. "The humidor is a device to keep the interior of the box humid. The vial contains water. When the sponge is wetted, the humidifying action starts. The effect is temporary, but it should enable us to escape from a difficult situation."

"I still don't understand."

"You will, in due course. If there is a crisis, and you see me opening the box, gather the rest of the party in close. This is important. Can you do that?"

"I'll try," Wenda said bravely. She was thoroughly confused.

"With luck, I won't have to invoke the humidor."

But almost immediately the luck went bad. The first sign of it was the return of Meryl and Dipper.

"Harpies!" the bird exclaimed. "A squadron!"

"Carrying baskets," Meryl said as she landed on her tail. "We don't like the look of this."

Their minds are hostile, Jumper's thought came.

"Maybe they're just passing by," Wenda said hopefully.

But they weren't. "There they are!" one screeched. "Bomb them!"

The flight zoomed low, passing just overhead. The harpies passed just overhead, releasing eggs. The eggs exploded as they struck the ground. Balls of putrid smoke roiled up.

Jumper appeared as the giant spider. "We're lucky their aim was bad," he said. "But they'll zero in next time. I'll try to catch the eggs before they strike."

"There are too many," Wenda said. "Some will get through, and hurt us."

Ida brought out her box.

"Gather in close!" Wenda cried. "All together, right here!"

The others didn't understand, but obeyed. They gathered closely around as the harpies turned in the sky, orienting for another pass.

Ida opened the vial and shook a drop of water into the sponge. Immediately mist emerged, expanding into a fog that formed a ball around them. In the fog a door formed.

"Open it!" Ida cried. "Go through it!"

They piled through as the harpies dive-bombed again. Ida slammed the door behind them just as the bombs detonated. They were safe.

"Where are we?" Meryl asked in wonder.

Wenda looked around. They were on a sloping blue field. To one side was a stand of yellow trees. To the other was a red stream.

"I don't think we're in Xanth anymore," Dipper said.

"We are on the world of Comic," Ida said. "I'm sorry we had to come here, but those harpies were ruthless."

"Why were the harpies after us?" Jumper asked. He

remained in giant-spider form, but Meryl was no longer freaking out.

"They know or suspect our mission," Ida said.

"Then why not just go for the Knot? Why waste eggs on us?"

"They don't know where the Knot is. They were out to stun and capture us, so as to make us lead them to it."

"That's not nice!" Wenda protested.

"And they want the Knot Gneiss," Jumper said, radiating a telepathic smile. "Though it's not gneiss."

"So someone has leaked," Wenda said.

"Isn't that a bad word?" Meryl asked.

"Very bad," Wenda said. "It means that someone who knows our Quest has told others, so that now there are wrong hands eager to have the Not fall into them."

"Who would do that?" Meryl asked, frowning.

"Oops," Jumper said.

"Not you!" Wenda said sharply.

"Not me. But when we passed Sesame Serpent, the moat monster, I caught an awareness in her mind. I think Soufflé told her, so she would know not to eat us, and she did not realize it was supposed to be secret."

"So it got out among monsters," Meryl said. "And to the winged monsters. We do like to gossip."

"You call yourself a winged monster," Wenda said, "but you're beautiful."

"It's not an insult. Dragons, griffins, rocs, harpies, fairies, winged centaurs, crossbreeds like me—we're all winged monsters, and proud of it. We're all beautiful to each other."

"Harpies think they're beautiful?" Wenda asked.

"Oh, yes! It's just that some other species don't properly appreciate them."

"As we don't," Ida said. "Not at the moment, at least."

"So now we know what we're in for," Wenda said.

"But about this world—Comic, you called it?—we can't stay here if we want to accomplish the Quest. Is there a door back to Xanth?"

"There are many doors to Xanth," Ida said. "But reaching them is awkward."

"Awkward?"

"They are cunningly hidden in the Strips."

"I've heard of those," Meryl said. "Hopelessly infested with abysmal puns. But aren't they on your moon, Terra?"

"Ptero," Ida said. "Yes they are, as boundaries. But Comic is a sister world where the great majority of the Strips exist. It's almost unpopulated, for some reason."

"I can't think why," Meryl said, and the others laughed. Puns were a natural part of Xanth, but the Strips were so concentrated nobody could stand them for long.

"So the Good Magician deemed this world a good place to put the Doors, as they would not be abused by others. They serve as a way to escape difficult situations. The return Doors open randomly in Xanth, so they are not convenient for traveling; a person would be lucky to find himself anywhere near his destination. But when there is danger, they can be useful."

"That's why you're on this Quest!" Dipper explained. "To help us escape danger!"

"Yes, in part," Ida agreed.

Wenda kept silent. It was important that Dipper not know about Ida's talent of making Ideas come true. She was a full Sorceress, though she did not act like it.

"And you just did that by conjuring the Door that brought us here," Jumper said. "But we shouldn't dawdle here too long."

"Actually it doesn't matter," Ida said. "Time is frozen. That is, when we return to Xanth, no time will have passed. That's part of the magic. We could remain here for months, and it wouldn't make a difference there."

"Something else," Meryl said. "If this is a sister world to Ptero, how can you be here? Isn't it orbiting your head?"

"That is complicated to explain completely," Ida said. "But I will try to simplify it. Ptero looks small, and for a long time we thought it really was small, but actually it's a full-size world. People on it see another world orbiting the head of Ida on it, and so on, each tiny in comparison. But appearance is not reality; via the magic of perspective they look small in the distance, but are not. They form a phenomenal loop, so it is possible to complete it and return to Xanth. I have done it. They can be visited conveniently by souls, but it is also possible to travel to them physically with the right magic. So the Doors are a way. I retain my connection to the chain via the image of Ptero, but that does not limit me."

"Okay," Meryl agreed uncertainly. Wenda could appreciate why; this was indeed complicated.

"Still, we have no reason to delay," Jumper said. "We have to return to Xanth and complete our mission. We may not know where we will land, but once there we should be able to find our way."

"We surely will," Ida said agreeably. But Wenda knew that this wasn't guaranteed, because Jumper knew Ida's talent. His suggestion would not magically become reality. Not unless Dipper suggested it. And they couldn't ask the bird to do that; it was too likely to give away the talent.

Ida brought out her carpet, unrolled it, and got on it. They walked, floated, and flew toward the nearest Comic Strip. "In there?" Meryl asked dubiously.

"We need to find a Sidewalk," Ida said, putting away her carpet again. She seemed to feel that the carpet would be more of a liability than an asset in the Strip. "Then we walk sidewise to find the Door."

"Have any of you been in a Comic Strip before?" Ida asked.

None had.

"Then I need to warn you that it rapidly becomes tiresome. Fortunately the Strips are not deep; if you feel overwhelmed, try to get outside, and the effects will cease. Meanwhile we will need to stay grouped, so that we can go through the Door together, because once a Door is used, and closes, it orients on a different spot in Xanth. We don't want to get separated."

The others shared a glance of agreement. Still, Wenda didn't see what could be so bad about innocent puns. They might be annoying or embarrassing or inconvenient, but surely they were harmless.

"Maybe we should link hands," Meryl suggested. "Then two others can pull me along just above the ground."

"I would have to change form," Jumper said.

"Maybe I can handle that now."

He assumed naked manform. Meryl took one hand and Wenda took the other. Ida took Wenda's free hand. Neither Meryl nor Ida looked directly at Jumper.

"I can't change form," Dipper said.

"Perch on my shoulder," Wenda said. "And don't let go."

Dipper flew to her and perched.

Thus linked, they stepped across the marked border that delineated the Strip.

Immediately they were in a patch of green, yellow, and red plants that were shaped like pepper mills. They were flinging up colored coins, which puffed into clouds of dust.

Wenda took a breath—and choked. It was pepper!

Then all of them were coughing and sneezing violently, their eyes tearing so badly it was impossible to see. But they dared not let go of one another, lest they get separated in the Strip and be lost. Whatever they suffered here, they had to be together.

They had to get out of this pepper patch. But how, when they couldn't even see?

"This—*sneeze!*—is peppermint!" Meryl exclaimed. "Minting—*sneeze!*—coins! We have to—*sneeze!*—nullify it!"

"But—*sneeze!*—how?" Wenda demanded.

"I have a—*sneeze!*—idea," Dipper said. He was not immune to the clouds of pepper. "Find a—*sneeze!*—salt mint."

"But we can't—*sneeze!*—let go of each—*sneeze!*—other," Meryl protested.

"I will—*sneeze!*—have to change," Jumper said. Then his hand in Wenda's hand changed to the foot of the giant spider.

Through bleary eyes she watched him spread out his other legs, searching through the patch. Then he found something, and lifted it high. And in barely a moment the clouds of pepper dissipated.

"Salt mint," he said, as they all recovered their breaths.

Salt to abate the pepper. That made sense in this crazy region. "Thank you," Wenda gasped.

Jumper remained in giant-spider form. Meryl still held his foot, now acclimatized to that shape.

They were through the peppermint patch. But they were not out of the Strip, and they had not yet found the Sidewalk.

Before them was a narrowing path between mountainous slopes. It was a V-shaped valley, blocked by what looked like a giant stone ear. There was no way around it, especially since they had to remain linked by the hands.

"This is surely a pun," Ida said. "Because everything

here is puns. But fathoming its nature is only part of the problem; we will need to find a way to nullify it so we can pass."

"What would nullify a stone ear?" Meryl asked.

"Maybe a really nasty sound," Dipper said.

That gave Wenda an idea. She knew of the nastiest sound in the forest, based on a pun. There ought to be one here, since all the most villainous puns were here. She gazed around, and spied one growing on the steep slope. But it was out of reach.

"We need that stink horn," Wenda said.

"I could fly up and get it," Meryl said. "But I'd have to let go."

"Maybe not," Jumper said. "I have the talents of size and form, thanks to my beloved Eris. If you don't mind standing on me, I can lift you up."

"I'll do it," Meryl agreed. She spread her wings and flew up to sit on him, without letting go of his foot.

Then Jumper expanded, becoming twice his prior size, then three times, carrying Meryl upward until she could reach the plant. She extended one hand, carefully.

"Handle it gently!" Wenda called. "Very gently!"

But then Meryl lost her balance, and instead of carefully lifting the horn from its mooring, she punched it. The thing blasted out a foul-smelling noise and issued a bilious colored smell. Both spread disgustingly out to fill the V of the valley. The people could not escape the sound or the cloud. Suddenly they were dipped in nausea.

Their pile collapsed in a sickly heap. But the job was done: the giant stone ear, similarly oppressed by the awful noise, was melting. Wenda could hardly blame it; all of them were retching. There was nothing quite as offensive as a ruptured stink horn.

They dragged themselves to their feet and scrambled

over the sagging stone before the ear could recover from the awful sound. They were not much better off than it was.

But they were not yet through. "I don't think I like these puns," Dipper remarked, shaking his head to clear a dribble of vomit from his beak.

"That is the heck of it," Ida said. "No person in his or her right mind would enter a Strip unless desperate. Unfortunately, we *are* desperate. We have no other way to return to Xanth."

As their sickness from the dreadful stink horn eased, they saw that they faced a pleasant scene where assorted hoodlike hats floated. "What is this?" Meryl asked suspiciously.

"It must be a pun we won't like," Dipper said.

"But there seems to be no way through except there," Jumper said, reverting to manform. This time the mermaid glanced at his body and did not protest or freak out. In fact her expression seemed appraising. Jumper glanced similarly at her bare body, and did not freak out. They were getting acclimatized. It was interesting seeing it happen, stage by stage.

"We shall just have to endure it," Wenda said. They were all still linked by their hands.

They forged together into the scene. The hats swirled, then flew to the head of each person, including the bird, and lodged there.

The effect was immediate. All of them became children.

"Oh, no!" a nine-year-old Ida exclaimed. "They are Child Hoods!"

"So what, dummy?" Jumper demanded.

"*You're* the dummy!" Ida retorted.

"Am not!"

"Am too!"

"Children!" Wenda said sternly. "Don't quarrel. It isn't nice."

Both turned on her. "Oh, yeah?" Jumper demanded.

"Yeah!" Wenda said. Then, realizing that she was being just as childish as they, she tried to correct it. "Those hoods are making us naughty children. We have to take them off."

"You first," Ida said.

"I don't have a free hand, dummy," Wenda said.

"I do," Meryl said, showing a trace of maturity. She put her free hand to her head, trying to lift off the hood. "It won't come off."

Wenda wanted to check her own hood, but didn't dare let go of Jumper or Ida. So she made a childish squeal of frustration.

"I'll check," Dipper said, putting a wing to his head. "Bleep!"

"It seems we can't get them off," Jumper said. "We're locked into Child Hood."

"This is all your fault," Dipper said to Wenda.

"Is not!" Wenda said, then caught herself. Somebody had to be un-childish. "I mean, I'm sorry."

Ida made an effort and spoke like an adult. "It's no one's fault. It's just part of the Strip. We just have to handle it. Does anyone have an idea?"

That shamed the others into momentary maturity. "There must be something," Meryl said. "This Strip seems to be like the Good Magician's Challenges: there's always a way, if you can just fathom it."

"That must be where the old gnome got the idea," Dipper said, cackling.

"I think it is actually that puns have an affinity for anti-puns," Ida said. "Opposites attract, and actions generate equal and opposite reactions. The effect is similar: we can nullify the puns if we just see how." Then, worn out by her effort of maturity, she lapsed into a childish giggle.

Wenda wracked her young brain. What would nullify a Child Hood? She couldn't think of anything.

"What's that?" Dipper asked. He was looking at a patch of fuzzy little plants that grew into the shape of the letters E or T.

"Those are mist E's or miss T's," Wenda said, because she had seen them on occasion in the forest. "They generate wisps of fog."

"What good is that?" the bird demanded truculently.

"Aren't human children afraid of the dark?" Jumper asked.

That crystallized a notion. "Yes!" Wenda agreed. "Meryl, get over there and stir up those E's and T's."

"You aren't my mommy," Meryl said. "You can't tell me what to do."

Wenda choked down her urge to shout, "Nyaa Nyaa fraidy cat!" and rephrased her request. "Please, pretty please with sugar on it, go mess up those plants."

"Well, in that case, okay." The mermaid flew over the patch, not letting go of Jumper's hand, and swept her tail through the patch.

The plants, outraged, puffed out a huge quantity of fog. It rose up in a roiling cloud and surrounded them. Suddenly everything was black.

Wenda was terrified. Children were indeed afraid of the dark, and she was a child. She screamed. So did the others, overwhelmed. But they all clutched one another's hands.

She felt something happen on her head. That was what she wanted. "Flee forward!" she cried, lurching forward herself.

They stumbled forward. In barely a moment and a half they plunged out of the shroud of fog.

"The hoods are gone!" Meryl exclaimed.

"Yes," Wenda said. "They didn't like being terrified, so they jumped off. Now we're beyond their range."

"You figured it out," Meryl said in a mature manner. "I apologize for my prior attitude."

"You were a child," Wenda reminded her.

"We were all children," Jumper said. "We all apologize. Wenda came through for us."

But they were not yet out of the world of Comic, or even the Strip. Now the way was barred by a large armored figure with a sword. He stood menacingly before them; on his chest was a sign: I AM THE SILENT KNIGHT. I HAVE TAKEN AN OATH OF SILENCE. I SHALL ALLOW NO TALKING PERSON OR CREATURE TO PASS.

"But we need to pass," Wenda protested. "We don't belong here."

The sign changed. TOO BAD FOR YOU. YOU SHALL NOT PASS.

"He means it," Ida said. "He is using sign language."

Wenda glanced at Jumper. "Could you maybe grow in size and move him out of the way?"

"No," Jumper replied. "I would have to let go of your hands, and we don't want to do that. Besides which, he would probably lop off a limb or two if I challenged him. Even in my spider form I wouldn't like that."

He was right. They needed to find some other way.

"Why did you take that oath?" Meryl inquired.

The Knight's visor oriented on her. It seemed to brighten. Was he gazing on her bareness and freaking out? That might be a way.

But Meryl was only the upper half of a woman. Wenda, though, was a whole woman. If Meryl could half freak him out, maybe Wenda could do the whole job.

"I think I need to strip," she murmured.

Meryl glanced at her appraisingly. "Maybe you do," she agreed. She helped undress Wenda, because she had a free hand. It was tricky getting her sleeves off without letting go of the two hands she held, but they managed it through extremely careful maneuvering.

Wenda stood in her bra and panties, slowly turning around. "Silent Knight!" she called. "Gaze on me a moment."

He did, but did not freak. Maybe his visor obscured the view enough to protect him. She had assumed the visor was to stop him from getting poked in the eye with an arrow or spear, but maybe it also served for dangerous visions.

She would just have to up the ante. With Meryl's help she removed her underwear and stood embarrassingly bare and blushing. As a species of wood nymph she had been normally nude, but now she was a whole woman, and that was different.

It didn't work. The Silent Knight remained immune.

"Mud and brambles!" she swore as she hastily donned her clothing. She was almost as angry about having exposed herself for nothing, as for the fact that they remained balked.

"We have a problem," Ida murmured.

Wenda looked. The Knight hadn't freaked out, but Jumper had. At least that showed that her body had not lost its power. Clothed, Wenda snapped her fingers, and he came out of it. "Did it work?" he asked blankly.

"Not the way we wanted," Wenda said.

The Silent Knight still stood guard, completely sober. His closed helmet did not give even the hint of a smile. "This guy's a barrel of laughs," Dipper remarked.

"Barrel of laughs," Jumper echoed. "I wonder whether that could be literal? And if so—"

"A wooden barrel," Wenda said. Wood was her domain. She sniffed the air. Sure enough, she caught a faint whiff. "That way," she said, pointing with her nose.

The valley had opened out somewhat. There was a vile

tangle of thorny mean-spirited vines on either side of the Knight, that would surely prevent any passage, but farther back the vegetation was halfway normal. There was an old dead beerbarrel tree in the direction Wenda was pointing. From it leaked a few muffled laughs.

"It got infected with bad humor and died," Wenda said. "Beerbarrels can't stand bad taste."

They made their way to it as a linked group. They pushed, and the old trunk fell over as a sealed barrel. They rolled it back to the path, then up to rest before the Knight.

"Now heave it forward," Wenda said.

They got behind the barrel and heaved together, so that it rolled right into the Knight. The Knight reacted automatically, swinging his sword and cleaving the barrel in two. There was an explosion of crude laughs.

They were contagious. In half a moment all the members of their party were rolling on the ground and helplessly laughing. There was nothing funny about it, but the bad humor had infected them and they had no choice.

And so was the Knight. "Ho ho ho!" he roared as he rolled.

"Move!" Wenda gasped between laughs.

They scrambled mostly to their feet and staggered past the helpless Knight. He had violated his Oath of Silence and was powerless to stop them. Soon they were beyond.

And there was the Sidewalk. "Sidle to the right!" Ida said. "That's the Door to Xanth."

"What's on the left?" Meryl asked.

"The Door to Elsewhere. We dare not risk it."

They sidled to the right, and in barely more than half an instant reached the Door. It was at the end of the walk, solid and closed. Meryl opened it, and they piled through.

They had won free of the Comic Strip. They collapsed in half a heap, recovering from the assault on their sanity.

"Let's not do that again soon," Jumper said.

"Never would be too soon," Meryl agreed.

4

PRINCE HILARION

They looked around. They were at the edge of a swamp. The Door behind them had disappeared.

"Where are we?" Jumper asked as he put on the clothes Wenda returned to him. They no longer needed to hold hands, being safely out of the Strip.

Wenda did not recognize it; this was not her part of the forest. She spied a small boy making some kind of a net. She went to talk with him. "Excuse me, do you live here?"

"Sure, for now," the boy said.

That was slightly odd, so she changed the subject. "What is it that you are making?"

"A hare net," the boy said proudly. "So I can catch a rabbit."

"That's very clever." Wenda looked around. "I am new here. Can you tell me where this is?"

"It is near the Otterbee Swamp," the boy said, proud of his knowledge. "The otterbees are taking care of me, because I'm an orphan, but I want to learn to forage for myself."

Wenda kissed him on the forehead. She couldn't help it; in the past year she had come to realize how much she liked children. She wished she could take this orphan boy home with her, but of course she couldn't, for multiple reasons. "That is very smart of you," she said.

The boy beamed with pleasure. Wenda tore herself away and returned to the group. "He says this is near the otterbees. I don't know what that means."

But Ida did. "The otterbees!" she exclaimed happily. "This is their swamp!"

"The whats?" Dipper asked.

"The otterbees are kindhearted swimming creatures who do what they feel they otter. They rescued me from the Faun & Nymph Retreat when I was a baby, so I wouldn't forget each day the way the nymphs do. They raised me, and brought in an itinerant centaur—his name was Cerebral—who educated me in the Human manner. The otterbees told me I otter bee looking for my destiny, so I left them."

Wenda realized that the otterbees were still doing what they otter, helping children. The little boy had departed with his hare net. He was surely being well cared for.

"Your destiny was to be the twin sister of King Ivy?" Jumper asked.

"Yes, as it turned out. We were twins, but the stork lost me, so only Ivy was delivered. I don't remember the details, only the way the otterbees helped me. Now I will see them again."

"So this is a harmless place the Door put us," Meryl said. "Isn't it?"

"Yes," Ida agreed. "Oh, I must talk with my old friends! I should have done this years ago." She clapped her hands. "Otterbees! It is Ida, with some Companions. It is safe to appear."

Wenda felt the magic as the masquerade spell was abbreviated for half a moment so that Ida's real name could be heard by others.

And a number of swimming creatures appeared. They had to have been in the area, but hiding, uncertain of the nature of these sudden intruders.

"Ida?" one asked. "She's a princess now. Not an old crone."

"I will show you for one instant," Ida said. "I know you will keep my secret." Then the magic flared again as she flashed as herself for exactly one instant.

"It is you!" the otterbees cried, coming out of the marsh to cluster around her. "What are you doing hiding as a crone?"

"I am on a Quest," Ida explained. "I can't tell you more, lest it be compromised. But I can tell you that I have a comfortable life at Castle Roogna."

"What was that ball beside your head?"

Ida smiled. "That is Ptero, a world where every character exists who has ever been in Xanth, or will be, or might be imagined. It orbits my head, at least in appearance, serving as an access to other realms."

"You must have found your talent!"

"My talent is the Idea. Ptero relates, as most of its inhabitants are just ideas here on Xanth."

"Are you married?" they asked.

"No. I simply never found the right man."

"Maybe some day," the otterbees said hopefully. "Every princess needs a prince."

"I'm sure that will be the case," Ida agreed.

Wenda kept her face straight. It was evident that the otterbees did not know the rest of Ida's talent of the Idea, so their suggestion could be confirmed. They had just allowed Princess Ida to finally find that right man. Whoever he might be.

"That reminds us," the otterbees said. "We have another visitor."

"This really isn't a social call," Ida said. "We must move on to our Quest."

"That's so sad," the otterbees said, looking unhappy. "We wish you would stay longer."

Wenda could see that Ida was moved. She did not want to disappoint her old friends. "Maybe we could meet their other visitor," Wenda said. "Before we go."

"Well, if it's all right with you," Ida said.

The otterbees hastily ushered their other visitor to the scene. Wenda was not the only one whose jaw descended. It was a young handsome prince!

"This is Prince Hilarion," the otterbees said. "He has a special Quest of his own." Then, to him: "This is our old friend Haggai." Wenda heard it as outsiders did, because of the masquerade spell.

"I am moderately pleased to meet you, Hag," Hilarion said politely. Obviously the politeness was an effort. Few people were truly pleased to meet an ugly old crone—which was, of course, the point of the masquerade. No one would ever suspect her of being a Princess.

"I think we need to be on our way," Wenda said. But then she saw the cloud. "Oops—I fear Fracto has spied us."

"He sees our gathering," the otterbees said. "He thinks it's a parade. Naturally he has to rain on it."

"Naturally," Jumper agreed. He was surely remembering how Fracto had chased them when he and Wenda were on their cable-repairing mission. Wenda was also remembering how Fracto had tried to ambush her more recently by the Gap Chasm.

"We have a shelter," the otterbees said. "We made it when we tried to help with a problem. Trolls were catching fish in a nearby lake, but their nets were harming doll-fins, a subspecies of water nymph. We couldn't make them stop; trolls don't listen well. But then a troll and a lovely doll-fin fell in love, and that motivated the troll, and he found a way to catch fish without harming the doll-fins. So that problem was solved, and we seldom use this shelter."

Wenda glanced again at the sky. The cloud was roiling horrendously. They would have an awful time trying to get out of the swamp with that drenching them. "Thank you," Wenda said for all of them.

Thus they found themselves under the spreading canopy formed by the tightly linked branches of a cluster of wicker trees. Wenda had to admire their intricacy; this was excellent woodworking.

The storm came splashing down, trying to wash them out, but the shelter was secure. They had merely to wait it out. Wenda felt guilty for appreciating the closeness of the prince. His sheer handsomeness was stirring her despite her determination not to be stirred. She suspected that the other women were experiencing similar emotions.

This is the way a man feels in the presence of a pretty girl, Jumper thought.

And if the prince got wet and disrobed, would Wenda and Meryl freak out? She couldn't be sure they wouldn't.

There was most of an awkward silence. Wenda stepped in to relieve the discomfort. "Where are you a prince, Hilarion? I mean no offense, but I never heard of you."

The young man smiled, becoming even more excruciatingly handsome. Wenda's heart gave an illicit flutter; it couldn't help it. "Naturally not, woodwife," he agreed easily. "I am from an island kingdom named Adamant that connects only occasionally to the Land of Xanth. Nobody knows me here."

This evidently stirred Ida's curiosity. "We know of the islands," she said. "Jenny Elf married a werewolf prince of one. But why are you traveling alone out here? Surely you would be more comfortable in your own castle, with all the royal comforts."

"Surely I would," he agreed with another devastating smile. "But I am missing something vitally important."

"A woman," Dipper said.

"You talk!" Hilarion said, startled.

"I have the gift of tongues. It helps."

He nodded. "You are correct. I am missing a woman."

"Aren't there princesses on your island?" Meryl asked.

"No. Just my father the King, my mother the Queen, a few relatives, and me. It's a small kingdom."

"A serving girl?" Meryl asked half mischievously.

"None I would care to marry. Anyway, my love is elsewhere."

"Elsewhere?" Wenda inquired, sensing an interesting story. "Where?"

"I don't know."

"Maybe you had better just tell us your story," Jumper suggested.

"True. Perhaps one of you will be able to help." Hilarion paused, gathering his wits for the narration. "When I was two years old, my parents took action to see that I would have a princess to marry when I came of age. There was a ceremony of betrothal to a worthy girl just one year old. They agreed that she would come to our island when she was twenty-one to marry me. But when the time came, she did not appear. Apparently she had forgotten. So I set out to find her, to bring her back to our kingdom and marry her, so she could be queen after my mother retired. Unfortunately I had a brush with a forget whorl, and forgot her name. But I am sure I will know her, and she will remember me, if I kiss her. So I am traveling around kissing suitable girls, in case any have brushed similarly with forget whorls and forgotten they are princesses. That is my Quest."

"Fascinating," Meryl said, intrigued. "Could she be a crossbreed?"

"She might," he agreed. "I don't remember."

"Maybe we should kiss, then."

"Very well." He went to her and kissed her. She seemed to float. But when the kiss ended, she shook her head. "I don't remember ever being a princess, unfortunately."

"I do not know you, either," he said. "I'm sure you're a worthy person, just not my betrothee."

"Not your betrothee," she agreed sadly.

Hilarion looked at Wenda. "You? You look to be of the age."

But she balked, not being the single maiden he took her for. "I am married elsewhere. But I would not qualify anyway; I have existed as a woman only a year. Before that I was a woodwife: only the front half of me existed."

"While I have nothing against woodwives," the prince said carefully, "I'm sure my betrothee would have been a whole baby. Still, we could kiss, if you wish, just to be sure."

Wenda was obscenely tempted, because he was so handsome. But she was sure she shouldn't. "My husband would not understand." It still made her feel odd to hear herself not say "wood knot."

"Who is your husband?"

"Prince Charming." Then she tried to bite her tongue, but it was too late: she had just surrendered her anonymity.

"Prince Charming!" Hilarion exclaimed. "I know of him. Then your companion must be the Little Mermaid."

They all had to smile at his understandable confusion. "Not so," Meryl said. "I never had the luck to rescue a prince. Besides, I'm not a regular mermaid; I'm a winged mermaid."

"Why so you are," he said, surprised. "I hadn't noticed."

"You didn't notice?" she asked, frowning.

"Your beautiful front side distracted me from any consideration of your backside. It's all I can do to stop from freaking out. I apologize."

She glanced down at her bare front. "No apology necessary," she said, pleased.

He returned his attention to Wenda. "So you are a princess."

"Technically, yes," Wenda agreed uncomfortably. "But I'm trying to travel anonymously."

"Why would you want to do that?" he asked reasonably. "Unless you are on a Quest of your own."

Worse yet, it was not in Wenda to tell an outright lie. "I am. But it's private."

"Of course. I did not mean to pry. I was merely inquiring whether you would like to kiss me, just in case."

Wenda suffered a siege of sudden resolution. "Yes!" she agreed giddily.

But now he balked. "Still, Prince Charming might not understand. Especially if you turned out to be the one."

"I can't be the one," she argued. "So it's all right. Kiss me." At the same time she was aware that she wasn't making a lot of sense. If men freaked out at the sight of women's whatever, so did women lose their common sense in the presence of a truly handsome man. But she held on to her equilibrium, somehow.

Hilarion did not seem inclined to argue the case. "Very well." He approached her, took her in his arms, and kissed her.

Now she freaked out. She found herself sitting on a stump where he had set her, little hearts spinning around her head. Some time must have passed: half an instant, or half a century.

"You are not she," Hilarion concluded. "Though you are marvelously rounded and supple. Prince Charming is a lucky man."

"Thank you," she murmured somewhat breathlessly.

The storm was abating. But before they could organize to move on, an otterbee splashed up to the shelter. "The trolls are raiding the Faun & Nymph Retreat!" he cried.

"Oh!" Ida exclaimed. "We must try to help them." Naturally she remained fond of her friends of childhood.

"I'll help," Prince Hilarion said bravely, putting his hand on his sword.

They scrambled out of the shelter and followed the otterbee. The Retreat was not far distant, and soon they came upon the scene. It was grim. Four huge ugly trolls were chasing after the fauns and nymphs, holding big bags to stuff them into. Both fauns and nymphs were fleet runners, being bare and healthy, but it was obvious that before long the trolls would succeed in catching one or more fauns or nymphs, and that would be the end of them. Trolls were notorious man-eaters.

"What a sight," Hilarion said, his eyeballs threatening to crystallize as they fixed on the bouncing nymphs. Wenda realized that nymphs would have that effect on normal human men, princes included.

"I can stop one," Jumper said, assuming his giant-spider form. "But I'm not sure what to do with him when I catch him. If he were a bug, I'd bite his head off, but I'd really rather not do that to a troll."

"They surely taste awful," Wenda agreed with half a fleeting smile.

"Well, I don't mind slaying a troll," Hilarion said, drawing his sword.

"No bloodshed, please," Ida pleaded.

"But madam," he protested, politely not calling her an old hag or crone as she appeared to be to him, "trolls are not known for listening to reason. They won't stop voluntarily, and the innocent fauns and nymphs will suffer grievously."

It was Dipper who got the key idea. "The humidor!" he exclaimed. "If we can put them through it."

Meryl had to laugh. "And make the trolls have to fight through all those dreadful puns. And if they get through it, they still won't land back here among the fauns and nymphs."

It did seem like the ideal solution. No bloodshed, no fuss nor muss, and they would be safely rid of the trolls and save the helpless fauns and nymphs.

Then Ida sobered them with a question. "How do we get them through the Door?"

How, indeed? They had no time to ponder; the chased fauns and nymphs were barely escaping their pursuers now.

"I'll do it," Wenda said. "Ida, set up the humidor. Jumper, run and rescue whichever faun or nymph is about to get caught. Meryl, Dipper, fly overhead and attract attention to me. I will lead the trolls to the Door."

Jumper bounded off on his eight long legs. Meryl and Dipper sailed into the air.

"What of me?" Hilarion asked, evidently feeling left out.

"You can't help me; you'll freak out," Wenda said, stripping off her clothing. "But you can discourage any fauns or nymphs from following me; we don't want *them* to go to Comic."

"Excellent point," he agreed, sheathing his sword.

Wenda, bare, ran out to join the nymphs, knowing that she now looked just like one. That wasn't surprising; she was really a forest nymph at heart.

"Hey trolls, look at this one!" Dipper cried. "Fat and slow. You can catch her easy."

That was the idea, though Wenda would have preferred a modified description.

"Over here, trolls!" Meryl called. "Catch this succulent nymph!"

That wasn't much better. But it did the job; the four trolls oriented on her. Trolls were not known for intelligence, fortunately, and did not question why any bird or flying mermaid should try to help them catch their prey. They lumbered in Wenda's direction.

Meanwhile Ida had set up shop. Her box was open, and she held the vial and tube in her hands. She wasn't concerned about being chased, as she looked to the trolls like a shriveled old bag of a crone with no tasty meat on her rickety bones. They didn't care what she did.

Wenda looped around and ran toward Ida, all four trolls pursuing her. Fortunately she could run as fleetly as a nymph, by no coincidence, and managed to stay ahead of them.

But now several nymphs were joining her, thinking this was some new game, and several fauns were chasing them, intent on the type of celebrating, as they termed it, they normally did. Hilarion stepped in, intercepting them. "No, no," he cried. "Go the other way!" He ran in a new direction, showing them how.

The nymphs followed him. He was after all a supremely handsome man. But then the trolls followed the nymphs. Oops!

Wenda was desperate. How could she attract the trolls without also attracting the nymphs? She had no idea.

"Scream," Dipper called.

So Wenda made the most piercing scream of her life. "EEEEEEEE!!!!" she screamed, putting a record eight E's and four exclamation points into it. Two E's and one point per troll. The effort almost turned her inside out.

It worked. The nymphs didn't react, as screaming cutely was routine for them, and this was hardly a cute scream. But the bloodthirsty trolls whirled around and charged, eager to pounce on the terrified morsel. To them, EE!

meant EEat! Their mottled jaws were covered with eager slaver.

Wenda put on a burst of nymphly speed and zoomed toward the forming humidor, the trolls in hot pursuit.

The largest and ugliest troll gained on her. He reached forth his gnarly hand and caught her by the hair. He hauled her up into the air.

She whirled around to face him, involuntarily, as she had no contact with the ground. He was still running, holding her aloft. His warty tongue slurped across his horny lips as his squinty eyes fixed on her chest. He was getting an idea, and biting off her face and stuffing her body into his bag was only the latter part of it. Wenda had had enough experience in the past year to derive a fairly accurate notion of the nature of the idea. She was definitely not interested.

Unless she could manage to increase his interest to the point of freaking out. Then she could escape him.

But if her chest didn't do it, what would? She wasn't wearing her panties at the moment, as nymphs didn't use them. Still, maybe she could emulate them.

She lifted her legs, spreading them before his face. He stared, but did not freak out. Probably all he saw was more fresh meat for his cookpot.

Then Hilarion ran up beside them. "Ho, varlet!" he cried. "Unhand that innocent maiden!"

At some other time Wenda would have had to laugh, or at least make an obscure smile. She was no longer an innocent.

But the troll glanced at Hilarion, then lowered his arm with her dangling by her hair, until her feet touched the ground. Then he let go, unhanding her, and she caught her balance and resumed her running. He had let her go!

The troll spied the other trolls running close behind, and fell in with them. Now the four of them were chasing her again.

She was close to the humidor. "Activate the Door!" she cried.

"But you don't want to go through," Ida protested.

"I won't! They will!"

Ida nodded, and dropped a drop of water into the tube. The ball of fog formed, and within it was the Door. Ida opened it just as Wenda and the trolls arrived.

At the last possible moment, Wenda dived under the Door, just missing the edge of the fog below. The four trolls, unable to dodge on such short notice, piled straight ahead through the open doorway. Ida slammed the Door behind them.

Wenda sat on the ground, catching her breath as the fog spread and thinned, dissolving the Door with it. Soon there was nothing left but dissipating wisps of mist.

"That was incredibly brave of you," Hilarion said, sitting down beside her. Jumper, Meryl, and Dipper rejoined them. The fauns and nymphs ignored them, as they were no longer doing anything interesting.

"I couldn't just let the trolls catch and eat the fauns and nymphs," Wenda said. "I had to do something."

"You certainly did something," Ida said. "I truly appreciate it. They don't remember, of course, but I have fond memories of running and playing with the nymphs in my youth. They are truly innocent creatures."

"There are those who might think otherwise," Hilarion said, observing the return of normal faunly and nymphly activity. The fauns chased the nymphs, who screamed cutely, flung their hair about, and kicked up their nice legs. When they were ready, they let the fauns catch them, and the pair would roll on the ground together, celebrating. Then the whole sequence would start over. That was what they did all day. The storks paid no attention; nymphs didn't count.

"It is innocent when nymphs do it," Ida said.

"I am sorry I kissed you, Wenda," Hilarion said.

This surprised her unpleasantly. "You found me un-pleasant?"

"By no means. The kiss was wonderful. Just not what I am looking for."

This mollified her only slightly. "Then why?"

"Because I would have preferred to imagine that you were the one, my lost princess, merely awaiting my discovery. You are such a wonderful woman."

"Oh," Wenda said, coloring. Normally she was unable to manage color, only a blush, but he had surprised her. "But I'm really just a wouldwife."

"You're a woman," he insisted. "A fine one."

"He's right," Jumper said. "You were a fine woman even when you were only half there."

This was embarrassing her, so Wenda tried to change the subject. "What happened out there?" she asked. "When the troll had me by the hair—and would have bitten off my face and celebrated in a way I would not have liked before stuffing me into his bag—suddenly he just seemed to change his mind, and I was able to lead them through the Door."

A glance circulated among the others. "We don't know," Meryl said. "Hilarion ran up next to the troll, and then the monster set you down. I was amazed."

"I was trying to charge over and rescue you," Jumper said. "But I knew I would not get there in time."

"I felt magic," Ida said. "It must have been something Hilarion did."

"But all I did was look him in the eye," Hilarion said. "I was trying to think of a way to stop him without bloodshed."

"You must have done so," Meryl said. "He would never have set her down otherwise. Trolls are not reasonable creatures."

"But I don't know what magic I could have used," Hilarion protested. "I have forgotten whatever talent I have, because of the forget whorl."

"That is unfortunate," Ida said. "You have helped us save the fauns and nymphs. Perhaps we can repay you by fathoming your talent. You will surely need it in your continuing search for your betrothee."

"It would help," he agreed, glancing again at Wenda with a certain appealing desire. She couldn't help regretting a bit that she was not the one. He was so handsome!

They oriented on it. "Picture the scene," Ida said. "The troll was dangling Wenda by the hair, making ready to do her serious harm. You ran up beside him. What did you say to him?"

"I told him to let her go," Hilarion said. "And he did. I was surprised."

"Maybe it was the way you said it," Ida said. "Some phrasings carry more conviction than others."

"It was dramatic," Wenda said. "He cried 'Ho, varlet! Unhand that innocent maiden!' I was surprised, because I'm really not innocent anymore."

Ida put her hand on Wenda's hand. "You remain delightfully innocent. But that was not about to stop the troll."

"I'm sure it wasn't," Hilarion said. "Yet he did as I commanded." He glanced at Ida. "You seem to have wisdom, crone. You must know what happened."

"Yes, I must," Ida agreed, startled. Wenda realized that was because Hilarion, unaware of her talent, had expressed a belief she could accept. "I believe you have a very special talent to influence others, even trolls."

"I don't think so. If I had that ability, my betrothee would have come to me by now."

"Unless she too got brushed by a forget whorl," Meryl said.

"That is possible," the prince agreed. "But I am not aware of influencing anyone else to do my will."

"We can perhaps find out," Ida said. "Make one of us do something."

He nodded. "Wenda, kiss me again."

"That's not fair!" Wenda protested. "I already want to kiss you." Then she quailed. "Oops."

"All you have to do to disprove it is to resist his request," Meryl said. "However reluctantly."

Wenda resisted. She remained where she was.

"Bleep," Hilarion muttered.

"Try me," Dipper said.

"Fly and perch on the head of a nymph," Hilarion told the bird.

Dipper sat tight.

"Try me," Jumper said.

"Change forms."

Jumper remained as he was, a giant spider.

"So it seems my idea was wrong," Ida said, faintly surprised.

That gave Wenda an idea. "Maybe not. Maybe we just have not figured out exactly *how* he influences others."

Ida nodded. "That is possible."

"The troll just seemed to forget about Wenda," Dipper said. "Or at least about celebrating with her."

"Forgetting!" Meryl exclaimed. "Hilarion makes people forget! Maybe not everything, but something. Like that troll—what he wanted to do with Wenda. So he put her down, but kept chasing her, because it was only the one thing he forgot."

A scintillating glance circulated among them. This was a really promising prospect.

"I am not aware of any such ability," Hilarion said. "But of course my own memory is suspect, after that whorl. I have the feeling that there are other important things I have forgotten."

"We can test this too," Ida said. "Make one of us forget something."

"But memories are what make us what we are," Hilarion said. "I would not care even to try to harm a person in that manner."

"I wish you could make me forget the horror of looking into that monster's face, and realizing the idea that was forging through his dull brain," Wenda said. "I'm afraid that image will haunt me for days."

"In that case, I will try," Hilarion said. "Wenda, forget that image."

Wenda blinked. "Forget what?"

The others laughed, for some reason. "Are you teasing me?" Wenda demanded. "I'm sure I don't know why."

"Let's try it again," Ida said. "What other memory would one of us like to forget?"

"How the other birds made fun of me when I took a swim," Dipper said. "They couldn't swim, so they tried to make me feel bad about it. I knew that, but still it bothered me. One of them was a Bird of Paradise I really liked, but after that she refused to have anything to do with me. She said I wasn't her type."

Hilarion looked at Dipper. "Forget that episode," he said. "Forget about the fickle Bird of Paradise."

"Those birds are fickle," Dipper agreed. "I'm glad I never knew one personally."

Another glance circulated. "I think we're making the case," Ida said. "But we should confirm it with one more."

"I'd like to forget the Demoness Sharon," Jumper said. "She played me along until I was ready to marry her, then abruptly dumped me. I am far, far better off with Eris, and remain endlessly glad she married me. I would not be here today, literally, without her; I'd be dead of old age. But still the memory of Sharon bothers me, and I'd like to be rid of it."

"Forget Sharon," Hilarion told him.

"Forget whom?"

The others laughed. Now it was Jumper who was perplexed.

"She was a . . . a person you once knew," Wenda said. "Who treated you unkindly. I was there; I thought so at the time. You are better off forgetting her."

"I will take your word, Wenda, because you are my friend and I trust you. The name means nothing to me."

"I believe we have established Prince Hilarion's talent," Ida said. "It is one we certainly can use. I wonder whether we should invite him to join our Quest."

Wenda saw the advantage immediately. Selective forgetting!

But Dipper didn't. "So he can make people forget things. He did us a favor by making that troll forget about despoiling Wenda. I'm sure we are all duly grateful. But his mission is not our mission. Why should he want to join us, and why should we want him along?"

Still another glance circulated, followed by subtle nods. Then Jumper assumed the mantle of explanation. "We have a very special situation, Dipper. Princess Ida's talent is—"

"The crone's a princess?" Hilarion asked, startled.

Jumper smiled, which looked odd on his spider face. "Yes, Ida is a princess. So is Wenda, as the wife of a prince, and I am technically a prince: the prince of spiders. We take it in stride. Ida's talent is the Idea: when any person who doesn't know her talent makes a suggestion, she is free to accept it, and when she does, it becomes reality. But she is limited, because those who know her, know her talent, and that makes it ineffective. But strangers don't necessarily make useful suggestions. It would magnify her power enormously if there were a way to make a person forget her talent. You might do that. You could work closely with her to facilitate her talent."

"I might," Hilarion agreed, trying with imperfect success to mask his aversion.

Jumper smiled again. "She is not as ugly as she appears. That is a facade, a mask, to protect her anonymity. She is of an older generation, but otherwise ordinary."

"I did not mean to imply—"

"We know, Prince," Jumper said. "If you care to join our Quest, Princess Ida will appear to you as she is, and we will share its nature with you. About all we can offer in return is the prospect of meeting people, including young women, along the way. We ask only that you not share the details with any outsiders, because there are dangers."

"Dangers," Hilarion said, not at all dissuaded. "Perhaps some good fights."

"Perhaps," Jumper agreed. "But we would much prefer to avoid confrontations than solicit them."

"Of course." Hilarion pondered no more than a moment and one or two instants. "Very well, I will join your Quest and do my best, hoping to find my betrothee along the way."

"We all have our incidental motives," Jumper agreed.

Then Hilarion's eyes widened as the scales of illusion fell away. "It is true! You are no longer a crone, and your name is not Haggai but Ida. You are Princess Ida, the sister of the King, with the little moon orbiting your head!"

"I am," Ida agreed.

"I have heard of you," he said, awed. "This must be a really important mission."

"It is," Ida agreed. "It is actually Wenda's Quest."

Hilarion looked at Wenda. "I am interested."

"It is for the Good Magician," she said. "There is a large petrified not of would that—"

"I beg your pardon?"

"A knot of wood," Jumper explained. "She normally

uses the forest dialect, but the Good Magician put a spell on her to nullify that, so that others will not recognize her. Unfortunately the spell is too effective."

"Ah, I understand," Hilarion agreed. "We call it the law of unintended consequences."

"Exactly," Jumper agreed.

"The Not terrifies all who approach it," Wenda continued. "But since I derive from would, I should be able to handle it. So my job is to transport it from the nook in the Gap Chasm where it is, to the Good Magician's Castle, without letting any bad creatures steal it. Because they might use it for ill."

"Like terrifying rivals," Hilarion agreed. "I appreciate the danger." He looked around. "I am glad to make your acquaintances, and will do my best for your Quest. This should be interesting."

"We would prefer it to be dull," Wenda said.

He laughed. "Life is not always as dull as we wish."

Wenda looked around. Much of the day had passed. "We can sleep here tonight, and proceed in the morning. With luck a couple of days will suffice to complete the mission."

Hilarion shook his head. "Quests are never completed on schedule. It is in the *Big Book of Rules*. I remember studying that in my days of training."

Wenda feared that was true.

They returned to the otterbees' shelter. The otterbees welcomed them, and brought all manner of food for their dinner. They, too, were pleased that the fauns and nymphs had been saved.

They set up beds of raised moss and settled down separately. Then suddenly there was an enclosure around Wenda's bed, and Prince Charming was there. He kissed her avidly—and drew back. "You kissed another man!" he exclaimed.

Wenda burst into tears of remorse.

He laughed. "Eris told me about it. You just wanted to be sure you weren't his betrothee, and you're not."

Wenda was relieved. "You're not angry?"

"How can I be angry? I love you!"

That wasn't quite the same, but before she could think about it he was kissing her again, and more, and in another six minutes he was asleep. Then he and the enclosure vanished, leaving her half bemused. She presumed Eris was similarly finished with Jumper. These spousal visits were fast and intimate, and they got the job done.

She was glad things were all right with Charming. The Quest was likely to be complicated enough without a problem there.

5

ANGELA ANGEL

In the morning they took turns washing in a pool of the swamp. First Wenda, Ida, and Meryl, then Jumper, Dipper, and Hilarion. The women agreed that Prince Hilarion was excruciatingly handsome, not that any of them would notice such a detail. "But the prince notices you," Meryl told Wenda. "Especially when you run bare."

"I wanted the trolls to notice me," Wenda protested. "So I could lead them to the humidor."

"And an excellent job you did," Ida said. "But it is true: you have a nymphlike figure, and males of any variety tend to notice."

"Well, a wouldwife is a sort of variety of nymph. The front half, anyway."

"I once heard a woodwife described as a half-assed nymph," Meryl said with three-sevenths of a smile.

"But wouldwives don't have donkeys," Wenda protested. "Not even half ones."

"I repeat," Ida said with the remaining four-sevenths of the smile. "You remain delightfully innocent."

There seemed to be something Wenda wasn't getting. That annoyed her, but she didn't want to admit it, so she changed the subject. "Now we have to plan our trip from here to the Gap Chasm. I fear it is a long walk."

"Too long a walk," Ida agreed. "We are near the Ever Glades, in southern Xanth, which would take ever and ever to traverse. Even those of us who fly, whether by wings or by carpet, might find it tedious."

"And the wilds can be dangerous," Meryl agreed. "Here there be dragons."

"But you're a winged monster," Wenda said. "Why should you fear flying dragons?"

"It is true that there is a camaraderie of winged monsters when there is a crisis or a convention," Meryl said. "But at other times, it's every monster for herself. A dragon would eat me as readily as you."

"We shall have to plan our journey carefully," Ida said. "I suggest that we use the trollway."

"But trolls chase nymphs!" Wenda protested, affrighted.

"There are trolls and trolls," Ida said. "Wild uncivilized trolls are dangerous, but the trolls who run the trollway are civilized. They don't molest travelers, as long as the proper fares are paid."

"What's a proper fare?" Meryl asked with half a trace of suspicion.

"They will accept tokens. Fortunately I have a supply, having anticipated such a need. They will work for a bus too."

"A buss?" Wenda asked. "I do not want to be bussed by a troll."

"It is a transport vehicle," Ida explained patiently.

Wenda realized that she had spent too long in the forest and castle. There were words in the outside landscape that she had not collected. "A bus," she agreed.

The males returned from their washup, bird, spider, and prince clean and clothed as required. "We have a long march ahead," Hilarion said.

"We will take a bus on the trollway," Wenda said.

It was evident that none of them knew what she was talking about. That pleased her.

Then Jumper figured it out. "A bus is for humans. I'd better change." He assumed manform, and Wenda gave him his clothing.

Ida knew the way. They bid farewell to the nice otterbees and set out along the appropriate path. Ida floated ahead on her carpet, keeping a pace suitable for the others.

Soon they came to a sort of station guarded by a troll in a box. Ida put her carpet away. Wenda hung back, preferring to let Ida handle it.

Ida approached a big sign that said STOP. PAY TROLL. "Here are six tokens," she said. "We're going to the Gap Chasm."

"You can't get there from here," the troll said gruffly. He looked typically vicious, but his voice was comparatively cultured. "The section crossing the Gap is currently under construction."

"But the trollway has been in existence for decades," Ida protested. "It traverses the entire length and breadth of Xanth."

"Deterioration of infrastructure," the troll explained. "Necessary repairs. The prior administrator was neglectful, paying too much attention to short-term advantage. We don't want valuable customers to fall into the Gap Chasm."

Ida considered. "How far can we get?"

"The link to Lake Ogre Chobee remains clear. That connects to river transport north. You can get an exchange."

"Then we'll do that," Ida agreed. She presented six metallic tokens. The troll accepted them, bit each one once, then hauled on a rope that lifted a barrier.

They entered the trollway section and stood by a

vast, long, paved road. Wenda had had no idea that such a thing existed in Xanth. For that matter, she'd had no idea that trolls could be businesslike, instead of ravening monsters. It was true: individuals differed.

Soon the bus arrived. It was a lumbering metal box-like vehicle with four black wheels and windows all around. It lumbered to a halt, emitted a naughty hiss of air, and opened its side door. A set of steps dropped down.

They stepped up into the bus. Inside it were two rows of seats aligned with the windows, so that passengers could look out. The driver was another somber troll who paid them no particular attention. He simply made sure all were safely aboard before he raised the steps, closed the door, and resumed the drive while they were walking down the central aisle to find seats. The scenery beyond the windows passed smartly to the rear like a projected illusion. The ride was so smooth that it seemed as if they were still while the scenery was moving.

Wenda noticed a small sign as she passed. YOUR DRIVER: TREVORR TROLL: SAFE RELIABLE TRUCULENT. Wenda decided not to inquire further.

There were several other passengers of assorted types. Wenda noticed one immediately, because she looked like a lovely angel. She wore an encompassing dress that reached from her wrists to the floor, with bands of color in the skirt. There was a yellow halo on her head, below which her pastel-colored hair descended. Her wings were like soft knitted cloth, resting behind her in gentle waves. There was a sash of pure white beads wrapped about her tiny waist. She was an utterly beautiful creature.

What was an angel doing here? The place beside the angel was vacant, so Wenda went there. "May I join you?"

"You may," the angel said. "I would like someone to talk with. I am not accustomed to this land."

Wenda sat beside her, Dipper perched on her shoulder. "I am Wenda Wouldwife, and this is my Companion, Dipper."

"I am Angela Angel."

"You are not a Xanth native," Wenda said. It wasn't a difficult guess, as she had never heard of an angel in Xanth.

"I am from Heaven," the angel agreed. "It is one of the Worlds of Ida."

Wenda considered, and decided it was premature to mention that Ida was here, complete with the first moon orbiting her head. Her masquerade concealed that.

"Why are you here?" Dipper asked.

Angela glanced at him, surprised. "A talking bird!"

"I was given the gift of tongues so I could join with Wenda and be useful. I am searching for meaning in my life."

"So am I, in effect," Angela agreed.

"But you're an angel!" Wenda said. "You already have the meaning the rest of us are searching for."

"By no means," Angela said. "Heaven is perfect. There is no challenge there. It is possible to find meaning only when there is something to achieve."

"So you came to imperfect Xanth," Wenda said. "That's so noble."

"Right now it's mostly confusing. I have no idea what to do. I wish someone could tell me or show me."

Wenda was developing a certain feel for the intricacies of the human condition. The angel's story did not quite align. "Please, I don't quite understand. You said you are searching for meaning, in effect. How can you qualify meaning? This makes it seem that this is not precisely what you seek."

Angela looked at her. "I did not want to bore you with my dull story. Heaven already is boring enough."

"Heaven is boring?" Wenda asked, surprised. "You said it was perfect."

"Perfection is dull. That's part of my problem."

"*Part* of it?"

Angela's eyes began to tear. "Please, don't press me. I am liable to burst forth with my entire pseudo-life history. You surely have better ways to occupy your time."

"I am not sure I do," Wenda said, now suspecting that their meeting was not entirely accidental. In Xanth, things had ways of working out, particularly on Quests. She had seen it happen on Jumper's Quest of the year before. A person just had to be alert to prospects, however obscure they might seem. "Jumper, Meryl, Hilarion, Ida—do you care to listen with us?" Because she wanted their confirmation of her suspicion.

The others came and introduced themselves to Angela. Then they settled in adjacent seats and listened.

"I was an ordinary angel in Heaven," Angela said. "We were all pretty much alike, differing only in minor details of feature or apparel. My friends Angel Gile and Angel Bull and I were part of the admittance team."

Wenda worked it out: Angel Gile would be A Gile, or agile. Angel Bull would be A Bull, or able. It seems puns infested even Heaven.

"We catered to the souls that come constantly to Heaven," Angela continued. "Providing them with harps and wings and little clouds to perch on, teaching them to sing hosannas, count their blessings, and so on. I was a tour guide, helping newcomers to orient. I am ashamed to confess that after an eon or two I got bored, and sought interest outside of Heaven. H*ll was adjacent, an awful place where the d*mned souls go. I encountered a tour guide for H*ll who was similarly bored. His name was Beauregard—Demon Beauregard. Of course our association was strictly professional; we needed to do some sorting when lost souls arrived in groups, directing some to my tour, others to his tour. Some groups received both tours, so they could decide for themselves, and Beauregard would tag along in mine, and I on his. Sometimes this led to dialogue, and even debate about the contrasting lifestyles, as it were."

Angela paused, her eyes misting. She blinked, and the mist floated away. "I preferred to drink nectar and eat ambrosia, while he preferred strong spirits and devils food. One day we were standing alone together by a spring, which we both thought was regular water, but it wasn't." She blushed. "It was a love spring. Our toes touched it, and suddenly we were each in love with the enemy, as it were. Naturally we didn't *do* anything." She blushed harder. "Not right then. But the urge was there. Beauregard's former lover, D Lusion, was jealous, and said horrible things. I was finally goaded into— into doing the unspeakable with him." Her blush became so hot that little wisps of steam rose from her face. "I showed him my p-panties. I let him t-touch them. Even l-look inside them. And I t-t-touched him where I shouldn't. And I *liked* it." She put her burning face into her hands, sobbing. That last was of course the worst of all. Innocent girls were supposed to never let a man near their panties, and to hate it if a man somehow touched them.

The listeners were silent. Angela was, after all, an angel. Angels were supposed to have no storkly interest. To do it with a demon was worse yet. It was her shame and her tragedy.

Soon Angela recovered enough to continue. "So now I am not welcome in Heaven, because I have . . . have . . . sinfully loved. So I set out to find somewhere where we can be together without being condemned by Heaven and H*ll for our association. Beauregard can't help me;

he's in trouble with his devilish superiors for not utterly humiliating me. He refused even to reveal my identity to them, so they couldn't harass me. I love him for that." She took a shuddery breath. "So this is my private personal quest. If I achieve reality here, he will join me, and H*ll will not be able to bar the way. But there is a problem. I am not real here. I have no body. I exist only as a once-pure soul without substance. Xanth requires substance."

"You look real to me," Wenda said.

"I am not. You see only my clothing, which is more apparent than real. My face and hands are illusion, but there was not enough to cover the rest of my body. I will show you." She lifted her voluminous skirt high, showing everything beneath it to the waistline.

Hilarion and Jumper in human body started to freak, then paused, confused. Because there was nothing there. Her skirt looked full from outside, but was empty inside. No feet, no legs, no panties. Just air.

Then Wenda realized that Angela's legs must be invisible. "May I?" she asked, extending her hand.

"You may," the angel said with a sad smile.

Wenda put a hand where there should be an ankle. Her fingers closed on air. She tried for a knee. Still nothing. Then for a thigh. Air. Finally she reached all the way up to where there had to be a juncture of the legs. No juncture.

"How can you walk?" Dipper asked.

"Like this," Angela said. She got up from her seat, moved to the aisle, and walked along it. Her skirt flexed with the apparent motion of her hips and legs, but there was nothing below it. It was as if she were floating.

"Like a ghost," Jumper said.

"Even a ghost is more real here than I," Angela said. "Because I will not be able to remain here. I have only one month to achieve a legitimate presence here. Then I must either return to Heaven, where I will be purged of all my memories of Beauregard, or fade away into oblivion. Of the two, I think I would prefer the latter."

"Purged of your memory of love," Hilarion said, interested for a reason the angel would not understand.

"Yes. Heaven will take me back, provided I am purged. But I don't think I want to return to that sterile existence."

"Kiss me."

Angela was startled. "I couldn't do that. I love Beauregard."

Wenda understood the prince's request. He wanted to ascertain whether she could be his bethrothee, by which she would definitely have a place in Xanth. His kiss could save her. "Trust me," she said. "Do it."

Confused, reluctantly, Angela proffered her face to be kissed. Hilarion kissed her. Then he drew back. "You are not she," he said with regret.

"Not who?"

"Not his fiancée," Wenda said. "He will know her when he kisses her. But you are not she, so he can't help you become real."

"Oh. Thank you," Angela said uncertainly.

"A month," Meryl said. "How much of it have you used so far?"

"Three weeks."

The six of them circulated a glance. The angel had only one week remaining to achieve her desire.

"This does not look good," Dipper said. "But I have an idea."

"That is one more than I have," Angela said. "I have been traveling Xanth, hoping to find a way, but without even half a modicum of success."

"Change places with me."

She looked at the bird. "I could not perch on Wenda's shoulder."

"I have been looking for meaning in my life," the bird repeated. "I think I can find it by giving you your chance. Take my place in our Quest. It is far more likely to help you than just riding the trollway."

"It surely is," Angela agreed. "Whatever the nature of your Quest. But I couldn't ask you to sacrifice yourself in this manner."

"Do they have birds in Heaven?"

"Actually, they don't, apart from birds of paradise," Angela said. "I'm sure you would be the center of attention there. But—"

"Then let me go there. It is something I want to do. Not because I care about Heaven—it obviously is not a birdly place—but because I think this is why I was sent to join the Quest. To reserve a place for you. Because you need that place more than I do."

"If you're sure—"

"I am. This is my destiny."

Angela looked at Wenda. "Could you agree to this? I would love to join your company. You seem like nice folk."

Another glance circulated, and landed hard in Wenda's left eye. "Yes," she agreed. "You may join us."

"Oh, thank you!" Angela turned to Dipper. "Here is my ticket to Heaven. Hold it and will it to activate, and you will be there."

The bird took the ticket in his beak. Then he vanished.

"But now you can't return," Wenda said belatedly.

"I didn't want to anyway. I only hope that regardless of my fate in a week, I can help you achieve your goal."

"We hope so too," Jumper said.

Then they acquainted Angela with their Quest, quietly so as not to be overheard by other passengers in the bus, and she came to see Princess Ida as she was. "I thought you suffered from Crone's Disease, but that's not so. You are the connection!" she exclaimed. "I see the next world around your head!"

"You do," Ida agreed. "Crone's Disease can only be reversed if a Bellyaching Old Crone discovers a young boy or two to fall in love with her." She sighed. "I am not interested in youths. I might be able to help you return to Heaven, if you wish."

The angel's delicate jaw firmed. "No. I will not return. I must make it here, or not at all."

"In that case, we all hope for the best," Wenda said. "I hope that we are able to help you find whatever it is you need."

The others returned to their prior seats. Wenda and Angela, now silent, couldn't help overhearing their brief dialogues.

"That was very interesting," the woman next to Meryl remarked. "I am Epi Nephrine. I stimulate hearts. But I don't believe I could affect a nonexistent heart."

"But it's nice of you to consider it," Meryl agreed politely.

"I am Prof Philactic," the man next to Jumper said. "Storks avoid me. But stork attention does not seem to be the angel's problem."

"Not at present, Professor," Jumper agreed.

Hilarion resumed his seat beside a robot, who issued a series of dots and dashes.

"I'm sorry, but I don't speak Morse code," Hilarion said.

The robot looked disappointed, but apparently was unable to speak any other way.

Angela looked out the window. "The scenery is not at all like Heaven," she remarked. "I see those animals eating those plants, but have no idea what either animals or plants are."

Wenda looked. "Those are cereal killers feasting on wild oats," she said.

"And that smart-looking tree, with all the people gathered around it?"

"That's a Pundit Tree," Wenda said. "It is full of wisdom."

"What about that one whose fruit people are eating while trying to burn it? That seems like odd behavior."

"That's a Tree Sonus whose fruits are candied dates."

"I don't understand."

"That's because you haven't been in Xanth long enough. Puns abound. Tree Sonus is Treasonous, and the candied dates are candidates. They stir up some fiercely negative emotions."

"You really know trees!"

"I do," Wenda agreed. "I'm a wouldwife. Would is my nature."

Conversation lapsed, and they snoozed as the long ride continued.

Wenda woke as the bus slowed. They were arriving at Lake Ogre Chobee. Hastily she got up and went to ask the driver for transfers, so they could transfer to a boat. She had almost forgotten that detail.

Armed with the transfer tickets, they debussed and stood at the shore of Lake Ogre Chobee. This was a vast shallow sea with toothy chobees swimming in it. No ogres were around, fortunately.

Wenda saw how Angela seemed to float just over the ground, her full skirt not quite touching. She had wings and could fly, but this was walking. The skirt flexed subtly as if being governed by moving legs. The overall effect was appealing.

There was a pier projecting into the lake, but no boat. What were their transfers good for?

Then Wenda spied a booth similar to the one the troll had used. She would inquire there.

But inside it was an ogre. She hesitated to approach

it. "I will go," Jumper said. "It may be that the ogres handle the river traffic."

He went, and in one and a half moments confirmed it. The ogre spread their transfers on his table and pounded his hamfist on them, once. Now they were stained with streaks of dirt: they had been duly canceled. "Wait to float, morning boat," he said.

"Morning?" Wenda whispered. "We need a suitable place for the evening."

"We are a party of six," Jumper said smoothly. "Four of whom are women. Where can we stay overnight?"

"Park your butts in yonder huts," the ogre said gruffly, pointing with a hamfinger.

They looked. There were several small cabins. Those would do. They selected two, one for the women, one for the men. Then they looked for somewhere to eat.

"There's a prospect," Meryl said, fluttering her wings. "Crossbreed Corner."

Wenda could appreciate why that would interest Meryl, who was a crossbreed. But was it really suitable?

Meryl went to inquire, then beckoned them in. It was a restaurant specializing in seafood. The proprietor was Nara Crossbreed, a composite of a six-species ancestry: human, sea serpent, nymph, brassie, dragon, and ogre. She could assume any combination of creatures in her heritage, but for now resembled a long-haired nymph with clawed dragon wings. Her talent was to summon water from any spring, into any container.

"What will you have?" she inquired when they were seated at the counter with tall glasses before them. "Healing elixir? Love spring water?"

"No!" Wenda cried.

The others laughed, and she realized it was a joke.

"We do carry tea," Nara said. "But right now the bags are being totaled, so they're not available." Indeed,

Wenda saw the tea-totaler totaling the tea bags to the side.

Nara conjured fresh ordinary water into their glasses, then took their food orders. Naturally Angela had angel food cake. It took Jumper and Hilarion a while to decide, because they were distracted by Nara's plunging décolletage, so Wenda ordered for them: humble pie. Not that they would appreciate her return joke.

Seven grizzled mining dwarfs entered and ordered hard drinks. There were several rocky bottles on the shelf, really hard stuff, but Nara refused. "You know miners aren't allowed hard liquor," she told them. Disappointed, they departed.

Nara delivered the pies, leaning gracefully forward. The men went comatose again, until she turned away. Then Hilarion returned to life. "Kiss me."

"Why should I do that?" Nara inquired.

"To ascertain whether you are the one."

Nara paused, perhaps contemplating a sharp retort. Then, observing his handsomeness, she leaned quickly across the counter and kissed him before he had time to freak out all the way from the view of her front. Stars radiated out from that contact like hot sparks.

But it was not to be. "You are not the one," he said with surpassing regret.

"Not the one for what?" she asked, faintly miffed. It had after all been a sparkling hot kiss.

"Not my betrothee. I can't marry you."

"Is that all? Have you any idea how many of my male customers want to marry me?"

"All of them," Wenda said, making a shrewd guess.

"All of them," Nara echoed. "So why should you be the one?"

"He's a prince," Meryl explained. "He was betrothed when he was two years old, to a princess who was age one at the time."

"Oh." Nara was evidently reconsidering. "I don't re-member any such event, but if I was in my nymphly form at the moment, I might have forgotten. Maybe we should kiss again, just to be sure." She leaned forward once more.

"No need," Wenda said quickly. Of course she wasn't jealous; she was married. "Unless you are twenty-one now."

"I'm seventeen."

"So it couldn't have been you."

"Actually—" Hilarion began.

"No need," Meryl agreed just as quickly. Naturally she wasn't jealous either, even if Nara was a prettier crossbreed, complete with legs instead of a tail, at least at this moment.

Ida and Jumper stayed out of it, and Angela merely observed, perhaps learning more about Xanthly inter-actions.

In due course they retired to their cabins. They even had illusion boxes showing scenes of Xanth. All part of the service of the trollway. Wenda was impressed.

"You seem like such nice people," Angela said. "I am enjoying your company, even if it is my last week of existence."

"I'm just a forest nymph who got lucky," Wenda said.

"What was it like, living in the forest?"

"It wasn't much, actually. I had to be wary of men, because they wanted only one thing and I didn't want to give it. I had a pet chuck made of would, like me, called Wouldy, and—"

"A what?" Angela asked.

"She used to speak in the forest dialect," Meryl ex-plained. "Now a spell blocks that. She is trying to say her pet was Woody Wood Chuck."

"Oh, I see," Angela said, though she didn't seem to see very clearly. "She certainly knows her trees."

"I will show you some tomorrow, if we have time," Wenda said.

"That would be nice."

They went to sleep watching a Big Band, which was a huge rubber band that vibrated to play popular music.

In the morning they rejoined the men and went to the pier. There was a boat there, but it was almost invisible. "I believe that is an air boat," Ida said. "It is made of compacted air, and is very light. It should be safe to use."

"But it's invisible!" Wenda protested. "I would not feel safe in it."

"I, too, have a certain insecurity," Hilarion said. Wenda flashed him a smile, appreciating the young man's support.

They went to the restaurant to inquire. "There's a new boat every hour," Nara said. "You'll have time for breakfast before the rowbot arrives."

Now it was Wenda who feared she had misheard. "Rowboat?"

Nara set a pile of pancakes and another of waffles before them. The pancakes looked like pans made of batter, and the waffles tended to shift positions, but they were good enough. "No, it's a robot boat. Stout and reliable."

"That's the one we want," Wenda agreed.

After breakfast, there was still a little time before the boat arrived, so Wenda took Angela for a walk at the fringe of the untamed forest beyond the way station. The first big tree was magnificent, but their feet started to slip as they approached it. "Slippery Elm," Wenda explained.

"Ah, now I comprehend."

The next tree had many furrly little flowers and made a mewing sound. "Pussy Willow," Wenda said. "Now we are coming to some pines."

Another made whispering sounds. "Whispering Pine," Wenda said. "If you listen carefully, it will whisper puns to you."

"I think I have already encountered plenty. In Heaven we don't have base humor; it is beneath us."

"There are doubtless plenty in Hell, though," Wenda said.

"I really wouldn't know."

"Still, it wouldn't hurt to learn some, if you are to associate with Beauregard."

"Oh! I hadn't thought of that."

The next tree extended small branches that hooked on their skirts and tried to lift them. They both had to jump back to avoid exposure. "Naughty Pine," Wenda said, smiling ruefully. "In the past I would have accented that differently."

"Knotty!" Angela exclaimed.

"Yes. Fortunately you don't need to worry, because it can't expose your panties."

"But I want to be able to worry! I need to get substance."

Oops. "I apologize. I forgot."

"No need. But I hope I can become a woman of substance soon."

They were interrupted by the toot of a horn. The row-bot was arriving.

This was a boat made all of metal, with arms that transformed into paddles. It was large enough to accommodate them all. Smoke drifted from its stack; it was indeed a wood-burning robot, with a pile of wood to consume. Robots had once been adversaries to the living creatures of Xanth, but now had been tamed and adapted to many purposes.

Wenda walked out along the pier and approached it, presenting her transfers. A bell sounded, and a gangplank extended to the pier. It seemed their tickets had been accepted.

They boarded. "We are going to the Gap Chasm," Wenda told it. A bell answered her. That seemed to be the language of this craft.

When they were all aboard, the paddles descended to the water and stroked it vigorously. The craft moved out, forging through the water of the big lake. Puffs of smoke rose from its stack and floated up into the sky, where they mingled companionably with the clouds.

They saw the green snouts of the chobees pacing them, but then Jumper assumed the form of an ogre, smiling, and the reptiles quickly departed. Evidently the chobees had brushed with ogres in the past, and learned respect by getting pulped into green paste. Ogres were not known for subtlety.

Later, as they were on the verge of the Kiss Mee River as it flowed into the lake, there was a storm that did not look like an ordinary tempest. This one made a howling sound, and let down a huge whirling tube that sucked up water. Then it came toward them and shot out a jet of water that splashed across the deck.

"It's a waterspout!" Ida said. "It is trying to wash us off the deck or capsize our boat so that we will fall prey to the hungry chobees."

"It is playing a mean game of Drench Mee," Meryl said.

"I can punch it," Jumper said, remaining in ogre form.

"You'd get sucked in and blown away," Ida said. "Waterspouts are dangerous."

Indeed, it looked dangerous, as it loomed closer, ready to spout again.

"Maybe I can help," Angela said. She spread her wings and flew toward it.

"Don't risk it!" Wenda cried, too late.

The angel flew right to the whirling spout. It spied her,

and shot a fierce jet at her. But the water passed right through the angel without affecting her.

Wenda was surprised. "How did it miss her?"

"She has no substance," Ida reminded her. "It can't touch her."

"Oh. Yes."

Immune to the jets, Angela flew right up to the spinning dark column. She put her sweet face forward and kissed it.

The spout was plainly surprised. Its tight column loosened. Then it lost control and flew apart, splatting them with flying water.

Angela, unaffected, flew back to the boat and landed neatly on the deck.

"What did you do?" Wenda asked, amazed. "A mere kiss by an insubstantial woman shouldn't have dented it."

"Yes it did," Angela said. "I could touch it, while it couldn't touch me. Sometimes mean-spirited things don't know how to handle affection. My kiss freaked it out."

"And the Kiss Mee River is certainly the place for a good kiss," Meryl said. "It must have had more power here."

So it seemed. Wenda realized the angel could indeed help their Quest, just by being what she was: a nice girl without substance.

They paddled on up the Kiss Mee River. No more waterspouts threatened them.

They ate the sea biscuits stored on the boat, watching the scenery forge by as the rowbot paddled ceaselessly. Angela didn't eat; she needed to develop substance before she could eat, ironically.

The sun was hot, and Wenda got thirsty, so she did what was natural in the forest: she cupped her hands and dipped out river water to drink. Meryl joined her.

"Don't do that!" Ida cried. "The water will—" But as often happened, she was too late.

Wenda sipped the water, and suddenly felt an overwhelming urge to kiss. She kissed Meryl, who was similarly overcome. Then the two of them got up and went after the others. Wenda kissed Hilarion while Meryl kissed Jumper, who had reverted to manform. Then they switched partners. Then they kissed Angela and Ida. Angela cooperated by actively kissing, because that made the illusion of her face just solid enough. Otherwise they would have fallen through her head. Finally, kissed out, they relaxed.

"—make you want to kiss indiscriminately," Ida finished. "The Kiss Mee is a very friendly river."

So it seemed.

"Still, if you girls are really thirsty . . ." Hilarion said, not at all averse to further kissing.

Ida threw a biscuit at him. "Neither of them is your betrothee," she reminded him sternly.

Dusk came, and the boat forged on. They spread mats on the deck and settled down for the night. Wenda had an idea, and dipped out a cup of river water, setting it beside her.

And Charming was there. Wenda hastily picked up her cup and gulped the water. Then she started kissing him so avidly that he was amazed. "You really miss me!" he said, pleased.

"I really do," she agreed around kisses.

Her ardor had effect. He was asleep in six minutes instead of seven. That wasn't quite what she had had in mind. Ah, well. It had been a wild six minutes.

In the morning the boat drew to a halt. They had come to the end of the river. Beyond it was the Gap Chasm.

"I believe we have completed our trollway trip," Ida said. "Hereafter, we must travel by foot and wing inside the Gap."

"Isn't the Gap dangerous?" Meryl asked.

"Not to us," Ida said. "I have a friend."

They did not question that. They would surely find out soon enough.

They stepped off the boat. "Thank you, Rowbot," Angela said, and gave its prow a hug. It almost seemed to Wenda that the boat blushed. The touch of an angel was special.

6

KNOT

They stood at the brink of the Gap Chasm. The land fell away in a virtual cliff, dropping into the shadowed depths so that they could not see the bottom. A young cloud floated serenely at ground level, which was cloud-height from the depths.

"This may seem like a foolish question," Hilarion said, "but how can those of us who can't fly safely descend?"

"There are paths down," Ida said. "I am familiar with them. There is one near here." She led the way to the east, and soon they came to a footpath that led up to the brink. And stopped. There was no angling ledge down the side.

"I fear this path has been terminated," Hilarion said.

"This may require some mental adjustment," Ida said. "Follow me." She stepped over the brink.

The others stared. Then Meryl leaped into the air, thinking to fly down and try to catch Ida as she fell. And paused, astonished.

Ida was not falling. She was standing on the cliff, her body at right angles to the ground. "It's magic," she explained. "The path provides its own orientation. Simply turn the corner and walk." She demonstrated by walking a few steps down inside the chasm.

Now Wenda remembered. The Princesses Dawn and Eve had shown how they handled the Gap Chasm, with Dawn crossing on the invisible bridge and Eve taking the low route, the path down into the void. Wenda had crossed on the bridge; Jumper had accompanied Eve into the depths.

"I will try it," Jumper said. "In my natural state, so I can post a safety line. That is what I did before." He became the large spider, dabbed a spot of web on the exposed rock, and clambered over. And paused much as Meryl had. "It works. It feels exactly like level ground."

Wenda trusted her friend, knowing he would catch her if she fell. He was explaining it as if it were new to him, reassuring her. She walked to the brink and stepped over. And turned the corner as if stepping over a ridge. Now she was standing horizontally. "I would not have believed this before trying it," she said, once again feeling slightly off because she had not said "wood knot."

After that Hilarion stepped over. "Remarkable," he said as he joined their orientation.

Meryl, still hovering, exchanged a generous glance with Angela. Actually it was more like a glance and a half. Then she flew to the Gap path and put her tail down. She stood aligned with the others, carefully balanced. Then Angela rounded the corner, not trying to fly. They were all on the path.

Meryl and Angela, having made their little demonstration of solidarity, lifted off the path and hovered nearby. Flying was really easier for them, for different reasons. Wenda saw Hilarion glance at them, perhaps hoping to see something interesting, but there was only a piece of tail as Meryl reoriented to the main chasm rather than the path, and of course there was nothing at all to be seen under Angela's widely spreading skirt. Wenda suppressed a private smirk of amusement. Hilarion was all right, but he was a man. That was his problem. He simply had to look.

They marched on down, following Ida. The princess was certainly proving to be helpful, with her knowledge of the most feasible route. It seemed like coincidence that they had encountered Angela on the trollway, but Wenda suspected that they had been magically guided. She also suspected that the angel needed them more than they needed her, but she was glad to help. Angela faced a horrible extinction if she did not succeed in her quest.

In time they reached the level bottom of the chasm. The path made a smart right-angle turn, and they resumed vertical orientation. The base was much like regular terrain, with bushes and a few trees dotting gentle hills. There were pie plants and pillow plants, so they would be able to eat and rest. It was actually rather pleasant.

Then they heard an odd puffing sound, interspersed by groud-shaking whomps. "That would be the Gap Dragon," Jumper said. "I believe he will remember me. You are on good terms, Ida?"

"Excellent terms," Ida agreed. "My sister Ivy tamed him decades ago, and now he accepts me as well as her."

"A dragon?" Hilarion asked, drawing his sword.

"No, please, no!" Ida said. "There is no need for that, and the dragon would simply steam you from well beyond sword range. Put it away."

He sheathed his sword, but did not look much reassured.

The green dragon whomped into sight. He had six legs, stubby little wings, and a huge hot head from which jets of steam puffed. He was a steamer, rather than a smoker or a fire-breather. Wenda knew that steam was quite enough to cook a person. He whomped because his legs weren't long enough for effective running, so he made snakelike curves up and down, moving forward section by section. It looked inefficient, but Wenda knew it wasn't; the Gap Dragon could catch what he chose to, in the chasm.

Ida went out to meet the dragon. She hugged the hot head without getting steamed. They did seem to be friends.

Then she introduced the others to the dragon. "Jumper Spider, whom you know from last year; he is now the Prince of Spiders, and married to the Demoness Eris. Wenda Woodwife, who is now the wife of Prince Charming. Prince Hilarion, on a Quest to find his betrothee. Meryl Mermaid, looking for she's not sure what. And Angela Angel, who needs to become a woman of substance."

The dragon nodded, accepting them.

"And this is Stanley Steamer, the Gap Dragon," Ida said, completing the introduction.

"We are glad to meet you in peace," Hilarion said, just a shade too politely.

The dragon puffed out a harmless cloud of steam in acknowledgment. Wenda knew that it could readily have been extremely harmful, had they encountered the dragon as opponents.

"We have an important mission here," Ida continued. "I would appreciate it if you made sure that no one interferes with us while we are in the chasm."

The dragon nodded again, puffing out a cloud of steam. Wenda realized that they would be quite safe in the chasm.

Now they oriented on the Knot, using Wenda's awareness of it. They followed the chasm west, then found a smaller split to the north, and followed that. But night, closing early in the depths, caught up with them before they reached the Knot, so they camped, harvesting pies and milk pods for dinner.

Angela was restless. "The approach of evening reminds me. Something happened last night that I don't understand. I was gazing at the stars, when they seemed to jump about seven minutes forward in their arcs. Was I imagining it?"

Wenda smiled. "You were not. You are not the only woman who ever showed her boyfriend her panties. Jumper and I had conjugal visits lasting that long. The rest of the party was put in stasis so as not to be disturbed. You were observant, noting the seeming jump of the stars."

"Well, I'm a Heavenly creature. I notice celestial events." She smiled sadly. "I envy you your visits."

That gave Wenda an idea. "Jumper, do you think Eris would be willing to arrange—"

"I believe she would," he agreed.

They said no more. But as they settled down to sleep under the stars, and Charming and Eris appeared, Wenda heard Angela's surprised voice. "Beauregard! However did you manage to escape your chores in H*ll?"

"I am a small-d demon," he replied. "Eris is a big-D Demoness. She can freeze Hell over, if she chooses, and maybe H*aven too. And she did. They won't notice the seven minutes I am gone."

"But why—?"

"It seems your friend Jumper sent her a telepathic message. Something about conjugal visits. She likes to please him."

"But we're not married!"

"Not yet," he said. "Don't tell."

Then he must have done something naughty, because Angela squealed with guilty pleasure and ceased talking. She might lack substance in Xanth, but evidently could relate to the demon with no physical difficulty.

In five more minutes things reverted to normal, except for the memories. Wenda had hardly noticed Charming's activity, this time, though she was sure she had satisfied him. She had been distracted by eavesdropping on Angela's affair. She knew she shouldn't have, but hadn't been able to help herself.

"Oh, my," Angela murmured, adjusting her halo, which had somehow been nudged askew. "What an experience! They will never let me back into Heaven now."

"Do you even want to return?" Wenda asked.

"No. I just want to be with Beauregard, even if it d*mns me to H*ll."

"I hope you succeed," Wenda said sincerely. Meanwhile, she was glad that the Demoness had elected to provide Angela with a bit of illicit joy, in case she didn't make it to substance.

The other three members of their party seemed unaware of what had happened, though they surely suspected. This was an unusual Quest, at least in this respect.

They slept at last, and the remaining night was uneventful. Wenda hoped they would reach the Knot next day, and that they would be able to move it. But she feared it would not be easy.

In the morning they handled morning chores and resumed travel into the narrowing gorge that was the Gap offshoot. Wenda understood already that getting a boulder out of this would be a chore. Would they be able to roll it along the path up the face of the cliff?

At last, as the crack narrowed almost too much to allow them passage, they reached it. Wenda knew it, because she saw the other members of the party getting frightened. That could only be caused by petrified reverse wood.

"I seem to be in the grip of an unfamiliar emotion," Hilarion remarked.

"It is fear," Wenda said. "We are approaching the Not. It petrifies all who come near it."

"Weird. I always wondered what fear felt like. I can't say I like it."

"Nobody does," Ida said.

"I forgot," Wenda said. "We will need reverse would—a lot of it."

"I thought you said the Knot was made of reverse wood," Angela said.

"Petrified reverse would. That changes its qualities. Its substance will feel like rock—actually much like nice—"

"Gneiss," Jumper murmured.

"Thank you. And its effect is fear rather than reversal. So I will have to clothe the Not in reverse wood, to change its effect on the rest of you."

"That will surely help," Meryl said tightly. She was looking somewhat green about the gills, despite lacking gills. Nobody liked being afraid.

"First we must locate the would," Wenda said. "I have no idea where any would be. I really should have anticipated this problem."

"Stanley Steamer will know," Ida said.

Wenda turned to Meryl. "Please, would you fly to Stanley and ask him where there is reverse would?"

"I'm afraid he'll steam me," Meryl said.

"He won't," Ida said. "He knows you now. It is the nearby Knot that is making you afraid."

"Of course," Meryl agreed nervously.

"I can ask him," Angela said. "He can't steam me."

"We'll go together," Meryl said, evidently relieved to have company.

The two winged females flew off down the crevasse.

"You wait here," Wenda said. "I will go to check the Not. It does not affect me."

"Which is why this is your Quest," Jumper said appreciatively. "The Good Magician always knows whom to send."

"He does indeed," Ida agreed. She too was plainly fearful; she was not immune.

Wenda walked on around the bend in the cleft and came into sight of the Knot. It was a massive boulder that seemed almost to glint with stony malice. She was not afraid, but she was definitely wary. This was physically inert, but not emotionally passive. It would mess them up if it could. It was her job to make sure it could not.

Beside it stood the wagon, stout enough to support the Knot. Somehow the Good Magician had managed to get it there.

She stood before the boulder. Now she could see the curling grain of it. It had indeed been part of a huge tree before getting buried eons ago. Surely a tree like no other. She could feel its lingering power radiating out to infuse the very air with fear, horror, revulsion, and other benumbing emotions. Had she not originated as wood, she would indeed have been petrified.

"Well, Not," she said boldly, "I am here to move you to a safe place."

It responded with an added blast of malevolence. *It understood her!*

This set her back, but she was determined not to let it gain any advantage. "We can do this the easy way or the hard way, Not," she said. "You can draw in your invisible fangs and let us transport you, or you can extend them and force us to nullify you. Either way, you will be moved."

The answering blast was so fierce that she knew it would never relent. The Knot was definitely not nice. In fact, it might not be much of an exaggeration to call it an evil artifact.

"So be it," she said with regret. "I think you understand me despite a certain problem I have with some words. As you may have guessed, I am a former would-wife, made whole by love and fulfillment, but I retain my ability to work with would. That includes immunity to your power, though ordinary reverse would can affect me. So you can't terrify me with your ambiance." She turned and walked away, feeling the virtual heat of its ire against her back. It was like a muzzled dragon, desperate to express its devastating internal fire. That was really too bad, because she had to respect wood this powerful. She would much rather have worked with it than against it.

She rejoined Jumper, Hilarion, and Ida, who were holding grimly firm against the horror of the Knot's radiation. "It is the Not, and it doesn't want to be moved, but the only power it has is the aversion it can generate in others." She paused an instant or two, struck by a question. "I wonder why it objects? Surely the Good Magician will give it a good home, and appreciate its special nature."

"It doesn't want to be caged," Ida said. "The Good Magician will keep it out of mischief."

Ah. That did make sense. "I told it we were going to move it regardless. I don't think it can stop us."

"I am wary," Jumper said. "The inanimate can be perverse and sometimes surprising. We shall have to be careful."

"We shall have to be," Ida agreed. "We can feel its ugly power from here. It may try to drive the rest of us off, so that you won't be able to cope alone."

"It is already trying," Wenda agreed grimly. "But the reverse would should nullify that."

"Can we be sure of that?" Hilarion asked. "It is my understanding that reverse wood can have different effects, not necessarily reversing things in ways that might be expected or wished."

"I think it will work," Wenda said. "Because the Not has only one power, petrification, so that's all that can be reversed."

"But what about the rest of us?" he asked. "We have multiple aspects."

"I had not thought of that," Wenda said. "I hope you will be able to cope."

"We shall have to," he agreed bravely.

There were things to like about this prince. If Wenda hadn't already been safely married, she might have found him interesting.

"I have an idea," Ida said. "We might use my carpet. That could float it out of the chasm."

That was an intriguing notion. "You don't mind walking?"

"I am here to help the mission. I can walk, especially at the slow pace likely when transporting the Knot."

"Then let me see if that will work," Wenda said.

Ida brought out the rolled carpet and gave it to Wenda. Wenda carried it back to the Knot. "You will get a ride," she told the boulder.

The Knot radiated a fresh burst of ire.

Wenda spread out the carpet, and put it against the base of the Knot. "Now just a little roll, and you will be on it." She pushed against the Knot.

To her surprise, the Knot rolled just enough, landing squarely on the carpet. Could it really be that easy?

"Up," Wenda told the carpet.

It lifted, but the Knot did not come with it. Wenda peered closely. To her horror, she saw that the Knot had burned a hole in the carpet. It had been ruined. "Oh!"

There was something odd radiating from the Knot. After half a moment, Wenda realized what it was: mean-spirited laughter.

"Bleep!" she muttered. The Knot had won this one.

Wenda returned to the others. "It burned the carpet," she said. "I am sorry, Ida. I did not know."

"It was my idea," Ida said graciously. "I did not know either. It was worth trying." There was no hint of blame in her tone.

Meryl and Angela returned. "Stanley Steamer's okay," Meryl said. "He's a winged monster, as I am. We were able to converse."

"I think he even likes her," Angela said. "He thinks she has a beautiful tail."

"He does think that," Meryl agreed, blushing.

"Well, you do," Hilarion said gallantly. "And that's not all." He had learned how to gaze at her bare front without freaking out.

"But about the reverse wood?" Ida inquired tightly. The baleful ambiance of the Knot was still affecting her.

"He has a cache," Meryl said. "He told us where it is."

"It seems he doesn't like to encounter reverse wood," Angela said. "It messes him up. We're not clear how, but it annoys him something awful. They all seem to be of the same variety. So he has packed away all the chips of it found in the chasm in a secluded grotto he never goes near."

"How did he do that, if touching it messes him up?" Jumper asked.

Meryl smiled. "He explained, in gestures. Sometimes elves, gnomes, goblins, trolls or other manlike cross-breeds stray into the chasm and he catches them. If he's not too hungry at the moment, he gives them a choice: get steamed for a future meal, or carry a chip to the grotto. Most of them decide to carry the chip, despite its effect."

"Maybe it reverses their personalities," Hilarion said. "Goblins and trolls hate to become nice folk."

Angela shook her head. "We got the impression it was more complicated than that."

"Well, let's find out," Wenda said. "We shall go to fetch the chips."

"How did he find them all?" Hilarion asked.

"One of the folk he made a deal with was Chris Cross, whose talent was to search an area and catalog everything there," Meryl said. "So Chris located all the reverse wood in the Gap Chasm. Now others are carrying it to the cache, bit by bit."

"That sounds like a fair amount of would," Wenda said.

"There's quite a pile, we understand," Meryl said. "We may need some way to haul it."

"I will fetch the wagon," Wenda said. She walked back to the Knot and took hold of the handle of the wagon. It was wood throughout, which she appreciated. She understood wood, even if she could no longer pronounce it correctly.

The Knot had no eyes, but somehow it managed to glare at her. It knew she was making progress despite its victory over the carpet.

She hauled the wagon to the others. It was heavy, and she was breathing hard. "Let me help you with that," Hilarion said, taking the handle. She realized that he had been looking at her chest. What was it about hard breathing that attracted men's attention?

Meryl and Angela flew ahead, showing the way. Hilarion and Jumper took turns hauling the heavy wagon. The way was bumpy, but manageable.

In due course they reached the grotto. It was indeed secluded, hidden by a tangle of vines. They would have missed it entirely had the winged girls not known exactly where to look. As it was, they had to maneuver the wagon over a ledge to enter.

They entered the grotto. There was the reverse wood: a good-sized mound of chips and branches. It looked like an ordinary brush pile, but Wenda knew it wasn't.

She had never before seen this much reverse wood in one place.

"Well, let's load it," Hilarion said. He stepped forward and picked up a fair-sized branch. And paused, dismayed.

His clothing hung loosely in some places, and stretched tightly in others. What had happened to him?

"You're a girl!" Meryl exclaimed, astonished.

"Oh, no!" he/she exclaimed, glancing down at a front that was fully as full as those he had been viewing on Meryl and Wenda. Apparently he/she wasn't completely thrilled to have one of his/her own.

"Maybe I had better load it," Meryl said. She flew to the pile and picked up a small branch. "Oops."

For she was now a winged merman, with broad shoulders, a flat chest, and a masculine midsection that caused Wenda to avert her gaze.

"I think we now have a notion what kind of reversal this particular variety of reverse wood accomplishes," Jumper said.

"But it should be a temporary effect," Ida said. "Only when we are actually touching it. We can load the wagon, then avoid direct contact. It is not an unbearable situation." She marched forward, picked up a branch, turned male, put the branch on the wagon, and let go. Sure enough, he/she reverted to female.

Angela tried to help, but was unable to touch the wood, let alone pick any of it up, so she was not changed.

That showed the way. They fell to with a will, piling the reverse wood on the wagon. Wenda was unaffected, being immune to the effect of reverse wood. "I wood knot have asked this of yew, had I known," she said as she placed the last chip. And paused. "What did I just say?"

"You are back in the forest accent," Jumper said. "The wood reversed your dialect."

"But I'm immune!" she protested.

"But the Good Magician's language spell isn't," Ida said, catching on.

That explained it. When Wenda stood away from the wood, she could no longer say "wood" correctly. "So when there's not a gender to reverse, it reverses what it can," she concluded. "I can live with that. I do not have to touch it at the moment."

"Yew dew knot," Jumper agreed with a smile.

Jumper and Hilarion pulled the loaded wagon together, while the winged girls spied out the best route for them and Wenda and Ida walked behind to salvage any pieces that got jiggled off. Ida changed genders as she worked, but reverted promptly as she dropped the wood on the wagon. The remarkable change was becoming routine.

They encountered a group of men. Hilarion immediately stepped forward to intercept them, his hand hovering near his sword. Wenda appreciated his boldness; if these men meant ill, they would soon be discouraged. "What are you doing here?" Hilarion asked.

"We can ask the same of you," one man answered. "How did you escape the dragon?"

"One of us knows the dragon from way back," Hilarion said. "Stanley Steamer let us pass."

"Us too," the man said. "We are performing an errand for the dragon, rather than get steamed. We are the Tractor family. I am Pro; I am very good at turning circles. This is my brother Con; he undertakes projects. And my brother Dis—" He broke off, because Dis was straying. "Get back here!" Dis returned to the group. "He tends to get interested in the wrong things. And Subcon, who finishes the jobs others don't get to. Not that any of this relates well to what we're doing for the dragon. But it's better than getting steamed."

"I'm sure," Hilarion said. These men were evidently

no threat, and were taking time from the mission. "We'll be moving on now on our own errand."

They moved on. Wenda wondered briefly what the Tractors were doing for the Gap Dragon. Then she realized it was obvious: they were fetching more reverse wood for the cache.

By evening they reached the vicinity of the Knot. They camped far enough away from it so that its baleful radiation did not affect them strongly. It obeyed the magic of the square cube law, diluting significantly with distance.

And as they settled for the night, Charming appeared, along with Eris and Beauregard, this time not putting the others into stasis. Again, Wenda was participating physically while paying attention mentally to the others—mainly the other two uncoupled members of the Quest.

"I admit to being jealous of their joy," Hilarion remarked to Meryl as she rested on her tail. "Do you suppose you and I might pretend to be a couple for seven minutes? You are an attractive creature despite not being my betrothee."

She considered. "And you are a handsome prince despite not being a merman. I have an idea. Suppose we pick up reverse wood chips, change genders, and then pretend? That would leave our normal forms pure for our beloveds at such time as we find them."

That made him pause. "I don't think I would appreciate it in that form. I wouldn't know what to do."

Meryl sighed. "Neither would I. So I suppose we'll have to suffer through alone."

"Anyway, it wouldn't be polite, when Ida lacks a partner," he concluded.

"I will manage," Ida said.

"How is it you never married, Princess?" he asked. "You are surely attractive for an older woman."

"Thank you," Ida responded a bit shortly. Maybe

they weren't far enough out from the Knot. "I simply never encountered the appropriate man. I like to think that it is not yet too late. That some day, when I least expect it, there he will be."

"I sincerely hope you find him," Hilarion said. "I am familiar with the experience of not encountering the right one."

"Yes, you are," Ida agreed, and smiled, her shortness dissipating.

"You never can tell," Eris said. "I waited for a century, and must confess I never anticipated marrying a spider. But he was indeed the one." She was ethereally beautiful, as perhaps only a being of her class could be.

The others were startled. "Aren't you supposed to be busy with that spider?" Ida asked.

"I put him blissfully to sleep in only four minutes this time. I think that's my record." Eris glanced in the direction of the Knot, though it was out of sight. "That is some bole you have to handle."

"It certainly is," Ida agreed.

"I have two thoughts that could materially simplify your Quest. Unfortunately I must not voice them, lest I be guilty of interfering with the internal affairs of another Demon's domain. As it is, these conjugal visits are skirting the limit. It's too bad." She glanced around. "I think the others are done. We must depart." Suddenly she was gone, and so were Beauregard and Charming, both sound asleep.

"We should tell Wenda about those thoughts," Meryl said.

"Why?" Hilarion asked. "Why tease her when we have nothing useful to offer? She has enough challenge already, without that added frustration."

"Point taken," Meryl agreed.

"She's certainly not taking that Knot for granite," he concluded with a bit of a smile in his voice.

Now Angela was stirring, finding herself alone. She hastily applied some an-gel to her mussed hair. Wenda stirred too, as if only now becoming aware of her surroundings.

"We three single individuals are envious of you three committed folk," Hilarion said. "We hope one day to be as satisfied with our relationships as you are with yours."

Angela blushed all the way into her halo. Wenda tried to blush too, but after a year of marriage such a reference lacked sufficient force. "Thank you," she said for them both. "We hope you find them."

Wenda elected not to reveal that she had eavesdropped. But she wondered what those unvoiced thoughts of the Demoness were. What was she missing? She would have to be alert for anything that could make the Quest easier.

Fortunately no one questioned her. Jumper was sound asleep, and the others soon were slumbering too.

Wenda continued to ponder the mystery of those two thoughts. Demons with the small d were often mischievous, like Metria, and could not be trusted. But big-D Demons were serious, and Eris more than most; she was genuinely grateful to Jumper for rescuing her from isolation. She probably wanted to help, but was constrained by Demon Protocol. So this was no tease; she had something in mind. What could it be? Not one thing but two.

It was both promising and frustrating that Wenda had overheard that dialogue. But that made her wonder: why hadn't the Demoness mentioned it to her, instead of to Ida, Hilarion, and Meryl? Wenda was the leader of this Quest, the one most concerned.

Then it came to her in a double flash that she hoped did not wake any of the others. Flash one: Eris had not mentioned it to her *because* she was the leader. Eris was constrained by Demon Protocol, and giving a hint to Wenda could have violated it. Mentioning it incidentally to others might have fallen just below the threshold of violation. They might not relay it, not thinking it important, so it would be wasted anyway.

Flash two: Eris had *wanted* Wenda to overhear. She must have known Wenda was listening, but pretended not to. Women of any type were good at that sort of thing. So she had given a hint in a masked manner. If Wenda could figure it out on her own, that was no violation.

Which left her with the two thoughts. Two ways her Quest might be simplified. What could they be? Surely she could fathom one of them. If she could just cudgel her simple woodwife brain to evoke it.

Could the people the Demoness had spoken to be relevant? Ida, Hilarion, Meryl. All three of them looking for meaning in their lives, whether in the form of a compatible companion or something else. All needed for the Quest, whether to fly to get information, or to use their talents.

A third bulb flashed. Hilarion's talent was to make people forget spot memories. Ida's talent was to make things real by agreeing with someone who made a suggestion without knowing Ida's talent. Wenda had been forgetting how those two talents could interact. Jumper had spelled it out when Hilarion joined the Quest: how he could work with Ida to magnify her power. It made terrific sense. Yet somehow that thought had gotten lost in the other complications of the Quest. Eris must have seen that, and tried to remind Wenda. That would certainly simplify the Quest. That had to be one of the thoughts.

So what was the other thought? Wenda tried to focus on it, but drifted off to sleep before she could come to proper grips with it.

In the morning they organized for the project. "My talent is to craft reverse wood," Wenda said. "That is why I am immune to its effects. Now I am going to shape a shell to surround the Knot." She smiled, because her dialect returned while she was holding reverse wood, a small benefit. "And that should reverse its petrifying radiation, and make the rest of you able to approach it. Then we will be able to haul it on the wagon to the Good Magician's Castle."

"How can we help?" Jumper asked.

"I think I need to shape the wood into long strands, and weave them together to make a wicker cage. If someone could weave them as I form them, that wood help. But yew dew knot need to dew that; yew dew knot want to suffer the change in gender when yew touch it."

"We can handle it," Jumper said, and picked up a branch.

Then the others were doing it too, teasing one another about how handsome or lovely they were in their reversed roles. They handed suitable branches and chips to Wenda, and took the strands she crafted, weaving them into a large wickerwork mat. The job took hours, but they stayed with it, and by early afternoon it was done. They had a sheet they could wrap around the Knot to nullify it.

The next step only Wenda could do. They rolled up the mat, and put it on the wagon, and she hauled the wagon around the bend to the Knot. She knew it was aware of her approach; she could feel not only its radiation, but its anger. But it couldn't stop her.

She hauled the reverse-wood wickerwork mat off the wagon and spread it on the ground before the Knot. It radiated so much anger that it almost seemed it might set the mat on fire. That it might at least burn a hole in it, as it had with the magic carpet. But that was unlikely, because the reverse wood converted the anger to friendly acceptance. Already it was working.

Now she had to wrap the mat around the Knot. What

was the best way to do that? She could throw it over the top, but then it wouldn't connect at the bottom. So it would be better to roll the Knot onto the mat, then lift up the edges and tie them together at the top. But how could she move the Knot? It wasn't as tall as she was, but the Good Magician had said it weighed a hundred and fifty pounds. She knew it would exert its maximum passive resistance, refusing to be rolled anywhere. It knew this was not the carpet.

She wished she had some elbow grease. When a job was too difficult, some of that applied to the elbows made it possible to accomplish. But there was no grease of any kind here. Would Princess Ida have some in her collection? Wenda was tempted to go and ask.

Then she remembered some garden-variety magic: leverage. A lever could move something by magically multiplying the force applied. That should do it. No need for elbow grease.

Naturally she had no lever. So she went to the wagon, worked out the wooden pin holding the tongue to the main body, and separated the tongue as a prospective lever. She carried it to the Knot, set the end against a rock in the ground, and pried. "I'm going to use my tongue to give you a licking," she said as she heaved.

The Knot resisted, but couldn't reverse the leverage because reversal was no longer its magic. Grudgingly, it rolled onto the mat.

Abruptly its anger seemed to become pleasure. The reverse wood was reversing the effect of the radiation.

She picked up the edges of the mat and drew them together over the top of the boulder. She wove their loose ends together to make the enclosure complete. She had succeeded in nullifying the baleful power of the Knot.

She put two fingers to her mouth and made a piercing whistle. Wood-whistles had always been natural to her.

The other members of the party heard and came

around the bend. They came right up to the wrapped Knot. "Oh, it's darling!" Meryl said, hugging it. "Oops." For she had suddenly turned male.

"Do not touch the would," Wenda said. "Because then it acts on you as well as on the Not." She put her hand on the mat herself, demonstrating. "I wood knot dew that to yew," she said, smiling.

The others laughed, and kept their hands off the mat despite their obvious urge to get close to the seemingly friendly and positive Knot. Its glare had become a smile, filtered by the lattice of reverse wood.

Getting it loaded on the wagon was no problem, now that they had many hands. Jumper, in manform, and Hilarion took hold of it on either side and lifted it up. Both became female, but even so they were strong enough to manage it. Ida, turning male, took an extra band of wood and tied it over the top, anchoring the Knot in place. Wenda put the tongue back on the wagon and replaced the pin.

They were ready to travel.

7

TRAVEL

Before we start hauling," Jumper said, "I have a question. How are we going to get it out of the Gap Chasm?"

"I thought we would retrace our route here back to the vertical path, and use that," Wenda said. She winced internally, thinking of the lost magic carpet.

"Maybe that would work," he agreed. "But it's a long, tedious trip, and I am nervous about hauling a thing of this mass on such a devious trail. Suppose the path's magic is overwhelmed or reversed?"

"We could crash," Hilarion said. "If we could even get started. I don't think we should risk it."

Wenda had to concede the validity of their concern. "Does anyone have a better idea?"

"What about that humidor you used before?" Hilarion asked. "Didn't that transport you from one place to another?"

Wenda shuddered. "Please not that. You don't know what Planet Comic is like."

"I don't understand the reference," Angela said. "Are you talking about a world or a travel route?"

"It is both," Ida explained. "Comic is one of the worlds in the loop to which I relate." She indicated the moon that orbited her head, and it promptly tried to hide behind her hair. "The humidor connects directly to it, and there is another door returning directly to Xanth. But there are two problems. One is that the return is random; we could land anywhere. That might be inconvenient."

"But that same randomness can be an advantage," Jumper said, "because we are unlikely to return here, or anywhere in the Gap Chasm. So it does represent a convenient way out."

"If we don't land in a swamp or a lava lake or a wild wind storm," Meryl said somewhat sourly. She naturally preferred clear air and open water.

"What is the other problem?" Angela asked.

"The door is hidden in a Strip," Ida said. "This is a section of atrocious puns that can be really unpleasant to navigate."

"But puns are natural to Xanth! What's so bad about them?"

"You would have to be there to properly appreciate the problem," Meryl said.

"Yes. I would like to see it." Angela seemed to feel that they were fussing about nothing of consequence.

A little girl wandered by, holding a handful of straws. Wenda, glad for the interruption, went to her. "Excuse me. Are you lost? This is a dangerous place."

"I know," the child said. "But the dragon is letting me go if I find all the straws."

"The Gap Dragon wants straws?"

"These are special. I know how to find them. Each one is a straw that breaks a camel's back."

A pun. "Why does the dragon want these straws?"

"Because they might break his back, if they thought

he was a camel. So he wants them out. He'll steam them to death. Then I can go."

"That's one careful dragon," Hilarion remarked.

"Where is your mother?" Wenda asked.

"I have no mother. I'm an orphan."

Wenda's heart clenched. But she couldn't adopt this child. She had a dangerous mission to complete. "I hope you find a good home."

"I hope so too." The girl moved on, searching out special straws.

Wenda gazed up the wall of the canyon. The top seemed impossibly high. It was bright above, while already the gloom of evening was encroaching on the base. Did they really have a choice?

"I believe we shall have to do it," Ida said tightly. "Maybe the reverse wood will nullify some of the puns."

"That's an idea," Jumper agreed. "It seems a better prospect than getting the vertical path nullified."

"Then we had better do it," Wenda said. "We can go there and spend the night, preparing for the onslaught of the puns. Maybe Angela will be able to spy out the worst ones so we can avoid them."

"Or simply ignore them," Angela said. Clearly, she did not properly comprehend the problem.

"Be ready to roll the wagon through the door," Wenda told the others. "There may not be much time, and we definitely want to pass through as a single party."

Ida brought out the humidor, opened it, and put a drop of water into the tube. The fog boiled out, forming the cloud. There was the door. Ida opened it.

Jumper and Hilarion, remaining masculine, hauled on the tongue. Wenda and Ida pushed on the wagon behind. Meryl and Angela hovered closely above. They moved through as a group. Ida closed the door behind them. The fog dissipated, leaving no trace. They were through.

They were in a glade in what appeared to be a dense purple jungle. It was not at all like the open blue field and yellow trees of the prior visit. But of course this was a planet; it had a varied terrain. They would make do. They parked the wagon with the shrouded Knot and relaxed, to a degree.

Wenda sniffed the air. "This is an ordinary forest, apart from its color, without bad threats," she announced. "We can camp safely right here. But I detect some puns that must have leaked from the Strips, so beware."

"We will scout the wider territory," Meryl said. She and Angela flew up to look around.

"Meanwhile I'm hungry," Hilarion said. "I presume there are pie plants in the vicinity."

"That is uncertain," Ida said. "But we can forage for whatever exists."

"There is a nearby pine apple tree," Wenda said.

"We don't want that," Jumper said.

Wenda smiled. "There are different varieties. This is a sad tree bearing apples, not explosives."

"Ah." He went to harvest some sad apples.

After a moderate time and a few moments, Angela and Meryl returned. "There's a Strip wending its way not far from here. The forest does not touch it, for some reason." She smiled, knowing the reason.

Ida and Hilarion returned with a collection of edible fruits. Jumper brought apples, which seemed to be perking up now that they were separated from the unhappy tree. Meanwhile Wenda had explored the ground and located a nest of fire ants, the kind that started small fires for controlled burns to clean up hazardous areas. They had death matches, and she borrowed a match from them to start a cooking fire for Ida to use while Wenda foraged for more sticks of ordinary wood.

Ida fried single- and double-yoked eggs from an eggplant they had found, and waffles from a corrugated waffle bush.

Before long they settled down to eat. Then the mischief started.

"This is an excellent waffle you found and cooked, Ida," Hilarion said.

"Thank you. But the credit should go to Wenda for making the fire for it." Ida took a nibble herself.

"Yes, of course." Then his mouth burst open and he let out a resounding burp. "Oops."

Ida followed half an instant after with an unsuccessfully stifled burp of her own. She colored, embarrassed. Elder princesses were not supposed to have impolite digestion.

Suspicious, Wenda checked. She knew all the forest products. "Oh, no! You harvested Belchin' Waffles!"

Meryl stifled a giggle, then bit into her pepper. And froze, her mouth turning blue with cold.

"And that's a chilly pepper," Wenda said, horrified anew. "Spit it out before you freeze!"

Meryl did, and the color slowly returned to her face.

Jumper, in manform, took a bite of his own pepper. Suddenly he heard a ringing sound, so loud the others heard it too.

"And that's a bell pepper," Wenda said.

Hilarion finished his egg and bit into a warm moist pastry. And fell flat on his back, looking flat.

"Steam roll," Wenda said.

Jumper had found a sandwich plant near the pine apple tree. He took a bite of a sandwich—and got invisibly whacked on the head. "Club sandwich!" he said ruefully. "I have seen them before. I just wasn't thinking."

Wenda looked around. "I think in future I had better do the foraging. It is evident that puns have infested this region, probably because of the nearby Strip."

The others nodded, ruefully agreeing.

Wenda foraged. She found a patch of vegetables. She was about to harvest some when she saw a child, a little boy, reaching for one. "Don't take that one!" she exclaimed. "That's cough-fee. That's for adults only. It will just make you cough."

"Then what can I take?" the boy asked. "I'm hungry."

"Take the one next to it. That's to-fee. It tastes good."

The boy took that one and chewed on it, showing no emotion.

That bothered Wenda. "Who are you?" she asked.

"I am Alex. Short for Alexythemia."

"I don't think I understand."

"I am named after my condition. A- means without, lexi- means words, themi- means emotions or feelings. I am unable to express emotions."

"Oh, you poor thing," Wenda said, her sympathy overflowing. "I wish I knew how to help you."

"No one can help me," Alex said with neither joy nor sorrow. "Thank you for the to-fee."

"You are welcome," Wenda said. But Alex was already departing. Wenda was sorry she had been unable to address his main problem, but she had no idea how. She returned to her foraging.

Soon she found a patch of sun flours. Those would do for one course. Their ripening flowers contained many seeds that powdered into edible flour. That flour could be baked into bright warm cakes that radiated their sunny nature.

By the time Wenda had scouted out truly edible things, it was late, and they settled down for the night.

Wenda remembered something. "Soon our significant others will visit," she said delicately. "I have a suggestion for the three of you who are unfortunately left out."

"No, the Prince and I decided not to," Meryl said, blushing.

Wenda had to smile. "Not that. This: I remembered something the three of you can do together. If Hilarion makes Meryl forget about Ida's talent, then Meryl can make suggestions that Ida can make real. That could be extremely useful. We discussed it before, but never followed up. Now, considering the hazards of travel, I think we should work it out in more detail."

Hilarion, Meryl, and Ida circulated a glance. They were interested.

Then the visitors arrived, seemingly having no trouble locating them on this other world, and Wenda, Jumper, and Angela were pleasantly occupied. The three singletons were in animated dialogue, working it out.

This time Wenda, tired from the day's activities, fell asleep herself, and did not wake until morning.

"Did you work things out?" she asked Meryl.

"Work what out?"

So her memory of the matter was gone. "The most feasible route to the nearest Strip."

"Oh. Yes. There's actually a path to it. Not that I'm eager to get into it."

"It's a necessary evil," Wenda said. "And it should be an education for Hilarion and Angela."

Wenda foraged for safely edible food for breakfast, and found a regular pie tree. They ate, then moved out. The men hauled the wagon, the fliers scouted the way ahead, and Wenda and Ida followed behind.

"You did work it out?" Wenda asked Ida.

"Yes. Meryl volunteered, but that memory was erased. Hilarion will encourage her to come up with ideas. We will just have to see how well it works, if at all."

There were tight squeezes, rocks, and boggy sections along the path, slowing the wagon. "I wonder whether there is any way to make the wagon lighter?" Meryl remarked. "Maybe we can find a lighter along the way."

"I'm sure we can," Ida agreed immediately.

And there, beside the path, was a lighter. Wenda picked it up, flicked its wheel, and a flash of light emerged. She put it near each of the four wooden wagon wheels, flicking the light on them. Sure enough, they became lighter, and the wagon lifted higher. Now it was easier to haul across the mushy sections. That was just as well, because the small lighter was exhausted, and could not be used anymore.

"It does seem to work," Ida agreed, as if pleasantly surprised.

It did. But that served to remind Wenda that the Demoness had had two thoughts. One Wenda believed she had figured out, about the use of Hilarion's talent. What could the other thought be? She had no idea, and that bothered her. It was surely highly relevant.

They emerged from the jungle in late afternoon. There was the blue field with scattered yellow trees, and a red stream in the distance. Such a landscape now seemed familiar.

"This is nervous business," Hilarion remarked.

Nervous? He had not found it so before. Not since Wenda had covered the Knot.

That gave her the clue. She approached the wicker mat and put her finger to the wood. "I would not do that to yew," she said. Only the last word had reverted.

"Does that mean what I fear it means?" Jumper asked.

"That the reverse wood is losing its effect," Wenda agreed grimly. "Touch it."

He did. His face wavered a bit, but his body did not turn female. "It is no longer working."

Ida joined them. "The Knot is a very powerful, dense, potent artifact. The shell of reverse wood is thin. The constant radiation must be wearing it out, depleting it."

That made unfortunate sense. They would have to replace the shell before they went farther. The Strip would be bad enough without the malign influence of the Knot.

They held a brief conference. "We must find more reverse would," Wenda concluded.

"Is there reverse wood on this world?" Hilarion asked.

"There should be," Meryl said. "After all, it's got puns and pie trees."

"I'm sure you are correct," Ida agreed.

Their ploy had just worked again. "We must search it out," Wenda said. "Quickly."

"I have an idea," Jumper said. Wenda knew this would be a practical one, not a suggestion for Ida. "I can take my small spider form and ride with Meryl as she circles over the landscape. When I spot reverse wood, I can notify you telepathically. There's only one problem: I don't know what it looks like, as I'm pretty sure it won't be in a grotto of branches and chips."

"I know," Wenda said. "But I'm too big for Meryl to carry."

"If you maintain telepathic contact," Ida said, "you can have Wenda gaze through your eyes, recognizing it."

"I can!" Jumper agreed, pleased. He changed form and jumped to Meryl's hair.

Meryl flew up in a spiral. She used her tail to stabilize her motion through the air. Jumper looked around with his full-circle spider's eyes. He opened his mind to Wenda, and she saw what he saw.

She knew what to look for. *Fly toward that isolated copse,* she thought.

Jumper relayed the request to Meryl, who flew that way. And there was a live reverse-wood tree, with a number of fallen branches around it. Bugs and animals tended to leave reverse wood alone, not appreciating its effects.

That's it, Wenda thought. *Reverse would. Come on back. We'll have to work with it there, away from the*

Not, then bring it to the wagon. That way the Not won't deplete it before we're ready to travel again.

They returned. "That worked so well, I'm almost suspicious," Meryl said. "I wonder—doesn't Hilarion have a talent to—" She shook her head. "I forgot what I was going to say."

Hilarion smiled obscurely. He was not the only one.

"You folk sleep," Wenda said. "I will work alone during the night."

"No, you won't," Jumper said loyally, returning to regular-sized manform. "I will help you."

"Thank you," she said gratefully, handing him his clothing.

In the end they all joined her at the copse, leaving the Knot by itself. It wasn't as if it would be going anywhere, and they were more comfortable being away from its growing effect.

Eris appeared. "Not that I would seek to interfere, but aren't you supposed to be moving the Knot?"

"It wore out the reverse wood," Jumper explained. "So we came here to fetch more, away from the Knot, so it can't be depleted before we use it."

Eris nodded. "That is one tough Knot. But you can surely spare seven minutes or less." She stepped into him with an embrace and kiss.

"Ooo, I'm jealous," Meryl said, smiling.

"I do try to be fair," Eris said. She embraced and kissed Meryl also. The funny thing was that as she did so, she became a handsome winged merman. Wenda was reminded how the Demoness could assume any form she chose.

"Thank you," Meryl said faintly as it ended. Little hearts orbited her head.

"I borrowed the form of your eventual lover," Eris said. "I hope you don't mind."

"Not at all." Then her eyes widened in pleasant surmise. There was a winged merman for her?

Soon the visitors were gone and work resumed. Jumper, Wenda, Angela, and now Meryl all were feeling more positive. Only Ida and Hilarion remained low, but they bore with it without fuss.

Wenda used her talent to shape the branches as before, rendering them into flexible strips. The others wove them into a new wickerwork mat. They took turns foraging for food and sleeping. By morning they had it done.

But they suffered assorted reversals as they touched the wood. This was a new variety, and it did not reverse their genders. Instead it rendered Angela into a demoness with little horns and a mischievous nature. Jumper became a big fly instead of a spider. Meryl had the head of a fish and human legs, complete with panties that freaked out Hilarion. Hilarion became a ragged pauper instead of a well-dressed prince. And Ida became a child instead of a mature woman. They all bore with it and kept working, doing what they could. Except for Angela, who still was unable to touch the wood with any force, regardless of her form, and finally gave up trying.

"We are ready to move on," Jumper said. "But we're all tired. I think we should wait before tackling the Strip."

Wenda was of two minds. She wanted to get on through the Strip and back to Xanth, but realized that they could handle it better if they were properly rested.

"Let me help," Angela said. "I was unable to do anything, so got a good night's rest, which I really didn't need anyway, since I am ethereal. You rest while I explore the Strip and try to locate the Door. Then I can direct you to the most expedient route."

That made so much sense that all they could do was agree. Then they sank down on the ground and slept.

It was noon when Wenda woke, feeling somewhat but imperfectly refreshed. She assumed it was much the same for the others. Angela had returned with her report.

"It's awful," she said. "That Strip has no end; it seems to circle the planet. I could not see the Door, but I think I did see the Sidewalk. It is protected by really awful puns, too mind-rotting to remember. So even taking the most direct route, we shall have to suffer."

"So we shall suffer," Hilarion said. He had not seen the puns, so was not fazed. Wenda knew he would soon learn better.

They hauled the new reverse-wood wicker mat to where the Knot remained. Overnight its clothing of reverse wood had withered and curled as if subjected to intense heat. It was of course useless.

The others were unable to approach the Knot. Their fear and loathing might have no sensible basis, but it was genuine. This was Wenda's job, alone.

She couldn't roll the Knot onto the mat, because it was securely nestled in the wagon. So she threw it over the top, and drew it together in a ring at the base. This was effective; the dreadful radiation was converted to the semblance of friendship and pleasure.

The others came close, now drawn rather than repelled. They hauled the wagon briskly along parallel to the Strip, following Angela. Now Wenda saw that the various puns confined by the Strip were shrouded by its translucent border so that it was difficult to make them out. Angela had been able to actually enter the Strip and see without being governed by them, which helped.

"Here," Angela said, pointing to a section that looked like any other section. They would have been unlikely to select it on their own. Angela now was proving her worth to the Quest.

"Stay close together," Wenda reminded the others.

"Especially when we reach the Sidewalk. We'd never be able to find anyone who got stranded behind."

"Close," Hilarion agreed, beginning to appreciate the gravity of the situation.

"Once we go inside, I won't be able to point the way," Angela said. "I have been able to hover outside and peer in, but I will lose that perspective inside."

"We understand," Wenda said. "You have done what you could."

They nerved themselves and plunged in, hauling the wagon along. There before them was a tree with many band-like branches. It looked harmless, but when they tried to brush past it, the twigs reached into their pockets and tried to steal things. They had to pull back, because there were too many branches to block.

"It's a Banditree!" Ida exclaimed. "It means to steal from us."

"How can we stop it?" Hilarion asked, fending off a branch that was trying to steal his sword.

"There must be a counter-pun nearby," Wenda said. "I am good at trees; I should be able to find it."

She looked around. She spied a Coventree, where unwanted people or things could be sent, but how could she send a rooted tree anywhere? Then she saw something that might work. "There's an Infantree," she said, relieved that the dialect spell didn't prevent her from saying "tree." Maybe that was because there was no similar-sounding word with a different spelling. Well, not exactly. "It grows tough babies. If we can get them to march on the Banditree, they will keep it too occupied to stop us from passing."

"Infantree," Hilarion repeated, as if the word tasted bad. "Make the infants march."

"Exactly. A Coquetree could do it, luring them forward, but I see none here."

"Jumper!" Meryl said. "He can change form. Could he become a Coquetree?"

"Yes, I'm sure he could," Wenda agreed, sounding in her own ears just like Ida.

"Yes, I can," Jumper agreed. He became a tree with flirtatious foliage. It oriented on the Infantree, where tough babies hung. A platoon of infants dropped to the ground, formed a column, and marched toward him.

Jumper sidled toward the Banditree. This was not something a true Coquetree could do, but fortunately the babies lacked experience. They followed, marching in step. When they were close to the Banditree, Jumper changed back to spider form, effectively disappearing.

"Companee—halt!" the sergeant baby bawled. He looked around, and spied the Banditree. There was a suitable target. "Charge!" he bawled.

In half a moment the tough babies were attacking the Banditree, a natural enemy. It would soon wish it was in the Coventree.

Meanwhile, the party slipped past, unnoticed, trundling the wagon with the Knot. They had nullified an obnoxious pun. Wenda had the feeling that the Knot was disappointed; it had of course wanted them to be balked.

But immediately they faced the next pun. This was a statue of a vigorous robot blocking their way. "A Robust," Hilarion muttered. "I am coming to appreciate your dread of abysmal puns."

When they tried to pass, the Robust reached out with his robotic arms to stop them. "I need fuel for my tank," it said. "Your body fat will do." It seemed that not all robots burned wood.

"Maybe a female robot is near," Meryl said.

"I'm sure one is," Ida agreed.

And there she was: a wheeled Robust with a fine bare female chest with twin turrets. Hilarion's eyes locked in place.

The female Robust rolled up to the male and pressed her metal torso close. Sparks flew.

The party moved by during the romantic distraction, still hauling the wagon.

Now they came to a patch of lovely purple flowers. "Lilax," Wenda said, identifying the plant. "They never tell the truth. Don't smell them, or you will be unable to tell the truth either."

"Could we reverse that with a chip of our wood?" Jumper asked.

"We might," Ida said. "But I think we don't want to weaken the protective shield around the Knot even a trifle if we don't have to."

"What does encourage truth?" Hilarion asked.

"Truthlax."

"Is there any of that here?"

"There must be," Meryl said. "Because the pun antidotes are always close. Isn't that what you said, Wenda?"

"I did say that," Wenda agreed, again feeling like Ida.

"There must be," Ida herself agreed.

And there was a patch of yellowish-blue flowers. Truthlax. Their fragrance made them all eager to tell the truth. "Where is the Sidewalk?" Wenda asked it.

The truthlax flowers leaned to the left. The lilax flowers leaned to the right.

"Thank you." Wenda led the way left.

But there was no Sidewalk. Instead there was a burning house. No, it was a house made of fire. There were firemen, also formed of fire, and it was surrounded by a wall of fire: a firewall.

They approached, cautiously, as there was no other way to go. Immediately the two firemen on guard raised their weapons: firearms. One fired a jet of flame, a warning shot. They could not pass.

"I think we need another idea," Wenda said.

"What do firemen do for entertainment?" Meryl asked.

"I believe they attend firemen's balls," Ida said. "That's where their true flames are."

"Then maybe what we need is a fireball."

"We surely do," Ida agreed.

"Considering this environment," Hilarion said, "we may want to look in a ballpark."

That was a good idea. They cast about, and saw a park to the side. It was piled high with balls of every type. And there in a corner was a fireball.

"We need to get it to the firehouse," Wenda said. "But it looks way too hot to touch."

"I may be able to move it," Jumper said. He walked to the far side of the ball, then changed form, becoming a giant blowfish. He blew hard, exhaling a fierce gust of wind.

The fireball flamed up, but it also began to move. Jumper followed it on his flippers, blowing, keeping it going. As it came near the firehouse, it expanded, becoming as large as the house. Within it Wenda could see the dancing flames, writhing evocatively. They looked like burning nymphs.

The firemen spied the ball. They lost interest in all else, and ran to join their flames.

And Wenda's party pulled the wagon past the house. One more punfest had been defeated.

But still they were not finding the Sidewalk. "How much of this infernal mess do we have to put up with?" Hilarion demanded.

"Now you understand why we abhor the Strip," Ida said.

"I do indeed. I thought puns were harmless, but some of these are dangerous, and they are certainly inconvenient."

"We need more suggestions to navigate them," Ida said.

"I will see to that." He looked at Meryl. "You seem

to have a productive imagination. For every useful idea you come up with, to deal with these festering horrors, I will kiss you."

"Is this a promise or a threat?" Meryl asked with an undefined portion of a smile.

"Both."

"I will hold you to it."

Now they oriented on the way ahead. This was a seemingly harmless field of rye grass.

"I do not trust this," Hilarion said.

"Do we have a choice?" Jumper asked.

"No," Wenda said, and walked into the field. The others followed, hauling the wagon.

"Hay!" Meryl said.

Wenda turned to her. "What?"

"Hay hay hay! I think I've got hay fever," Meryl said, sneezing.

Then the others were doing it too. There was a chorus of hays interspersed by sneezes and arguments. What was happening? The group was not normally this fractious.

Wenda looked more closely at the plants of the field. "Now I understand. This is not rye, it's wry. It is making us react wryly. To be perverse or distorted."

"Then let's get the bleep on through it," Hilarion snapped.

They hurried, but soon came up against a fort with a nasty attitude. It sat directly across the path, and had embrasures with crossbows galore. Meryl flew toward it, and several bolts were loosed at her. Only the fact that their party was still out of range prevented them from striking her.

They halted, gazing at the fort. "I don't see anybody inside it," Jumper said. "Those crossbows seem to be operating on their own."

"That means we can't reason with them," Wenda said.

"Who is holding down the fort?" Hilarion asked.

"I'll go see," Angela said. She flew toward the fort. The crossbows did not loose at her, perhaps aware that she lacked substance and so could not be hit.

Angela landed at the base of the fort where the wall touched the ground. Then she flew back. "It is definitely being held down," she reported. "The walls are made of cloud stuff that normally floats, but they are pressing down the wry grass. Something is pushing it to the ground."

"An invisible giant!" Jumper exclaimed. "That's who is holding down the fort."

"Another confounded pun," Hilarion remarked wryly. He couldn't help it.

"How do we get an invisible giant to let go?" Wenda asked.

"Maybe Meryl has an idea," Hilarion said.

"For a kiss!" Meryl remembered. "If it works."

"If it works," he agreed.

Meryl considered. "I don't suppose we could just ask the giant?"

"We could try," Jumper said.

Meryl flew up to where the giant's head might be. "Please Mister Giant, stop holding down the fort."

Now they heard the giant's thunderous response: "HO HO HO!" There was a vaguely green tinge to the sound.

"So much for that," Jumper said. "These puns will not let go voluntarily."

Meryl fluttered back down. "Maybe that didn't work, but seeing the field below me gave me another idea. If we could get the giant to roll in the wry and get hay fever, he won't be able to keep holding down the fort."

"How can we get him to do that?" Jumper asked, interested.

"Well, if there's a summer salt pun nearby—"

"I'm sure there is," Ida agreed.

And there was. They saw a salt lick to the side, with winter, spring, and summer salt. Meryl flew there, picked up a shaker, and promptly flipped over in the air.

"Somersault," Hilarion agreed, almost smiling.

Meryl flew crazily upward, constantly turning over as the salt affected her. She returned to the region of the giant's head. Then she unscrewed the shaker's cap and flung the contents out into the invisible face.

"HO HO OOPS!" the giant sounded as the salt took effect. Then he must have somersaulted onto the field, because it flattened with his invisible contact. "BLEEP!" he cursed as the wry grass took effect.

The fort, loosed, floated up up and away.

In a large moment the giant overcame his wryness and ran after the disappearing fort. They saw and heard his giant footprints.

They didn't wait. They hauled the wagon rapidly across the field and through the region where the fort had been. By the time the giant returned with the fort, they were safely beyond.

"About that kiss," Meryl said.

"Ah, yes," Hilarion agreed. He enfolded her and kissed her so effectively that several little hearts flew up.

But Wenda's attention was taken by something else. "The Sidewalk!" she exclaimed.

Indeed, there it was at last. "Get on it, sidle right, and through the door," Wenda said, afraid that the Sidewalk would not remain there long.

The men hauled the wagon up to the walk, but the wheels stalled against the raised edge. They heaved the front wheels up, but the rear ones remained off. Wenda and Ida pushed and lifted together, and with a struggle managed to get them over the rim. Then they had to get the wagon turned sideways to move along the walk. It almost tipped over, which would have rolled the Knot off; they barely leveled it in time.

"I have the feeling that the Knot is enjoying this," Ida gasped. "I feel its underlying malignity despite the effect of the reverse wood."

"The Strip must have worn out the wood faster," Wenda agreed.

"It's a nuisance, having to keep changing it," Meryl said. "But what choice do we have?"

They rolled the wagon to the Door. "Open it," Wenda called.

Hilarion did so. Then they wheeled the wagon through. As it got clear of the doorway, Wenda made a last check to be sure all members of their party were present, then slammed it shut. They were back.

"That's a relief," Meryl said. "Those puns are corrosive."

"Something is odd," Hilarion remarked, looking around. "I have traveled Xanth somewhat, but have never seen this region."

"I agree," Jumper said. "This is new to me."

Ida looked. "Uh-oh," she said. "I fear this isn't Xanth."

"Of course it's Xanth," Wenda said. "Where else could it be?"

Meryl got an unkind notion. "Which Door did we go through?"

"The one at the end of the right Sidewalk, of course," Wenda said.

"I think it was the left one," Angela said. "I thought I had confused what you said when I saw it happen."

Oh, no! "The reverse wood," Wenda said. "It reversed our direction. We went through the wrong Door!"

"Then where are we?" Hilarion asked.

"That, I fear, remains to be discovered," Ida said

sternly. "The left door leads to parts unknown. It could be any world in the circuit."

"Any world in the endless loop?" Jumper asked.

"That is my understanding. I believe it is a random access."

They exchanged alarmed glances. What had they blundered into?

The Knot was grimly amused.

8

REVERSE WORLD

Actually the scene was pleasant enough: a gently undulating white cloud surface where a number of angels flew, perched, and sang sweetly.

"Can this be Heaven?" Hilarion asked. "We may be fortunate to have a native guide."

"This is not Heaven," Angela said. "At least, not any province of Heaven I know of. But I will inquire."

She flew to the nearest angel, a handsome male, while the others waited with the wagon. The two held a momentary dialogue. Then the male angel tried to grab Angela and throw her down on the cloud. Angela screamed and leaped free. The other angel's hands passed through her body without effect. What was going on?

Angela flew back to the group. "That's no angel!" she said. "That's a demon! He tried to—to r*pe me!"

"To rape you!" Ida said, appalled.

"Yes. But he couldn't hold me, because I am immaterial here, while he is material. His form is illusion. This is definitely not Heaven. It could be H*ll."

"How can this be?" Jumper asked. "How can Hell pretend to be Heaven?"

"I don't know. But now I realize it's not H*ll either, because real demons would have the same reality there that I do. It is something else."

"So it seems," Ida agreed, frowning.

"Before we go further, we need to know what we're up against," Wenda said. "Are the demons real or illusion?"

"I may be able to help," Jumper said. "I tend to forget it because I'm not used to it, but Eris made me invulnerable as well as giving me the power to change forms. So even a solid physical demon can't hurt me." He assumed the form of a male angel, complete with halo, and flew out to meet the thing that had attacked Angela. He had forgotten to scrounge for clothing, but maybe it didn't matter.

A female angel flew in to intercept him. The others of the Quest watched as she floated before him, speaking to him. Then she came forward to kiss him. Only as her face touched his, she opened her mouth to show sharply pointed teeth, and bit his face.

Jumper, unharmed, put his hands on her body and lifted her away from him. She struggled, but his spider strength held her captive. Now Wenda could hear their dialogue.

"Who or what are you?" Jumper demanded. "I think you're no angel."

"Of course I'm a blessed angel," she said. "See my body. Feel it." She put her hands to her dress and tore it asunder to reveal an extremely shapely torso. "Are you man enough to handle that?"

"That's a demoness!" Angela whispered, amazed. "That body, that attitude. Heavenly creatures never acted like that."

Jumper remained frozen in place. "Oh, bleep!" Wenda swore. "She freaked him out with that exposure."

"He's your close friend," Meryl said. "Can you reach his mind?"

"Yes, maybe." Wenda reached out telepathically, jogging his blank mind. *Jumper! See her through my eyes. A body with too much meat on it.*

Jumper revived. *Thank you. Stay connected, neutralizing her meat.*

Gladly, she agreed. *Now question her.*

"I am just looking for some information," Jumper said. "Why did you try to bite me?"

"I thought you were an angel. Now I know you are of harder stuff. I'd like to get a piece of it." She glanced at his midsection in such a way that he blushed. She was certainly no angel.

I am at a loss, Jumper thought to Wenda. *What do I do or say now?*

She's a demoness, Wenda thought back. *Ask her what world this is.*

Evidently perplexed, Jumper obeyed. "What world is this?"

"You must really be from the backwoods! It's Reverse, of course."

Then Wenda got an idea. *Read her mind.*

Jumper held the demoness before him another moment and a half. Then he threw her away and returned to the group. "Ugh! Demon minds are ugly."

"Did you learn anything useful?" Wenda asked.

"Yes. This is Reverse World, made entirely of reverse wood or its equivalent. It is shaped like a giant reverse-wood tree. We are standing on the trunk section. Nothing is what it seems. Demons seem like angels, and vice versa. They look, sound, and feel like their opposites. This is true for everything."

"Amazing," Hilarion said. "How will we navigate it, assuming we have any idea where to go to find a Door back to Xanth, or—ugh—Comic?"

"I think we shall have to learn to appreciate it for what

it is," Ida said. "That is, to know that whatever we encounter is actually its opposite. With that caution we should be able to travel."

"There was a Door here," Meryl said. "There must be a Door back."

"I'm sure there is," Ida agreed.

"The Doors on Comic are in the Strips," Jumper said. "But I doubt there are Strips here. The Door must be in the least likely place. That is, the reverse of what seems likely."

"I should think a Door would be set in the trunk," Wenda said. "So maybe it's in the foliage instead."

"That makes reverse sense," Hilarion agreed.

"So let's travel to the foliage," Jumper said. "If we can find it."

"I will find it," Angela said. She flew straight up, impossibly high. Wenda realized that she was trying to gain the magic of perspective so she could see enough of the planet to make out its outline.

Soon she returned. "That way," she said, pointing.

"Next question," Hilarion said. "How do we get there, when we can't even take a step without endangering ourselves?"

Now Wenda had an idea so bright that the bulb almost blinded the group. "Jumper can change to more forms than just the few he's had so far. He could become a big roc bird and carry us and the wagon swiftly there."

"I could," Jumper agreed, surprised. "I'm not used to multiple form changing, so haven't tried it. But I'd want to practice with the roc form first, lest I be clumsy and dump the rest of you into a volcano or something."

"Practice," Ida said encouragingly.

But now a dragon was approaching. It was a fierce fire-breather, monstrously huge, and it looked ready to toast them all with a single snort of fire.

"Maybe I'd better become a dragon to balk it," Jumper said.

"Wait," Ida said. "If nothing here is what it seems, we should check for its opposite. It may be harmless."

"That's right," Jumper agreed. "But how can we be sure? We don't want to get fried."

"Use your invulnerability," Wenda suggested. "Meet it as something harmless."

Jumper became a fluffy white lamb. He frisked out to meet the dragon—and the dragon reared back, turned about, and fled.

"So it was a lamb, or some other harmless creature," Ida concluded. "And it thought Jumper was a dragon, reversing to look meek."

That seemed to be the case.

"I wonder if the angel/demons would know where the Door is?" Meryl said musingly.

That was a question, rather than an opinion, so Ida could not agree to it and make it so.

"What do you think?" Wenda asked.

"I have no idea."

So much for that. "Let's camp here for now," Wenda suggested. "There must be some food the demons eat, since they are solid here. We should get some for us."

"I will look," Ida said. She brought out a basket from somewhere. Evidently she had joined the Quest well prepared for incidental chores.

"So will I," Wenda said.

"I will come too," Angela said.

That left the men and Meryl to watch the Knot. Wenda did not want to leave it unattended. It seemed too satisfied to be here, and she did not trust that at all. Could it have some devious plan for escape?

They soon found a lovely patch of green, red, brown, black and blue berries. Those would do nicely.

"Don't touch them," Angela said. "They have to be revolting sludge, or maybe poisonous."

"True," Ida agreed regretfully. "We must seek the ugliest food."

They found a ditch where sludge and bones had collected. It was a repulsive mess. They nerved themselves and collected a fair quantity. This would be dinner.

"I wonder," Angela said as they started back.

"Wonder what?" Ida inquired, evidently aware that the angel was hesitant to express herself too forcefully. It wasn't angelic.

"When I talked with the demon I thought was an angel—why weren't our words reversed?"

"What kind of reversal would that be? Speaking backward, so as to be unintelligible?"

"Or making truth a lie, and vice versa," Wenda said.

"I'm not sure. But I understood him well enough, especially when he grabbed me and said, 'Lie down, b*tch.'" She blushed blue, embarrassed by the unheavenly crude word. "So I don't think either kind of reversal occurred."

"Now that is interesting," Ida agreed. "Their appearance was reversed, as was that of the lamb or dragon. As is our blushing. But not their speech."

"Or their gender," Wenda said. "That was a male demon. That was clear by its nasty action."

"Oh, they aren't all nasty," Angela protested. "Beauregard isn't." She blushed blue again.

"Of course not, dear," Ida said. "Demons vary, as I am sure do angels."

"They do," Angela agreed. "Some in Heaven are almost mean-spirited."

"Which suggests that the reversal does not affect their underlying natures," Ida said. "Natural variation accounts for it, with most demons being nasty and crude, and most angels being nice and sweet."

"It's limited to one kind of reversal," Wenda said. "Which is curious, if this is Reverse World. Shouldn't there be all types of reversal? Sight, sound, gender, and so on? And why aren't we affected?"

"It is curious," Ida agreed. "Normally reverse wood affects anyone who touches it."

"And we're not touching it!" Wenda exclaimed. "We're wearing shoes, and Angela is flying."

"So we are," Ida agreed, looking down at her feet. "Indeed."

"Your shoes are reversed!" Angela said. "They look like gloves."

Wenda looked at her own. They were like mittens. But they felt the same as usual. "They, too, changed their appearance," she said. "But not their actual nature. That's why we didn't notice. They don't *feel* different."

"I confess to an unbecoming curiosity," Ida said. She stooped and touched the ground with one hand.

She became an ogress. Wenda would have been appalled, if she had not known it was Ida.

"You are reversed," Angela said. She descended and touched the ground with a hand. She became a demon, as she had before when they worked with the second batch of reverse wood. It seemed that the larger ambiance here could affect her, when it had been at best intermittent on other worlds.

"But I became a child, before," Ida said.

"That was a reversal of nature," Wenda said. "This is a reversal of appearance."

"I became a demoness before," Angela said. "And one now. Why is it the same?"

"I think I know," Wenda said. "That was a reversal of your nature. You became demonly mischievous, even trying to flash your panties. You couldn't, because they were still invisible. This is a reversal of your appearance, not your nature. Do you want to flash your panties now?"

"Heavens, no!" Angela said, appalled. She sailed back into the air, reverting to her angelic aspect.

"Sometimes appearances are similar," Ida said. "Then you were a demoness; now you merely look like one. It is an interesting distinction. And an interesting limitation. I would have thought that this world would apply all kinds of reversal, not merely one."

"I suppose it would be hard to function, if all types of reversal occurred at once," Wenda said.

They returned to the wagon. The men were standing beside the wagon, and Meryl was hovering above it, all looking somewhat disgruntled.

"Let us guess," Ida said with a suppressed quarter of a smile. "You sat down and became monsters."

"How did you know?" Hilarion asked.

"We had a similar experience. But it is only appearance, not reality, as we know."

"So you won't mind if we sit?" Meryl asked.

"Not at all."

"We have food," Wenda said. "We believe it is wholesome. It only looks repulsive."

"How does it taste?" Hilarion asked.

Wenda laughed. "We didn't have the nerve to try it." She reached into the basket and brought out a clot of greenish gunk. She put it to her mouth, forced herself, and bit into it. "Blueberry!" she exclaimed.

Now Angela thought of something else. "Why didn't it show itself as it really is when we separated it from the ground?"

"I believe I know," Ida said. Wenda was coming to appreciate how smart a woman she was, quite apart from her Sorceress magic. "We are from elsewhere, so change our appearance only when we touch the planet.

But the berries are of this world, so it is natural for them to retain the reversal magic."

"That does make sense," Hilarion agreed. He sat down, becoming an ogre. "I must say, you are a sensible woman, Ida."

"Thank you. I try to be." Ida sat too, becoming the ogress. She set the basket between them. Meryl dropped down to curl her tail on the ground, and became a horrendous kraken weed. Angela joined them, becoming the demoness. Wenda sat, and became a female troll.

But the berries were very good. How fortunate that their taste had not been affected!

In due course they settled for the night. All the worlds seemed to have similar air and days, which was another blessing. Their personal forms might look horrendous, but in other respects they were comfortable.

Suddenly an ogre stood before Wenda. She stifled her automatic scream. "Its appearance!" she cried. "I am Wenda. You are Charming!"

"You do sound like her," he agreed. "But your complexion has really deteriorated."

"This is Reverse World," Wenda said. "Everything is reversed. In appearance. I'm still the same nymph, really."

He stepped forward and touched her with a hamhand. "So you are," he agreed, relieved. "Still, a little more darkness would help."

She got to her feet, donning her wooden shoes, and returned to her natural appearance. Charming, evidently anticipating a different environment, seemed to be in bare feet.

"Shall we wait a bit, and chat?" Eris asked. She had not actually changed, perhaps being beyond the power of this world.

"Yes," Beauregard said. He too had not changed, as he was hovering above the ground. But if he had in mind anything of a lying down nature, he would become a seeming angel, and he perhaps preferred to avoid that.

"I am curious," Eris said politely. "Why did you come here, instead of returning to Xanth?" She could have read their minds; that's what made her query polite, indicating that she was leaving them the privacy of their thoughts.

"It was an accident," Wenda explained. "The reverse-wood shell reversed our direction, and we were through the wrong Door before we realized. Now we have to find the return Door."

Eris sighed. "I fear you will have trouble finding it, but I do not want to interfere with your Quest."

Wenda was almost inclined to request exactly such interference, but worried that it would indeed cause a rift between Demons, and that would not be smart. "We understand."

"Actually it's an interesting adventure," Jumper said. "It never occurred to me that such a world existed."

"Oh, it does," Eris said. "It's the source of most of the reverse wood of this sector, and even of some transplants so that more can grow elsewhere. There's a regular trade with other worlds."

"There's trade between other worlds?" Wenda asked.

"There is," the Demoness agreed. "Xanth is a bit backward in that respect, but surely enjoys its isolation."

Wenda was privately amazed. Not so much at the interaction of other worlds, but that the Demoness would actually chat with mortals. Her relationship with Jumper must have mellowed her.

Hardly, Eris's thought came. *It's that I love Jumper, and you are his best friend. Without you he would not have rescued me. So I treat you with the courtesy that will please him. Were he not present, I would pay you no attention.*

That was plain enough, if somewhat lacking in tact.

Demons normally hardly cared whether individual mortals lived or died, unless there was a Demon wager connected. But Wenda couldn't help liking the Demoness anyway. Maybe it was because without her, Jumper would have wound up jumping between weeds, biting the heads off bugs, lonely, and dead in months. Eris had rescued him forever from such a fate. Wenda truly appreciated that.

Now it was dark enough. They could lie down without showing their monstrous semblances. That evidently made a difference to Charming and Beauregard.

Six and a half minutes later Charming was asleep, and gone. The conjugal visit was over, and normal life resumed.

In the morning Jumper practiced with the roc-bird form while the others organized for the resumption of travel.

"Do you know," Ida said, "I believe that we can adapt to this reversal of appearances if we concentrate. We simply need to school ourselves to see the opposite of what seems to be there."

"Like seeing Prince Charming instead of an ogre," Wenda agreed.

"Yes. Then you would not need darkness to complete your conjugal tryst."

"Let's practice," Wenda said.

They took off their shoes and became apparent troll and ogress. Wenda squinted, trying to see Princess Ida instead of the ogress, but it was difficult.

"What is going on?" Meryl asked.

"We are practicing reversing our seeing," Wenda said. "So that we won't be fooled by this world's reversals."

"That makes sense," Meryl agreed, and touched her tail to the ground. There was the horrendous kraken weed.

"That does make sense," Hilarion said. He removed his boots and became the ogre. He looked at Ida. "Please do not be offended, but I suspect that if I were really an ogre, you would be beautiful right now."

"Thank you," the ogress said, grimacing. Wenda stifled her remark that Ida looked good regardless, for a middle-aged woman. Hilarion had not meant any offense. Men simply were not much for nuances.

Angela dropped down and touched the ground with her substance-less feet. As a demoness she was still pretty, but now in a smoky seductive way, rather than the clean innocent angel way.

Gradually they got the hang of it. The effect was imperfect, but Wenda could see a kind of outline of the true forms of the others within the reversals. It was as though they were wearing horrendous costumes.

Meanwhile Jumper was making his own progress. It was interesting to watch. When he touched the ground as a bare human being, he was a rough ogre. When he changed to spider form, he was a stupid fly. When he became a roc, he looked like a hummingbird. It seemed that the opposite changes were related to the form, not to the person. Wenda was halfway used to seeing Jumper in all his forms, large spider, small spider, and man, so it was not hard to extend it to the opposite forms.

"How are we going to ride on a hummingbird?" Hilarion asked dubiously.

Wenda wondered herself, but decided not to question it. She had a more pressing question to address: exactly where was the Door? Eris had let slip another thought: that they would have trouble finding it. That meant it was not in any obvious place. So their simple tour to the foliage of the planet now seemed unlikely to be effective. But what else could they try? She couldn't think of anything.

"I have a harness," Ida said. Where could she have gotten that? She must have a bottomless purse. Literally; with magic it was possible.

Meryl flew toward the Knot, and veered away. "We forgot!" she exclaimed. "Another day has passed, and the malign thing has burned out its clothing."

They had indeed forgotten, in the distraction of the new world. "There is plenty of reverse wood available," Wenda said. "But it will take hours to craft the shell."

"Maybe not," Angela said. "I spied an old beerbarrel trunk husk. Wouldn't that do?"

"It might indeed," Wenda agreed gratefully.

They fetched the barrel and set it over the Knot. The frightening radiation converted to warm appeal. "You're Heaven-sent!" Hilarion told Angela, who blushed blue.

They fastened the bottom rim of the barrel to the wagon so that it couldn't blow off in flight. The cargo was ready.

It was time. The Jumper hummingbird had made several takeoffs, loops, and landings, flashing into roc appearance while in the air, and was satisfied with his competence. *I am a roc, even if I don't look it,* he thought. *You will want to perch on my back.*

Wenda found the tip of his spread wing, well away from the apparent hummingbird. He was in effect invisible. She treaded carefully, and the others followed. Meryl and Angela took places also, because a roc's flight was swifter than either of them could ever manage.

There was indeed a comprehensive harness that fastened securely to the roc's body. It even had seat belts. No one would be falling off during flight. The harness had become invisible, because it was attached to a bird supposedly the size of a hummingbird. The reversal magic was doing what it could, but Wenda wondered whether its resources were not being strained.

They rolled the wagon with its barrel on, and secured the wheels in place on the harness. It would not roll off.

But it looked strange indeed. They were a collection of people who seemed to be sitting in midair, along with a wagon and a barrel. They retained their normal forms because they were not touching the ground; they were touching Jumper. He was touching the ground, so he was affected; they weren't.

When they were set, the roc lifted his wings, flapped, and took off. And abruptly appeared in full feather. They were on their way to the foliage section of the planet, for whatever that was worth.

The roc flew higher, much higher, as was the nature of this largest of all birds. The details of the land fuzzed out with distance. That was probably just as well, since those details were all reversed.

Nevertheless, Wenda gazed at the scene below. Now she could see that they had been on the thick solid trunk of the tree, and were flying "north" toward the spreading branches and foliage. This business of a tree-shaped planet seemed odd, but pleasant, because she associated with trees. And of course Xanth was a peninsula planet. Most others, she knew, were plain dull round, or, technically, spherical. Ball-shaped. Maybe they had no imagination.

Wenda.

It was the Demoness Eris; she recognized the mind. *I am here,* she thought back.

May we converse?

If you wish. Why did the Demoness want to waste time on her when Jumper wasn't watching?

You had a thought last night that I was lacking in tact.

Oh, no! She hadn't realized Eris was reading her mind then. This was surely mischief.

No mischief. I merely want to know how.

How to explain tact to a being who lacked awareness of many human interactions? What could she do except try to clarify with utter, tactless, candor?

Precisely.

It was that Eris had clarified that she paid Wenda attention only because Jumper was present. Demons generally did not care about the welfare or feelings of mortal folk, yet it was unkind for them to say so openly. But a soulless entity would have no basis to comprehend that.

Error. I inherited half of Jumper's soul when I married him. He had in turn received portions of the souls of the other members of his Quest. So it is a composite soul, and its nicest component is the part of yours. I am trying to understand it, as it affects me now.

Oh. Of course. Once a Demon received even part of a mortal soul, things like conscience and love became possible.

Yes. But it takes time to become proficient in such things. I am trying, because my half-soul tweaks me when I violate its principles. It tweaked me when I was straightforward with you last night. I want to know why.

That was where tact came in. The Demoness had been brutally candid about Wenda's place in her esteem. It had set Wenda back, before she reminded herself that this was the nature of Demons, whether big D or little d. A human person would have been more tactful, so as to avoid hurting feelings.

Feelings. There is another mystery. Jumper has feelings for you, and I know from your soul that is now part of mine that you have feelings for him. But since the only use a male has for a female relates to stork summoning, and this is not the interest the two of you share, how is it possible for you to have such feelings?

Suddenly Wenda appreciated the magnitude of the emotional challenge. Feelings between men and women were not limited to storks, though that was very important to men. Jumper saw in Wenda the same things she saw in him: selfless caring, generosity, dedication, commitment, and loyalty. They loved each other in a way that was independent of storks. Wenda was not jealous of Jumper's relationship with Eris, and he was not jealous of hers with Prince Charming. They understood each other in that respect, including the satisfaction each could get when stork summoning, without having to do it with each other. It was just a small part of their larger friendship.

Friendship.

That was when people knew and respected one another, and truly wanted what was best for the other.

I want that for Jumper.

But Eris wasn't Jumper's friend. She was his wife, lover, and protector. That wasn't the same, though it did not exclude friendship.

Friendship is independent of storks, Eris repeated from Wenda's prior thought. *So a way to know if it is friendship and not sexual love is to have a relationship that is not sexual.*

The Demoness had cast off the euphemism and gotten to the essence. Love without sex. That would do for a working definition.

I want a friend. That is the only way to learn the whole of it.

It probably was, considering that none of the human nuances of feeling came naturally to a Demon, even one with a soul. If Eris had a lover—Jumper—and a different friend, she would in time be able to work out the distinctions between the two relationships.

You.

What?

Friendships are not exclusive. You can be my friend as well as Jumper's. If I learn how to appreciate your nature, I will have 92.532 percent of the qualities Jumper values.

"But you're a Demoness!" Wenda exclaimed aloud. Fortunately the others were absorbed in the sights, not paying attention to her.

A Demoness and a mortal can be lovers. Can they not also be friends?

And of course that was the case: if the one was true, so was the other. But a Demon! It was like a roc being friends with a mite.

I asked Jumper if he would marry me. He accepted, and we married. I am asking you: will you be my friend?

And what could she possibly say to that? Except yes.

Thank you. Now I will retire and consider the implications.

So would Wenda. The Demoness was doing it for a practical, perhaps cynical reason: to grasp 92.532 percent of the qualities Jumper valued. But a genuine friendship would rise above any such number. Wenda only hoped she could measure up.

Time had passed, and now they were reaching the foliage section of the planet. It was time for a rest stop. The roc was coasting down for a landing at the base of a branch.

They landed in a suitably-sized glade by a pleasant river. Pie trees fringed it, and there was a fragrant breeze. Innocent rabbits hopped playfully about, playing bunny games. Naturally none of them trusted that.

"We must be ready to take off again immediately," Wenda said with alarm. "Those could be deadly monsters."

"Let me see," Angela said. She was the one who could fairly safely approach an unknown threat. She flew from her place, away from the nearest bunny.

"Oops," she said, correcting her course. She wee-wawed, and finally managed to fly toward the creature.

Wenda thought she might have gotten dizzy from the long ride on the roc.

They saw her reach out to touch the bunny. Angela could not be touched by ordinary folk, but she could touch them, to a degree. First she reached away from it, then tried again and managed to touch it. She looked surprised. "It really is a rabbit!" she called.

"But what about the reversal?" Hilarion asked.

"It's not reversed."

This was significant news. Hilarion jumped to the ground, reached up, then put his hand down, and touched the turf. He did not change.

"The reversal's gone," Meryl said, amazed. She flew down, touched the ground with her tail, turned away from them, then around to face them. "Gone," she repeated.

Wenda walked down the wing, which remained visible, and to the ground. She removed her shoes. "Am I still me?" she asked.

"You are," Hilarion said.

She meant to reach down to touch the ground with her hand, but instead she reached up toward the sky. Startled, she reversed, and got down. She still didn't change. She turned to face the roc, but found herself facing away from it.

Then she caught on. "Direction! We're reversing directions!" That explained the peculiar motions of the others and herself.

She put her shoes back on, and then was able to point or walk in the directions she chose. It was contact with the ground that brought it on.

"I wonder," Ida said. "If the nature of the reversal is different, here on the branch, what about the wood we carried from the trunk?" She walked to the wagon and touched it. And became the ogress.

"That wood is from the trunk," Hilarion said. "It retains its properties. Wood from the branch will reverse directions."

So it seemed. Now they knew that different parts of the tree had different reversal properties.

They completed their break, then boarded the roc again. Jumper tried at first to plow into the ground, then corrected and managed to lift. Once he was airborne, he was all right.

"That was odd," Hilarion remarked. "Will we face a third type of reversal in the foliage?"

"I suspect we will," Ida said. "That may complicate our search for the Door."

Wenda was very much afraid it would. Eris had mentioned that the Door would be difficult to find, and she surely knew. Wenda would not ask her to clarify, because she didn't want the Demoness to compromise her nonengagement protocol. They would have to find it by themselves.

Is that decision a consequence of friendship? Eris asked.

Wenda was startled. It wasn't, but maybe it should have been. Friends did not try to get friends in trouble.

Should I risk a Demon consequence to give you the information, for the sake of friendship?

"No!" Wenda exclaimed aloud.

Meryl looked at her. "Are we going in the wrong direction?"

What could she say, except the truth? "I am talking to the Demoness Eris, mentally. She asked whether she should risk a Demon consequence, for interfering with another Demon's domain, by telling us where the Door is hiding. I told her no."

You're in touch with Eris? Jumper's thought came.

She is, Eris responded to them both. *Do you object?*

No. I am merely surprised. What do you care about her?

I am trying to learn how to be more human, so I can better please you. I enlisted Wenda as a friend.

Good enough, Jumper agreed. *She's the best friend a person could have.*

"You did right," Hilarion said. "Eris has helped us tremendously, notably by enhancing Jumper. We wouldn't want to get her in trouble for helping too much."

"I agree," Ida said. "We must handle our mission ourselves. We will find that Door."

You are all friends! Eris exclaimed to them all, mentally.

"Yes, we are, to an extent," Meryl said. "We don't know each other as well as Wenda and Jumper do, but we're working on it."

But this is not rational. You could suffer mischief because of it.

Hilarion shrugged. "Friends do."

Demons do not.

"We aren't d*mons," Angela said, with an angelic smile.

Indeed you are not. This passeth understanding.

"If you explore your piece of my soul more carefully, you may be able to gain some understanding of it," Wenda said. "We're simply not very rational."

I will do that. The Demoness's mental presence faded.

"She must be interesting to be with," Hilarion remarked to Jumper.

She is. But I think this will make her more interesting.

"More?"

She has assumed that all I want from her personally is stork summoning. I do want that; she is phenomenally good at it. But I want more, and she doesn't understand why or what.

"I think she envies me," Wenda said. "Because Jumper likes my company without storks."

I do, Jumper agreed. *I liked you from the start, and*

*would have accepted storks with you, but our friend-
ship is better. That's really why I came on this Quest: to
be with you again.*

"That's why I asked you," Wenda confessed. "To be
with you."

"I think we all understand," Meryl said. "We interact, we struggle, we kiss, but these are mere superfici-
alities. We like each other's company."

There was a general murmur of assent.

As evening approached, they were well into the foliage section. Jumper glided down for a landing on a green
section that seemed to be a giant leaf, so big that it soon
extended beyond the horizon. He touched ground.

Wenda realized that she was holding her breath. But
nothing happened. There seemed to be no reversal of
appearance or direction. That was suspicious.

Hilarion jumped down, then turned and held up a
hand to help Ida down. She accepted it, and joined him
on the ground. In one and a half moments they all were
standing there, and Jumper changed to normal manform. "This is disgusting," he said.

"What?" Wenda asked, surprised.

That isn't what I meant to say, he thought to them all.
*I thought I was commenting on the pleasure of not be-
ing reversed.*

"Let me check," Ida said. She removed her shoes and
stood barefoot. "You're crazy, you idiotic bug." Then she
put her hands to her face, evidently appalled.

"Reversal!" Wenda said. "We are reversing what we
say." She removed her own shoes. "We are doing no such
thing. We are all enemies."

Then they all touched the ground. "I can't think why I
associate with such a paltry lot of misfits," Hilarion said.

"That's because you're such an ugly, crude lout," Meryl
said.

"As if you are any judge, you winged hussy," Ida said.

"You're all wretches," Angela said.

Wenda made an effort. "We must all—say the opposite of what we mean. So that it comes out true."

"Reversing the reversal," Hilarion agreed. "That is very stupid—I mean, smart of you, Wenda."

"Forget it, dope!" Wenda snapped. Then tried again, "I mean, thank you."

Meryl started crying. Then she caught herself, and managed to arrange the laugh she had intended. "Or maybe just let it reverse, and understand that it is the same—I mean, the opposite."

"No!" Hilarion said. "I mean, yes. It may be harder—easier to just let it happen and make allowances."

They did that, and soon had no further problem as they routinely exchanged insults. They foraged for pies, and found a nice pond to wash in.

"This seems like a truly wretched world," Meryl remarked as she finished her slice of greenberry pie.

"Horrible," Ida agreed.

They settled down. The consorts arrived. "Charming!" Wenda exclaimed. "How awful!" She had quite forgotten, in the distraction of the language. She was in contact with the ground.

He paused, taken aback. In the background she heard Angela talking to Beauregard in distinctly unangelic language, setting him back too. At least Jumper would not have to explain to Eris; they had telepathy.

"I mean, how nice," she said quickly. Then she spoke carefully. "Charming, here the reversals are of sound. It's easier just to understand."

"Understand," he repeated uncertainly. "What kind of sound?"

"Like this," she said. She kissed the back of her wrist, audibly. It made a sound that would have done a stink horn proud. "Try it yourself." For now he was sitting down on the ground.

He kissed his own wrist. And recoiled at the obnoxious noise. Then he put his hand under his armpit and pumped his arm. It made a lovely kissing sound. He smiled; he had caught on.

After that it was actually fun, though it sounded as if they were fighting in a garbage dump. By the time the seven minutes were up, she was asleep too.

It had been quite a day.

9

FRIENDSHIP

In the morning they exchanged further insults, boarded the roc again, and took off for the north of the tree. Their speech reverted to normal. It was almost disappointing. The insults had become fun in their perverse way.

I am slowly coming to understand friendship, Demoness Eris thought. *Thanks to your clarifications, your soul fragment, and Jumper's efforts to explain. Friendship is not entirely rational.*

"Yes," Wenda murmured. It was a point she had made before, evidently difficult for the Demoness to assimilate.

I want to be your irrational friend.

Wenda had to laugh. "Welcome."

I will seek an avenue to complete my comprehension. Her mental presence faded.

Wenda wished the Demoness luck. She had had her own problems relating to human things, when she was a true woodwife. It had been her association with Jumper that enabled her to become emotionally whole before becoming physically whole, despite the fact that he was not human, but a spider. She owed him that. His presence on this quest supported her and gave her confidence to continue that she would have lacked otherwise. She owed him that too.

Thank you, Jumper's thought came.

Well, it's true.

I know. That's why I appreciate it. You need me in a way Eris does not.

They slept, as there wasn't much else to do. When Wenda woke, they were landing again, at the top of the tree.

Now there were giant flowers that gave off a scent that made Wenda think dizzily of every kind of possible reversal, and some impossible kinds. She was used to plants, but quickly learned to avoid these. The other members of their party were overcome before they could retreat. They sat beside the wagon, little curlicues and spirals emanating from their heads. All except Angela, who was not material enough to be strongly affected.

"I don't see a Door," Angela said.

"It must be at the other end of the tree," Wenda agreed. "We'll have to go there. But first I think we need to find more reverse wood to shield the Not."

"Yes. Will old flower petals do?"

"They may. But I have another idea. There should be fruits, and seeds. Seeds could be very strong."

"I will look," Angela agreed, and flew off.

Wenda went to Jumper where he sat in human form, smiling deliriously. "Jumper! You're intoxicated with fumes. Snap out of it."

He just continued to stare vaguely into space, little squiggles surrounding his head.

"Jumper! You're supposed to be invulnerable. Doesn't that include your mind?"

That got through to him. "It does not," he agreed. He

concentrated, and the squiggles faded. "Thank you for nothing."

"You're my friend," she reminded him, making due allowance for the reversal that affected him now that he was back in contact with the ground. Her shoes protected her. "Besides, we need you to take us away from here, once we find some reverse seeds."

"Door?" he asked.

"No Door. I want to check the roots next."

"That makes no sense." He was agreeing with her.

Angela returned. "I found fruits! But they're some distance away." She pointed the direction.

"Awful problem," Jumper said. He assumed roc form. They got on, and he took off in the wrong direction. *Oops!* He corrected. The directional reversals remained in effect in the foliage region.

They came to the fruits. There were several adorable dear eating them, spitting out the seeds. Wenda collected a considerable number of seeds and stored them in a bag, feeling their considerable reversal power. Her impression was that they featured all kinds of reversals, so that each could make a whole reverse-wood tree with all its parts.

They returned to the wagon. Wenda made a net of thin vines, speckled with seeds, and spread it over the Knot in place of the worn-out shell. It worked; Jumper and Angela knew the difference immediately.

Satisfied that the Door was not here, they organized for an overnight flight to the south of the tree: the roots. Jumper transformed to roc form, and they rolled the wagon on and anchored it. Then they all took their places, and the roc took off.

The sound reversal stopped. They were normal, for the time being.

There was nothing much to do but snooze. They did, as the roc winged steadily onward.

Wenda woke when Charming appeared. "Charming! What are you doing here?"

"It is dark. Conjugal time."

She realized it was true. She had slept through the night and day. "But we're still in the air!" she protested.

"Yes. Poor Eris can't be with Jumper. But Beauregard and I have no problem."

Wenda saw that the others were asleep, except for Angela. So she embraced Charming. And in seven minutes he was asleep and gone. Sometimes she almost wished he would stay awake another minute or two, so they could talk when the urgency of his physical interest had been abated. But that seemed to be too much to ask of marriage.

What could she do? She went back to sleep.

She woke in the morning. They were now flying above the base of the trunk, approaching the root. They had breakfast, washed up, and used closable privy potties Ida produced, so that the flight did not have to be interrupted.

"What kind of reversal will we face when we touch the root?" Wenda inquired.

Gender, Jumper replied mentally. *Eris told me.*

Evidently incidental information was not a violation of the Demon Protocol. Eris couldn't tell them where the Door was, but something they would soon discover on their own was all right.

"We can wear shoes, and avoid it," Hilarion said. "That I think is to be preferred."

"Or remain in the air," Meryl said.

No, Jumper thought. *Eris says there are folk there we will want to interact with, and the moment we touch them, we will change, so it's better to change at the outset and be consistent.*

"What folk?" Ida asked. "We are merely looking for the Door off this world."

The gnomes. They will know where the Door is.

Oh. "So we'll go barefoot and change orientations," Wenda agreed, not entirely pleased. "But we must make clear to the gnomes that all we want is the Door."

"I lack experience with gnomes," Meryl said. "Exactly what is it they do?"

"They are normally miners," Ida said, "working underground, and crafting things there. The men are rather squat and ugly, but the females, the gnomides, are petite and beautiful. They have a reputation for honesty and hard work. It won't be like dealing with trolls or goblins."

"Actually the trolls of the trollway were all right," Meryl said. "They did their business properly."

"They did," Ida agreed. "But I think goblins would not."

"Wasn't there a decent goblin?" Hilarion asked. "I believe I heard a story about one who married a goblin princess."

"That was Goody Goblin," Ida said. "He was an exception, because he drank a reverse-wood beverage when young and got reversed. So he was nice, and reviled by other goblins. Fortunately Gwenny Gobliness was looking for a nice male, and she made a play for him, and of course took him."

"I have heard about goblin females too," Hilarion said. "It is said that some are so beautiful that a man must wear protective glasses when looking at them, lest he suffer eye damage."

Ida laughed. "Surely an exaggeration. But it is true that the females are both lovely and nice, in considerable contrast to the males. Gnomes are similar in such respects, but less so."

Conversation lapsed as they moved on toward the root. Would they find the Door there? Wenda was not at all sure they would. But where else was there to look?

Then she became aware of an increasing nervousness among her fellow passengers. Oops—it had been more than a day since the last reverse-wood shell update. The Knot was making its nasty power felt.

Wenda got up and touched the net shell. "I wood knot dew that to yew," she said. "That wood bee cruel." Sure enough, the shield was almost gone. The words had meaning only as a test of the shield's effect.

Quickly she got out new seeds to replace the old ones in the net. She felt the brooding anger of the Knot. It had perhaps hoped to drive the people off the roc, then make the roc himself panic and crash. Fortunately Wenda had been at least belatedly alert. The bad feeling faded as she completed the replacements.

Thank you, Jumper thought. *It was becoming uncomfortable.*

"You are welcome," Wenda murmured, noting that the dialect spell was functioning again.

She settled back into her place and relaxed. She hoped the Door would be found soon, but knew she couldn't count on it. They would simply have to keep slogging on until they somehow found it.

Hello, Wenda.

"Hello, Eris," Wenda murmured. She was coming to like these occasional private dialogues with the Demoness.

Thank you. I believe I am making progress in my study of friendship. I discover that I like conversing with you. That is a pleasure I had not imagined before I came to know you. Now I would talk to you even if Jumper were not near. He has become irrelevant in this respect.

"Thank you," Wenda said. "But I am nothing special. I'm just a wouldwife with a job to do."

And you are doing it well. You have kept your mind on your mission, and maintained the organization necessary to accomplish it.

"I have just muddled along, unable to do anything else."

You are an effective leader. The others depend on your constancy.

"Thank you," Wenda repeated, unable to think of anything else to say, though she felt she was being given more credit than was due.

Jumper learned much of humanity from you, and I am doing the same. The others need you. So do I.

"But you're a Demoness!"

A Dwarf Demoness. I do not need you physically or intellectually. I need you emotionally. You have the simple, honest, nice feelings that made you the best of friends for Jumper. Feelings I want to share.

"You're welcome to them." Wenda still felt overcredited.

Your very contact enhances my mood. Now that I have discovered you, I do not wish to lose you.

"Oh, I will not reject you!" Wenda protested. "I just think I am not the only one who could help you."

Perhaps, the Demoness agreed, and faded.

The Demoness was becoming familiar, but Wenda suspected she would never lose her awe. She was keenly aware that even a Dwarf Demon had power beyond anything imaginable by mortal folk. The only constraints on it were the powers of other Demons, in their Demon Protocols that governed their interactions. That was perhaps fortunate for mortals.

It is, Jumper agreed. *I have come to know her to an extent, and her full powers are miraculous. I occupy only about one percent of her attention, and that's more than I can compass. Yet I know she is merely one of a great number of minor demons.*

"One percent!"

You occupy a similar amount of her attention. She is really taken with you. I understand that; you are worthy.

"Thank you," Wenda said once again. It was obvious she knew next to nothing about Demons.

I value my friendship with you above all else. I think that is what first attracted her attention to you.

Eris had said much the same. Wenda still felt unworthy.

In due course they reached the root section of the tree. Jumper glided down to a suitable landing place. He found a valley with brown plants growing thickly. That would do.

The moment Jumper touched ground, he transformed to a female roc, slightly smaller, with glossier feathers. *I'm a chick,* he thought. That confirmed the nature of this region.

The others removed their shoes and set bare feet on the ground. Ida became a man, with her dress ill fitting, loose around the chest and hips. Meryl put her tail down, transformed, picked up a chip of wood, and flew back into the air, retaining her transformation. Angela touched and did not seem to change. But that was because her body was invisible. Hilarion became a lovely woman, his clothing tight where Ida's was loose, his/her hair growing down to her waist. Jumper changed to manform, and was a handsome bare woman. What had been mere flashes before as they worked with reverse wood was now permanent for the duration, and that was less comfortable.

Wenda of course would not be affected, but she put her bare foot on the ground to join the others. And felt something uncomfortably strange. What was happening?

"You're changing!" Jumper told her.

"But I can't be," she protested. "I'm immune."

"You may be immune to chips and branches, but not an entire landscape," Ida said. "This is the reverse-wood heartland, surely the most potent environment of all. In fact I suspect it is more than wood, but the reverse soil from which the wood springs. The root essence of the tree and this world."

That seemed to be the case. Wenda's chest and hips shrank, her shoulders and arms turned muscular and her body became lean and hard where it had been rounded and soft. The hair of her head shortened drastically, and a mustache sprouted on her upper lip. Her delicate human feet had become hard hooves. She was now not a nymph but a faun. Physically; she would never be male in spirit. "Ugh!" she exclaimed.

The others laughed. "That does sum it up," Meryl agreed, glancing down at her own blank chest.

Hilarion glanced at Ida. "Would you like to exchange clothing?"

"Yes, I believe I would." Ida went to Hilarion, and the two removed their awkward clothing and donned each other's outfits. They did fit reasonably well, for Ida had gained stature as a man, and Hilarion had lost some as a woman. Wenda noted that they had become comfortable enough with each other to make such an exchange without retreating to private areas. They were what they were, reversed.

Then Wenda produced Jumper's clothing from her purse, donned it, and handed him hers. Again the fits were reasonable, considering. They were decent again.

They scattered to separate groves to dump potties and such. Wenda had to get used to the male hardware that had replaced her female software; it was awkward, physically, esthetically, and emotionally. Then they organized for a search for the Door.

"I don't suppose you could conjure it with the humidor?" Meryl inquired.

"Unfortunately, no," Ida said. "The humidor conjures only the Door going out, not the one returning. We have to find an existing Door."

Jumper transformed into a female quack and flew out to canvas one outer quadrant. Meryl flew to check another. Angela covered a third. Ida, Hilarion, and Wenda spread out and paced the closed-in area. It seemed hopeless, but they knew there was a Door. They would simply have to keep looking until they found it.

"Hello, faun."

Wenda jumped; she had been so focused on looking around that she had not looked ahead. There was a gnome, short, knobby, dour in the gnome fashion. He bore a gnarled wood staff, but did not seem unfriendly. "Hello, gnome," she replied.

"I am Gnever Gnome, chief of the Gnarly Gnomes. What brings you to our territory?"

"I am Wenda, from Xanth. We came here by accident, and are seeking the Door home."

"Ah, a world traveler. You will not find the Door here."

"You know where it is?" Wenda said eagerly.

"Perhaps," he replied cannily. "Your party will want to visit for a while; perhaps you will elect to remain here."

"I don't understand."

"There are not many of us, and we have a heavy burden of demand for our carvings, which are exported to many other worlds. We would like to augment our numbers. Perhaps we can persuade you to stay."

Wenda realized that it might not be expedient to deny him directly. They needed the gnomes' cooperation. "Possibly," she agreed. "But how is it that you speak our language? We are from worlds away."

Gnever smiled. "We colonized this world from Xanth, generations ago, to set up a viable trade with reverse-wood artifacts. Naturally we retain our home language, and are eager to have news from the old world. But we do need more colonists."

Oh. That did make sense. "We will be happy to share whatever news we have."

"Call in your several minions, and we will treat you to a visitors' welcome. We can get to know one another."

"That seems fair," Wenda agreed cautiously. How had he known she was the leader of this party? Unless he had been observing them before making himself known.

Wenda lifted her voice and called, using her forest voice. "Folk, come in! We have a contact!" She sent a separate thought to Jumper, knowing he would read it in her mind. She was slowly becoming acclimatized to this leadership business.

Soon the others gathered, and Wenda introduced them to Gnever. They seemed suitably impressed. Jumper, in female manform, caught her eye in passing; he had gotten her message. He would conceal his several special abilities until they were better acquainted with the gnomes.

Then Gnever tapped the ground with his staff, and a hinged portal opened, with solid wood stairs leading down. He led the way down into the depths. It seemed that they had landed almost on top of this access, coincidentally.

Wenda distrusted coincidence. There was usually magic involved, and not necessarily friendly magic.

I knew there was something here, so I oriented on it, Jumper thought. *I hoped it was the Door. But it seems to be the wrong door.*

The wrong door. Wenda hesitated, not liking the idea of getting trapped underground. But gnomes did generally live below, so this made sense. She followed, and the other members of her party followed her.

The stairs led to a subterranean hall, which led in turn to a larger chamber. Here there were a number of gnomes and gnomides, the female of the species.

Gnever introduced them, having an uncanny memory for names. In barely three moments each member of their party had a friendly gnome companion. Had the gnomes somehow been expecting them? They had been on the world for a while now, so news must have spread.

Wenda's companion was Gnaughty Gnomide, a remarkably fetching little creature. Now that Wenda was male, she was better able to appreciate such qualities in a female. "Come this way," Gnaughty said, leading Wenda to another chamber where there was a huge banquet table.

The others were there with their guides. Wenda noticed that each guide was of the opposite gender, and attractive. The meal was wonderful, with tasty courses and drinks. The gnomes were going to an extraordinary length to make the visitors welcome. Why?

Gnaughty did not keep her in doubt long after dessert. "We want to persuade you to stay. We need new blood. We can make you happy here."

"So Gnever said. But we have other business and must move on." Wenda saw similar conversations occurring around the table.

"We can offer you so much," the gnomide pleaded. She turned to Wenda, and her robe came slightly open, showing her marvelously bare bosom beneath.

This electrified Wenda. She was appalled in more than one respect. First, because she reacted so strongly to the exposure, which she knew was intentional; her male body was reacting in a fully masculine manner. Second, because it signaled how far the gnomes would go to convince their visitors to stay. She had no doubt that Gnaughty would eagerly oblige her in any way she desired, and of course her body had only one desire at the moment. And she couldn't afford that.

"I see what you offer," Wenda said carefully, "but I am human and you are a gnome. I am twice your height, and about four times your mass. Such a liaison is not physically feasible."

"We have accommodation spells," Gnaughty said, inhaling.

Wenda almost freaked out. She had always been privately amused by the way men foolishly freaked at the sight of women's panties or breasts. Now it was not funny at all; it was dangerous. "Those are temporary effects. They don't actually change the nature of the folk."

"But they do make stork summoning feasible and enjoyable," Gnaughty said. "Yet I hope to satisfy you that we won't even need a spell, once we get private." She shifted her position slightly to provide a better view.

Wenda knew she couldn't afford to freak out; she would be lost, with or without the spell. The gnomide already had her in thrall, and surely the other companions were doing the same to the other members of the Quest, of whatever gender. This was a choreographed campaign.

She clapped her eyes closed. "Gnaughty," she said urgently, "I'm married."

"On another world? That doesn't count on this one."

"And I am female."

"Not here."

"I may have the body of a man here, but I am really a woman. That will always be true. I couldn't marry another woman even if I were free to do so."

"And I am male," Gnaughty said, unfazed.

Wenda's eyes popped open involuntarily, and were trapped. The view remained, locking her gaze in place. "What?"

"We are all reverse-gendered here. We make the best of it. If any of us ever leave the root, we'll change to our true genders. So we won't leave."

"You're all—" But of course it was true. How could it not affect the natives? "But then—"

"Understand, it takes place at birth or before; we

don't know. So I have always seemed female, to myself and others. But I would be a male gnome away from here. So if we married, and departed, we would change together. We will always be of opposite genders."

This was almost overwhelming. "Well, I am used to being a woman. I mean to return to being one as soon as possible. I can't help you. We can't help you. We must go now."

"Please," Gnaughty said desperately. Tears began to form in her lovely eyes.

But Wenda knew she could not afford to relent. Tears were another female weapon that could demolish her male resistance. She had used them herself when necessary. She had to act immediately.

She stood up. "Folks, we are departing now. The Door is not here." This was a desperate guess, but necessary. The gnomes were not about to let them find or use the Door. "We must go look elsewhere. Now."

The others, having caught on similarly, did not hesitate. They knew they were on the brink of disaster. They stood up and made their way to her.

"You can't do this," Gnever protested.

"It is not that we feel you are bad folk," Wenda said, still trying to be careful. "You could surely make us very comfortable here. But we have a mission to accomplish. We thank you for your hospitality, and will now resume our search for the way home."

"I appreciate your phrasing," Gnever said, "but I was speaking literally. You can't do this, because we will not let you out until you are properly committed to our community. Our access is closed."

Wenda didn't argue with him. She led the way through the chambers to the hall to the stairs, and up the steps.

The portal was locked shut, with a magical bond. They could not open it.

"We ask you to reconsider," Gnever said.

Now each gnome companion approached his or her guest. Gnaughty flashed her décolletage, effectively freezing Wenda in place, then stood on a step that brought her face to the level of Wenda's face, and kissed her. It was no amateur effort.

Wenda freaked out, overwhelmed by little flying hearts.

When she recovered, she and the others were locked in a bedroom chamber. They had all been similarly captured.

"What a creature," Ida remarked, brushing away a heart that clung electrostatically to her shirt. "If I had a quarter of that expertise, I would have been married long since."

"I can only hope that my betrothee has some similar ability," Hilarion said. "And that when I am male again, I can impress her in the manner my gnome impressed me. He may be short of stature, but he's one romantic figure."

"What do we do now?" Meryl asked.

Wenda had come to a realization during her freaking-out. "We wait."

"We what?" Angela asked.

"I think they will let us go in the morning."

The others stared at her in perplexity. Then Jumper smiled in a fetchingly female way, having read her mind.

They used the suite bathroom to wash up, and settled onto the various beds.

The nuptial party appeared, and promptly changed genders. "Oh, my!" Charming said as his clothing bulged in particular sections.

Demon Beauregard was similarly confused as he discovered himself to be a demoness. Angela took hold of him. "I have a surprise for you, you ravishing creature," she said.

And Eris was now male. Wenda knew that the local

reversal could not affect her; she was merely going along with it. "You look very pretty, Jumper," she said, and took hold of him.

Wenda caught Charming and hauled him into the suddenly curtained bed. She gave him no chance to protest. And in seven minutes she was sound asleep while he remained amazed and awake. It was glorious.

In the morning the chamber door opened. Gnever stood there. "It seems we have a problem," he said.

Wenda affected innocence. "Whatever can that be?"

"That object you left on your wagon. The gneiss rock."

"It's not nice," she said, not caring that the local reverse wood was not nullifying her dialect spell.

"Correct. It is a terror. We are fearful to approach it."

Now the other members of the Quest were catching on. The Knot had burned through its shield and was radiating its petrifying malice.

"Fancy that," Wenda remarked without sympathy.

"Could you—would you move it?"

"Why should we want to do that?" She was enjoying this, and the others were stifling smirks and snickers.

"It is obstructing our exit! We fear to go near it."

"It is merely a not of reverse would," Wenda said reasonably. "You surely have seen similar things before."

"Not like this! What have you done to it?"

"Nothing. It did it to itself. It's petrified."

Now he began to understand. "Old wood. Transformed by time."

"That's right. Now that you understand it, you should have no further problem. Just ignore it."

Gnever looked pained. "We can't. The effect is too strong, too close to our door."

"That's odd," Wenda said. "We do. It would be no trouble for us to move it. But we can't."

"Can't?"

"We are confined to quarters here. Don't you remember?"

The gnome was starting to look ill. "If we—if we let you go?"

Wenda considered. "Actually we are coming to like it here. We are in no hurry to go."

Gnever knew he was being manipulated. "What—what do you want?"

"What do you have? Aside from winsome damsels?"

"We made many reverse-wood artifacts for export. Swords, arrows, or simply arrowheads. Those can be devastating on other worlds."

Wenda considered. "Perhaps we could use a supply of those. Give them to Prince Ida."

Hope flared. "Then you will move it?"

"We will take it with us when we go. Provided there are no further complications."

"No complications!" he agreed eagerly.

Wenda shrugged. "Perhaps we should have breakfast before we go."

Soon they were at the morning banquet, with their gnome companions of the day before. "You were magnificent," Gnaughty murmured. "I've never before seen Gnever sweat like that." She was showing no freakish flesh.

"You aren't angry because we are not staying?"

"We do what we have to do." Gnaughty lowered her gaze. "I have a boyfriend I'd rather entertain, no offense."

"None taken."

The Knot was no trouble. Wenda went first and replaced the seeds in the net, nullifying its baleful glare. Then the others joined her. Jumper changed to roc form, and they wheeled the wagon onto his back. They reverted to their natural genders as they left contact with the ground.

The assembled gnomes stared. "He's a Magician!" Gnever exclaimed, staring at the monstrous bird. "If he had done that underground—"

"There was no need," Wenda said cheerfully. "We knew you would reconsider in the morning, being nice people."

Gnaughty was not the only gnome to stifle a giggle. They were, after all, good sports.

Then Jumper got to his feet, taxied, pumped his wings, and took off. The gnomes below and behind waved.

"We forgot to demand the location of the Door!" Meryl said, stricken.

"Not so," Wenda said smugly. "Jumper took it from them telepathically. We are flying there now."

Hilarion, changing to his masculine clothes, nodded. "You are truly a princess."

The others applauded. Wenda blushed.

But he's right, Jumper thought. *You showed real leadership qualities throughout. Right from the start when you told me to get that Door location.*

Wenda continued to blush. She had merely seen what she had to do, and done it.

They descended a relatively short distance up the trunk where there was a mountain range of bark masking a winding valley, a crevice in the bark. But as they approached, the scale of it became evident: the formation was huge. This was after all a planet, whose details were landscapes. In that valley was a lake, and on the lake was an island. On the island was a single hill, like an overgrown branch, and in the side of the hill was a cave. It looked exactly like a knothole, by no coincidence.

Jumper landed neatly on a plain beside the hill. They dismounted and rolled the wagon off. Jumper reverted to manform.

As their feet touched the ground, the scenery changed.

The hill became a giant pit, the cave an ugly boulder. But they knew it was the familiar image reversal.

"The Sidewalk and Door are within," Wenda said. "There is a path. All we have to do is follow it."

Buoyed by the success of their search, they rolled the wagon down into the masked cave.

As they entered the cave things changed again. *The wood is situational reversal,* Jumper thought. *I picked that up from the gnomes.* His body was now that of a fly, so he had to speak telepathically.

"Completing the five aspects of Reverse World," Hilarion agreed. He was now a pauper.

"It is surely bearable," the child Ida agreed.

"But hardly comfortable," Demoness Angela said.

"I agree!" Meryl said. She had resumed the fish-headed, human-legged form, complete with the panties that threatened to freak Hilarion out. She quickly donned a skirt Ida provided.

And Wenda, overwhelmed by the ambiance, discovered herself to be a reversed woodwife: only her backside existed, while her frontside was hollow. "We shall endure," she said bravely, not at all pleased.

They resumed motion—and walked carelessly into trouble. The path was there, but reversed; what looked like a rise was a descent. Before they knew it, the wagon was rolling ponderously down.

Hilarion and Jumper labored to hold it back, while fish-headed Meryl and Demoness Angela ran helplessly beside it. The child Ida, behind, could do nothing. All of them were hampered by their unfamiliarly reversed bodies.

Wenda, walking beside it, saw a chasm to the side. She tried to push the wagon away from it, but lacked sufficient substance to move it. Her footing gave way and suddenly she was falling into the gulf.

It had all happened so suddenly there had been no time to figure out a better course. Wenda, falling, knew she was done for. She might be only half a woman, but the fall would crush and splinter what remained of her. She was doomed.

Then someone caught her. It was the Demoness Eris, carrying her back up to the path where the wagon had finally halted. Things were abruptly back to normal, at least as normalcy was defined by this region.

"You saved me!" Wenda exclaimed. "I would have died."

"I had to," Eris agreed. "It is what friends do."

"But now you will be in trouble with the other Demons," Ida said.

"Will they hold a trial?" Meryl asked, bemused.

"I'm sure they will," Ida said. "In their fashion. Capital-D Demons can be very possessive of their territorial imperatives."

A somber courtroom formed about them. Now Eris was confined to a booth marked DEFENDANT. The rest of them were their normal, unreversed selves, except for Wenda, who remained hollow in front. This was definitely Demon business.

The Demon Reversal appeared, in the form of a tree. "I hereby charge the Demoness Eris with Infringement on my Domain," he said. "That is a Violation of Demon Protocol. The penalty is the forfeit of one Status Point and elimination of the change she made."

Wenda knew that was a serious matter to a Demon, because all they really cared about was Status. It was even more serious to her personally, because elimination of the change would mean that she would not have her life saved. But she couldn't protest, because she, like the other members of the Quest, was now relegated to the Witness section and was unable to speak or move. What would happen would happen.

A panel of three Judges appeared. One had a vaguely human body and a head like a small planet; another was female with an aspect like a small distant galaxy; the third was in the form of a dragon ass, with the body of a dragon and the head of a donkey.

Suddenly Wenda realized whom that last one was. The Demon Xanth! He was said to like the dragon-ass form, though it was hard to fathom why.

"We are the Demon Panel for this Decision: Xanth, Fornax, and Pluto, selected by our interest of the moment. Who is to be your Defense Attorney?" Xanth asked Eris.

"Angela Angel."

Angela flew up out of the Witness section, surprised almost out of her wits. "But I know nothing about legal matters," she protested.

"Here is what you need to know," Xanth said. "Win and you will be rewarded. Lose and you will be punished. Now proceed with your case."

Angela looked as if she was about to wet her nonexistent panties. "But—but—I'm an angel! This is Demon business. I can't possibly—"

"Do not argue," Eris murmured from the booth, "lest you and I both suffer grievously. Call your Witnesses. Make your case."

Angela moved her hands about, collecting the wits that remained in reach. She evidently realized that she was stuck for it. "First we must establish exactly what happened," she said. "I call Wenda Woodwife to the stand."

Wenda found herself in the Witness Stand, now free to speak. "I fell," she said. "I was about to perish, when the Demoness Eris rescued me. I owe my life to her."

"Why did she do this?" Angela asked.

"For friendship."

"What nonsense is this?" the Demon Reversal demanded. "I do not know this word."

"It means being on good terms with another person," Wenda explained boldly. "Being respectful, affectionate, caring."

"This is not rational."

"Yes."

"So why did she really do it? To spite me?"

"To save me."

"You're a mortal!" he exclaimed, as if that refuted her statement.

"I am." Wenda was almost beginning to enjoy this. The Demons were reacting a tiny trifle like the Gnarly Gnomes.

Reversal turned to the Panel. "The Witness admits it. The Defendant did it for no rational reason. She must be Penalized."

Xanth turned to Angela. "How does your client plead?"

"She did it," Angela said. "But it was justified on the basis of friendship."

There was a visible stir among the Judges. "We have not before encountered such a Defense," Xanth said. "Have you no more comprehensible rationale to offer?"

"No," Angela said. "I feel this is sufficient."

"Then we will proceed to the Deliberation leading to the Vote," Xanth said.

The Demoness Fornax came forward. She glanced at the Witnesses. "You," she said to Hilarion. "Who are you, and what is your business here?"

What was going on? But Wenda, no longer the Witness, was unable to speak. It was Hilarion who was free to do so now.

"I am Prince Hilarion, looking for my lost betrothee."

"You are a handsome mortal man. As such, you have a certain incidental appeal."

If he was taken aback, he did not show it. "Thank you."

"Are you also Wenda's friend?"

"Yes, I like to think so."

"Would you save her from death if you could?"

"Yes."

"Are you Eris's friend?"

"No, I would not presume to so aspire. I respect her and appreciate what she did, but that's not the same."

"Would you prefer to see her exonerated?"

"Yes, because she saved my friend."

"Understand this," Fornax said. "If Eris loses, she will forfeit one Status Point and what she did will be undone. Your friend Wenda will die. If Eris wins, she will not forfeit a Point and Wenda will survive as she is now, a half woman. That is the standard compromise when a mortal inconveniences a Demon."

"I didn't know," Hilarion said, taken aback.

"Marry me, and I will vote Yes for exoneration."

Wenda was amazed and appalled by this extreme cynicism. The Demoness was openly selling her Vote! Why did she even want to marry a mortal man?

Hilarion looked surprised. "I respectfully decline."

Fornax considered. "I will amend my offer. Marry me, and I will vote Yes and give you immortality."

Hilarion gulped. "No."

Fornax was unfazed. "I will amend again. I will give you those two things plus ultimate sex." Now her form changed to that of a blindingly beautiful human woman.

Hilarion's eyes started to crystallize. "No," he gasped.

"Are you sure?" The Demoness's dress faded out, so that she was standing in bra and panties, both amazingly supple and well filled.

"N-no," Hilarion gasped.

Fornax pounced. "You are not sure?"

He struggled to get out the words. "K-k-kiss me."

The Demoness smiled a smile of incipient victory. She approached him, embraced him, and kissed him. Hearts, planets, and stars shot like rockets out of the contact of their lips, and a wisp of perfumed smoke rose. She let him go and he sank back limply, hardly aware of the universe, let alone his immediate surroundings.

"Now what is your answer?" she asked imperatively.

His mouth struggled valiantly to form the words. "You are not she."

"Not what?"

"Not my betrothee."

A small dark cloud formed over her head. "What is your answer?"

"No."

"Then I will vote No." She returned to the Judges' Panel.

What had Hilarion done? It defied comprehension.

The Demon Xanth spoke. "What governed your decision, Hilarion?"

"Friendship."

"You could have garnered a vote to save your friend's life, and had immortality and ultimate sex for yourself. How does turning down the deal benefit your friend?"

Wenda wondered too.

"I could not endure seeing my friend reduced to such a wretched state. How could she exist as half a woman?"

He thought this would be torture for Wenda? Then Wenda realized that he had never known her in her original woodwife state. He had a horrible idea of it, having seen only her recent reversed variant. And she was unable to speak to tell him that she would much rather live as a half woman, whichever half, than die as a whole one.

"So you did this for friendship?" Xanth asked.

"Yes."

"I remain curious about the strength of this irrational feeling." Xanth looked at Meryl. "Who are you?"

Now Meryl alone could speak. "I am Meryl Winged Mermaid."

"Are you also friends with Wenda?"

"I am."

"I will summon your ideal male, a handsome and virile winged merman, to join you and be your mate, if you will renounce that friendship."

"No!" she explained, pained.

"He knows you exist, but does not know where to find you. The two of you may never get together otherwise. That would be unfortunate, as he is already half in love with you just from the knowledge of your nature. He is a fine and generous man. Will you make the deal?"

Tears flowed down Meryl's face. "I can't."

"Interesting." Xanth looked to the side. Wenda was able to follow his gaze. There was a beautiful young mortal woman. She nodded slightly.

"I vote Yes," Xanth said.

Then Wenda realized that the woman was the Demon Xanth's mortal wife, Chlorine. He had half her soul, so he could understand friendship if he tried. Chlorine certainly understood, and had signaled him to vote Yes. She had much more concern with mortals than a Demon did.

The Demon Pluto took the floor. "I too am curious about the limitations of this mortal phenomenon." He looked at Ida. "Who are you?"

It was Ida's turn to speak. "I am Princess Ida, sister of King Ivy."

"You have an interesting talent. We came here because of it. No mortal talent can control Demons, but we felt its intriguing tug and decided to honor it. What exactly is it?"

"It is the power of the Idea," Ida said. "The planet that seems to orbit my head is Ptero, where the Idea of all living or theoretical characters exists. This is a link rather than a literal orbiting. It links in turn to a large loop of other worlds with other characters and rules of magic. All are connected by the Idea of their association. In addition, I am able to confirm any Idea locally, provided it is suggested by someone who does not know about this aspect of my talent."

Meryl could not speak, but Wenda was aware that she was startled. Hilarion would have to delete her memory of this dialogue, when he got the chance.

"You are nevertheless unmarried."

"I am." Ida smiled wishfully. "Not entirely by choice. I simply never encountered the right man."

"I will introduce you to your ideal man, who will be smitten with you the moment he recognizes you, and you will marry him and live happily ever after, as long as you both shall live, etc. In return you must renounce your friendship with Wenda."

"Absolutely not!"

"If your ideal man does not locate you, he will never marry any other woman, and will live out his life in solitary sorrow. He knows there is only one woman for him, and that you are that one, though he does not know your identity. Do you wish to do this to him?"

Now the tears were on Ida's face. "No."

"Then will you make the deal?"

"No," Ida sobbed.

"You will give up your happiness and his for the sake of your friendship with a forest nymph?"

"Yes," Ida whispered.

"Interesting," Pluto said, as Xanth had. He glanced to his side, where a fair young princess sat. Wenda recognized her: Princess Eve! She had married him last year, and given him half her soul. He too had a basis to understand, if he chose to.

Eve nodded. Pluto spoke. "I vote Yes."

The Demoness Eris had won, two votes to one. She would receive no loss of a Point. And Wenda would live.

The courtroom and Demons vanished. They were back in the dusky cave, their bodies no longer convoluted, except for Wenda. Wenda was a true woodwife again, except that she was hollow in front, just as she had been the moment the Demon Court convened. All the rest of them were now back to their natural forms.

"I'm so sorry," Hilarion told Wenda. "I did not want this torture to be visited on you."

"Dew knot bee concerned," she said. "I was a wood-wife for most of my life. I can bee one again. I appreciate yewr sacrifice to try to spare me." For the Demoness Fornax had offered him everything that Eris had given Jumper, and she knew how happy Jumper was. But Hilarion did have half a case: she was devastated by her loss of full reality. What would Charming think?

"And you, Meryl," Hilarion said. "You gave up your ideal male companion."

"I couldn't let Wenda die," Meryl said simply.

"Yes, of course. And you, Ida—you also gave up your ideal male companion."

"It had to be," Ida said shortly. "The Demons were testing us. We have to be true to our friendships."

Then Angela screamed. They all looked at her. She was flying just above the cave floor, her feet almost touching. They were dainty feet, on nicely shaped legs. But why had she screamed?

"I'm whole!" Angela cried. "My legs have substance!"

That was it. Her legs and feet had become visible. How had that happened?

"The Demon Xanth said I would be rewarded if I won," Angela said. "This must be how."

"You got Wenda's lost substance!" Meryl said.

Angela looked at Wenda's hollow frontside. "Oh! I didn't know. I never would have taken it that way!"

Wenda realized that her loss was not total. "I'm glad yew got it," she said. "Yew needed to get it before yewr time ran out."

"Wenda," Ida said. "Your forest dialect is back."

Wenda realized it was true. "My reversion must have nullified the spell," she said. "I have nothing to hide anymore."

"You never did," Ida said.

"I think it's quaint," Hilarion said.

Wenda shrugged. "It's me, anyway."

Now it was late in the day, for all that they were in the gloom of the underground. They camped where they were, on a wide ledge, eating from their supplies, and were ready when the conjugal visiting party came.

"Angela!" Beauregard exclaimed. "You've got legs!"

"And that's not all," Angela said, hoisting her skirt to flash him with her visible panties. Maybe her recent experience as a demoness had made her bolder about such un-Heavenly details.

Meanwhile Charming was embracing Wenda. Like Beauregard, he had not changed his situation. Maybe the Demons had nullified that aspect of this region when they set up the courtroom, and forgotten to revert it when they left. So Charming was neither a child nor a pauper, but a man with desire and hands. She braced for his exclamation of dismay as those hands clasped nothing behind. Then she would have to explain how she had reverted. How would he react?

Then she remembered that she had her backside. It was her frontside that was missing. So she turned in his embrace so that her full side was facing him, as it were.

He kissed her neck and dropped to the floor with her, having no objection to the changed position. In seven minutes he was safely asleep. He hadn't even noticed! Wenda wasn't sure whether to be pleased or annoyed.

The visitors were gone. It was time to settle for the night.

Then Meryl screamed, bringing them all alert. "The Sidewalk!"

Sure enough, there it was, crossing the path ahead. They had found it when they least expected it.

Hastily they trundled the loaded wagon to the Sidewalk, and onto it, sideways. This time they made sure to take the right fork. Jumper opened the Door, and they squeezed through. They had escaped Reverse World.

10

GOBLINATE

It was dark but quiet. "There is no nearby threat," Jumper reported, ranging out telepathically. "We are on an island in a lake."

"The Door connected from one island to another," Meryl said.

"That may be coincidence," Ida said, "but it is convenient." She produced a small tent from her handbag, and they set it up. Then came pillows and blankets. Soon they were sleeping comfortably.

Except for Hilarion and Ida, who sat up a little while, talking in the darkness. And Wenda, whose reverted condition made her restless. So she quietly listened, feeling slightly guilty for snooping. "Should I renew the forgetting for Meryl?" Hilarion asked.

"I believe you should," Ida answered.

"Forget what?" Meryl asked, hearing her name.

"You volunteered to allow Hilarion to work his magic on you," Ida explained, "so that you could forget something it is important to forget."

"Oh. Like being fish-headed. That's fine." Meryl slept, satisfied.

"You have a certain touch for discretion, Ida," Hilarion said.

"Thank you. I must say that it was a noble thing you did, surrendering your discovery of your betrothee in order to save Wenda's life. Fornax offered you everything Eris gives Jumper. I realize how tempting that must be to a young man."

"No more noble than your own sacrifice of your ideal man. Anyway, Fornax was not my betrothee, so it would not have worked out."

She laughed without humor. "We seem to be similarly foolish. I hope you find your betrothee when no one's life is on the line."

"I hope so too, and I hope the same for you. The Demons did not actually say we would not find them on our own."

"They did not," she agreed. "At least now we have confirmation that they exist, and are presumably alive and well. That's worth something."

"Yes, it is," he agreed. "Maybe we can locate them after we get the Knot delivered."

"That is an idea," she agreed. "Perhaps we should plan to make those searches together, as they are of similar nature and our talents mesh well."

"They do," he agreed thoughtfully. "I would like to do that, hoping for success for us both."

"Then it is perhaps a date," she said, and they both laughed. Wenda was glad that the young man and older woman were getting along so well. She wished them both success.

In the morning the Knot was making its malice known again. Wenda replaced the seeds in the net, and the wagon became seemingly friendly.

They rolled the wagon into the red water. It wanted to float, being wood, but the Knot was more like heavy rock and would not let it float. So Jumper transformed to a giant fish and carried it across to the blue mainland.

Now all they had to worry about was the Strip.

Angela and Meryl flew ahead, searching for evidence of the Sidewalk or Door. But this time they found no clue.

"We shall just have to plunge in and look for it," Wenda decided.

They nerved themselves and did it. Immediately they were in a chaos of sound. A bell was ringing, deafeningly loud. Wenda oriented on the loudness and saw a man walking toward them. He had ears shaped like bells, and they were ringing as he walked. Loudly.

"Excuse me!" she yelled over the sound. "Can you turn that off?"

"I can't hear you," he shouted back. "My ears are ringing."

Just so. Normally any ear-ringing was internal. This was an animated pun, and they had to get past it to reach the Door. But the man was in the way, and when Wenda tried to push by him, the ringing got worse. She fell back, putting her hands over her ears. Her ears fed into her now-hollow skull, but the sound was painful anyway. She knew it was just as bad for the other members of the party.

What would get rid of this tormented man? She looked desperately around. All she saw was another man. Well, at least his ears weren't ringing.

She approached him. "Hello," she shouted. "I am Wenda Woodwife, as yew can see." She turned around briefly so he could see her full backside, now decently clothed. Unfortunately she couldn't clothe her hollow face. "Who are yew? What's yewr pun?"

"I am Anthony," he shouted back. "I'm no pun. I just wandered into this dreadful Strip and now can't find my way out. It's awful!"

Another sufferer? She did not fully trust this. "What's yewr talent?"

"Summoning and banishing the Demoness Metria." He shrugged. "I know it's useless, but there it is."

Wenda knew of Metria, who was always into mischief. She did not want Metria complicating this problem.

Meryl was behind her. "Maybe Metria could help," she said.

Ida was behind Meryl. "I'm sure she could," she agreed.

Now that was interesting. There should now be a way Metria could help them, if she would. That was two questions: how could the Demoness help, and how could she be persuaded to do so?

Then Wenda suffered a double notion as twin bulbs flashed over her head. "Summon her!" she shouted.

"Are you sure?" he shouted back. "She'll be in a bad mood. She doesn't like being summoned."

"Reasonably sure," she said. "I want to trick her into getting you out of here."

Anthony smiled. "Say no more." He concentrated, and a bathtub appeared.

The Demoness Metria was in it, having a bubble bath, scrubbing her bare back. She glared around, realizing that she was suddenly public. "Who did this assail?" she demanded threateningly.

Wenda was ready. "Did this what?"

"Violate, ravish, rape, assault, dishonor—"

"Outrage?"

"Whatever!" Metria agreed crossly, her temper not improved half a whit.

"I did it!" Wenda said. "With the help of these two miscreants." She indicated the bell ringer and Anthony, both of whom had freaked out at the sight of her bare heaving wet front. "What are yew going to dew about it?"

Metria squinted. "I know you! You're that woodwife with the funny dialect. Only what's with your face? Did somebody punch you in your wooden nose?"

"Yew're right," Wenda agreed, ignoring the face remark. "I'm guilty. Let the two men go. Haul me out of here instead."

"Oh no, you don't! You're trying to trick me into extricating you from the Comic Strip. I'll mess you up instead."

"No, please! I'm the one to punish."

But Metria was already reaching out to catch the two freaked men. She hauled them both into the tub with duplicate splashes. The shock of the water made them recover. They gazed again at her front and freaked out again.

"I *am* punishing you." Then Metria, the tub, and both men vanished. And the awful ear-ringing had been silenced.

"Onward," Wenda said, pleased.

"You are developing a rare talent in management," Ida murmured.

"Thank yew. But we still have knot found the Door."

But already another pun was upon them. A large wild woman was barring their way. "You shall not proceed, you civilized tenderfeet," she declared. "I am Harberian Barbarian, and my talent is changing local seasons. You will stay here forever and three days unless you have a seasonal pass."

Wenda was taken aback. "Aren't yew exaggerating? How can we stay longer than forever?"

"It's hyperbole, you tiny little nit. If ignorance were a molehill, you'd be a mountain."

"She's a hyper-bully," Jumper said.

"And I love harp music, and know where every harbor is," Harberian agreed. "Now observe my power, you insignificant mites." She waved her arms.

The season had been summery. Now it was fall, with the trees turning colors. And winter, with snow flurries blowing at them. And spring, with flowers popping out of the ground.

Wenda looked around again. There was another man. Could she somehow use him to cancel the barbarian?

She approached the man. "I am Wenda Woodwife, passing through. Are yew another lost traveler?"

"No, I'm Eric, enjoying the scenery. I am Harberian's boyfriend. My talent is to find the question for any answer."

"Knot the answer to any question?"

"No. I know the questions to ask to get folk to come up with specific answers."

This seemed to be no help at all. But Wenda was desperate. She cudgeled her hollow brain, and managed to evoke another bulb flash. She noticed incidentally that the flashbulb was half hollow, like her head. Maybe she could use his talent after all.

"The answer is Right Here," Wenda said firmly.

"The question is, Where is the Door?" Eric said immediately.

"Sheer genius!" Hilarion murmured admiringly.

And there was the Sidewalk leading to the Door. They trundled the wagon hastily to it, made the right turn, and came up against the Door. In little more than a moment and an instant they were piling through it.

"That was a remarkable recovery," Ida said. "I agree with Hilarion: you showed genius, Wenda."

"With my hollow head?" But Wenda was pleased, and she knew the back part of her head was blushing.

"Maybe we shouldn't celebrate yet," Jumper said.

Ida looked around. "Indeed we should not. This is, if I remember my geography correctly, the dread Hate Lake of the Goblinate of the Golden Horde. A deadly dangerous place."

"At least we are back in Xanth," Meryl said.

"We had better move on out of here," Wenda said. She knew of the Goblinate; it was reputed to be the worst goblin band in Xanth, utterly ruthless and cruel, buttressed by the hate spring, which they used to torture captives.

"I can assume roc form and carry us out," Jumper said.

"Too late," Hilarion said. "They have surrounded us. You don't have takeoff room, and if you did, they would pepper you with arrows."

Indeed, there was now a wide arc of goblins extending from the shore on one side to the shore on the other side, and closing in. They were trapped.

"Dew knot change form," Wenda told Jumper. "We dew knot want them to know yewr ability."

"I see an air boat," Angela said, hovering above them.

Wenda glanced up and saw that the angel's flaring skirt was no longer empty; her nice legs showed right up to the heavenly panties. "Dew knot look up," she snapped to Hilarion and Jumper.

She was too late. Both men had freaked out.

There was no time to snap them out of it. "Can yew show us the air boat?" Wenda asked Angela.

"It is right here, beached by the water. It is invisible because it is made of air. I can see it because I remain partly ethereal." The angel flew down to perch on it.

"How big is it?"

"Big. It could hold us all, plus the Knot. The goblins must use it to haul freight."

"Roll the wagon to it. We'll cross to the island before the goblins catch on. Dew knot touch the water."

They snapped the men out of their freaks, and the two of them hauled the wagon to the boat. Wenda and Ida pushed from behind, while Meryl and Angela hovered nearby, watching the goblins.

"They're catching on," Meryl called. "They're bringing up some sort of contraption. Get the boat moving!"

There was an invisible ramp for the freight. They hauled the wagon across it and lifted it clear of the beach. Hilarion pushed off with an invisible pole. They had made it.

Meryl screamed. Wenda looked, and saw her ensnared in a flying net. That was what the contraption was: a catapult that had hurled the net and caught Meryl in the air.

Angela flew toward her, but Meryl saw her and called a warning. "Don't get close! They'll catch you too! Leave me and get out of here!"

"She's right," Ida called. "You can't help Meryl. Stay with us. We'll think of something."

Distraught, Angela came to land on the air boat. "We've got to rescue her."

"We'll dew it," Wenda said. But she had no idea how.

There were air oars on the boat. The men wielded them, careful not to splash, and the craft moved smartly across the deadly lake. The goblins did not try to follow; they well knew the nature of the water.

But Meryl was a captive of the most brutal goblins in Xanth. What could they do?

They watched as the goblins swarmed over the net and hauled the struggling Meryl into their ugly mound. They did not seem to be hurting her. Yet.

They held an impromptu council of war as the boat continued to move across the lake. "We have to save her!" Angela said tearfully.

"I could change to roc form," Jumper said. "But the moment I attacked the mound, they could kill her."

"And they would riddle you with arrows," Hilarion said. "This is a hostage situation. We shall have to negotiate."

"Negotiate?" Wenda asked. "With what?"

"They want something from us," Hilarion said. "Otherwise they would not have taken her captive. They would have killed her immediately, probably while we watched."

"What could they want?" Ida asked.

"I don't know. I think we shall have to wait until they contact us. We are unlikely to like what they have to say, but I fear it is our only course at the moment."

Wenda suspected that he was right. The goblins did want something, and it was unlikely to be anything nice.

"They are not fools," Jumper said. "They may know about my transformation abilities, and fear that if they kill Meryl, I will bomb them to oblivion regardless of their arrows." He smiled grimly. "And they are correct."

"We'll just have to see," Wenda said morosely.

They reached the island and debarked. The Knot was starting to break down the reverse-wood shield, but Wenda did not refresh the seeds yet, not wanting to waste them.

"Don't we need Meryl to suggest something Ida can agree to?" Angela asked.

Ida nodded. "That is a minor part of our problem. The major part of course is how to save her from the awful clutches of the goblins."

"Yes. I thought that if she can't suggest a way, maybe I can. Only I know about your talent, so—"

Ida caught Hilarion's eye. He focused on Angela, who was evidently volunteering.

Angela shook her head. "I'm sorry. What was I saying?"

"I think yew were about to make a suggestion about rescuing Meryl from the goblins," Wenda said. "Because the rest of us have no idea."

"Oh, yes. For some reason I thought it wouldn't work." Angela pondered an angelic moment. "It's not really a rescue idea so much as a way to figure out a way by getting more information. If Jumper can reach her telepathically—"

"I'm sure he can," Ida agreed.

"—then he could tune in on what's happening to her now. At least we could find out exactly where she's being held, so that we would know where to strike."

"Dew it, Jumper," Wenda said. She doubted Jumper's telepathic range had been far enough before, but now she knew it was. Hilarion and Ida were working beautifully together again.

Jumper concentrated. "I've got her," he said. "I'll put it on the hologram."

"The what?" Hilarion asked.

Then it appeared: an image of a dusky dank cell with an iron-bar gate, guarded by a bulging-eyed goblin. It was what Meryl was seeing at the moment. The hologram was where Jumper was, replacing him. He was projecting the scene he was receiving, to all their minds.

It occurred to Wenda that Eris had given Jumper talents that would come close to making him a Magician if they were permanent. Apparently this did not constitute a Demon Violation, because she had done it at the outset, and already had a close relationship with him. The Demon Xanth had given Chlorine similar gifts; Wenda understood that Chlorine had been an unpretty and bad-tempered woman before her association with the Demon. It was only when Eris intervened to change the outcome of another person's accident—Wenda's own—that the Violation occurred.

Correct, Eris thought. *The extra courage and intelligence I lent you when I let him go with you did not count, and neither do our nuptial visits, because they don't change history but merely make your lives more comfortable. Demons don't care about mortal comfort, one way or the other.*

She had given Wenda extra courage and intelligence? That explained a lot! Wenda, like a fool, had never suspected. She had thought she was merely rising to the challenges as the occasions demanded.

You were never a fool. Merely inexperienced. I wanted to be sure you would not do something that would stress Jumper, like falling off a cliff.

But Wenda had done that anyway, she remembered wryly. So Eris's precaution had not been sufficient.

That was an unusual accident. But yes, then I had to act, because of our friendship.

And Eris *had* acted, and thereby put her Demon status in peril. Exactly as a friend would.

I'm glad I got it right. I'm sorry the compromise brought a penalty on you.

Which had given Angela something she desperately needed: substance. Had Wenda realized that would happen, she would have chosen it.

Exactly as a friend would.

Wenda had to smile. The Demoness had gotten it right, again. She was a fast study.

Thank you.

And Wenda really did like her, quite apart from the rescue. She had made Jumper happier than he could ever have been otherwise, but that was only part of it. She was nice to communicate with, not being coldly arrogant like the other Demons.

I am learning from Jumper—and from you. I regret I can't rescue Meryl. If I intervened again, I would have no recourse. I'm on probation.

That figured. The Demons had suffered the inconvenience of the Violation hearing, and did not want it repeated.

"Would you stop staring at me?" Meryl demanded of the goblin guard.

"Can't help it. I'm Goggle Goblin." He continued goggling between the bars. The orientation of his gaze suggested that it was focused on Meryl's bare chest. That figured. He was male.

"Then may I have a cloak?"

"No. If you covered up, I wouldn't be able to goggle."

Wenda appreciated Meryl's discomfort. But if that was the worst she suffered, it was bearable.

"That seems to be a low cell," Hilarion said. "I wonder whether Jumper could transform to a tunneling vole and give us access from below."

"I doubt it," Ida said with regret. The idea had come from the wrong person.

"Oops," he breathed, realizing.

There was the sound of tramping boots. A new goblin appeared. This one was older, stouter, uglier, and nastier than Goggle. He put one black hand on the bars and ripped it open, the lock tearing apart.

"You always gotta do it the hard way, Gorilla," Goggle griped. "I got a key."

"Shut your staring face," Gorilla replied politely, "before I push your eyeballs out through your ears."

Goggle shut his face, as it was evidently no bluff.

Gorilla stood and peered at Meryl. "What a piece of tail!" he exclaimed, gazing at it.

"What a crock of spit," Meryl replied defiantly.

"Har har har! I like them spirited. They last longer." Again, he was evidently speaking literally.

Then another goblin appeared, the fattest and ugliest yet. He wore a small smudged iron crown. "At ease, Gorilla. You'll have your turn." Gorilla shut up with surprising dispatch.

"You must be the head honcho," Meryl said bravely. But the hologram was quivering; she was frightened.

"King Gauche," he agreed, hawking and spitting to the side. He squinted at her, seeming to be impressed by neither her front nor her tail. "You will tell me everything."

"I will tell you nothing," she retorted.

He formed a gap-toothed smile as he picked his nose. "Let me rephrase, crossbreed. You will tell all, or suffer hostile witness procedure, which of course we prefer."

"And what is that?" she asked. The image was shuddering, because she knew she would not like the answer.

"Number one: rape by Gorilla Goblin. We'll hold him back after five or six efforts, just in case you are by then inclined to cooperate. Otherwise, when you recover from your internal injuries, we will do number two: clipping your wings at the shoulders, so you will never fly again. It will be painful, especially when we burn the stumps; you will be free to scream. We love the sound of screaming."

That truly terrified Meryl on more than one level. The hologram suffered glitches across its surface, and almost faded out with intermittent losses of signal. But she somehow maintained a defiant pose. "And what else?"

"If you still are difficult, we will douse you with hate elixir and put you into the cell of another innocent captive." He paused as if considering. "Maybe that winged merman. That should make for an interesting combat."

The hologram grayed out entirely. The brutal chief had scored.

"Tell her to cooperate!" Wenda cried.

Jumper sent the thought. "Oh!" Meryl exclaimed, realizing that she was not alone.

"Is there a winged merman there?" Angela asked.

Jumper checked. *No. He lied to make her squirm.*

This was a really nasty goblin. "Tell her that too," Wenda said.

"Oh!" Meryl repeated, perversely relieved.

"Tell her that we mean to rescue her, somehow," Wenda said.

Jumper did. "Oh," Meryl said, this time relieved.

"What's it to be, crossbreed?" Gauche demanded. "Or would you prefer to wait before deciding? Gorilla is eager to start the torture. He likes raping crossbreeds. They scream in interesting ways."

"Yeah, yeah!" Gorilla agreed eagerly. He was clearly ready to commence the torture immediately.

"I'll—I'll cooperate," Meryl said, making an attempt to feign reluctance.

"Awww," Goggle and Gorilla said almost together, disappointed.

"Well, maybe later," Gauche said, scratching his behind. He was plainly disappointed.

"What do you want to know?" Meryl asked quickly.

Gauche belched. "Your party of six arrived without warning in our territory. We know you didn't just march in. How did you travel, and why did you come here?"

"We came through a Door between worlds," Meryl said. "It's complicated to explain; you probably wouldn't understand."

"Right," Gauche agreed, blowing out a disreputable noise from somewhere obscure. "Goblins aren't as stupid as ogres, but we try."

"He is not stupid at all," Ida murmured. "He is crude, cunning, and ruthless. He is playing a game. Maybe he wants her to try to trick him, so he'll have a pretext to torture her despite her cooperation."

"Tell Meryl," Wenda said tersely.

Jumper did.

"The Door takes us to the world of Comic," Meryl said quickly. "The return Door dumps us randomly in Xanth. It landed us here. We never wanted to be here; we detest your hate spring and your whole awful tribe."

"Why are you traveling?"

"We have to transport the Knot to the Good Magician's Castle."

"The what?"

"It's a big knot of petrified reverse wood. It terrifies anyone who approaches it. Anyone except Wenda Woodwife, who derives from wood and understands all kinds. She nullifies it with reverse wood so we can get close enough to haul it on the wagon."

"You reverse reverse wood with reverse wood?" he asked alertly.

"You're right," Hilarion murmured. "The rogue's no fool."

"The Knot is petrified," Meryl said. "It is changed, and seems more like a big rock. It doesn't reverse, it frightens people. But Wenda puts a shell of regular reverse wood around it. That doesn't change the Knot, just its malign radiation, reversing that so that the thing seems friendly. But it wears out the reverse wood in a day or so, and it has to be replaced. It's a challenge."

Gauche wiped his wet nose on his sleeve. "It terrifies anyone who comes near it?"

"Yes, except for the effect of the shell of reverse wood."

"And if a chip of that should be catapulted into an enemy camp, what would be the effect?"

"I suppose it depends on the size of the chip. It would scare anyone who tried to pick it up."

Gauche scratched under a grimy armpit. "Suppose half a slew of chips were hurled into the camp?"

"Instant chaos would erupt as people fled in mindless terror."

He nodded. "We can use that Knot."

"But I told you! You can't approach it, let alone chip it. Your workers would panic."

"With shields of reverse wood?"

She reconsidered. "Maybe then, yes."

"We will offer your group an even trade: you in good health for the Knot."

"But they can't give up the Knot! That's the Quest."

"Too bad for you, then." Gauche glanced meaningfully at Gorilla.

"But I suppose you could ask them," Meryl said quickly.

Gauche sighed gustily. "I suppose I could," he agreed. "Come on, then."

"What?"

"*You* are going to ask them, and describe the alternative. They will see that you have not been harmed, yet, and know that you will be doomed if they balk. I suspect they will see reason."

"Maybe they won't," Meryl said uncertainly.

"Then we'll let Gorilla start in while they watch. They might change their minds soon, if not unduly titillated."

Horrified, Meryl was silent.

"Tell her that now we are forewarned," Wenda said tightly. "We'll figure out a way."

The hologram continued, but neither Wenda nor the others paid much attention to it. They were holding an intense dialogue. They had very little time to come up with their response to the dreadful deal to be offered.

"I do not trust Gauche," Hilarion said. "I have had some experience with military campaigns, I don't remember when, but I know that no male goblin can be trusted. My guess is that he wants to get the Knot and keep Meryl for torture. His word is worthless."

"How can you think that?" Angela asked. "A deal is a deal, even for a bad chief."

"You're an angel," he said. "What do you think your demon fiancé would say?"

She shook her head. "Exactly what you just did," she confessed.

"So I think Gauche wants to lure us back across the lake with the Knot, then renege. We need to fathom exactly how he will play it."

"Couldn't Jumper read the goblin's mind?" Angela asked.

"Yes!" Ida agreed.

"I'm not sure," Wenda said. "Suppose we go there, read his mind, and it's too late to escape the trap?"

"It would be a mistake to underestimate goblin cunning," Hilarion agreed.

"We perhaps need one of us to cross alone," Ida said. "Keeping the Knot here. Then if it turns out that it's an honest deal, the rest of us can cross."

"No," Wenda said firmly.

The others looked at her.

"Because we can knot give them the Knot," Wenda said. "The whole point of the Quest is to keep it out of bad hands like that. We can knot make the exchange."

"But Wenda—" Angela said.

"We need to rescue her. Just knot by giving up the Knot."

"And I don't suppose you want us to pretend to be considering yielding the Knot," Hilarion said.

"That's right. They may knot be honest, but we are."

"Then what do we have to bargain with?"

"I do knot know."

But now the goblins emerged and came to the shore. They carried a small dirty white flag of truce.

"And our time is up," Ida said.

"We dare not cross to negotiate," Hilarion said.

"I agree."

"Let me go!" Angela said. "Because I can fly across alone, and not risk the Knot. Maybe I can negotiate something else." Then, before Ida could agree, she reconsidered. "Whom am I fooling? I have nothing to offer."

Then a bulb flashed over her head. "But Jumper can read the chief's mind while I talk with him. Then we'll know for sure whether it's a trap."

"That's brilliant!" Ida agreed.

The hologram faded and Jumper reappeared in manform. "Ask him key questions so he'll think of the answers even if he's lying, and I can read the truth."

"I will," Angela said. "But if you see danger for me—"

"I will send you a thought to flee," Jumper agreed. "If I do, don't question it. Flee instantly."

"I will," Angela repeated. She flew across the water.

"Give us the hologram again," Wenda said. "This time from Gauche's mind, if yew can."

For answer, the hologram reappeared. This time it showed the scene from the goblin chief's perspective.

He watched the angel flying across the lake. "I must get her to bring the others," he said to himself. "She's not enough by herself."

Angela flew closer, and more of her legs showed under her flaring skirt. "Then again, she's got nice gams. I hope she keeps her elevation as she gets closer, so I can peek at her panties."

"He would," Ida muttered.

Angela, inexperienced and concerned about possible capture, did maintain her elevation, showing more of her legs. She was not even thinking of such exposure. Wenda thought of asking Jumper to warn her, but decided not to, for two reasons. She was concerned that Jumper might lose focus if he had to do two different telepathic things simultaneously, and realized that the distraction might give Angela an advantage. This might be naughty strategy, but was tolerable.

Gauche did look, and was increasingly distracted. But his cunning goblin mind remained in control. He had seen enough legs and panties in his day to appreciate them without freaking out. Indeed, the sight stirred memories of goblin girls whose beauty threatened to put the sun's glory to shame.

"Wow!" Hilarion breathed, viewing those memory girls in the hologram. "Goblin males may be ugly, but goblin females are contrastingly lovely."

Angela came to hover almost above Gauche. "I have come to—to negotiate," she said hesitantly.

He hardly blinked. "How much to drop down here and let me grab your ass, cutie?"

This was so far out of bounds that the angel couldn't understand it. "What is your proposition?"

"Just spread your legs wide and settle down right here."

Now she began to get it. She blushed from her face to the tips of her toes. "Oh! I forgot my legs show!"

"They sure do, honey! Bring 'em down."

Angela closed her legs. "We want to—to—recover our companion, Meryl Mermaid. We will consider any reasonable—"

"That too," Gauche said, concealing his irritation at the loss of the panty vision. "We want the Knot. We'll trade it for the mermaid."

"We can't do that," Angela said.

"Okay. Let her tell you the deal." He snapped his stubby fingers. Gorilla Goblin advanced, carrying a struggling Meryl.

Meryl spoke her piece, repeating what they had learned telepathically. "So they want an exchange," she concluded. "And if they don't get the Knot, they will t-torture me."

"We can't make that deal," Angela said.

"Yeah?" Gauche smiled. "Gorilla, you may begin."

Gorilla held Meryl before him. "Ha!" he said hungrily.

"I mean we have to discuss it," Angela said desperately. "We need to agree about making the exchange."

"Just tell the rest to come on over and we'll do it," Gauche said. "It's not complicated."

"Yes, it is. We have five remaining members of our party, and they all have to agree. We can't possibly decide on the spur of the moment."

The goblin chief gazed at her closed legs. She seemed innocent, and she was an angel. That meant she wasn't trying to deceive him. He might yet get the whole party to come across. He made a snap decision. "Okay, cutie. I'll give you a day and night. After that, Gorilla starts in on the crossbreed, and we'll go on from there. You think about that. Think about it hard, because you know what we'll do if we don't get that Knot."

"I—I will tell them," Angela said. She spun in the air and flew back across the lake.

"Take her back inside," Gauche told Gorilla. "You can't have her yet."

"But tomorrow—" Gorilla said hopefully.

"Tomorrow we'll all score," the chief assured him.

The hologram dissolved. "We've got trouble," Jumper said. "I read his deeper mind. He doesn't just want to get the Knot and keep Meryl. He wants to get our whole party."

"Our whole party!" Wenda exclaimed.

"He had goblins hiding in ambush. If we had crossed today, they would have thrown a net over us all, doused us with hate elixir, and captured us individually while we fought among ourselves. Then his men would have started raping and torturing all the women of our party. You don't want to know the details."

"What of the men?" Hilarion asked.

"We are to be given to the goblinesses to play with before execution. Execution would be by dousing us both with hate elixir and locking us into a cell together. The winner lives to be doused with another captive, and so on."

"We can't afford to be captured."

"But neither can we leave Meryl to be tortured," Wenda said.

"We have a day and night," Ida reminded them. "We can fashion a plan."

Hilarion looked at her. "I am not sure our combination of talents will be effective in this instance."

"What are you talking about?" Angela demanded. "Can't you make the goblins forget about Meryl?"

"Not from this distance, and not in a mass," Hilarion said. "Were I close to the chief goblin, I could make him forget her, but the others would remember. That would not be much of an improvement."

"Well, then maybe I should try it," Angela said angrily. "I can fly in there at night and unbar her prison, and the two of us can fly out of there."

Wenda could see that Ida wanted to agree, but couldn't manage it. The angel would most likely be caught and cruelly ravished. Gauche had already eyed her panties.

But that gave Wenda an idea. "Jumper could dew it. He could assume the form of Gauche, and say he's taking Meryl for fell purposes, then lead her out."

"Fatal flaw," Hilarion said. "What would the real Gauche be doing while Jumper was emulating him?"

Ouch. He was right. Something had to be done about the real chief goblin.

"I know!" Angela said. "I could go and distract him so he wouldn't be checking on anything else."

"Another flaw," Hilarion said. "No angel could do what that miscreant would require. Only a demoness could do that."

"We have reverse wood," Angela said. "I could use it to reverse my nature and become a demoness."

"And forever soil yourself, if you even survived his degradations," Hilarion said.

"Better that, than to let Meryl suffer."

The angel was demonstrating her friendship and loyalty. But the thought of subjecting her to that session with Gauche appalled Wenda, and she was sure the others liked it no better.

"Yet it might work," Ida agreed reluctantly.

"Yes, it might," Wenda agreed. "I will dew it."

Hilarion turned to her with much the same concern as he had for Angela. "This is not a thing to inflict on any damsel. It is likely death and sure degradation."

"You and your d*mned gallantry!" Angela flared.

"The safety of the members of my Quest is my responsibility," Wenda said. "I will dew it."

"Wenda, please," Jumper said, pained. "I couldn't bear to see you hurt."

She appreciated his concern, but had little patience with it at the moment. "Then figure out a way for me to avoid getting hurt."

A bulb flashed over Ida's head. "Reverse wood!"

The others looked at her, not seeing it.

"We have all kinds," Ida said. "And only Wenda is immune, at least as far as the chips are concerned. She could do it."

"Please explain," Hilarion said.

Ida explained. And before long they had a plan. It was daring and chancy, but had a fair chance of working.

Jumper checked on Meryl, and made the hologram of her surroundings. She was now in a much nicer suite, with a roommate/guard: Gossamer Gobliness, delicately lovely in the manner of her gender. They were playing card games. It seemed that the goblins were honoring the delay. But that did not mean that Gauche had relented; the torture would commence on schedule.

Jumper picked up on something else in the chief's

foul mind: "He *expects* us to raid at night. Guards are lurking to capture us when we do. Then they will cross to the island and capture the Knot. They are just pretending to be unaware. It's all part of their plan."

Wenda winced. They could not afford to forget for a moment that they were dealing with dangerously cunning little monsters. But they were going to raid, regardless. Just not quite in the expected manner.

They waited until nightfall, meanwhile organizing their camp, foraging for pies on the island, and locating a small spring that was not hate elixir.

And the nuptial party came. Well, why not? If Wenda was going to risk her life soon, it was better to let Charming know now.

The others felt the same way. Each explained to the spouse or equivalent.

"If you are wiped out, what will become of me?" Charming asked, worried.

"If Wenda loses, you will take her place?" Beauregard asked Angela, not at all easy about it.

"You are invulnerable," Eris reminded Jumper. "But I may have forgotten to tell you that the talents I lent you are limited. If you use them too often, they will expire."

"Expire!" Jumper exclaimed. "I had no idea!"

"It's in the fine print of the Demon Protocols. We can't give too much to mortals. It might give them delusions of significance."

He considered. "I'll have to use one shape-change tonight, and limit it to that. And be far less free hereafter, saving my talent for an emergency."

"That makes sense," Eris agreed. Then she kissed him, and Beauregard kissed Angela, and Charming kissed Wenda's left ear as she unobtrusively turned her back. Six and a half minutes later the visitors were gone.

Wenda, Jumper, and Hilarion paddled the air boat

across the lake, while Angela hovered above, serving as liaison. Ida remained with the Knot to make sure no goblins sneaked across to the island to steal it. If she had to, she would invoke the humidor and push the wagon through, rather than allow the goblins to get the Knot.

They landed, and walked boldly toward the goblin hill. Soon the goblin guard spied them. "Halt! What simpleton goes there?" he demanded.

Hilarion focused on him, and in half a moment the sentry forgot that he had seen anything. They walked on.

"I will go first," Wenda whispered. Coordination was essential.

"I will go second," Jumper agreed. He changed form, assuming the likeness of Gauche Goblin.

"I will wait here, and be ready to make any pursuers forget," Hilarion said.

"I will hover here and watch," Angela said. "And flee to tell Ida if anything goes wrong." She shuddered prettily.

Wenda donned a white scarf to signal truce, girded her hollow loin, and marched to the main entrance. A goblin guard oriented on her, but he was in sight of Hilarion, and immediately lost his memory of her. She walked on in, unchallenged.

Now she was on her own. She followed the twisted passages toward where she knew the chief's chambers to be. Jumper had identified it from the awareness of the goblins, and Wenda had rehearsed the route. The passage was lighted by guttering torches, and was high enough so that she did not have to stoop, though she was taller than any goblin.

"Hey, nymph!" a goblin challenged her. "You're an outsider!"

"Hey yewrself, snot for brains," Wenda responded

politely enough for goblin dialect. "I'm going to see Chief Gauche. Want to make something of it?"

The chief's name was magical in this domain. The goblin went on, staying out of it. A goblin who messed with the chief could get hung upside down and force-fed hate elixir until he vomited it out the wrong end. Jumper had picked up the memory.

She came to the chief's door. She closed her hollow wooden fist and pounded on the door. "Open up, fecal face!" she called. "I'm here to talk to yew."

The door opened. There was Gauche, glowering. "Woodwife!" he exclaimed, amazed. "What the bleep are you doing here?"

"I come under flag of truce to plead for the release of my friend the winged mermaid," she said.

Gauche considered. "What will you do to get her back?"

"I thought I wood talk to yew. I'm sure we can come up with something."

"Come in." He stepped back to let her in, then closed the door firmly behind her. "I never had a woodwife before."

Naturally there was only one thing on his evil mind. But she needed to distract him, and keep him distracted long enough for Jumper to emulate Gauche and take Meryl out to safety. She half turned so that he could focus on her full rear outlined by her tight skirt, instead of her hollow front. She was padded in front, but that would be lost the moment he tore her clothing off. "Why knot?"

"Couldn't catch one. They're slippery woodland creatures." He smiled as he scratched his rear. "But you are catchable."

Wenda touched her white scarf. "I am here under truce. I am knot for yewr interest."

"Not even to save your friend?"

Wenda hesitated. "Knot necessarily."

"Enough of this bourgeois courtship! Rip off your clothes!"

"I wood knot dew that to yew," Wenda protested, alarmed. "It wood knot bee right."

"Of course not, nymph. I'm doing it to you." He grabbed her and threw her roughly facedown on the bed. It didn't hurt because she had no frontside to bruise. In three quarters of a moment he was on top of her, still clothed, slobbering expectantly. He caught at her skirt, trying to haul it up or down.

"But I wood dew this to yew." Wenda brought out the chip of reverse wood she carried. She tucked it into his boot beside her thigh, wedging it against his dark ankle.

Gauche converted to a gobliness.

It took him a good moment and a half to catch on. He was still busy trying to get into her skirt. "What—what?" he sputtered.

Wenda lifted him off her, as he now weighed perhaps a third what he had. "Yew are now Gaucherie Gobliness," Wenda said. "Enjoy the condition."

Gauche scrambled off the bed and went to look in the wall mirror beside it. He was now a very fetching gobliness in very baggy male clothing. "Oh, horror!" he wailed.

"But yew look quite gneiss," Wenda said. "Yew will knot bee in want of male companionship for long."

"What have you done to me?" he demanded.

"I thought that since yew like the female form so much, yew wood bee happy to have more of it." She walked to the door. "I will leave yew to admire yourself." She opened the door, stepped out, and closed it behind her.

Now to rejoin Jumper. He had sent her a flash thought

to let her know where he was. She hurried, knowing that there would soon be ugly chaos in the mound.

She rounded a corner—and saw Gauche carrying a frightened Meryl over his shoulder. Then she remembered: it was Jumper, emulating the chief, and Meryl was pretending fright. This was the rescue in progress.

Wenda stepped forward to join them. But a hulking goblin shape intercepted her. "What have we here?"

Oh, no! It was Gorilla Goblin.

Then a bulb went off over Wenda's head. "Gorilla!" she said. "Go to the chief's chamber immediately. He has a new female captive who needs breaking in. Dew knot listen to anything she says."

"Huh? The chief's right here."

Jumper turned his head. "Get over there, poopface! I'm busy with my own captive."

Gorilla went.

Wenda felt almost guilty. Yet she was sure the converted chief more than deserved what was about to happen to him.

They moved on out. Whenever a goblin guard thought to approach, Jumper glared him back. "Mine!" he said. "Both girls mine. Wait your turn." That was clearly persuasive.

They forged on out of the mound. By then the goblins were developing more resistance, suspecting that the chief would not take the captives outside. But as they boiled out of the entrance, Hilarion caught them with spot forgetting. They milled about, uncertain what they had been about to do.

Jumper lifted Meryl off his shoulder. "Fly," he said tersely. "We'll make our own way back."

Meryl flew up to join Angela, and the two headed out across the lake. Jumper, Wenda, and Hilarion strode rapidly on foot. They found the invisible air boat, jumped in, and rowed into the lake.

The goblins swarmed to the shore. Now they were remembering, and knew that it was not really Gauche. But it was too late for them to do much about it. Some went back for weapons, but it was too late for that too.

They had made the rescue.

11

TOURISTS

They rejoined Ida on the island. "Oh, I'm so glad you are safe!" Ida exclaimed, hugging Meryl.

"I'm glad too," Meryl agreed. "I was really scared, and not because of the Knot."

"Now we can rest," Wenda said, relieved. "I wood knot care to go through that again."

"I am not sure we should rest yet," Ida said.

"It has been a really hard evening," Jumper said. "If anything had gone wrong, we would have been in serious trouble. I don't dare depend on my special powers anymore; I need to save them for emergency use."

"Yes, of course," Ida agreed. "But let me share my thoughts with you first."

Wenda realized that there was something on Ida's mind, and Ida's ideas could be serious matters. She would not inconvenience them for no reason. "Yes, please bee candid."

"While I was alone in the darkness I had time to think," Ida said. "I wondered about the air boat. It was remarkably convenient, yet the goblins paid it no attention. If they have such craft, why did they not pile into others and pursue us across the water, firing their arrows?"

"Ida, you are making sense," Hilarion said. "Not that you don't always. It was almost as if that boat had been placed there for our use. The goblins would never do that, unless they thought it would spring a leak and dump us in the hate elixir. But the boat is sound. It is as if the goblins are unaware of it. Considering that this is their territory, that is remarkable."

Ida's voice had a smile in the darkness. "You have expressed my concern very well, Hilarion. Unexplained conveniences make me nervous; they may be like the pleasant paths leading to tangle trees. My other concern was why the goblins did not cross to the island by other means. They do have ordinary wooden boats; I saw them by the shore. Yet they made no effort to use them, despite the fact that they were eager to capture us."

"And they tried to trick us into crossing back, so they could capture us all," Hilarion said. "Jumper read in their minds about that. Why should they employ such a ruse when it would be easier simply to swarm across and grab us on the island? Subtlety is not their forte."

"Again you have nicely amplified my concern," Ida said. "What we have seen does not seem to make much sense. And that leaves me unsatisfied. I fear that there is something we do not understand that may be dangerous to our health."

"I agree emphatically," Hilarion said. "It was very intelligent of you to come up with these aspects the rest of us overlooked."

"You are kind to say so." Wenda suspected Ida was invisibly blushing.

"These are excellent points," Jumper agreed. "It might make sense for us to depart this island now and find somewhere else to spend the night."

"Readily accomplished with the air boat," Hilarion

said. "We can row away under cover of night, and be well away from the vicinity by morning."

"We can't," Angela said. "I have been scouting around. The goblins are really angry about our escape, and maybe about what happened to Chief Gauche." She paused, possibly for an un-angelic smile. The chief had gotten his just desserts, before managing to lose the chip of reverse wood, and they surely had not been pleasantly tasty. "They have surrounded the entire lake. You can see their hundred torches in the evening dews and damps."

Wenda looked. There in a great circle was the glimmer of distant lights. The lake was indeed surrounded.

"Can Jumper become the roc bird and carry us away by air?" Meryl asked.

"No," Jumper said. "I can't safely take off by night; I need to see where I'm going. Also—" He hesitated.

"Also, we have learned that Jumper's borrowed talents are limited," Wenda said. "When he uses them up, they will no longer be available. So we feel he should save them for emergencies only. If we can possibly find another escape, we must do so."

"Oh! I didn't realize."

"None of us did," Wenda said. "We were letting him use them wastefully. We shall bee far more careful henceforth."

"Which leaves us in a dill of a picklement," Hilarion said. "We don't want to stay here, but it seems we can't conveniently depart. There is little to sustain us on the island; maybe the goblins expect to starve us out."

"Angela and I can fly in supplies," Meryl said.

"No," Wenda said. "They will shoot yew down with arrows. Only Hilarion's talent of making them forget us on a spot basis prevented them from dewing that before. That will knot work, now that they are fully alerted."

"Then we shall simply have to find another way," Ida said.

It was a long shot, but Wenda tried for it. "Meryl, yew have come up with good ideas before. Do yew have any now?"

"Not really," the mermaid said. "Unless there is something special about this island that we have not realized."

"Like maybe a secret passage that leads to somewhere safely far away," Angela said. Wenda remembered that in Meryl's absence, Angela had become their idea person.

"That might be the case," Ida agreed.

They checked in the dark, canvassing the entire island, thumping on the ground with their feet or tail. The island wasn't large, and they were able to cover it. And found no hollow section, no portal into the ground.

"Yet there must be something," Hilarion said, frustrated.

"We have two mysteries," Meryl said. "The presence of the air boat, and the absence of anything on the island. Could they be connected?"

"They surely could," Ida agreed.

"But how?" Hilarion demanded.

"An avoidance spell!" Angela said. "It keeps the goblins from finding the boat, even by accident. And it keeps them from the island. They don't even know they're avoiding these things; they just don't go to them."

"That makes sense," Ida agreed. "Yet—"

"Yet we found it," Angela said. "Probably because we are not goblins. The spell must have been oriented specifically on goblins. Who else would come here?"

Who, indeed!

"But why reserve a special boat to go to an empty island?" Hilarion asked.

"A way station!" Meryl said. "The boat goes to the

island, where someone else rendezvous with them and takes them off. Like a troll bus stop or exchange station. They don't want goblins messing with it, so they keep them away."

"That too makes sense," Ida agreed.

"It could be a landing field for rocs," Jumper said. "At certain times."

Angela dropped down to the boat; they could tell by her descending voice. "I'm thinking how we don't even notice the trollway until we're traveling on it," she said. "Maybe this is similar."

"We have used the boat," Jumper said. "And noticed nothing special except its invisibility and sturdiness."

"There's something here," Angela reported. "Knobs, like controls. They—oh!"

"What?" Wenda called, alarmed.

"There's a lighted boulevard!"

"Knot that we can see," Wenda said.

"Come into the boat!"

Wenda went there, found the boat by feel, and climbed in.

And saw the boulevard. It was a lighted highway touching the center of the island and rising over the water to either side. Where it touched ground, a side lane diverged, leading to the water where the boat was.

"We have found the bus stop," Wenda reported breathlessly. "Yew can't see it from outside."

The others joined her, and became believers. The boat was magic in a way they had not suspected.

"How do we use the boulevard, when we can neither see nor touch it?" Hilarion asked.

"We use the boat!" Angela exclaimed. "That's what it's for!"

"That must be the case," Ida agreed.

Hilarion settled into what seemed to be the driver's

seat and twiddled knobs, which now glowed in soft pastel colors. They did seem to be controls of some kind. One was a larger circle.

The boat lifted. Hilarion hastily reversed his turn of the knob, and it sank again. In a moment and a half he had it floating just above the ground.

He tried another knob. The boat nudged forward. He twisted the other way, and the boat slowed, paused, and moved backward.

"This is like a sophisticated magic carpet," Hilarion said.

"And to think we rowed it across the lake," Jumper said.

Then the boat sank to the ground. The knobs had ceased working.

"We're off the boulevard," Angela said. "We need to be on it."

Wenda, Jumper, and Ida got off the boat, got behind it, and pushed it forward. When it came to the edge of the lighted section, it lifted. That was it: the boat was a magic highway craft, losing much of its magic elsewhere.

"I think we have our way off the island," Ida said.

Wenda replaced the reverse-wood seeds in the net around the Knot. Then they rolled the wagon onto the ramp and onto the boat. They settled in around the Knot.

Hilarion moved the boat forward. He followed the access road, then used the wheel to steer it onto the main boulevard. He increased the speed. The boat floated up the rise over the water, traveling more swiftly.

"And the goblins can't see us at all," Meryl said, satisfied. "We can see out, but no one can see in."

"This is remarkable magic," Ida said. "But whoever can have set it up? It is surely a considerable project."

"Not the trolls?" Jumper asked.

"This does not seem to be their type of trollway," Ida said. "I suspect it was crafted by some other agency."

"I dew knot want to be a wet blanket," Wenda said, "but maybee we should find a safe landing and get off the boulevard before we find out who made it. Just in case."

"Good idea," Jumper agreed.

But the boulevard continued over the nocturnal terrain of Xanth, not dropping down. There was no ready exit.

"I think we'll just have to pull over to the side, and sleep there," Hilarion said.

"And hope for the best," Ida agreed.

"Maybe there's something ahead," Hilarion said.

Wenda looked. There was a huge pattern in the sky, like a complicated ribbon bow. Each ribbon was outlined by lines of lights along its sides.

"I have heard of this sort of thing," Ida said. "They have it in Mundania. It's called a cloverleaf intersection."

The boulevard divided. Hilarion took the right fork. This led up into the higher sky in a huge graceful loop. Wenda was afraid they would fall, but it was as though they remained level.

"Like the path down the Gap Chasm wall!" Meryl exclaimed.

So it seemed. They looped up and over the rest of the pattern, seeing other loops below, their lanes heading in different directions. Then they looped beneath the pattern, and came out on a lane traveling at right angles to the first one.

But still there was no landing place.

Angela looked back. "I think I see a ribbon leading to a place," she said. "If we can find it."

Wenda understood what she meant. There might

be an avenue, but how could they select the right one amidst the complicated tangle of lanes?

They tried. When the lane divided again, Hilarion took the left one. This led into another loop that threaded the center of the giant flower, passing other ribbons to left and right, above and below, in a bewildering array of curves.

They saw another boat. It was sailing along another ribbon that passed close to their own without touching. "Maybe they can tell us how to find the correct route," Meryl said, and waved.

Then they saw that the occupants of the other boat were not remotely human. They were masses of colored tentacles: land-going squid.

There was a little squid in front. It waved back with a pink tentacle. Then their boat was out of range.

"I think we're not in Xanth anymore," Ida murmured.

Then their ribbon emerged from the tangle and came to the rest stop they had wanted to reach. Hilarion steered into it and brought the boat to a halt. There was a glowing minipark with a pleasant pool, several comfortable moss beds, pie trees, boot rear roots, milkweed pods, and high bushes marked with silhouettes of a human man and human woman. Clear enough.

"Let's rest here," Jumper said. "We can discuss our situation in the morning."

Wenda was happy to agree.

In the morning, refreshed, they assembled for a discussion. "You surely have relevant further thoughts, Ida," Hilarion said.

"I do," Ida said. "They are not as comfortable as our present lodging. It occurs to me that we may have blundered onto a reserved boulevard similar to the trollway, but with different proprietors. Those squids were like nothing seen on Xanth. I fear we don't belong here."

"This parallels my own concern," Hilarion said. "We discovered a very special boat that the goblins seem not to know of. Why should it have been there, and to whom does it belong? I fear we have unknowingly absconded with some other party's property."

"If there were a tourist boulevard for alien creatures," Ida said, "it might resemble this. In which case the island in the hate lake would be a tourist stop, where they could go safely to land and see the local sights. I conjecture that they—being not of this world—would, in the manner of Angela Angel, be insubstantial in Xanth, so could walk about freely without being harassed by the goblins or other local creatures. The boat would be an interim stage, invisible but with enough substance so that it could float on physical water."

"Exactly," Hilarion agreed. "They floated their boat across the lake, then left it as they went to explore the goblin mound, never thinking that anyone else would be aware of it, let alone take it. I daresay there are sights of interest there as the goblins go about their normal business."

"Working, eating, torturing prisoners," Meryl said with a grimace.

"We do not know the tastes of the aliens," Hilarion said, "but it seems not beyond the bounds of possibility that they might enjoy snooping on locals summoning storks."

"That's disgusting!" Angela said.

Meryl smiled indulgently. "Normal folk have secret desires that are beneath the notice of angels. They like not only to summon storks, but to watch others doing so, especially when the others do not know they are being observed. You have now had some experience with mortal desire. Can you say you would not look if you could secretly see two other people signaling the stork?"

Angela blushed furiously. That seemed to be answer enough.

"So perhaps we understand the motive of the alien tourists," Ida said. "There remain questions. Why didn't the dissuasion spell affect us as it did the goblins? That is, why limit it to the goblins? Creatures with the power to make such a highway should readily have been able to make it apply to all creatures. We should have avoided both the boat and the island."

"We're not goblins," Jumper said. "The spell must not be on the island or boat, because that would drive away the tourists too. It must be limited to the goblins, the only menace in the area, as a practical matter. The goblins would dissuade all other creatures. If the aversion spell had wider compass, the tourists would not be able to find their way back to the boulevard, once they left it."

"That does seem to make sense," Hilarion said.

"And by sheer chance we got deposited right there," Jumper said. "If you believe in chance."

Ida smiled. "The Muse of History once told me of a rule in telling a story: You can use chance to put a person into trouble, but not to get him out of it. So chance put us into trouble. We found our own way out of it."

"Still, it was a remarkably mixed site," Hilarion said. "Very bad because of the goblins. Then perhaps good because of the boat and the boulevard. The chance of our landing right there, in all of Xanth, seems remote. A story writer would have to be really bad at his trade to write that."

"That boat was using chance to get us out of trouble," Jumper agreed. "That's against the rule."

"So it is," Ida agreed. "Perhaps we need another explanation."

"Or two," Meryl said. "The Knot is malign and wants to mess us up. So if it had any influence, it would choose the worst of Doors. That accounts for the bad.

And the Doors may not open perfectly randomly on Xanth. They are magical, and may tend to orient on spots of high magic or significance. The boat, the dissuasion spell, the hate elixir—magic galore."

"This is a genius idea, surely viable," Hilarion said. "I'm so sorry you are not my One."

"Well, you're not a winged merman," Meryl said, blushing moderately.

"But the prior time we used the Doors," Wenda said. "What accounted for our arrival at the home of the otterbees?"

"That may have been a nexus of magic too," Jumper said. "The otterbees are magical creatures, near the Faun & Nymph Retreat, and Princess Ida had lived there for years, and Prince Hilarion was there. So there were significant crosscurrents."

"Lo, I am answered," Hilarion said. "Encountering Wenda's Quest seems to be changing my life."

"Except that it hasn't helped you find your betrothee," Ida said.

"True. But my association with this Quest is not yet done. There is time yet."

"At any rate, if we took someone's boat we should return it," Ida said. "They may need it."

"We don't know that someone was using it," Meryl said. "Maybe it was there to be used by whoever needed it. As we did."

Hilarion was troubled. "I'm not sure. It should have been on the island, waiting for a tourist party."

"And we may have stranded just such a party by the goblin mound," Ida said morosely.

"Yet I am not eager to return there," Meryl said, shuddering. "The things they were going to do to me—"

Ida put her hand on Meryl's. "We understand. We must not go back."

"But we should settle this matter of the boat," Hilarion said. "I wonder whether it has a distress signal?"

They looked at the small control panel. "What's that button?" Wenda asked.

"Let's find out." Hilarion pushed on it with his thumb.

The boat made a steady bee-beep sound, and a light flashed.

"I think that's it," Ida said with half a smile.

"But who answers the signal?" Jumper asked.

"We are about to find out," Angela said. "Something is approaching us, flashing."

They waited nervously. It was another boat, cruising swiftly along the ribbon, colored lights blinking. It zoomed up to the rest stop and came to a halt. Two tentacled bug-eyed monsters got out.

"Mxtplkty sctkzzt?" one asked.

"We don't understand," Wenda said.

The monster used a tentacle to twiddle with a dial on its belt. "We are the Bem Patrol. Why did you summon us?" he asked.

They had a translator! "Sir, we—we found this boat," Wenda said with proper humility. "We needed it to escape the goblins. But we fear we may have stranded the owner there."

"Check the boat registry," Bem #1 said out of the side of its head.

Bem #2 twiddled with his belt. "It is registered to a tourist party of snails from Beta Slime."

"Do these look like snails to you?" Bem #1 asked.

"Not much," Bem #2 said. "These look more like ignorant locals."

"Then their story checks out. Send a boat to the goblin station to pick up the snails."

The other monster twiddled some more. "On its way."

Bem #1 eyed Wenda with several facets. If she hadn't

known better she might have suspected that it was mentally undressing her. After all, what would a bug-eyed monster want with a nymph? Yet this made her conclude that it was male. "How did you access the boat and boulevard?"

Wenda explained what had happened, including about the Knot, which was starting to radiate hostility. "We really did knot mean to cause any trouble, sir," she concluded.

"But you did generate mischief," Bem #1 said. "You stole a boat and stranded a tourist party. That's a No. You have no pass to tour the Boulevard. That's a No-No. You will have to answer to the full extent of interplanetary law."

Before Wenda could protest further, Bem #2 spoke again. "The snails are declining to press charges. They appreciate that the intruders sent help."

Wenda was getting to like alien snails. "Then it's all right?"

"By no means," Bem #1 snapped, irritated. Evidently he liked to enforce the law to its full extent, and now he couldn't. "The No-No remains. You will have to pay."

"How can we pay?" Wenda asked meekly.

The Bem considered. "You are locals."

"Yes."

"You have local substance."

"Yes."

"As it happens, we need to set up another tourist site on this world. But local labor is unreliable."

"We're reliable!" Wenda said quickly.

The Bem might have smiled; it was hard to tell with his corrugated slit of a mouth. "We will program your craft to travel to that site. Your job will be to level the access so that tourists can debouch there and appreciate the sights. Accomplish that and you may exit the Boulevard at an access of your choice."

"Thank yew, sir," Wenda said. She had learned how to be as humble as she had to be.

Bem #2 touched the boat controls. Then the two of them returned to their own boat and departed.

"You handled that very well," Hilarion said. "I suspect we got off easy."

"Thank yew. I did knot want to antagonize them."

Wenda replaced the reverse wood seeds in the Knot net, and they got in. The boat started moving without Hilarion's direction, and proceeded confidently through the flower formation of ribbons. It zoomed past several rest stops, and came to a lake in a mountain.

"Lake Wails!" Ida exclaimed. "It may be the filled caldera of an extinct volcano. This will be awful to set up."

"Why?" Hilarion asked. "Are there dangerous monsters?"

"Not exactly. The Wailing Monster doesn't go beyond the lake. But it's so steep we'll have trouble making a proper landing."

The boat drifted to a stop where the Boulevard touched the edge of the lake. There was almost no room; the mountain slope outside was steep, and inside was filled with water. It was indeed a challenge.

Hilarion considered the situation. "We might make a landing by dredging gravel from the interior of the lake. The question is how deep it is, and whether there is enough to make a sufficient landing."

"I can check," Meryl said. She removed her clothing, flew up over the water, and dived in.

"I hope it is safe," Ida said. "We really don't know what is below. It is an ancient lake and very deep."

But before long, though well after short, Meryl reappeared. "There are all manner of fish," she reported. "Ted wants to talk to you, Wenda."

"Who?" Wenda asked, startled.

"Theodore Sturgeon. He's a consummate stylist, very

sharp on details. He does not want the lake desecrated by hacks."

"A fish," Wenda said.

"But not just any fish. He's the leader of the local school. He can help us if he chooses to. You must talk to him."

"I can't go down there," Wenda protested.

"Sure you can. Just put rocks in your feet to weight you down."

"But I'd drown!"

"I don't think so. You're made of wood now."

Wenda remembered it was true. As a woodwife she could talk, but without breathing. She was a magical creature. She had become accustomed to the state of being a real woman. Real women needed to breathe to better show off their bosoms. "Why does Theodore want to talk to me?"

"I told him of our Quest, and how we need to make a landing here. I said you are our leader. He's interested, but he must protect the lake."

"Doesn't the Wailing Monster do that?" Angela asked.

"It protects the surface," Meryl said. "But the landing will be built up from below."

"Then I will talk to him," Wenda agreed. "Except I dew knot know water talk."

"We anticipated that problem. Ted gave me a sea biscuit." She held it forth.

"A biscuit?"

"It's a linguistic accommodation spell. Like the gift of tongues you gave Jumper. This does it for the sea."

Oh. Wenda took it and chewed it up. "Is it working?"

"Yes."

"How dew yew know?"

"Because now we are talking sea talk."

"It seems just the same."

"The translation makes you hear it in your own tongue. Now weight your feet."

They foraged for suitable rocks, and fitted two into the hollow fronts of her feet. Then Wenda stepped off the edge into the water.

She sank swiftly. She saw fish all around: a hammerhead chasing after several nailheads, a sawfish sawing a boardfish, piggish hogfish, a pole-like pike, a dangerously sharp swordfish, a little birdlike perch on a strand of seaweed, a crowned kingfish, several gold- and silverfish, a colorful banded rainbow trout, a sailfish sailing blithely along, a pair of skates sliding along a ledge, and a shining ray coming from a bright sunfish that illuminated the whole region.

"The sea horse even let me ride him," Meryl said, having no trouble speaking under water; she was after all a mermaid. She was flying, her wings propelling her smoothly through the liquid. "Ah, here we are."

They were at the bottom, before a large sleeping shell. A sign said WAKE SHELL. Meryl grasped it by two edges and shook. It woke and opened wide, revealing a dark tunnel.

Oh. It was a pun on Shake Well.

"This way," Meryl said, swimming into the hole.

Bemused, Wenda followed, walking carefully so that her feet did not lose their stones.

They came to a chamber that looked like the aftermath of a bad battle. It was piled high with arms and legs.

"What is this?" Wenda asked uncomfortably.

"A loan shark's den. He takes all the arms and legs people let him get, and stores them here."

Oh. She should have known.

"Halt," a deep voice said.

"This is the bass," Meryl murmured. Then, to the fish: "We have come to see Ted."

"Very well," the bass boomed.

Then they were before Theodore Sturgeon, a large beautiful fish. "I am Wenda Woodwife," Wenda said. "I wood like to ask a favor of yew."

"You *are* a woodwife," Ted said. "Not just an empty head."

"I am," she agreed, realizing that her dialect came through in sea talk.

"You care about nature."

"Yes, I dew."

"So why do you want to build a landing in our pristine lake?"

"We have to, to make up for stealing a tourist boat."

"You are thieves?"

"No. The goblins were after us. We took what was offered. Now we have to pay."

"You have a hard roe to hoe."

"Yew speak the sea dialect!" But how could it be otherwise? This was his medium.

"Just as you speak the forest dialect," the fish agreed. "So I know I can trust you. But I need your assurance that you will not despoil our unspoiled lake."

"All we want is to make a landing. We thought we wood dredge gravel from the bottom."

"Dredge!" Ted exclaimed, appalled. "Never! It chews up the bass something awful."

"Then maybe if there are rocks we can pile."

"There are volcanic rocks, fragments of old lava. But there is a problem."

There was always a problem. "What might that bee?"

"It is the abode of the kraken. He does not like intruders."

She knew of the dread kraken weed, that could make large whirlpools just by waving its tentacles around. "Then we are lost," she said regretfully.

"Not necessarily. He might listen to you, because you're a winsome wood nymph. He doesn't get many visitors. I think he's a bit lonely. All you have to do is persuade him."

Wenda quailed. "I'm afraid he wood eat me."

"He wouldn't eat wood. Just flesh."

She had forgotten her reverted nature again. It had its advantages. "Then I will talk to him."

"But I think I won't," Meryl said. "Because I am flesh."

"Delightful flesh," Ted agreed. "Stay and visit a while. We don't get too many winged mermaids here."

Meryl smiled. "Do you get *any*?"

"A winged merman once. Does he count?"

"You must tell me more," Meryl said eagerly.

The sturgeon nodded. "I shall be glad to. But first let me send your friend on her way."

"Yes," Meryl agreed. "Wenda, if you get lost, simply get your rocks off and float to the surface."

"But I have knot talked to the kraken yet."

"The coelacanth will take you there and introduce you. He has been around a long time." Ted turned his head. "Seel! Are you dead? Rouse yourself."

Another large fish roused itself from a coffin-like alcove. "Reports of my extinction have been greatly exaggerated." It swam close. "What's a pretty wood half-nymph doing down here?"

"I have to talk with the kraken," Wenda said.

"Take hold. Hang on."

She put her arms around the solid body. "Like this? Will it knot hamper yew when yew swim?"

"The embrace of a nymph never slows me down," Seel said gallantly.

Wenda would have blushed if she were able to in this medium. So the fish was male. *Every* male liked nymphs. He was nevertheless doing her a favor. She hung on.

Seel flexed his powerful tail and moved forward. In a quarter of a moment they were past the loan shark's cache, and in half a moment they were out of the awake shell and forging through the lake. In three-quarters of a moment they came to a region of tumbled lava rocks. And in a full moment they were before the awesome kraken weed.

"Who dares intrude on my domain?" the kraken demanded.

"This is Wenda Woodwife," Seel said. "Don't eat her. She doesn't taste good."

"Ha ha ha," the weed said sourly. "Your humor is eons out of date, fishhead. Canth you come up with better?"

"While yours is only a few centuries dated," Seel retorted.

"We need to make a landing by piling up rocks," Wenda said nervously, being not absolutely sure krakens did not eat wood. "So we can pay our debt to the alien tourist authority and bee on our way. Will yew help?"

"Why should I help?"

That stumped her. Why should the weed care what she might want? Then a bulb flashed over her head. The water quickly extinguished it, but not before she caught its notion. "Yew dew knot get much respect," she said.

"I'm a big ugly rapacious weed. Folk fear me. They don't like me."

"Yes. But yew can win respect. All yew have to dew is pile lava rocks up to make a landing by the edge of the lake. Then the tourist Bems will come. Yew can come to the surface and grab at them. Yew will knot catch them because they have no substance here, but it will thrill them to bee threatened by a fearsome local monster. You will bee a major attraction. Maybee as much as the Wailing Monster. How is that for respect?"

The weed was impressed. "As much as the Wailing Monster?"

"It could bee, if yew are ferocious enough. The dreadful kraken will bee known throughout the local worlds and attract more tourists."

The kraken considered. "I will do it. Show me where."

Wenda gambled that this was not a cunning ploy to get her in reach. "Take me in a tentacle, and I will show yew where."

The kraken wrapped a tentacle around her body. She pointed up, and the giant weed rose grandly toward the surface.

They arrived some distance around the rim from where the Bemway touched. A horrendous snaky head rose from the water and eyed Wenda. It salivated, then launched toward her, jaws gaping.

Wenda screamed, but slightly too late. The mouth bit down on her left shoulder. And jerked back, surprised. A front tooth had broken on her wooden frame.

"It is knot gneiss to bite visitors," she reproved it. Then she turned to the rest of the kraken. "Did yew bring me here just to feed me to this ilk? I thought we had a deal."

The kraken made a weedy growl. A tentacle wrapped around the serpentine neck, squeezed it horrendously tight, and jerked the head off. This was evidently the kraken's way of showing annoyance.

Then two small heads sprouted from the severed neck. Six other heads rose out of the water to see what was going on. It was a hydra, a seven-headed sea monster.

The eight heads surveyed the situation, then sank quietly out of sight. Wenda realized that if there was one thing that could make a fearsome immortal monster like a hydra back off, it was the kraken.

"Thank yew."

"It wasn't supposed to bother you," the kraken said. "Maybe one of its scatterbrained heads got confused. So I reminded it."

"Yew did," Wenda agreed, relieved. "The place is around the rim, to the south."

The kraken slid smoothly through the water. It might be a huge ugly tangled weed, but it was graceful in motion.

They arrived at the site. Jumper, Hilarion, Ida, and Angela stood there, watching anxiously. Wenda waved.

Soon she was explaining the deal. The others nodded; it made sense.

The kraken set her down on the rim and got to work. In an hour it hauled a small pyramid of rough lava stones, piling them rapidly on top of one another. The landing was taking shape.

Meryl reappeared. "I talked to the hydra," she said. "It suffers from lack of respect too. It will put on its own show for the tourists. And Theodore too."

"Theodore wants to put on a show?" Wenda asked, surprised.

"He's a craftsfish. He does everything with style. But hardly anyone sees his talent while he remains below. So he will come to the surface and do some fancy leaps out of the water. The tourists should love it."

"Thank yew," Wenda said. "Yew have really helped. The Bems should be pleased."

The Bems were. They arrived as the landing was getting its finishing touches, and the creatures put on their show. The sturgeon leaped high out of the water and splashed back in, the hydra hissed and lunged for them with several heads, the kraken threw myriad tentacles at them, and the Wailing Monster, attracted by the commotion, came running across the surface of the water, leaving its little round prints of wails behind.

The Bems agreed it was a fine tourist stop. They expiated the charges against the party, and as a bonus gave them a pass to whatever connecting way they chose.

Wenda was relieved. Was there a connection leading to the Good Magician's Castle? No. She sighed, unrelieved.

12

FUN HOUSE

They sat in the boat, with the brooding Knot in the center, slowly cruising nowhere in particular, and discussed it. "So what connection do we take?" Hilarion inquired.

The others looked at Wenda. They expected her to decide. But she, sunk in a momentary funk, had no answer. All she wanted was to deliver the Knot to the Good Magician's Castle, rather than traipse around tourist sites. Things kept getting in the way.

Jumper stepped in. That was one big reason she had wanted him on this mission: he generally had an idea what to do. "Since we hardly know what offers, maybe we should simply watch the intersections and see what looks most promising."

"That makes sense to me," Hilarion agreed, and the others nodded.

"Thank yew," Wenda breathed. It seemed so simple, once he had clarified it.

They cruised along, watching intersections, which were plainly marked. The first one was not promising:

HELL'S HOLE. It seemed to consist of towering flames, which lapped at the entry itself. "No!" Angela squeaked.

"No," Wenda agreed. It would be awful for any of them, but worse for an angel.

They went by. The next intersection was labeled MONSTER'S APERITIF. "Why do I suspect that *we* would be the tasty delicacy?" Meryl murmured, gazing at the monsters crowding the sides, slavering their chops.

They passed it by. But the next one hardly seemed better: GOOZLE GIZZARD. None of them were certain what it meant, but they didn't trust it. The region looked swampy, with pairs of sparkling balls floating in the muck. Balls? Wenda suddenly realized that those were eyes. She hesitated to imagine what might lie beneath those eyes, but suspected it had many teeth and powerful jaws.

The next was NEUTRON STAR. "Eris has mentioned things like that," Jumper said. "We dare not go near. We would be squished down to the size of grains of sand."

Then HORROR HAREM, with a nice enough looking palace and cloaked figures walking through its gardens. "There might be girls there," Hilarion said.

"We're not going there," Ida said tightly.

"Eris wouldn't let me," Jumper agreed. The others were unified: no.

There was MOSQUITO DELIGHT. It seemed to be another giant swamp, with islands of trees, seemingly pleasant enough. "I would surely find many bugs to bite," Jumper said. "But I doubt the rest of you would be comfortable." They agreed to let that go.

And SLIME MOUND, with a mountain of slime quivering. It was halfway pretty in its glistening greenish yellowish fashion, and slurped eagerly in their direction, but they decided not to risk it either.

Then came FUN HOUSE. They slowed, considered,

and took that exit. Fun was something they had been short of recently. Even if it didn't help them deliver the Knot, it might be a place to relax.

It led into a pleasant yard girt by trees, bushes, and walks. But there was no structure.

They paused, remaining in the boat. "How can it be fun if there's no house?" Meryl asked.

"Maybe someone will see us and come," Wenda said uncertainly.

"Maybe it's along one of these walks," Jumper said. "This may simply be the landing place."

"I will explore the paths from above," Meryl said.

"I'll help," Angela said.

The two girls flew up, hovered over the paths, then split and flew away.

"It occurs to me that we were perhaps too trusting of the Bems," Hilarion remarked. "They gave us free passage to a site of our choice, but did not actually say we would like it or benefit from it."

"I was making an effort not to voice a similar sentiment," Ida said.

He smiled wryly. "It seems unfortunate that we can't agree on something more positive."

"Maybe you can," Jumper said. "Let's discuss this when our winged friends return, hoping to evoke some suggestion we can find useful."

"After making sure they have no notion of Ida's talent," Wenda said. "This approach may seem devious, but may bee more promising than trusting further to the good will of aliens."

Hilarion and Ida exchanged a glance, nodding together. The young prince and the older princess seemed to be finding similarities of perspective despite their dissimilar natures, and their talents meshed nicely.

After a while Angela and Meryl returned. "The paths simply loop around in a seeming maze," Meryl reported.

"They don't go anywhere," Angela agreed.

"So it seems that whatever is here for us, needs to be found," Jumper said. "I think we should discuss prospects, and check out any promising ones. What do you think?"

"Could it be underground?" Angela asked.

Wenda saw Ida getting ready to agree, but hesitate. She knew why: they had had enough of underground challenges.

"Did you see any portals, like the one on Reverse World?" Jumper asked.

"No," Meryl said. "So whatever is here is invisible."

"Now that might be the case," Ida agreed.

Wenda realized that it *would* be the case. She kept silent.

"I was being facetious," Meryl said. "I just meant that this seems to be an empty park."

"But maybe invisible makes sense," Angela said. "If they didn't want strangers spotting it."

"It makes sense," Ida agreed.

"But how could anyone have fun in a house they can't see?" Meryl asked.

"Well, if it was a maze," Angela said. "Like finding your way in darkness, except that it's not dark, just invisible. That could be fun."

"Yes it could be," Ida agreed.

"But what would be the point?" Meryl demanded. "Just navigating a maze for its own sake isn't much. There needs to be a reason for the challenge."

"There could be prizes," Angela said. "Maybe things we really truly want, that we can have if we just solve the maze."

"Solving the maize," Wenda agreed.

"What do we really truly want, apart from getting this awful Knot delivered so we can relax?" Meryl asked.

"What about your winged merman?" Angela asked.

That set Meryl back. "I would do an invisible maze for that," she agreed.

"So maybe that's a prize," Angela said, smiling.

"Perhaps it is," Ida agreed.

Wenda saw that this was taking shape. "Maybee we should make wishes, each of us, then see whether we can find them as prizes."

"My winged merman," Meryl agreed.

"Finding a fast, easy root to the Good Magician's Castle," Wenda said.

Hilarion smiled. "Finding my betrothee, of course."

"I suppose I would wish for something similar," Ida said.

"The rest of my substance," Angela said. "I am at present only half solid. Beauregard notices. But not at Wenda's expense."

Wenda realized that she had lost only half of her body, so that was all that Angela had gained. The angel was more apparent than real.

"A Status Point," Jumper said.

The others looked at him. "How's that again?" Hilarion asked.

"For Eris," Jumper explained. "She's a Dwarf Demoness. With enough Status Points she could become a full one."

Wenda nodded. "Yew dew love her."

"Oh, yes. And you, in a different manner." He looked around. "Did you notice that she did not wish for her own lost substance back, but only for the completion of her mission? None of the rest of us are that unselfish."

Wenda felt herself blushing, for no particular reason. "Yew were unselfish too. Yew wished for a favor for yewr deer."

"My dear," Jumper agreed. "I owe her everything."

Hilarion shook his head. "I am surely not the only

one who envies you such a relationship. I am not thinking of her power, but of her love."

"Surely not the only one," Ida agreed.

"Now we have established our wishes," Meryl said. "Now all we need is an invisible fun house with prizes."

"I wonder," Hilarion said. He got out of the boat and walked to the fence that surrounded nothing. There was a gate. He opened it and stepped through. And stopped. "There is a structure here."

"The house?" Wenda asked.

In hardly more than a moment the others had joined the prince. There was indeed something, invisible but solid.

Hilarion reached out to touch it. And a picture formed before him, like an image in a magic mirror. A picture of a lovely young princess, complete with gown and crown. "Well, now. That would be her."

"Your prize," Jumper agreed. "Should you choose to pursue it."

"I do." Hilarion stepped forward, into the picture. He tripped on something, but caught himself. "It is a doorway, and a stairway," he said. He stepped up, and up again. Soon he was standing at head height. "Perfectly solid." He felt ahead, then to the sides. He turned to the left, paused, then stepped up again. "It is indeed a maze. My prize must be at its end, if I find the right route."

"Let me try that," Meryl said. She balanced on her tail before the door, which now showed a handsome merman. She entered, felt about, then spread her wings and flew upward. "I have flying space," she announced. "But I can feel the nearness of barriers."

Angela approached the door. Now the picture showed a mound of what looked like blubber: her missing substance. She stepped into it and through it, discovering invisible stairs downward.

They seemed to be discovering the rules of this game.

Would it really deliver the prizes? They would just have to find out.

Jumper stepped up. He'd remained in human form, ever since learning that his magic changes were limited. "May I gamble?" he asked Wenda. "I would really feel more comfortable in my natural state."

"Gambol," she agreed.

He became the giant spider and touched the picture space. A shining numeral appeared, the number 1. One Status Point. He stepped into it, and evidently discovered a web network, because suddenly he was using all eight legs to climb an invisible scaffold.

That left Ida and Wenda. "Can it really deliver a Demon item?" Wenda asked.

"Not unless it has Demon endorsement."

"Is that possible?"

"It is possible," Ida said. "Though I think unlikely. We don't know the background of this alien network."

"We dew knot know," Wenda agreed.

"Let's see what it offers me," Ida said. She approached the gate, touched the picture place, and gazed at the forming picture. It was of a handsome older prince or king. "I think he would do, if real."

"Yew judge by appearances?"

"When there is no other information. I would of course need to come to know him first."

"There is something vaguely familiar about him," Wenda said. "But I can knot place it."

Ida focused. "Could it be Hilarion's father, the king of his isle?"

"That might bee it," Wenda agreed. "Though he did knot say his father was widowed."

"His uncle, perhaps."

"Yes. He should have similar sterling qualities."

Ida entered the invisible maze. Her path turned

abruptly right, then left. Wenda saw her feeling her way with her spread hands.

Now it was down to Wenda. "I dew knot like leaving the Knot unattended," she murmured. Then she had an idea. She returned to the boat, made sure it was firmly docked off the alien highway, and peeled away the remaining sheath of reverse wood, which was pretty much depleted anyway. That allowed the Knot to have full effect, petrifying anyone else who approached. It should be safe from molestation.

She returned to the gate. But still she was bothered. "Someone should bee in touch with the others, to bee sure they dew knot get lost or need help," she said.

Then she had an idea. The picture seemed to be guided by thought. Could it be guided by hers?

Her picture showed the Good Magician's Castle. She reached to its sides and took hold of the invisible frame. She felt that frame gradually shrinking in her hands, until it was relatively small.

"Hilarion," she murmured. And there was his picture, the size of her hollow palm. He was still making his way through the maze. She looked directly, and saw him in the distance, above the ground, in the same position as the picture. So it seemed to be valid.

"Hello, Hilarion," she said. He did not respond, which did not surprise her; this was a picture of him, not a communication with him.

"Meryl," she said, and the winged mermaid appeared. She had disappeared from the original "house" but the picture showed her flying over a mountain vista. There in a high valley was a small lake. She flew down toward it.

"Angela," Wenda said. Again, the original had disappeared in the gloom below, but showed clearly in the picture. The angel was now in a vast subterranean cave whose stalagmites had been sawed off to make level tables. On each table was an object, a seeming work of art. Angela touched the nearest, a figure of a catlike creature, and it expanded and animated, becoming an ancient tome. It was titled *Cat-Egories of Interest*. She turned the pages, which showed pictures of cat-related things, such as a double-hulled boat or a device to hurl rocks into space, or an underground cemetery, or a wild natural disaster. She obviously could not make anything of this, and neither could Wenda. She put the book back, and it returned to its animal statue form.

The next object resembled a goat. Angela touched it, and it became another book, this one with pictures of goat-related things. A human man with a small pointed beard. A bearded fish. A small bird. An herb. A person obviously being seriously annoyed by another. Neither Angela nor Wenda could make anything of this, either.

One of these objects should relate to Angela's missing substance, but which? How? It was a mystery.

"Jumper," Wenda said. He, at least, remained visible directly; he was climbing some giant invisible web. It seemed to stretch from star to star, spanning the scene.

But there was a platform, a shelf anchored nowhere, and on that platform was a collection of bundles of glowing 1's. Those must be the Demon Status Points. Jumper was climbing steadily toward it. But Wenda saw what Jumper could not: there was also a ferocious ogre guarding the bundles. How would the spider handle that?

"Ida," Wenda said.

Ida was still making her way through the invisible labyrinth. But she seemed to be approaching some person-sized object; Wenda saw its shadow. So she peered in Ida's direction in the real maze—and saw that she was now in the same area Hilarion was. Were their two convoluted passages going to intersect?

So it seemed. Ida stepped up to a passage while Hilarion stepped down to the same passage from a different direction. They saw each other and spoke together, gesturing. Wenda could not hear what they said, but presumed it was a surprised greeting. They talked; what was it about?

Then Wenda pieced it together. It seemed that the two of them were not actually in the same passage, but at adjacent intersections. It further seemed that a section had to be rotated to let them pass, like one of the magic revolving doors in Mundania. And that whichever one got the use of that access, the other would not. Only one of them could proceed.

They discussed it for some time. Wenda suspected that each was courteously deferring to the other. Well, they would work it out somehow.

Wenda focused on her own path. This twisted and turned and folded back, doing its best to confuse her, but she plugged away and finally won through to what appeared to be a mountain path. It seemed that only the original maze was invisible; its several passages led to visible routes.

She walked along the path. It curved around the side of the mountain, and then became a straight ramp leading down to—the Good Magician's Castle. This was her access! If she got the wagon with the Knot here, it would be easy to roll it down to the castle, and her mission would be accomplished.

Then she saw the dragon. It seemed to be made of string or cord, with many loose ends, but it was definitely a dragon. And it was definitely barring the way.

Wenda paused, considering. Had it been a forest dragon she might have reasoned with it, because she understood all forest folk. But this was an alien thing.

Still, maybe it was not truly hostile. She walked toward it.

The thing flung out a spreading tangle of string that

just missed her. It was trying to catch her so it could consume her at leisure. It was a dragon-net.

She retreated, reconsidering. How was she to handle this creature? Obviously she needed to get it out of the way if she were to roll the wagon along this route.

She decided to check on the others. She held the invisible mirror before her. "Hilarion."

Hilarion had evidently resolved his issue with Ida, because now he was moving on at a great rate. In fact he was sliding down an invisible chute to somewhere.

"Angela."

Angela was paging through another book. This one was titled *Doggerel*, and it had pictures of dog-associated things, such as a very opinionated person, a determined person, a kind of flowering tree, a kind of swimming, and a kind of slow running. None of these seemed relevant.

Angela touched another figure, but this one did not convert. It seemed she had a limited number of choices, and once she used them up, she was through.

Yet she did not look dismayed. She moved on to other figures, searching more carefully. Maybe she had not actually touched the last one; Wenda had not seen closely.

"Meryl," Wenda said.

Meryl was now apparently in the lake, swimming through underwater caverns, searching for where they led. Their windings were marvelously devious, but the mermaid seemed confident; it seemed that she could handle such twists.

"Jumper."

The spider had discovered the ogre and taken him on. Wenda remembered that Jumper in his big spider form was one of the few creatures who did not fear ogres. The ogre was bashing gleefully—ogres loved to bash—but Jumper was avoiding each smashing hamfist and flinging a line of silk around it. Soon he had the ogre hopelessly wrapped in strong silk lines and largely helpless. The ogre was none too pleased; the fight was supposed to finish the other way around.

Jumper pushed the swathed ogre off the platform. A line went taut; he was suspended in a kind of cocoon below the platform, unable to smash anything except air.

Jumper started examining the glowing bundles. All he needed was one point, but it was possible that it was hidden among hundreds of fake ones.

"Ida," Wenda said.

Ida had found her way to an open plain with thousands of circular holes, as if a giant with a pogo stick had been bouncing around. There was a castle in the distance, surely the one containing her promised prince or king. All she had to do was walk to it.

Two people appeared, young men. "Hello," Ida said, though she was not pleased to see them. At least, that was the way Wenda interpreted it, seeing her mouth move with two syllables and without a smile.

"You look as if you distrust our motives," one of the men said. At least, that was what his expression seemed to indicate.

"I do. You seem most likely to be obstacles to my progress."

"That is true. I sense a person's deepest fear." He focused intently on her. "And in this context, yours is bad weather." Or at least it must be something like that. There was a kind of threat in the man's expression. The weather statement Wenda figured out by what happened next.

Wenda saw Ida wince. Yet what was so bad about weather?

"And I bring it to life," the other man said.

"I'm sure that is a very nice set of talents," Ida said. "Now I must be on my way." She walked past them.

Immediately a storm came up, with roiling gray clouds and flashes of lightning. The young man had invoked the bad weather. Ida would have to hurry, lest she get soaked. But could that be the extent of it, Wenda wondered? Getting wet wasn't fun, but it didn't seem to be a serious threat.

Ida hurried. But so did the storm. It intensified by bounds and leaps, sweeping closer. In no more than two and a half moments it caught her. The wild winds pulled at her hair and clothing, and rain sluiced down in drenches. In three-quarters of another moment she was soaked, and still it poured.

Wenda wished she could help, but she couldn't. So she focused on her own problem: the string dragon. At least she could try to talk to it.

She stepped forward. "Dragon!" she called. "I am Wenda Woodwife, and I am here to—"

It flung out a net and snared her. In no more than a moment and a quarter she was hauled into the air, bagged by the net. The dragon was slavering stringily.

"Yew dew knot want to dew this," she warned it.

The dragon paid no never mind. It opened its ropey maw and bit her on the right foot.

And dropped her, groaning. For of course her foot was not maidenly flesh, but hard hollowed wood.

"I tried to warn yew," she reminded it as she got to her feet and removed the net. "Woodwives are knot edible. Now why dew yew knot go away and leave this path clear so I can use it?"

For answer, the beast pounced on her, trying to bite off her head. It succeeded only in further damaging itself. In two instants it was rolling on the ground, moaning with several awful toothaches.

"Please go now," she told it. "I dew knot want to hurt yew anymore."

But the dragon roused itself and attacked her again.

Apparently it was too dull to realize what it was up against. A fire-breather could have burned her up, but string could not hurt her.

Still, she realized that they would not be able to roll the wagon through this pass as long as the dragon remained. Its string could foul the wheels, and it could bite other members of their party. The thing was too stupid to know when to quit, and that gave it the victory. It was annoying as spit, but she was not going to win her prize.

With that realization, she felt herself sinking. It wasn't just emotional; she was physically descending into the forest floor. She fell down and down, the earth sliding by, until she was back in the invisible maze. Then she was out of it, landing un-neatly at the entry gate.

"Let me help you," Hilarion said, helping her to her feet.

"Yew are supposed to bee in the maize," she protested.

"I yielded the right of way to Princess Ida. It was the princely thing to do."

"That's why yew were sliding," she said, realizing. "Yew were beeing washed out."

"Yes. I am sorry to see you suffering the same fate."

"It was knot fated to bee," she agreed. "Ida—I am surprised she agreed to take yewr path."

"She didn't. She wanted to yield to me. But I worked the rotary door to favor her, and she was through before she realized. I regret playing such a trick on her. I hope she finds her king."

"Yew are really a pretty decent person."

"I do what I feel is right," he said. "As do you. She's an elder princess with diminishing prospects, while I could marry some other young woman than my betrothee if I chose to. Her need is greater."

That seemed to cover it. "Let us see how she is dewing," Wenda said, lifting up the mirror.

Not well, as it turned out. The storm was so thick that it was difficult to see immediately ahead, let alone across to the castle. Ida tried to avoid the holes, but their slopes had become larger, so that there was hardly room to step between them, and erratic gusts were pushing her that way and this. Now Wenda understood why Ida feared the storm: it made her route become too treacherous to navigate.

Then she lost her footing and fell, sliding into one of the holes. Suddenly she was zooming helplessly down and out of the maze.

Hilarion and Wenda were there to assist her as she emerged at the gate. She was soaked and obviously miserable, but she put on a smile. "Hilarion, is your father a widower?"

Startled, Hilarion considered. "Not that I know of, though it may have been some time since I last saw him."

"Dew yew have an uncle?" Wenda asked.

"I do. But I don't understand your interest."

"It's that Ida's ideal man might bee him," Wenda explained. "In which case she will know where to look next."

"I suppose that is possible," he agreed. "Princess Ida, you will be welcome to join me when I return to my home isle for a visit after this mission is complete. I'm sure my uncle would consider you more than worthy."

"Thank you. I regret that you gave up your chance for nothing."

"I must act in a princely way," Hilarion said seriously. "Else I risk *becoming* nothing."

"I appreciate the point."

"I am sure you do, being a princess in your own right."

She shrugged. "We are all constrained to be what we must be."

"We are indeed," he agreed. "Though on rare occasion there might be a tinge of regret."

"Exactly."

Wenda, a princess by marriage, found it interesting to see how those to the manner born behaved. They understood nuances of behavior that she was still struggling to learn.

But there were things to do. Wenda activated the mirror. "Jumper."

The big spider was still examining bundles of numerals. But Wenda saw that the ogre, too stupid to know better, was still struggling with ham-minded determination. He had succeeded in biting through some of the silk bindings and had worked a hamhand free. Then he started swinging. What was he doing?

Now Wenda saw a dangling cord. It had a red ball on the end. The ogre swung toward it, away from it, and toward it again, gaining momentum. This was surely mischief.

"Jumper!" Wenda cried. "The ogre's knot tied anymore!" But he couldn't hear her.

The ogre caught the cord and yanked on it. Suddenly the entire platform collapsed, dumping Jumper into a nether chute. In barely three moments he landed at the gate in a tangle of debris.

"I'm so sorry," Wenda said, helping him up. "I tried to warn yew."

"I should not have been so distracted by the bundles," Jumper said. "I thought I was so close to finding the right numeral."

"You surely were," Hilarion said. "But the fun house does not make it easy."

Jumper looked around with two or three eyes. "The three of you washed out?"

"We did," Wenda agreed.

"Literally," Ida said. She remained thoroughly wet, her hair in a mess and mud on her gown.

"But Meryl and Angela are still in it?"

"They are," Ida agreed.

"Then all is not yet lost."

"Knot yet," Wenda agreed. "Dew yew have another dress?" she asked Ida.

"As a matter of fact, I do. I will try to clean up and change now."

"I will gaze elsewhere," Hilarion said. And he did, providing Ida some privacy. So did Jumper.

Wenda lifted the mirror. "Angela."

Angela had found a promising figurine. It was of an impossibly fat nature goddess. She touched it, and it became a volume titled *Women of Substance*.

"I think she's got it," Hilarion said.

Angela paged through the tome. There were pictures of assorted human women, some of them queens of ample girth. Then she came to a picture that made her pause.

"That's Angela!" Ida said.

So it was. Somehow Angela herself had gotten into the book. Did this mean she had won her prize?

Angela touched the picture. Suddenly the whole book came up around her hand and arm, as if consuming her. Then it disappeared into her. And her body filled out.

"She got the substance of the book," Jumper said. "She won!"

"She won," Ida said. She was now in an alternate dress, with very little mud left on her. She had cleaned and changed efficiently, as well as was feasible in this awkward circumstance. "Now she is whole."

"It seems we were wrong to doubt the constancy of Bems," Hilarion said. "I am glad to see it."

"As am I," Ida agreed. "I did not like suspecting ill of any creature. It is unprincessly."

"You were never that," Hilarion said.

Now Angela was sliding down the exit chute. Unlike the others, she was happy. Soon she appeared at the gate.

"I got it!" she exclaimed. "Look! Feel! I am thoroughly solid."

Jumper and Hilarion were appropriately diffident, though they might have liked to oblige her, but Wenda and Ida felt Angela's arms and legs. They were fully fleshed, not spongy. Angela was indeed now a woman of substance.

One remained. "Meryl," Wenda said, holding the mirror.

Meryl was still flying lithely through the watery caverns. Tendrils were reaching for her from crevices, but she was avoiding them. She seemed to know where she was going, and was determined to get there soon.

She came to a new cave, and there above her was the flatness of the surface of the lake. This cave was only half full of water. Within it was an island formed from a nether projection of rock, and on that isle was a figure.

In fact it was a winged merman. The one who had shown in the picture.

Meryl must have called, because the merman turned and saw her. Then he slid into the water and joined her. They held an animated dialogue.

"I was just flying along, minding my own business," Hilarion said, mimicking the presumed merman's voice. "When suddenly I was caught here in this cave with no idea of the way out."

"Fortunately I know the way out," Ida said, mimicking Meryl's voice. "I have an excellent memory for travel details. I will show you."

"I would be so grateful," the merman said.

"I am just glad to be of help," the mermaid said.

Then the two embraced, there in the water, and kissed.

Wenda and Jumper looked at Hilarion and Ida. "Will yew dew that too?" Wenda asked.

But the two, abruptly embarrassed, did not.

Meryl was as good as her presumed word. She led the way back through the underwater caves, and the merman followed. He could have escaped alone, had he had any idea of the route, but it was such a labyrinth that he must have feared getting lost, and caught by hungry sea monsters.

"They will surely be here soon," Jumper said. "So our party has won two of six prizes. That seems worthwhile."

"Oh, yes," Angela said, admiring her own full flesh.

"Which means it is time to consider where we should go from here," Wenda said. "We can knot expect any further help from the Bems; they have fulfilled their end of the deal."

"And it seems they know it," Hilarion said, glancing toward the boat. The others looked.

The boat was gone. The Knot sat alone on the wagon.

"I suspect we will not be able to use the Bem highway without the boat," Jumper said. He went to the highway access and poked it. His leg passed through it. It had become illusion, as far as they were concerned.

They explored the edges of the park. They faded into nothingness. There was no other exit path.

"I fear we shall have to take an uncomfortable route," Hilarion said.

"The humidor," Ida agreed, similarly distressed.

"At least we can camp here overnight and consider," Angela said.

Two figures arrived at the gate. "I found him!" Meryl exclaimed jubilantly. "Merwyn Merman! Isn't he wonderful!"

There was a flurry of individual introductions. Merwyn seemed happy to have been rescued by such a charming creature of his species. His expression indicated that Meryl was everything he had ever dreamed of, but feared didn't exist.

"Will you two fly happily into the sunset?" Jumper asked.

"No way!" Meryl said. "I want to stay with the party until the Knot is delivered, and have conjugal visits. I have been jealous of those all along."

The others laughed. Now all but Hilarion and Ida could have hot visits. Wenda was sorry for the two left out, yet happy for Angela's substance and Meryl's companion.

They broke out their stored supplies and ate, for the day was now late. And just at dusk their companions appeared.

"Too bad the rest of you did not win your prizes," Eris remarked. "And I'm not just saying that because of yours, you hopeless romantic," she said, kissing Jumper on the carapace. "But you folk have one remaining significant adventure to get through before you can retire."

Then Wenda was in a separate little tent with Charming. He still did not seem to notice her reverted condition, masked as it was by her clothing, and she was not about to call it to his attention. She liked his enthusiasm. In seven minutes he was asleep, and then gone.

Wenda was interested to see that Merwyn Merman was asleep. Evidently that relationship had progressed rapidly.

In the morning they consulted. "You won't want to be along on this," Meryl told Merwyn. "Those puns are atrocious."

"But how will I ever find you again, if you reappear randomly in Xanth?" he asked.

He had a point. "Then come along," Wenda said. "Just bee prepared."

Ida brought out the humidor.

13

MAY I

They landed in a deep blue valley near yellow jungle-overgrown ruins. Planet Comic had seemed uninhabited, and maybe it was, but there had been some sort of civilization here once.

Hilarion cupped his ear with his hand. "Is that baying I hear?"

Meryl and Merwyn sailed up into the sky. "We'll see," Meryl called back. She remained flush with happiness about finding her man. Wenda was glad for her, and for Angela, and that helped ease her discomfort about her own hollowed condition. She reminded herself that she was better off this way than dead. But for Eris . . .

"Baying," Ida said uneasily. "Does that mean wolves?"

"Or dogs," Hilarion said. "The dogs of war."

"I don't know whether to hope that's a pun," Angela said.

"This is a world of puns," Jumper reminded her. "But they are mostly confined to the pun Strips."

"But some dew escape," Wenda said, remembering their awkward meal with pun food.

The winged merfolk glided down. "Definitely dogs,"

Meryl called. "They look absolutely vicious. We had better take precautions."

Wenda swung into action. "Yew two—survey these ruins, quick. Find a section that can bee sealed off rapidly. Jumper—we will need yewr power to roll some stones into place. Ida—yew surely remember some good castle designs. Figure out one for what we have here, defensible against animals. Angela—forage for some food, as we may bee cooped up for a while. Hilarion—keep listening. Tell us when they are getting close."

They got busy. The merfolk soon located an ancient temple whose roof had collapsed, but whose high green stone walls were still standing and solid. Ida considered it. "This will make a defensible dungeon," she said. "Except for this one broken-down section of wall."

"The Knot can block that," Wenda said, hauling on the wagon.

Jumper heaved some of the fallen roof sections to the main entry, where they made a barrier.

"We should also make a battlement," Ida said.

"A what?" Jumper asked.

"A sort of serrated wall," Hilarion said. "Alternating high and low sections, merlons and crenels, so we can peer out between them without exposing ourselves unnecessarily. We can't be sure how high those dogs can leap."

"Exactly," Ida agreed. "You know about castles."

Hilarion shrugged. "Necessary princely background information."

Jumper got on it, heaving tiles to the top of the walls, some high, some low. Wenda parked the Knot in the gap, heedless of its radiating resentment at being made useful, then helped heave green tiles as well as she was able.

"And weapons," Hilarion said. "Sticks for spears, rocks for missiles. This may become ugly." Merwyn and

Meryl foraged quickly for suitable sticks and stones. There were many lying around, so the collection quickly grew.

Angela flew in with an armful of pies. "I found a pie tree just outside the Strip," she said, dumping them down. "But those hounds are coming awfully close."

"Man the defenses," Hilarion said. He clambered up to the top of the wall, stood there, and drew his sword. "Oh, yes," he muttered, gazing down.

Wenda climbed up to the top of the wall and looked out through a low spot. There were the dogs, surging through the jungle, their eyes glowing red.

"I am relieved that we don't have to encounter those directly," Ida said.

"It wood knot bee fun," Wenda agreed, shuddering. One or two bites would not hurt her, but the pack of animals could tear her wood apart.

The dogs heard them. They leaped up against the wall, snarling, slaver flying. They did seem to be mindless beasts.

Ida screamed. A ravening dog had managed to scramble over the tile-blocked entrance and was menacing her from the inside of the wall.

Hilarion leaped down from the wall, sword extended. "Ho, beast!" he cried. "Depart the way you came, or perish."

The dog whirled, understanding the challenge. There was nothing it liked better than a good fight. It leaped directly at Hilarion. Ida screamed again.

The prince's sword moved so swiftly it was almost invisible. The dog yelped and fell to the ground, mortally wounded. It had been sliced through the neck, and its lifeblood was pouring out.

"I gave fair warning," Hilarion said sternly.

The dog nodded, then died. Hilarion wiped and sheathed his sword, then picked the dead animal up and hurled it back over the tiles. "Any more for this route?"

he called. No more came. The dogs were vicious, not stupid.

Ida looked faint. "You saved me," she told Hilarion.

Now he was embarrassed. "I do what is needful. I regret you had to see the bloodshed."

"So do I," she said. "But it was instead of *my* blood being shed. That makes a difference."

Wenda went to try to comfort Ida. It occurred to her privately that this ugly incident had been the proof that Prince Hilarion was no paper prince; he had been quite ready and able to use his sword when it was, as he put it, needful.

"I think there will be no reasoning with these animals," Jumper said. "They seem to understand only lethal force. But we will need to divert them, if we are ever to make our way to the Strip."

"How can we dew that?" Wenda asked.

"I wonder," Angela said. "It may be a foolish notion—I'm not sure I have myself properly together yet, mentally—but if those dogs are a pun, maybe they escaped from the Strip."

"They surely did," Ida said, wincing as another leaping canine smacked into the wall just below her spot. Wenda remembered that Angela's memory of Ida's talent had been deleted, so she could make useful suggestions without realizing it.

"So there must be a hole in the Strip," Angela continued. "Since the anti-puns are generally near the puns, there might be something there, similarly escaped, that could nullify the dogs."

"I'm sure that is the case," Ida agreed.

Wenda pounced on the moment. "Why dew yew knot fly out and see if yew can find it?"

"I will try," Angela said.

"But do not go near the ground," Hilarion said. "You are no longer unbiteable."

Angela glanced at the dogs, and winced. "I won't." She flew up, up, and away.

Wenda made her way around the perimeter, making sure their defenses were tight. They seemed to be; the only open space was around the Knot, and the dogs were shying well clear of that.

She paused at the Knot. "Yew know, yew're a lot of mischief," she remarked.

It responded with a blast of sheer malice.

She was intrigued. "What wood yew dew, if a loving couple perched on yew and kissed?"

The Knot almost seemed to swell with rage. The remaining chips of reverse wood around it steamed and curled.

"I suppose I should knot tease yew," she said. "It is knot gneiss. Yew may bee knot gneiss, but I am supposed to bee gneiss. I wood like to deliver yew to some situation yew really liked, provided it did knot harm Xanth."

The Knot continued to radiate ire. It was having none of this sniveling dialogue.

Wenda moved on. She had difficulty understanding anything so perversely inimical. The Knot seemed to hate everything.

The defenses seemed tight. She completed the circuit just as Angela returned.

"I found it!" Angela exclaimed. "Doves of Peace!"

"I dew knot understand," Wenda said.

"Look."

Wenda climbed the battlement and peered out. A flock of birds was following Angela. In a moment and a half they spied the raging Dogs of War and angled down to join them.

"The birds'll be torn apart," Meryl said, hovering anxiously above the battlement.

But it was not so. Each Dove oriented on a particular Dog, flew down, and kissed it on the muzzle. The dog then stopped snarling and became peaceful. Soon the entire pack was wandering off through the forest, sniffing roots, tugging vines, and doing other doggy things. While the Doves, their peaceful urges dissipated, explored the ground cover, picking up seeds. Dogs and Doves had become normal.

"I dew knot quite trust this," Wenda said. "Suppose they are pretending, so we will come out unprotected?"

Hilarion nodded. "It was a brilliant ploy, Angela, but you will surely forgive us for our caution."

"Certainly," the angel agreed angelically.

"I propose we remain here for the day and night," Jumper said. "If the dogs have not reverted to war, then perhaps we can assume we can safely make it to the Strip."

"And if we have to," Ida said, "we can cluster close around the Knot. We are accustomed to it; we can surely move closer to it than other creatures can."

"That seems excellent," Hilarion said. "We can use the rest."

They ate the pies Angela had foraged, not going outside the fort, but they were not enough. Members of the party remained hungry.

"Maybe I can help again," Angela said. "Now that I have the rest of my substance, my beads should work."

"Beads?" Meryl asked.

"My sash," the angel explained, touching it. "It is made of seed pearls. They can grow into things I need." She removed a bead, held it up, and breathed on it.

The seed pearl expanded, becoming a loaf of freshly baked bread. She breathed on another, and it became a jug of wine. Soon they were sharing bread and wine, and lemon and lime stones to flavor their cups of water, and they filled out the meal very well.

Angela also found some soapstone, and they passed

the bar around so that each could wash with a basin of water.

They took turns sleeping in the afternoon, while others watched at the battlement. The snarling dogs did not return, but all of them were aware it could be a trap. Angela, Meryl, and Merwin flew out to forage, and did find some more fruits and square roots. Ida made a fire and baked the roots, and they were good enough for a square meal.

At dusk their conjugal visitors arrived. "You folk travel about," Eris remarked. "I would have thought you had had enough of this world."

"We have," Wenda said. "But we did knot have much of a choice."

Then they were separated into their private chambers. "I envy you," Prince Charming said as he eagerly addressed her wooden and fleshly charms. "You have so much adventure."

"Thank yew," Wenda said, not saying that she was eager to be free of this adventure and safely home again, and with her full body. He would not understand, as he seemed not yet to have realized that any of it was missing.

In seven minutes their party was alone again, except that Merwyn remained beside Meryl, sound asleep. Jumper was also asleep, alone, though his multiple spider eyes were not closed. Things were back to normal in that respect.

Wenda took the first watch of the night, perching on the battlement and watching carefully for any dogs. She saw none. She hoped that was good news.

In due course Hilarion relieved her. "I wanted to mention my appreciation for your leadership in the crisis," he murmured. "You did the job that needed to be done to safeguard us all."

"Me!" she exclaimed. "Yew organized the defense!"

"After you established the parameters. You acted instantly, and that saved us all from likely mischief."

"Thank yew," she said, blushing. "I never thought about it. I just knew we had to get safe, quickly."

"You are a princess. By marriage, true, but you do possess the qualities. I hope when I find my betrothee, she will have qualities similar to yours."

Wenda couldn't think of any response, so quickly retired to her spot on the ground so she could sleep. Part of her problem was her sudden realization that Hilarion was more of a prince than Charming was. She didn't want to find herself wishing that Charming could be more like Hilarion. That unknown betrothee was a luckier woman than she could know.

Wenda slept. At first it was peaceful, as it normally was; her wooden mind, such as it was, was at home in the forest, and this was a kind of forest.

Then there was a disturbing element. Something was coming, and the walls were not stopping it. In fact it was a troop of ghosts. Should she be afraid?

The ghosts were male, female, and juvenile, garbed in loincloths and brief headdresses. They were handsome enough, but oddly troubled in their expressions.

"Who are yew?" Wenda asked, not fearful so much as curious and wary. Ghosts could be of any type, from nostalgic to horrendous.

"We are the May I," their leader answered. "I am Steven Wolf, the leader of this remnant." He made a gesture to include the several plainly adoring, lovely women beside him. "We, that is, our people, built this grand city that is now in ruins because of our folly."

"We did knot mean to intrude," Wenda said, finding herself mysteriously attracted to the man. "We were in trouble, and had to protect ourselves. Otherwise we wood have been destroyed."

"You are a forest nymph!" a ghost woman said.

"I am," Wenda agreed, turning around so they could see her full backside as well as her hollow frontside. "I am Wenda Woodwife, passing through on a special mission. I speak in the forest dialect."

"But nymphs are typically empty-headed," the woman said.

"My head is empty, as yew can see," Wenda agreed. "But I have a job to dew."

"What is that job?"

"I must deliver that Knot of petrified reverse wood to the Good Magician's Castle, so that it can knot bee used to harm anyone."

The May I contemplated the Knot, the women inspecting it from one side, the man from the other. "That is one sullen artifact," Steven Wolf remarked.

"Yes," Wenda agreed. "It seems to hate everything in its presence."

"The opposite of my talent," Steven said. "I attract women who are madly in love with me in my presence, but who completely forget about me when I am absent."

"Is that true?" Wenda asked the women, surprised.

The women looked perplexed. "Is what true?" one asked.

"About you and Steven Wolf?"

"About who?"

Wenda realized that the women were standing where they could not see the man. They had forgotten him. That also explained her own attraction to him: it was his talent.

"That must bee frustrating," Wenda said to Steven.

"It is, in death as well as life. But it is incidental. We have a serious favor to ask of you. But we must pay for it."

"I will help anyone I can," Wenda said. "I dew knot need to be paid."

"Ah, but it is part of our protocol, which we can't violate. We must come to terms."

Wenda shrugged. "What is it yew need?"

"First you must understand our history," Steven said, "because the favor must be done with knowledge of its significance."

Wenda began to be concerned about the nature of the favor. If it involved touching Steven, she would have difficulty restraining herself from hugging and kissing him. So he was a ghost; this was a dream, and he would seem solid to her. It would be a violation of her commitment to Charming, and her hollow face might turn Steven off. "Then tell me yewr history," she said, hoping that would clarify that the favor was of some other nature. Yet also guiltily hoping that it wasn't.

The women finished their inspection of the Knot and circled it to rejoin the man. "Steven!" one exclaimed, delighted. "How could we have forgotten you!"

Then all three of them were clustering about him, one kissing him on the face while another hugged him from the side and the third patted his rear rather more intimately than seemed appropriate in public.

Wenda held her place, though she desperately wanted to join them. It was as though he were a big magnet, and she made of metal rather than wood. The pull was fierce.

Steven sat on a fragment of tile, the women sitting closely around him. Wenda noticed that their loinskirts barely covered their full bottoms in that position, and that if Steven had looked, he would have seen inside their flexed thighs to their panties. Assuming they wore any. But his gaze was fixed on Wenda. She wasn't sure whether to be relieved or disconcerted. She also wished she could sit like that, but it would show the hollow frontsides of her thighs right up to her hollow belly, ruining the effect. She had in the past year become accustomed to the advantages of having a backside, notably in the presence of a man, but now it was her frontside she missed.

"The history of our people extends back thousands of years," Steven said. "We even had two calendars to track our civic and routine events, and they hardly even overlapped. We were excellent farmers and warriors. We sacrificed regularly to our gods, and they rewarded us with fine harvests. Always we asked their permission for any key decisions we made. Our priest would stand before the statue of a god and ask 'May I?' and if the god did not say no, we would do it."

"Did the god ever say no?" Wenda asked, curious.

"Sometimes. The gods did not speak in words, but in signs. If there was a sudden close crack of thunder, that was no. If the earth shook and a building fell, that was no. If a bird smacked into a tower and fell dead, that was no. But usually there was nothing, so we knew it was all right."

Wenda realized that in the great majority of cases, it would be all right, even if there were no gods. But she did not want to annoy the believers by pointing that out.

"Then a prophet came and told us that there were no gods, that nature was everything, and that we were wasting our resources by sacrificing our best and brightest to these imaginary deities. That no sensible god would relish receiving a beating heart in a stone dish. That we were taking the silence of gods that were no more than stone idols as permission, and attributing our naturally good weather to their intercession. 'Cease this nonsense!' he cried. 'Just be great warriors and farmers without soiling it with supernatural crap.'"

Wenda realized that that must have been some prophet. To go against thousands of years of culture; to speak what to Wenda was plain obvious truth, crediting nature rather than gods—that would have taken intelligence and courage.

"We believed him," Steven continued. "We stopped the sacrifices, thereby sparing the lives of many doughty warriors and beautiful maidens. And for a time all was well, and we prospered. The days were fine and sunny, one after another. Then came the drought. Fine sunny days are not so great if not interspersed with dark rainy days. We dug wells, and irrigated, tiding through, but the drought continued. The water table lowered, requiring us to dig our wells deeper."

He sighed, and the women sighed with him, their bare breasts rippling in a manner that made Wenda almost incoherent with envy. She had no such equipment herself, now, only a hollow that matched the curvature of her back. She had stuffed her clothing, so as to look complete, but was able to show no actual flesh. Sooner or later Prince Charming was bound to wonder why she no longer removed her shirt when embracing him.

"We had been at peace," Steven continued. "But war broke out as the drought intensified, as people fought over the diminishing number of wells that still provided copious fresh water. The green fields shrank. Hunger spread. Until at last no producing wells remained, and the last crops dried up in their fields. Folk fled in masses, but the drought was everywhere. There was no place to survive.

"Then belatedly we realized that this was the gods' answer to our infidelity. We had renounced the gods, so they renounced us, and ceased providing the water we so desperately needed. We should never have listened to that false prophet. But he was gone to some far distant land, with wealth and lovely women, leaving us to our folly. We had no recourse but to perish with what little remaining grace we could muster."

"That is so sad," Wenda said, feeling a teardrop formed of sap on her face.

"Naturally once the last of us was gone, the water returned. There were heavy storms washing out many of our remaining traces, and the jungle trees overgrew our cities. Now our only visitors are wild animals, and abysmal puns from the Strips. We are still being punished." He grimaced. "Pun-ished. All we want at this stage is to let our spirits fly to another world, where we can perhaps form a new culture. But we have been unable to do that."

"Yew can knot just go?"

"We cannot. That is our problem."

"I dew knot understand."

"We must be given leave. We must ask 'May I?' and be given leave by an understanding, living mortal person. It is our nature."

"I can dew that," Wenda said, relieved yet with a tinge of disappointment.

"Yes, you can," Steven agreed. "But you must be recompensed. What wish do you have that we can grant? Understand, we are unable to offer you anything physical."

What she most wanted was to complete this mission, recover her frontside, and go home. But she was pretty sure these ghosts could not handle that. Then she thought of something that might be within their compass. "We barricaded ourselves against the Dogs of War. We think we nullified them, but can knot bee sure. Can yew tell me whether we can safely make our way to the nearest Strip?"

"That is no problem at all, nymph. Once a pun has been nullified, it is without power. But why would you ever want to go to a Strip? We found them sickening, when we lived, and avoided them in droves."

"It is where the Door back to our world is," Wenda said. "We must brave the awful puns to find it."

"You poor thing," one of the women said.

The dead were being sympathetic to the living. But Wenda appreciated it. "Thank yew."

"I think that reassurance is our return favor," Steven said. "Now may we depart?"

"Yew may," Wenda said, hoping that her accent did not foul up the permission.

"Thank you." Steven and the three women faded.

Wenda's urgent desire to clasp the man dissipated. In fact she could hardly remember his name or anything much else. Just the dialogue.

Wenda woke. It was morning. They had some traveling to do.

The others stirred. Merwyn was on guard. "I believe I saw some ghosts," he said.

"Yew did," Wenda agreed. "I talked with them in my dream. They say we can safely trek to the Strip."

"Then let's get to it," Hilarion said.

As they organized for the trip, Wenda overheard Hilarion and Jumper talking. "I am pretty sure my betrothee is not a ghost," Hilarion said. "Otherwise I would have loved to clasp one of those women and kiss her."

"Eris is not a jealous female," Jumper said. "And I am not in human form. But had I been, those bare-breasted, short-skirted women would have freaked me out."

"I believe I did freak out when one of them swung her knees in my direction. The May I may have been great farmers and warriors, but they surely were great lovers too."

"That man—what's his name—Steven, was surely so," Ida said. "Even I felt the attraction, and he is not near my generation."

"I simply wanted to comfort him," Angela said. "My newly solid flesh would surely have helped." She blushed.

Wenda knew exactly how it was.

They moved out. The Dogs of War did not show up,

and the trip was uneventful. By noon they were at the fringe of the Strip.

"I dread this," Hilarion said candidly. "An ordinary enemy can be dealt with by sword or persuasion, but those puns erode a person's self-respect."

"True," Ida agreed.

They peered through the shimmering border of the Strip, trying to see whether the Sidewalk and Door were there. Instead all they saw were piled-up puns. The nature of many of them was not clear just from the murky images, but they were able to make some guesses.

"That patch of water," Ida said. "That resembled the Brain Coral's pool, where surplus characters are stored until needed. The pretty coral snake would be guarding it."

"What's that bird?" Meryl asked. "It doesn't look quite like Dipper."

"That is the pet peeve," Ida said. "A notorious bird of indeterminate gender who insults everyone within range. It is said that it wore out its welcome in Hell and was expelled. It is also said that only crackers from a vigorous crackerbarrel tree will shut it up even temporarily. We don't want to go near it."

"And these bees buzzing around," Angela asked. "Are they dangerous?"

"No, those are wanna-bees," Ida said. "They are filled with unrealizable ambitions."

"I dew knot think we will ever find the Sidewalk or Door by looking from the outside," Wenda said. "I fear we shall have to plunge in and find it by trial and error."

"Mostly error," Jumper said. "Merwyn—you have not experienced this before. Stay close to Meryl and try not to be disgusted out of your mind."

"I don't see what can be so bad about puns," the winged merman said.

No one argued with him. He would learn.

They picked what looked like a less obnoxious spot, linked hands, and plunged in.

There before them was a sad-looking donkey. "You must be desperate to come here," he said.

"We are," Wenda said shortly. The very presence of the animal was making her feel depressed. She tried to brush by it, and it balked her.

"And you are a wood nymph out of your forest," the creature said. "How can you stand it?"

The awful thing was, suddenly Wenda seriously doubted that she could stand it. The longer she remained close to the donkey, the worse she felt.

Then she recognized it. "Yew are a beast of burden! Yew make people heavyhearted."

"Justifiably," the beast agreed. "When you think about it, don't you realize that routine existence is barely worth it? To be depressed is to be realistic."

"Where have I heard that sort of reasoning before?" Hilarion asked.

"The May I prophet who denounced the gods," Ida said.

"Ah, yes. We must be rid of this."

"Lotsa luck, lonely prince," the beast said.

"I'll look," Meryl said, taking off.

"We'll look," Merwyn said, following.

"Dew knot get lost!" Wenda called.

"It should be close by," Meryl reassured her.

The two landed by a brightly colored log. It seemed to have been dyed by an artist with paint to use up. "We must talk," the log said.

"No need," Meryl said.

"You may apply new colors to my bark while we talk," the log said.

"We don't want to talk, we want to stop the beast of burden."

"That is too bad, because I am an excellent conversationalist."

"You're a Dye-a-Log!" Merwyn exclaimed. "You talk colorfully."

"How very true."

An angry older woman burst on the scene, the first of several. "What are you strangers doing here?" she demanded. "You ought to be ashamed of yourselves, bothering innocent things."

"Oh, let it rest, harridan," the log said. "That diet you're on has made you foul-tempered."

"Foul-tempered. Me? How dare you!" Now the woman was haranguing the log, and her companions were supporting her.

"Diet. Tribe," Merwyn said. "I think we've got it."

"Stay out of this, fishtail!" a woman screeched.

"Right this way," Meryl said, flying slowly backward. The women followed, diatribing all the way.

They came to the beast of burden. In a moment they were all around him, berating him unmercifully.

"As if life isn't bad enough on its own," the beast muttered. They kept after him, fulminating constantly. The beast tried to escape by walking away, but they followed.

And the way was clear. "Thank yew," Wenda murmured, leading the rest of the party through.

Except that the moment one pun obstacle was nullified, another took its place. Now they were balked by several ogres working in a garden. One was twisting young trees into knots. Another was squeezing juice from assorted colored stones. A third, an ogress so ugly that her face resembled the rear end of a cow with diarrhea, was pruning thorn bushes. But she was not using clippers or her bare hamhands. She was carefully squeezing juice on the stems, which promptly severed.

Curious despite the danger, Wenda spoke to the ogress. "What is that you are using? It is very effective."

"Me use prune juice," the ogress said, the second and fourth words jammed into unwilling rhymes. Ogres were rough on anything, physical or intellectual.

Prune juice to prune. And why not? Ogres could squeeze juice out of anything. "Thank yew."

But this did not get them past the ogres, who blocked the way by no accident. What would distract ogres, who were justifiably proud of their stupidity?

"I will look," Hilarion said.

"Take care," Wenda said warily. In a Strip, it wasn't just the obvious that was dangerous.

He explored the vicinity, searching for suitable puns, knowing there was bound to be one if he could just fathom it and its relevance. But all he saw was a swarm of bees going about its business. It did not seem smart to mess with those.

"Could bees sting ogres?" he asked musingly, then answered himself: "If the ogres even felt it on their horny hides, they would simply smash the bees into oblivion. No chance there."

Yet there seemed to be nothing else. He studied the bees more closely. They did not seem to be gathering pollen for honey; instead they circulated around a metallic rod angling up from the ground. It was almost like a handle to some buried object or chamber.

Cautiously, he touched it. "The bee lever!" he exclaimed. "Now I am a bee lever!"

"A believer in what?" Wenda asked, not quite trusting this.

"I believe I can lead us out of here," he said. "We have merely to forge ahead with confidence."

"Unjustified confidence is dangerous," Jumper said.

"Not to a believer. My strength is as the strength of eight or nine, because my belief is pure." Hilarion marched up to the ogres. "We are looking for a Sidewalk and two Doors," he said. "Where are they?"

Dully startled, the ogres hesitated. Then one pointed to the side, where there was a wall of bushes.

"Thank you," Hilarion said. He turned to the others. "This way." He marched toward the bushes.

"It is not like him to be rash," Ida said, "so I will suppress my doubts for the nonce."

That seemed to be the best policy. Wenda and the others followed the prince.

The bushes turned out to be illusion. Beyond them was—the Sidewalk.

Wenda realized that Hilarion had played on the natural stupidity of the ogres. He had asked them a direct question, and they had been unable to think of a reason not to answer it. The bee lever had given him the confidence to do it. Such a ploy could work only once, if at all, but he had done it.

Jumper and Wenda slowly pulled the wagon to the Sidewalk, half expecting it to fade out as more illusion. But it held its place, and soon they were on it. "Turn to the right," Wenda said, conscious of the way they had gotten reversed once before. She wanted never to have to go through this again.

They sidled to the right and came up to the Door. Wenda opened it, and helped push the wagon through. The others crowded after.

But Wenda, having learned caution the hard way, made one more check: a head count. There were six.

But their party now numbered seven. Who was missing?

It was Merwyn. Inexperienced, he evidently had not realized the importance of staying together.

"I will find him," Meryl said.

"No. Yew hold the Door open," Wenda said. "I will find him." Because she knew she was the least likely person to get lost in the awful mass of puns. She would not be distracted at all.

She went, stood on the walk, and looked around. There was only the hedge of illusory bushes. She would have to go through it. That was risky.

"Silk!" Jumper said. "Take a line!" He extended a leg with a gob of spider silk on it. "So you can't get lost."

"Thank yew!" she said, taking it. Trust Jumper to come through again.

She forged through the bushes, trailing the line, which spun neatly after her as the ball in her hand thinned. And there was Merwyn. He was facing a nymphlike figure, but wasn't freaked out. Instead he was being violently ill, vomiting on the ground.

"Merwyn!" Wenda called. "Come with me!"

"I—can't," he gasped, heaving out whatever was left in his stomach. "All I can do is—heave."

"At the sight of a nymph?" Wenda demanded. "Ridiculous."

"No. Sickening," he said. "She's a flu-Z."

Wenda had heard of them. They were nymphs who delighted in flashing their panties, not to freak out men, but to give them flu-like symptoms. They delighted in sickening men to death, if they could. This one must have intercepted Merwyn as he was bringing up the rear, and taken him out with her stomach-flu magic. She was bending over, flashing her mottled bilious green panties, which had a large scarlet letter Z on them.

It was time for firm action. Wenda could not be affected by such a sight, both because she was female and because she was wood. She strode to the flu-Z, picked her up, and hurled her into the grunge of ogres. She landed in her normal position, panties up.

"See shee!" one male exclaimed, just before he got sick. Then the ogress swung her hamfist and knocked the flu-Z right out of the Strip. She knew how to handle competition.

Wenda grabbed Merwyn's hand and hauled him

back the way she had come. The illusion hedge seemed to have put forth new branches to confuse her, and would have succeeded, except for the silk line. She followed that, tuning out most else.

And there was the Sidewalk. She had been half afraid it would vanish behind her, as she did not know how long it remained in any one place.

"Sidle," she said urgently, guiding him. He shuffled along on his tail flukes, not really understanding. Fortunately he was still too sick to think for himself.

She pushed him through the doorway, and followed. "All here?" she asked.

"All present," Jumper reassured her.

She yanked the Door shut behind her and stood against it, her hollow wooden knees feeling as weak as flesh. "Then we are safe."

"Perhaps," Hilarion said.

Wenda did not much like the sound of that. "There is a problem?"

"There may be," Jumper said, rewinding the last of his ball of silk. "We are in very strange country."

"Just so long as it's Xanth," she said, "we can handle it." Had she been less distracted, she might have wondered why the others lacked confidence.

14

MAIDENS

Wenda gazed out across a small pleasant valley with a lake in the center, surrounded by giant trees. To one side was a little human village, and near it was an outlying collection of huts. There seemed to be just a single road out, passing through the village, around the lake, and between the steep slopes of a narrow pass.

"What is strange about this country?" she asked.

"We did a winged reconnaissance," Meryl said. "That lake is a love spring. Those large trees are tangle trees or some closely related species; they're not quite the same. The villagers . . . are weird."

"This is an isolated hamlet," Wenda said. "They could have special conventions. It does knot matter, as we will knot be staying long."

"No one is leaving the valley," Jumper said. "And the way the villagers interact with the trees—maybe you should see it for yourself. I found a spectacle bush and made a spyglass." He handed her a crude tubular device with lenses at each end.

She took it and peered through it. It magnified the scene enormously. Suddenly she could see right into the village, as though the people were within speaking distance. They were oddly garbed, with shirts and flaring short skirts, male, female, and child alike. The tangle trees grew right around the village, yet the villagers did not seem concerned. "Must bee mock-tanglers," Wenda said. She had encountered plants that mimicked more fearsome plants, for their own protection. The plants of the forest were just as varied and devious as were the creatures.

"Keep watching," Jumper said.

She did. She saw a village man walk right under a tangle tree. The tree sent its tentacles down and wrapped them around the man, lifting him from the ground. The man did not struggle as the tree enfolded him in its foliage. He disappeared into it with seeming equanimity. That was indeed odd.

"Drugs!" Wenda said. "Are the villagers drugged? Or is there a pacification spell?"

"Not that we can see," Jumper said. "Keep watching."

"But the tangler has eaten the man!"

"Not exactly."

After a brief time, the foliage rustled and the man emerged. He seemed unchanged. The tentacles set him gently on the ground and withdrew. He walked back into the village.

"It let him go!" Wenda exclaimed. "It did knot eat him!"

"That is what is strange," Jumper said. "We have seen several examples. The villagers seem to offer themselves to the trees, and the trees take them, then return them unharmed."

"This is knot the nature of tangle trees!" Wenda protested.

"So we conclude that they are not exactly tanglers," Jumper said. "But surely closely related."

"Why should the tree even take the villager, if it's knot going to eat him?"

"That is the mystery," Hilarion said. "We do not care to enter that village until we understand."

"Lest it turn out that the trees inspect all passers, but eat only strangers," Ida said.

That did make a kind of sense. "I agree," Wenda said. "This is a strange country."

"We note that those outlying shacks are not near the trees," Merwyn said. "We might talk with those folk."

But he was looking pale and weak from his siege of Z flu. "I will dew it," Wenda said.

"We did not mean for you to risk yourself," Meryl said. "Merwyn and I can do it, and fly away if there is danger."

"No. It is my responsibility. I wood knot have someone else take such a risk."

"Then I will go with you, to guard you," Hilarion said.

She was constrained to agree. She had seen how expertly he used his sword. The two of them walked down to the shacks, which were not far, being at the edge of the valley.

They reached the closest shack. "Hello!" Wenda called.

A man emerged. She was relieved to see that he was conventionally garbed, rather than skirted. "Ah—new refugees," he said. "You must be perplexed."

"We are," Wenda said. "I am Wenda Woodwife, and this is Hilarion. We landed here randomly, and wonder about the villagers and the trees."

"I will explain about them in due course," the man said. "But first I would prefer to get to know you. Let's exchange stories."

"Briefly," Hilarion said.

"Briefly," the man agreed.

"I am on a mission for the Good Magician, to deliver a boulder of petrified reverse wood," Wenda said. "I have several companions. We used a magic portal that put us here. Now we are knot sure it is safe to use the trail out of this valley."

"You are correct to be wary," the man agreed. "I am Michael. I was once a carefree adolescent, doing whatever evoked my fancy. I discovered a giant trapeze, so my friends and I were using it to swing through the air. But suddenly I was attacked by a hot tomato. It splattered my shirt, setting me afire. I fell, burning, only to be struck by a boulder hit by a baseball-playing ogre using an ironwood tree as a bat. Scorched and broken, I fell into a healing spring I hadn't known about. That enabled me to recover, and soon I was back on my feet. But the experience left me with two things that changed my life. First, I now have the talent to heal with my hands, having absorbed so much of the elixir. Second, I am trapped in this valley, unable to escape."

"What is it that stops you from departing?" Hilarion asked.

"That is the thing about this valley," Michael said. "Have you noticed how a few of us reside apart from the regular villagers?"

"This is why we approached yew," Wenda said. "There is something strange about those villagers."

"There is indeed."

"It occurred to us that the tangle trees might spare villagers but eat strangers," Hilarion said.

"Not so. They will treat you exactly the same. You are in no physical danger here."

"No physical danger?"

"There's the rub. Some few of us do not care to be subjected to the emotional danger entailed."

"Emotional danger?"

"You have seen the villager apparel? Not for nothing is the village named Scoop."

"They all wear skirts. Even the men."

"Precisely. And nothing under those skirts."

"Why?" Wenda asked.

"It facilitates production for the trees."

"I dew knot understand."

"At some time in the past near a love spring a tangle tree crossed with a call-to-nature bush. The result was a crossbreed we call the toilet tree. That variety prefers animal manure. Am I clear?"

"No," Wenda said.

"It is the normal custom for all animals, including people, to eat, drink, and produce natural wastes. The trees crave those wastes. So they trade security for those wastes."

"I still dew knot—"

"Poop!" Hilarion exclaimed. "From Scoop!"

"Precisely. The tree collects it and lets the person go. It seems to be a compatible exchange, for those who are amenable. Some of us are not."

Wenda found herself blushing as she figured it out, though in her present state she was not vulnerable to the tree's demands. "So when the tree picked up that man, it made him . . . give it his wastes. That was all it wanted."

"We would not care to become part of that system," Hilarion said.

"Unfortunately you will not have much choice. The trees guard the exit trail. They intercept anyone trying to use it. They have elixirs that will make any person perform urgently. They will hold him suspended until he performs. So to try to depart is to find oneself abruptly contributing. If his clothing interferes, too bad. Then they put the emptied person back in the village. That is why we don't try to escape, though we wish we could. It is a matter of emotional preference."

"But we have a mission to complete," Wenda protested.

"The trees don't care. They see people as mere content providers."

"Thank yew," Wenda said tightly. "We must return to our group and consult."

"Welcome," Michael said. "If you find a way to escape without humiliation, by all means let us know. We will be happy to cooperate in any way we can."

Wenda and Hilarion returned to the group and explained the situation. "This is disgusting," Ida said.

"We must find a way safely out," Jumper said. "Three of us can fly, but the rest of us need a strategy."

They discussed it, and Meryl came up with a suggestion. "That's a love spring in the center," she said. "Suppose those of us who can fly take buckets and carefully dip out the elixir, then dump it on the trees and villagers? It may make them both eager to interact in their special manner, and that could distract them long enough for us to use the trail out."

"That could work," Ida said, though she looked a bit pained. This was not the kind of subject princesses normally discussed, and the idea was far-fetched. But it was possible that the trees and villagers had a particular kind of love of their own. Ida's agreement made it more likely.

"Let's dew it," Wenda agreed. It might be risky, but no more so than remaining captives of the valley.

The three fliers flew down to talk to the nonvillagers, and soon were able to borrow buckets. Meanwhile the four groundbound members of the party eased the malign Knot down the slope to the shacks. "Dew knot be afraid of Jumper," Wenda said. "He is a tame spider."

"Thank you for advising us," Michael said, maintaining his distance from the spider. "Here are the other valley captives: Shenita Life Guard, whose talent is to warn people of trouble next day, so they can escape it. But she can't warn of trouble today, or warn a person more than once. So far she has been confined to warning us against attempting the escape."

"But if you can do it today, maybe it will work," Shenita said. She was a well-structured woman, evidently used to helping out at beaches. Wenda wondered how she had gotten trapped here. Maybe her talent did not apply to herself. "I did not see you coming, because you are not bringing trouble."

"And Metro Gnome," Michael continued, indicating a gnome. "He is very time-oriented."

The gnome nodded, his motions precisely timed.

"And Care," Michael said, introducing a cautious-looking woman. "As long as you walk with her, nothing bad happens."

"But evidently fate does not consider what the trees do with villagers to be bad," Care said.

"Still, it will bee good to know that other bad things can knot happen," Wenda said.

The three fliers were up in the sky. They flew over the trees and dumped their buckets, whose liquid twisted, spread out, and became writhing clouds that splatted into the foliage. Then the three flew down to the lake and dipped again.

"We must wait until they finish with the villagers," Wenda said. Because of course they did not want their own party to get doused.

The three doused the villagers. Immediately they flocked to the trees and were taken in by the tentacles and foliage. "Now," Wenda said.

They moved smartly along, pulling and pushing on the wagon. The un-villagers wanted to help, but could not bring themselves to get close to the Knot. Hilarion, Jumper, and Ida had built up a certain tolerance, though they did not look comfortable.

They moved through the village. No one bothered them. But the worst of it was ahead, at the pass. It would be uphill, and with the tangle trees overhanging. If they had calculated wrong, they would be in trouble. Even if fate did not consider it so.

They approached the first tree along the trail. Michael, Shenita, Metro and Care edged closer to the wagon despite their fear. It was a question of which they feared more: the Knot or humiliation.

The tree's tentacles quivered, but did not descend. It was aware of them, but busy elsewhere. There was evidently only so much content it could handle at a time. Maybe it had only one content pot.

They slowly pushed on. They passed the first tree and approached the second. Again the tentacles twitched, but did not descend.

There was one more tree to pass. As they pushed by its tentacles, Shenita thought of something. They all saw the bulb flash over her head. "That horrible Knot!" she exclaimed. "It is driving away the trees!"

Wenda felt her wooden jaw drop. Of course! The Knot radiated constant malignancy. Tangle trees were wood, but very special wood, and their conscious, mobile tentacles must be subject to the Knot's effect. They could have rolled the wagon through any time. Maybe the love spring deluge helped, but maybe it didn't. The Knot had saved them. That surely infuriated it.

They moved on into the pass. They had escaped the valley and village of Scoop. Without becoming content providers.

As they descended the other side of the pass, now having to hold the wagon back so it wouldn't lurch ahead and crash, the three flying members of their party rejoined them.

"We are grateful," Michael said. "What return favor may we do you?"

"There is no need," Wenda demurred. "You provided the buckets, and Care surely helped keep us safe as we went."

"I will walk with you farther," Care said. "At least until we reach a village where you can safely rest."

"There will be a castle in precisely 2.35 hours," Metro said. "I do not know whether it is safe."

"It associates with a Demon," Shenita said. "But I foresee no mischief on the morrow if you stay there."

"You folk are already being very helpful," Hilarion said, "just by your presence."

"Why would a Demon have a castle here?" Ida asked.

"I certainly wood like to know," Wenda said. "But if it is safe for us, that is what counts."

They moved on, and in 2.35 hours they reached the castle. It was tall and windswept, with tassels flying at its towers.

"I wood like to bee in a safe castle overnight," Wenda said. "Recent adventures have been wearing. How dew the rest of yew feel?"

"Much the same," Hilarion said. "Though I remain nervous about entering a Demon castle."

"I wonder if I should change to manform?" Jumper asked.

"Save yewr magic," Wenda said. "If they dew knot accept yew, I will knot accept their hospitality either."

"Good compromise," Ida agreed.

Wenda lifted the ornate metal knocker and knocked on the massive oaken front door. In barely more than a moment it opened. There stood a lovely, dark-haired, dark-eyed princess.

"Wenda!" she exclaimed, hugging Wenda. "Jumper!" She hugged the big spider too. "Aunt Ida! And friends."

It was Princess Eve.

"But I thought yew married Demon Pluto and went

to the underworld," Wenda said, belatedly taken aback. "I saw yew briefly at the Demon Trial of Demoness Eris. Yew made Pluto vote to save her—and me."

"I did. I could not let either of you be doomed. You're my friend, and Eris is Jumper's wife, and Jumper is my friend too." Eve smiled briefly. "And Pluto has learned not to cross me when there is something I care about. But I am mortal, at least in background. I wanted a mortal castle as well, for summer guests and such. So I am renovating the old Storm King's residence, Castle Windswept. Come in, come in! I am so glad to see some familiar faces."

Wenda understood. As Jumper had discovered, a mortal who married a Demon became immortal. But a mortal remained mortal in outlook, with mortal tastes. Eve had been part of Jumper's party, as had Wenda, and they had come to know each other well. In fact, Eve had seduced Jumper, with no ill intent, and given him a fraction of her soul. They surely still loved each other to a degree.

They paused to introduce the rest of the party, which had grown to eleven. The Scoop Valley escapees seemed diffident, but Wenda and Jumper reassured them that Princess Eve was to be trusted. She wanted to show off the premises.

Wenda explained about the Knot. "We will need to park it somewhere safe, and knot too close to people," Wenda concluded.

"We have a fine nether dungeon guarded by an ill-tempered dragon," Eve said.

"A dungeon and a dragon," Wenda agreed. "That should bee fine, if the dragon can stand it."

They entered the castle, discovering magnificent wood-paneled hallways with pictures of storms, fires, floods, and other wind inspired activities. Eve had not remade the castle, but restored it to its former grandeur. It carried an aura of century-old times.

"Let's see," Eve said. "I have restored nine guest suites, but there are eleven of you. Someone will have to double up, I'm sorry to say."

"We are a couple," Meryl said, indicating Merwyn. "We will share."

"Of course," Eve agreed. "That means only one extra. Aunt Ida, will you join me in the Mistress Suite? My husband is in Hades at the moment and I shall be glad to have the company. You can catch me up on events at Castle Roogna since I left."

"I will," Ida agreed.

Servants appeared, lesser demons garbed as footmen, butlers, maids, and hostesses. Wenda realized they were probably denizens of Hades, allowed topside as long as they behaved. Eve was now Mistress of Hades. She was a Sorceress in her own right, but this was special authority.

Each member of their party was shown to his or her guest suite, which was a cluster of rooms including a magic kitchenette and lavatory. Wenda suspected that despite its seeming age, this was as modern a facility as existed in Xanth.

Wenda had a nice bubble bath, which she really appreciated, because her rear half had gotten soiled and her hollow frontside was clogged with debris. A maid helped scrub her and fit her with fresh clothing, neatly padded in front. Eve had known her in her woodwife state, so understood her needs.

Then they attended a sumptuous banquet with many courses. The waiters brought Wenda steaming platters containing nothing, understanding that she didn't need to eat. But the others feasted.

Wenda saw Ida, seated beside Eve, murmur something to her as the meal finished. Eve smiled, then made an announcement. "Dusk is nigh. There will be a pause of seven minutes before the evening dance." Eve understood about the needs of visiting male companions too.

Just in time. The Demoness Eris appeared with several companions. Before temporary compartments formed, Wenda saw that Eris was garbed like one of the exotic May I women whose appearance had tempted Jumper, showing just as much flesh. But her body was closer to the shape of that of Princess Eve. She was teasing Jumper for his past imagination or activity.

Then Wenda was alone with Charming, who made short work of her fresh clothing. Fortunately the stuffed bra was of superior design, and withstood his attention until Wenda turned around. He wasn't even curious about the castle; his whole attention was on Wenda. She decided that was flattering.

In seven minutes he was asleep and gone, and things reverted to the way they had been just before the visiting party arrived. The Scoop Valley folk were neither surprised nor dismayed; they were not aware that any time had passed.

Now the evening dance proceeded. Competent demon partners guided each member of the party, and it worked well. There was even a demoness jumping spider for Jumper, who still had not changed. She was so competent that Wenda suspected that Eris had quietly taken her place.

Other demons served punch, a tasty drink that was like boot rear, except that it socked the drinker in the front.

When the dance was done, they retired to their suites, pleasantly tired. Wenda dropped onto her bed and slept, though ordinarily as a woodwife she did not need to.

In the morning there was a royal breakfast. Eve was evidently pleased to be able to entertain, being mistress of her castle. She was making it a point to get to know each of the visitors. During breakfast she tackled Prince Hilarion, eliciting his story.

"So your betrothee should be about twenty or twenty-one," she said.

"Yes."

"I am twenty."

He smiled. "I would dearly like to find a princess like you, beautiful and a Sorceress. But you are already taken."

"But my twin sister Dawn isn't. I know all about anything I touch that is not alive. She knows all about anything she touches that is alive. She is as lovely as I am, only she has bright-red hair and green eyes. I am a spirit of evening; she is a spirit of morning. And she remains single."

Wenda could see Hilarion's interest quickening. "Could she have gotten betrothed young?"

"I am not aware of it. But it is possible. We have always been mischievous, and she might have liked your look."

"I would like to meet her. To kiss her."

"To verify her," Wenda said quickly. "He will know his betrothee when he kisses her."

"Dawn remains at Castle Roogna. Once you complete Wenda's mission, you must stop there. That might complete your personal Quest."

"I shall be sure to find my way there."

"I will be glad to guide you there," Ida said. "I will be returning there."

"Thank you, Ida," he said. "Then I will guide you to my home kingdom, to meet my uncle. With luck, we both will find our fulfillments."

"With luck," Ida agreed, though she seemed unconvinced.

"But first we must deliver the Knot," Wenda said. "Can yew tell us the most direct route there from here?"

"I can," Eve agreed. "But there are constraints."

Wenda sighed. "There always are. I wood knot expect it to bee entirely easy."

"What constraints?" Jumper asked.

"The maidens."

"Maidens?"

"Between here and there is Maiden Country. You might prefer to route around that."

"What is constraining about maidens?" Jumper asked.

Eve glanced sidelong at him. "You have not noticed?"

But Jumper was in spider form, largely immune to her potent flirtations. "Do they mean ill?"

"No. They are very nice. But they will seek to involve you in their projects."

"We will simply pass through," Wenda said firmly. "No side projects."

"As you wish," Eve said, subtly amused.

The Scoop Valley escapees thanked Eve and departed, seeking their homes after their captivity. Then Wenda's group thanked her too, and set out toward the Good Magician's Castle, which was only about a day's travel away.

"What do you think Princess Eve meant about the Maidens?" Hilarion asked.

"It is not like Eve to be obscure," Ida said. "Perhaps there are social complications."

The path led to the edge of the great Gap Chasm. "We have been here before," Jumper remarked.

"But we dew knot need to cross it," Wenda said. "We are south of it, and so is the Good Magician's Castle."

"Then we should have no problem," Hilarion said.

Wenda wished Angela or Meryl had said it, because then Ida could have agreed and made it so. As it was, they were at some subtle unexplained risk. Wenda was developing a distaste for that sort of thing, especially after Scoop Valley. All she wanted at this point was to deliver the Knot and be done with it.

The path entered a cultivated region with many types of vegetables growing. Someone was maintaining a garden. In fact there was a woman working there, watering a section. She looked up as they passed.

"Why, it is Princess Ida!" the woman exclaimed.

"The Maiden Taiwan!" Ida responded. "I had no idea you lived here!"

"Oh, I do, along with my sisters Japan and Mexico," Taiwan said. "We generally prefer privacy, so our domicile is invisible and partly hidden in the Gap. But we know you, Ida, and have admired your sorceries for decades. I would recognize that orbiting planet anywhere."

And of course that did identify Ida. The Maiden Taiwan evidently had had no difficulty penetrating Ida's disguise. That suggested there was something special about her.

Could she be one of the Maidens Eve had warned them about? Yet surely a friend of Ida's would not be any trouble.

"I am glad to see you again, Taiwan," Ida said politely. "I gather this is what you do in the time you are not married to Magician Humfrey."

"That is correct. Humfrey rescued five and a half of us from Hell. Actually I was just visiting the others at the time, having established my own base elsewhere. But he does need someone to tend to him. After all, he is 177 years old. He covers it up with spot doses of youth elixir, but he does get grumpy and forgetful. He can't even keep track of his socks."

"And how old are you, Taiwan?" Ida inquired gently.

"One hundred and seventy-six. But age wears better on a woman."

"One hundred and seventy-six!" Wenda exclaimed, astonished. "Yew look thirty!"

"And who do you think handles Humfrey's supply of youth elixir?" Taiwan asked archly. "None of us look our age." She returned to Ida. "We must catch up on old times. Come, you and your party, accept our hospitality this day and night. We have excellent accommodations."

"But we are on our way to the Good Magician's Castle now," Wenda protested. "We wood knot want to impose."

"I insist," Taiwan said, and there was something in her tone that hinted slightly of her age and more than slightly of her iron will. They were going to visit with her, like it or not.

Wenda sighed. She was beginning to understand Princess Eve's quiet amusement. As a neighbor, she must have experienced this. Foes could be fought, but not well-meaning friends.

Jumper tried to intervene. "As you can see, I am not human. And the Knot we are transporting is not at all nice. You would not want it in your home."

Taiwan oriented on the Knot. "Fascinating," she breathed. "Genuine petrified reverse wood. I must study this."

Which was worse. They were evidently stuck for it.

Taiwan ushered them into her invisible house. As a courtesy, she waved her hand, and the walls appeared, scintillating in pastels. It was a mansion with many levels, far more elaborate than anything short of a palace. How could an incidental part-time wife manage this?

They rolled the wagon into an attached shelter and closed it in. The Knot would be secure for the duration.

"And here are my sisters, the Maidens Japan and Mexico," Taiwan said as two more women of her seeming age appeared. "We share the residence compatibly. Now come and settle in, and we will exchange life histories."

Life histories! That would take something short of forever. "No need!" Wenda said desperately.

"I am sure each of you has a fascinating story," Taiwan said, settling them in couches. For Jumper there was a weblike structure he could cling to with all eight legs. She was being a good hostess.

Soon they were eating delicious snacks and telling their stories. The three Maidens were enthusiastically fascinated, even applauding at the more intriguing parts, such as when Jumper had encountered the Demoness Eris and married her, and the way Wenda had been saved by the Demoness because of friendship, and then seen Eris put on Demon trial for interference, and Meryl's finding Merwyn. Wenda had to admit that their stories did seem more interesting when told to this rapt audience.

There was a curious turn when Hilarion recited his search for his betrothee. "I remember," Taiwan said. "You passed by here, and kissed all three of us. We didn't have the heart to tell you how old we were. We could not possibly be the one for whom you search. But you do kiss well, and we enjoyed it. You were a perfect guest, very courtly."

"I do not remember this," Hilarion said, disconcerted.

"I understand you had a later brush with a forget whorl. That would account for it."

"It would," Hilarion said. "When was this? Last year?"

"More like a decade ago. You have had a long search."

Hilarion was silent, obviously perplexed. Wenda could appreciate why. He had been searching for a decade?

Then it was the Maidens' turn. And again Wenda had to admit it was a most interesting personal history. She closed her eyes and saw the three Maidens as they had been historically.

Once upon a time in Mundania there lived three beautiful ladies who were also extremely bright and shared a love of science, specifically physics, chemistry, and computer science. But apart from their passion for technology, their lives were miserable. Because they were beautiful, boys and then men were constantly seeking their company. The boys and men hardly cared about their minds or the content of their character; they simply wanted to get their hands on those bodies. Especially their upper fronts and lower backs. This annoyed the Maidens, for no reason they could get the men to understand.

Worse, it was a time in Mundania when women were not expected to have serious occupations, let alone scientific ones. They faced constant discrimination in a male-dominated world of school and science.

Then things changed, to a degree. The three of them had lived in their respective Mundane countries, but had applied for scholarships elsewhere, hoping to discover a more enlightened society. They received scholarships to attend colleges at the same university: Squeedunk, where Magician Grey would go years later. It was largely unknown, and trying to establish its credits, so was generous with grants to students showing real promise around the world. Including women. That showed how desperate it was.

They flourished there, advancing to the top of their classes. Their prospects for finding work remained meager, because of their gender, but at least they had hope.

They met each other during Spring Break of their senior year at a popular resort in Florida, which was somewhat like Xanth, only without much magic. They compared notes, discovering a striking similarity of experience. It wasn't that they didn't like men, it was that they wanted men to like them for their brains instead of their torsos, and no man even inquired—other than some professors, who actually turned out to be interested in the same thing, as a side dish. And of course the professors were married.

They decided to form a sisterhood, where they would pool their expertise and form their own company upon graduation, to create truly extraordinary inventions. They would enlist a few men to serve as figureheads for the company, so it would be accepted by other companies. There would be no problem enlisting the men; all they had to do was grant some limited access to their torsos, and the men would cooperate completely. If the men got inconvenient ideas, a little more access would freak them out, bringing them back under control. They were converting the disadvantage of male tunnel vision to an advantage.

Alas, fate intervened. The airplane they took to return to college encountered severe wind shear from a mundane cousin of Cumulo Fracto Nimbus, and exploded in a spectacular fireball when it smashed into the runway.

At the last possible second, a minor Demoness from Xanth assumed the form of a female leprechaun, stopped time on board the airplane, and talked to the terrified Maidens.

The Demoness, Nan O'Tek, was more than capable of building things from atoms by mere thought. But she had no creativity whatsoever, so could not usefully participate in the games that Demons played against one another for power and status. Nan saw the impending crash of these three talented and creative girls to be a meaningless waste, and offered them a deal: an oath of lifetime loyalty to her, in exchange for a rescue and an excellent life to come. The girls made the oath and were spirited off the plane the instant before impact. No one in Mundania knew.

Nan helped the girls set up shop in the Gap Wilderness, unknown to others. The four of them pooled their knowledge and power to selectively breed the small indus-trees they collected across the Gap. They developed a giant and robust breed of trees called Heavy Industrees, which were capable of producing massive amounts of refined materials such as steel or plastic, in a completely nonpolluting manner.

The girls designed their first atomic assembler, which

they named after their patron, called a Nan O'Assembler. An array of assemblers took the refined materials from the heavy industrees to create all manner of useful non-magical products and toys to be marketed across Xanth and Mundania.

Thus was devised the first, if secret, Xanth company, the Mai-Den Corporation Industrial Park. It was chartered by King Ebnez, and proved to be a source of untold wealth for the Maidens, and a source of ideas for Nan O'Tek. It later became the primary armorer for the King of Xanth and his Army. Others in Xanth never knew or questioned the source.

Given time and virtually unlimited resources to explore the limits of science in the magic realm of Xanth, the Maiden Japan designed and created the ornery self-willed contraption known as Com Pewter.

"Com Pewter!" Ida exclaimed. "He is notorious!"

"Imperfect, I know," the Maiden Japan said modestly. "It was a learning process. I could do better today, but my interests are elsewhere."

Wenda was amazed. These largely unknown Maidens had become virtual Sorceresses.

"Taiwan, didn't you marry the Good Magician at some point?" Ida asked.

"Why, yes. It seemed like a good career move at the time, especially considering our work for prior kings," Taiwan agreed. "But then he abdicated the throne, ruining the connection, and I had to abdicate the marriage. Then later I was visiting my sisters in Hell, when Humfrey rescued us all. So I had to accept remarriage, fortunately on a part-time basis. It really isn't bad. We do a good deal of work for Humfrey now too. He's one man who can keep a secret."

"So you work for the king and the Good Magician," Ida said. "That must keep you busy."

"Not really. We tackle other projects that interest us.

For example a knowledgeable engineer in Mundania wanted to design a ship of space that would travel to Alpha Centauri. He had made a deal with the centaurs, but had a problem delivering because they wanted it to travel faster than light. Science forbids that, for some reason, so he had to go to magic. That was where we came in."

"A ship—to another star—faster than light?" Jumper asked, intrigued. "How could that be done?"

"It requires use of the Magic Law of Similarity," Taiwan said. "Suppose you have a sheet of space-time fabric, actually called the ether, upon which you impose a map of the universe. Since the centaur's ship is part of the universe, it will be shown on that fabric. Then—"

But Wenda was unable to follow it any further. It was vastly too technical for her. And, she suspected, for the others. So she just smiled and nodded as if she understood, and let it go at that.

Time passed. At one point they gathered around the Knot, the three Maidens approaching it as closely as they could, intrigued by the fear and disgust it inspired. "There is a lot of power there," the Maiden Mexico said.

"We could take it off your hands," the Maiden Japan said. "We would like to study it at length."

"No," Wenda said firmly. "It must go to the Good Magician's Castle. Only then will our mission bee done."

The Maiden Taiwan nodded. "I will see it there, in due course. That will do."

Then Eris was there, bringing the nuptial visitors, so Wenda knew it was evening.

"Those Maidens are intriguing," Eris remarked. "I understand their sister, the Maiden China, survived in Mundania, and now is showing her power there."

"Things are more complicated than I ever suspected," Wenda said.

"Well, yes, of course. Few folk even suspect the real

sources of power or information, in Xanth or Mundania. That is perhaps just as well."

"Just as well," Wenda agreed, realizing that they were talking while their males were busy with their bodies. Wenda was really coming to appreciate her incidental discussions with the Demoness.

"Thank you," Eris said, leaving Jumper asleep. Then she collected the other sleeping males and disappeared. "You have, I think, just one more day before your mission is complete."

What a relief that would be! "Thank yew," Wenda said as the Demoness faded.

15

FULFILLMENT

In the morning they were on their way, the Knot freshly clothed in the last of the reverse-wood chips. The Maidens had promised that there would be no more delays; the way to the Good Magician's Castle was clear. They were in a position to know, as they used it often.

Wenda had to admit that the Maidens had not been bad. Their history was interesting, teaching Wenda much about Xanth that she had neither known nor suspected. They had been good hosts, and Wenda and the party were refreshed. Even the Knot had benefited, as a Maiden had managed to approach close enough to apply some grease to the wagon's axles, and it was rolling more smoothly.

About the only unpleased member of their party was the Knot itself. It knew that delivery was incipient, and it hated that. Wenda had no sympathy.

"We are at last nearing the conclusion of our mission," Hilarion said as he helped Ida pull the wagon. They were taking turns, as the chore became tiring after a while.

Wenda was walking beside the Knot, being the one best able to tolerate its malevolence.

"We are," Ida agreed.

"I wanted to say that I almost hope that Princess Dawn, however beautiful and talented she may be, is not my betrothee."

"But Hilarion, I know her," Ida protested. "She is a fine young woman, and an outstanding Sorceress. You could hardly find a better match."

"There is the key: she is young."

"She and her sister have been known to be mischievous, even naughty on occasion," Ida said. "But in a manner you would surely appreciate. I understand they teased Jumper, when he was in manform, something awful, flashing their panties when he was bare."

"They did," Wenda agreed. She had been there. Those panties had just about set fire to the landscape.

"But that relates to the impetuosity of youth," Ida continued. "As they age, their mature potentials will emerge. Eve is already showing hers. And Dawn—she was the one who realized how to save the Demoness Eris by making Jumper the Prince of Spiders. Eris had to marry a prince, you see. Dawn would make any man a very fine wife."

"I have no doubt of it," Hilarion said. "But the problem is with me. In the course of this mission I have come to know you, Princess Ida. I realize that you, too, are a full Sorceress, with powers unimaginable to ordinary folk. But setting that aside, and with no affront intended to the women of this party, you are still more woman than any I have known. You have shown me what a woman can be, and that is like a Sorceress compared to the incidental magic of an ordinary girl. When I finally discover my betrothee, I fear I will see a girl, when what I now desire is a woman. You may have spoiled me for her."

"Oh, Hilarion, I'm sorry! I never thought . . . I never meant to—"

"Of course you are innocent of any evil intent," he said quickly. "That is part of your mature nature. It is your very presence, your essential nature, that has educated me and made me see beyond the mere appearance of a girl. It is definitely not your fault. It merely explains my attitude."

"I am not sure I understand." But Wenda could see that Ida was at least on the verge of understanding. She just did not want to acknowledge it.

"If Dawn is not the one, I will then have a pretext to continue looking. To travel with you, Princess Ida, as we have agreed. To keep further company with you."

"This is foolish," Ida said. "You must find your betrothee."

"Yes. But I try to be honest with all people, myself included. I would be satisfied to look for some time yet, in your company."

The tears flowed down Ida's face. "So would I," she whispered.

"I am glad to hear it."

"You are young, yet you exemplify princely qualities of courage, commitment, and nobility that I fear have similarly spoiled me for my own man, once I find him. I doubt he will be better in such respects than you, and I will be aware of the lack."

"It is ironic," he said. "We have nothing but the greatest respect for each other, and this is perhaps our tragedy. To mess up each other's lives by sowing dissatisfaction."

"Unfortunately true," Ida agreed.

Their dialogue lapsed, leaving Wenda to ponder. What each had said was true: they were in key respects ideal for each other. It was too bad they were of different generations, destined for other relationships. Each needed to find a companion of his or her own age.

By noon they crested a hill, and there before them, in the next valley, was the Good Magician's Castle. It was all downhill from here.

They paused for lunch, relaxing, basking in the near completion of the arduous chore. The Knot radiated so violently that already the morning's shield of fresh reverse wood was curling.

"Something the Maiden Taiwan said," Hilarion remarked as he sat beside Wenda. "Could I have been searching for ten years?"

"Yew did run afoul of that forget whorl," Wenda reminded him.

"I did. I thought it was merely a glancing blow, as it were. But now I am almost beginning to remember."

Ida came up on his other side. "You remember? That suggests that you are older than you seem."

"I may be," he agreed. "I do remember that when I set out to find my betrothee, I invoked a spell to freeze my age, as a matter of convenience. I will revert to my current age, whatever that may be, once my Quest is complete."

"Assuming that the Maiden Taiwan's memory is accurate," Jumper said, "you have been at it for at least a decade, and probably longer. There's no telling how long a span that forget whorl wiped out."

"True," Hilarion agreed. "But I think that dose of forgetting is wearing thin. Perhaps the Knot or its sheathing is affecting it, reversing it."

"Try standing closer to it, if yew can," Wenda suggested.

Hilarion did. He got up and stood nervously close to the boulder. "It—it *was* longer," he said. "Twenty years."

"But that wood make yew forty," Wenda said.

"Forty-two. I remember now."

"Forty-two!" Ida said, startled. "I am forty-one."

He gazed at her with a dawning surmise. "Is it possible?"

"Yew can readily find out," Wenda said. "Kiss her."

"I never thought of you in that way," Hilarion said to Ida. "I thought you were well outside the age my betrothee had to be. Now I feel almost guilty. But yes, I would like to kiss you, Princess Ida."

But now Ida demurred. "It still seems far-fetched. I would hate to spoil our compatible relationship by proving that there is no match."

He considered that, and nodded. "I agree. It is not a worthwhile risk. There needs to be some further indication. We need to believe that it could be the case, before risking the refutation of it."

"Your memory," Meryl said. "It came back for your age. Surely you knew the name of your betrothee. Can you remember that?"

Hilarion concentrated. "Yes, it is coming back. An odd name. Nirp, I believe. Adissec Nirp."

"She must be from a far kingdom," Jumper said.

"I know of no one by that name," Ida said sadly. Wenda realized that she had just started to entertain the idea that they might be for each other, only to have it dashed by his further memory.

"I have an idea," Angela said. "Hilarion went close to the Knot to remember. It is made of old reverse wood, with a sheathing of new reverse wood. Could his memory of the name be reversed?"

The others stared at her. Then Wenda smoothed a place in the dirt and printed out the name, backward, letter by letter. P-R-I-N-C-E-S-S I-D-A. "Princess Ida!"

"It *is* you!" Hilarion cried.

"Then perhaps we should . . ." Ida said, blushing.

"Oh, yes! To verify." Ever a man of action, he stepped up to her, gently enfolded her, and kissed her.

There was a coruscation of brilliance from the touching of their lips that radiated out to brighten the scene, warming them all. It intersected Ida's moon, causing it to radiate a burst of colors. The ground glowed, and the nearby trees, and then the sky itself. It caught Wenda, warming her hollow frontside and to a lesser degree her backside. A giant beating heart formed, scintillating in rainbow colors, enclosing them in the center. Pastel hues coursed through it, making a fog of sparkles. The world faded out, leaving only that picture in the center.

There was the swamp where Princess Ida had lived. A stork flew low, carrying a double load. A stray wind buffeted it, and it almost crashed. It fluttered its wings valiantly and managed to recover elevation. But the content of one of the bundles rolled out and splashed into the water. By the time the stork realized what had happened, and turned back, the baby was gone. The stork had to go on with the one bundle it retained. There was after all a delivery to make on a tight schedule.

That baby was Ida, and she had been rescued by a passing nymph from the adjacent Faun & Nymph Retreat. The nymph took her to the retreat, where the others paused in their ongoing celebrations and clustered around admiringly. They had no memory of ever seeing a baby before, but they instantly adored it. They collected milkweed pods and fed the baby, and swaddled it in warm ferns. Baby care came naturally to them.

As the day ended, the fauns and nymphs settled down for sleep, as they normally did. They left the baby in a comfortable nest with plenty of milk, intending to return to her in the morning.

But fauns and nymphs have no memory of the past. Each day is completely new to them. They completely forgot about the baby.

Fortunately the nearest neighbors were benign water dwellers, the otterbees. One spied the isolated bundle, and investigated. Then the friendly creature, knowing the forgetful nature of nymphs, did what it otter, and took her to its den. There the mama otterbee did what she otter, and dried and swaddled the baby in soft dry leaves. The otters took care of her in the following year, teaching her to swim, then to crawl, then to walk. She was human, so they taught her the human language. They took very good care of her.

When she was a year old, a party from a far island came. Their magic had shown them that the ideal bride for their two-year-old son was here. So they set the little boy, Prince Hilarion, down beside Princess Ida and held a ceremony of betrothal.

"She's a princess?" the otterbees asked, amazed.

"And a Sorceress," the party's seer said. "Be sure she comes to consummate the marriage when she is twenty-one."

"We will," the otterbees promised.

The visitors put the two children together and had them kiss, sealing the deal, and there was that coruscation that bathed the swamp in lovely light. By the time it cleared, the prince's family was gone, and Ida was as she had been before, just another baby. Only now she had a glorious future.

Then a stray forget whorl forged through the swamp, wiping out all memories of the occasion. The otterbees still cared for Ida, but they no longer remembered her destiny.

She grew up into a fine and beautiful young woman. When she was of age, the otterbees told her that it was time for her to seek her fortune, for they were sure she had one. They just couldn't remember what it was. So she set out, and after many adventures discovered that she was the twin sister of Princess Ivy, daughter of the King of Xanth. She posed for one picture as she settled in to her suite in Castle Roogna. That picture looked exactly like the one the fun house had shown, of Hilarion's betrothee.

Later she acquired her orbiting planet, Ptero, the

connection to all the imagination of existence, and was recognized as a Sorceress. The magic of the planet interfered with pictures, and so there was never another made of Ida as she aged. That was why the fun house lacked any recent picture, and had to use the early one.

But she did not remember the betrothal.

Meanwhile in another part of the heart-shaped picture, Prince Hilarion undertook the considerable training required of a prince. He studied weapons and combat, and letters and literature, and logic and diplomacy. He became the very model of a royal scion. Everyone was proud of him.

When the day for his marriage came, there was just one hitch: his betrothee did not show up. What had gone wrong? So he did what he had to do: he set out to find her.

He searched for some time. He had a brush with a forget whorl—perhaps the same one, meandering through the territory—and it wiped out most of his memory of the search, so that he did not realize it was twenty years instead of one year. This meant that he was looking for and kissing twenty-one-year-old maidens, and not having any success.

Until this moment, when enough of his memory returned to identify his betrothee at last.

The kiss was one minute in one frame, and forty years in another. At last it broke, and the two parties separated. Slowly the heart and colors faded, and the other members of the party resumed breathing.

"You are the One," Hilarion told Ida. He was now showing his true age. He was a handsome man of forty-two. In fact he looked exactly like the fun house picture.

"I had that impression," she agreed.

Wenda glanced down at herself. The explosion of love light had melted her clothing and imbued her hollow front with a gentle warm glow.

Then Wenda heard a ticking sound behind her. "The Knot!" she exclaimed. "The love was too much! It is about to blow! Get under cover!"

The others threw themselves behind any cover available. Wenda stood facing the Knot, her arms spread wide, to shield the others to the extent possible. The ticking increased in volume.

Then it blew. The Knot exploded into fragments that blasted the ground, the trees, the sky, and the remains of the floating heart. It piled into Wenda's frontside, hurling her backward. The landscape darkened with the force of the blast.

When it seemed safe, the others emerged from their refuges. Everything was peppered with embedded specks of petrified wood. Wenda herself was . . . filled, from face to feet. She had caught the brunt of the detonation.

"Maybe we should have kissed with less force," Hilarion said. But he did not seem particularly regretful. Ida did not comment, but she looked vibrant.

"You are whole again!" Jumper said. "But the detonation must have reversed it, because you seem to be shapely flesh, not packed petrified sawdust."

Wenda checked her frontside. It seemed to be so. Her shapely bosom had been restored, and her limbs were rounded and whole. Even her hollow head was now solid, with a fully functional face. Jumper was right: she felt like living flesh, rather than shaped sawdust. How could that be?

"But I have lost the Knot," she said. "How can I deliver it to the Good Magician?"

"We will go with you to explain," Hilarion said. "It was my fault it happened."

"And mine," Ida said. "We should not have kissed so close to the Knot."

"We all will go," Jumper said.

That seemed to be all they could do. The party resumed travel toward the Good Magician's Castle, pulling the empty wagon. Progress was rapid, without that weight.

The scenery had changed. The trees, bushes and rocks seemed somehow enhanced, as if painted with a brighter brush. They also seemed to be making sounds, or at least the colors felt audible. Some were loud, some soft; some strong and bold, others pale and weak. Wenda even heard the footsteps of running colors. Even the ground was strangely colorful, with its own shades of sounds. But there were shadows of normal ground beyond the rocks and trees. There was also a subdued aura of fading menace, yet nothing tangible. They hadn't been that way before; what had changed?

Yet the effect was one-sided. The opposite sides were normal. Why were the odd sides all facing the travelers, as if orienting malignantly on them?

"The Knot!" Meryl said. "It exploded and sent tiny fragments into everything nearby. But only on the surfaces that were line of sight."

That was it, of course. Every surface in sight of the Knot when it detonated had been sprayed with petrified reverse-wood powder.

Now that they understood the pattern, it was rather pretty. The near side of everything scintillated with slight malice. Diluted like this, it wasn't really scary, but merely tangy.

Wenda realized that when she looked at a peppered surface, she saw reversed colors. When she listened to it, she heard those colors. They were not speaking or singing, just sounding off. The reversal had extended into another sense. That was curious.

"I think I understand," Jumper said, divining her thought. "The Knot exploded and spread its powder right after the kiss." He did not need to specify which kiss. "So now the two are mixed on all the surfaces they struck: the love from the kiss, and the malice from the Knot. They must cancel each other out. Except for the competitive interface between them, which generates the colors and sounds. So it is harmless and interesting."

"My frontside is neutral," Wenda said, relieved. "It was bathed with the light of the kiss, before getting filled by the exploding Knot."

"It must be," Jumper agreed. He eyed it with three or four eyes. "Yes. It is harmless and interesting. Prince Charming should notice."

That reminded her. "I must dress!"

"I have a spare dress," Ida said, coming to help put it on Wenda. But in a moment she shook her head. "That is the wrong one; I don't know how it got in the collection."

Wenda looked at it. The dress was covered with ads for different things. EAT AT SLURPEES, OLD SPELLS TRADED, CURSES ENHANCED. "What is it?" she asked.

"It is an ad-dress. It consists of assorted ads for things, constantly changing. Some young women like the attention it generates. But it's not right for you."

"Not right," Wenda agreed.

Ida got out another dress. That one made Wenda look like a princess. But of course she was one.

"Now you look complete, even a trifle salacious," Ida said as she applied the finishing touches. "Your restored front is very nice."

"But is it flesh?" Wenda asked, concerned. "I wood rather have real flesh to offer Charming."

It is, the Demoness Eris's thought came. *I arranged it.*

"Yew what?" Wenda asked, startled.

It was part of a Demon wager I made, which fortunately I won. That your lost substance be restored, in full rondure and fleshiness. Because it was my fault you lost it.

"But yew saved my life!" Wenda protested.

But still cost you some of it. That needed to be remedied.

"A Demon bet—just for that?"

And for a Status Point. That made it worthwhile for other Demons. Demons don't make wagers for nothing.

"What was the wager?" Jumper asked.

That Prince Hilarion and Princess Ida would discover each other before the Knot was delivered to the Good Magician's Castle.

"But that was sheer chance!" Hilarion protested. "Had not the Maiden Taiwan mentioned my contact with her a decade ago, I would not have realized how long I had been searching."

Yes. An even chance. Most Demon wagers are perfectly balanced. But fear not: the Good Magician planned to tell you at the completion of the mission, as a reward for your assistance.

"He knew, and did not tell?" Ida asked, her lip curling in what in a less nice person might have been taken for annoyance.

He has his ways.

That was certainly true. The Good Magician's grumpiness and obscurity were legendary.

"But why?" Wenda asked. "I can understand the Status Point, but why add to the risk like that? Yew really did knot owe me anything."

For friendship.

Wenda could not refute that. "Thank yew," she breathed weakly.

As they walked, the effect thinned, because there were fewer avenues for the flying debris. Finally it was gone.

But Wenda remained troubled. Finally she realized what was bothering her. "That bet," she murmured, knowing the Demoness would hear. "What wood yew have lost, if yew lost it?"

A Status Point.

She was not fooled. "What else?"

And Eris had to answer. *Forfeiture of all further association with mortals.*

"But what of Jumper?"

He is now immortal.

"But that wood have meant yewr association with me . . . yewr friendship—"

Would have been sacrificed. It would have been horrible. But I had to risk it, to get the wager.

"Yew risked yewr friendship—for the sake of friendship?"

The scales had to balance. It was the only way. Demons do not kittenfoot.

"I am knot worth it."

Oh, but you are, Wenda. Before I got half of Jumper's soul, which included part of yours, I never experienced love or loneliness. Now I need your friendship. You alone of all mortals, understand. You do not care that I am a Demoness, any more than you care that Jumper is a spider. You care only about the personal relationship. I can find that nowhere else.

And Wenda did understand. It was true: the origin or nature of her friends did not matter to her. Only her contact with them. The tears were streaming down her face. "Please—dew knot dew that again. I need yewr friendship too."

Not again, Eris agreed.

And that was where it had to be left. The Demoness had taken an appalling risk, for the sake of friendship. What better proof of it could there be? Not that Wenda had ever sought proof.

No one else commented, though they had heard her side of the dialogue and understood the general nature of it. It was something they knew she had to handle on her own.

Now Wenda realized something else. They were nearing the end of the mission, having done what they could. The several members of the group would be going to their various lives, most of them significantly enhanced. Wenda would be returning to the castle with Prince Charming. That was fine; she loved him and loved his passion for her. But it wasn't enough.

She had no friends at the castle. There were servants galore, but servants were not friends. There were royal visitors, but they were not friends either. She had not realized how lonely she had become, ensconced in her life of splendor.

But on the mission, with Jumper, Meryl, Angela, Ida, Hilarion, and Eris, she had had friends again, just as she had when on Jumper's mission. That had buoyed her despite the tribulations. That was almost over.

At least now she could continue her association with Jumper and Eris. That would make an enormous difference. Two friends were infinitely better than none.

Yes.

"Yes," she breathed. And walked on with a jauntier step.

Not far from the castle, they came across a young woman. She was sitting on a stone, sobbing. Wenda could not simply walk by a person in trouble, so she paused.

"Please—I dew knot like to see sadness," she said. "I am Wenda Woodwife, on the way with my companions to see the Good Magician. Is there anything I can dew for yew?"

"The Good Magician!" the girl repeated, and her sobbing increased.

"This is odd," Hilarion murmured.

"Are yew having trouble finding him?" Wenda asked. "We can show yew. His castle is almost in sight."

"I've been there!" the girl wailed. "That's my problem."

Wenda glanced around. "Let us take a break," she suggested.

The others smiled, knowing her soft heart. They settled down to rest.

"Tell me about it," Wenda said.

"I . . . my name is Liz. I went to the Good Magician because I was afraid for my little girl."

"She is in danger?"

"Not exactly. Well, maybe. You see, my talent is to sniff souls. I can smell the difference between them. I can even identify people blindfolded, when I know them, because of the odors of their souls."

"That is an interesting talent," Wenda said encouragingly.

"It isn't much, really, because it's easier just to look at people. But then I noticed something. When my little girl lost her first baby tooth, I smelled it."

"It had a soul?" Wenda asked, surprised.

"Yes, or part of one. It had a fragment of my child's soul. I realized that the soul infuses all the body, and when part of the body is lost, so is part of the soul. So my little girl was losing a bit of her soul with her tooth. That bothered me."

"I never thought of that," Wenda said.

"So I went to see the Good Magician, to ask him if this was really doing my daughter harm. She has many teeth to go, and I didn't want her soul to be depleted."

"That makes sense," Wenda agreed.

"But I never made it through the Challenges," Liz wailed, "so I couldn't ask him. Now I'll never know."

Wenda looked around, at a loss to help. Ida stepped up. "Souls regenerate in living people," she said. "So your daughter will not suffer. She is probably replacing the parts of her soul as fast as she loses them."

"Oh, that's such a relief to know!" Liz said.

"What happens to those lost teeth, and their bits of souls?" Meryl asked.

"The Tooth Fairy collects them," Ida said.

"But what does she do with them?" Angela asked.

"Why, I don't know. She must pass them on somewhere. Especially if they have attached soul fragments."

"Where? Who would want them?"

That made them all wonder. "Maybe Liz could sniff out where her daughter's tooth-soul went," Angela suggested.

"That should work," Ida agreed.

And of course now it would work. Liz got up and sniffed. "It's close," she said. "I never thought to trace the tooth fragment."

They followed Liz to a slope with a cave. It looked like a lion's den.

"No, it is a tiger's den," Jumper said. "I will investigate."

Because he remained invulnerable, one of Eris's temporary gifts to him for the mission. Except that that could end at any time.

"When dew those gifts expire?" Wenda asked nervously.

Oh, not long now. A century or two.

"A century! I thought it was any day, any hour, any minute."

A century to a Demon is like a minute to a mortal.

So it seemed. They had run afoul of differences in perspective.

Jumper stood at the den entrance. "Ho, tiger!" he called. "I would like to talk with you."

The tiger emerged. He had bright orange stripes and tremendous long tusks. "You and who else?"

"Me and my friends here. We come in peace. We merely want to know, what does a tiger want with baby teeth?"

"I am the Save-a-Tooth Tiger," the creature said. "I collect teeth that would otherwise be lost, and their soul fragments. It is my business."

"What do you do with the soul fragments?"

"I save them for otherwise worthy babies who may be denied souls by glitches in the process. Sometimes the storks or the soul-assignment demon foul up. It happens. That's when I enter the picture, to be sure wrong is not done."

"That's beautiful," Wenda said.

The tiger glanced at her. "Thank you. You look good enough to eat."

Hilarion stepped forward, drawing his sword.

But Wenda recognized it as a compliment. "Thank yew."

"Eris," Jumper murmured.

I am here, beloved.

"Your concern about our baby. The tiger may relate."

"What's this concern?" the tiger asked.

Now the Demoness addressed the tiger. *It is that I want to have a baby with Jumper. But I am a Demoness with only a borrowed half soul, and he is a spider whose soul was cobbled together from sharings by his friends. I now appreciate the value of a soul, and want our baby to have one. But considering the sketchy nature of our souls, I fear that the effort of sharing with our baby will stretch it beyond reason, and it will dissipate and become nothing. So I don't dare risk it.*

The tiger oriented on her, evidently having no trouble perceiving her. "Your soul is indeed a patchwork. But fear not. If it doesn't take, I will provide a soul for your baby. It fits the profile for my service."

"Yew can tell just by a look?" Wenda asked.

"Souls are my business. Just as your friend can smell them, I can see them. They are affected by the way a person lives. Some souls get stained by bad decisions. The spider's composite soul has been enhanced by seriously positive actions the past year, and the Demoness's share of that has been enhanced by high risks taken for friendship. There can hardly be a better recommendation. A child of such a union is worthy of a soul; that soul will not be abused." The tiger paused. "Another tooth is being lost; I must fetch it before the silly Tooth Fairy loses it." And he was abruptly gone.

"That is amazing," Liz said.

Amazing, Eris agreed.

"I thank the group of you for your reassurance and assistance," Liz said. "Now I will go home, reassured."

So will I.

"I am so glad things worked out well," Wenda said.

"It was because of your soft heart," Jumper said. "That did several of us some good."

They resumed their trek to the Good Magician's Castle. Wenda remained worried about the loss of the Knot; she could think of no way to replace it.

But when they got there, Humfrey was unconcerned. "I wanted the Knot brought here to be sure it was safe, and could not be exploited by unworthy parties. You nullified it instead. That will do. Your mission is done."

Wenda was relieved. Now at last she could go home. "I am eager to start my own family," she confided to Rose of Roogna.

"Oh, that's too bad," Rose said sadly.

"Bad? I dew knot understand."

"Humfrey asked me to tell you. You have paid a subtle price for your adventures. Your origin as a wood-wife, followed by your reversion, and then the unusual manner you regained your lost substance, have left one detail imperfect. Your signals will not reach the stork."

"But they have to, so the stork can deliver."

"Yes. There will be no delivery."

Wenda was appalled. "But I want a baby!" she wailed. "I love children!"

"I am so sorry," Rose said, hugging her. "But I can tell you that your fulfillment will come from friendship."

There seemed to be no help for it. Her hope for the future was doomed. Now she would have to go home and tell Prince Charming. She was not at all sure how he would feel about it. He had never commented on the prospect of children. Would he be disappointed or relieved? Neither prospect appealed to her.

Her numbness was gradually fading into grief. She needed to be alone, before she dissolved into an orgy of explendiferous self-pity.

Not yet, the Demoness Eris's mental voice came. *Ida wants you for the wedding party.*

"The what?" Wenda asked, confused.

Maid of Honor. You can't decline.

"But I'm knot—there must bee hundreds of better—"

"There are not," Ida said. "You made this possible. You are the woman I want."

"I'm knot even dressed," Wenda protested. Actually she was in the princessly dress Ida had lent her, but that would never do for a wedding. "I wood knot know the first thing about it."

Jumper transformed to manform and kissed her. "You will manage, I'm sure."

How could she tell them that she would just be a wringing wet blanket? How could she be properly happy for the happy couple, when all she wanted to do was weep for her own misfortune?

Then she was at Eris's hidden castle, dressed fetchingly in a forest green gown. Everyone else was there too. Looking around, Wenda saw the Good Magician Humfrey with his Designated Wife Rose of Roogna, the Maidens Taiwan, Japan, and Mexico, Princess Eve with Demon Pluto, Princess Dawn, and King Ivy with her consort Magician Grey Murphy. This was indeed a royal wedding.

And beside Wenda were Meryl Mermaid and Angela Angel, hovering in fetching white dresses. "Bridesmaids," Angela explained. Both of them looked genuinely happy. Wenda tried to stifle her jealously, knowing it was unjustified.

Then she saw Jumper, in manform and in a uniform. "He's the Best Man," Angela said. "Hilarion asked for him."

"But he's knot really a man," Wenda protested weakly. "He's my best friend, but for an occasion like this—"

"He's a prince, and Hilarion's friend."

That did seem to cover it. Wenda realized that it was her own loss that was making her negative about other things. She would have to suppress that, at least for the duration of the wedding.

She looked at the seated audience, and saw many other people, and a bird. That was Dipper, who had given up his place in the Quest so that Angela could join it. She wondered how he liked it in Heaven. Then she saw that he was perched on the shoulder of a lovely angel. He probably liked it very well.

There was a brief confusion while things got organized. Wenda went to assist Ida, as that was what a Maid of Honor was for, but Ida's twin sister King Ivy was already doing it. Wenda felt a bit out of sorts, apart from her private personal misery. She had had a royal wedding herself, when she married Prince Charming, but servants had arranged everything and she had been largely oblivious, transported by the moment. She wanted to be useful, but had little idea how.

It is a figurehead role, Eris's thought came. *You represent moral support for the bride. All you need to do is stand there, look pretty, and smile.*

She had never before realized how hard it could be to

smile! "But I dew knot look pretty," Wenda said. "I am a hollow woodwife."

Not anymore. Your frontside is now decorously covered by your dress, but retains its impact. Covertly observe the male attendees.

Wenda looked around, pretending a blank gaze. She saw several men's eyes orienting on her front. Some were glazing.

I can make your dress become translucent, if you wish, so that your bra shows.

"No!"

Just as well. Not only would they freak out, their popped eyeballs would bounce on the floor.

"But my frontside did knot ever have that kind of power."

It does now.

Wenda realized that when a Demoness made a gift, it was something to be reckoned with. "Thank yew." What else could she say? If only that compelling appearance could encompass full functionality.

Wenda, nothing is too good for you. Jumper has made it plain many times that without you, he would never have completed his mission, and would not have discovered me. I owe you everything.

"But I dew knot want everything, or even anything. I just like yewr company." In fact she wished she could be alone with the Demoness, and pour out her broken heart to her.

I know. And I like yours. Eris paused. *Oh, I was not looking. Now I see what is bothering you. Wenda, that's awful! Come, I will take you on a tour before you dissolve into a sodden lump.*

"But the wedding is about to happen."

I will put it on Pause. Only the Demon Pluto will notice, and he will not interfere.

Wenda realized that this was readily within the power of the Demoness. "A tour?"

Eris took her hand. *A distraction, and we can talk.*

Suddenly they were flying up, up, and away, out of the palace and the subterranean enclave. Up into Xanth. Now Eris assumed her human form, a lovely lady garbed as another bridesmaid, still holding Wenda's hand.

"This is Xanth," Eris said, no longer needing to confine herself to mental communication. "A marvelous magic land. And here is Mundania, relatively dull but it does have its points. They are two of a huge loop of worlds connected by Ida's moon."

Somehow the scene had shifted, and they were flying over a spherical planet, rather than the peninsula-shaped world that was Xanth. There above it floated a maturely handsome male figure. "Snooping, Eris?" he inquired.

"Touring," Eris answered. "Demon Earth, this is my friend Wenda Woodwife of Xanth. She is a nice person."

"Very nice," he agreed, contemplating Wenda's frontside.

"This is the home world of the Demoness Venus," Eris said, as the scene shifted to a cloud-covered planet.

"Thank yew for getting the Demon's eyes off me."

"I am long accustomed to avoiding such attention, though normally a Demoness finds it a useful distraction."

"I think I wood knot bee a good Demoness."

Eris laughed. "And the home of the Demon Pluto." This was a smaller, colder planet. "Considerably warmer below the surface, where Hades is. I believe Princess Eve is learning to like it."

"She wood," Wenda agreed, remembering how smoldering Eve could be when she tried.

The Demon Pluto appeared. "Amazing what a blast of petrified wood can do," he remarked as his gaze fixed on Wenda's frontside. Obviously he was seeing through the material of the dress.

"And this is my home world," Eris said as the scene changed again, leaving Pluto behind. It was a dark cold planet, far away from anything. "You can see why I maintain my alternate residence in Xanth. Jumper prefers it."

"Yes." But Wenda was bothered by something. "Are *all* males going to bee staring at my frontside?"

"Yes, when they're not staring at your backside. But you will get used to it. They are wired to focus on certain things. It is the nature of their gender. Without that fixation, women would not be able to control the violent foolishness of men."

There was truth there, but it reminded her of another aspect. "I love Prince Charming, of course," Wenda said. "And I am glad to please him, any way I can. He really likes my—my front and backside. But sometimes I wish he was interested in more than my—my body."

"You wish he were more like Jumper."

"Yes!" Then Wenda reconsidered, embarrassed. "That is—"

"I understand. Jumper is a spider, but he is a more rounded person than most straight human males. You came to know him well, and that spoiled you for ordinary men."

"That may bee so," Wenda agreed. "Sometimes I wish that Charming had other interests than . . ." She trailed off, not wanting to seem disloyal. After all, Charming had made her a princess, and provided for all her material needs.

"He needs social rounding," Eris agreed. "It will not come naturally. He will have to be trained. I am not sure how to arrange that."

"Maybe Jumper wood know."

"Jumper." And there he was, floating in space with

them, still in his wedding suit. "How can Prince Charming be trained to be interested in more than a woman's frontside or backside?"

"Encourage him to cultivate new interests."

"What interests, beloved?"

"Well, children, for example."

"He has been trying!" Wenda said, bursting into new tears. "But that will bee slow. First the storks have to bee alerted, and they refuse to bee rushed." She took a breath, then blurted out the rest of it. "In fact they will knot come at all, for me."

Jumper was taken aback. "You can't get a baby?"

"She can't," Eris said. "She learned at the Good Magician's Castle. She is devastated."

"But Wenda, you care so much for children. You want to adopt every orphan child you see."

His sympathy just made her cry harder.

"So all she has is Prince Charming," Eris said. "And he pays more attention to her body than to her personality. How can she change that?"

Jumper considered. "Shortcut it."

"I dew knot understand."

Jumper faced her seriously. "Wenda, you have a palace, with servants, and a husband who needs new interests. You have an excruciatingly caring nature. But you can't have children of your own. Your situation is ideal."

"For what?" she demanded, tearfully frustrated.

"For being den mother to a group of orphan children."

Astonished, Wenda could not speak. She did like children, and had seen some along the way she had wished she could help. But she had been too busy with the mission. Now she was about to have much more time. Too much time! But if she gathered in some children who needed a home, that would not only fulfill her, it well might get Charming involved. Now her future situation was opening out before her, and she was thrilled.

"How would she find children?" Eris asked.

"The Save-a-Tooth Tiger would surely know of a number. You could ask—"

They were in front of the tiger's den. The tiger appeared. Wenda opened her mouth.

"Yes, as it happens I do know of a number of orphans," the tiger said. "Ones with special needs, or character problems stemming from neglect or abuse, so they are unadoptable. They lose teeth too. It would take a very special person to handle them." The tiger focused on Wenda with disturbing insight. "And you are that person. Set up your castle, childproof it, warn your husband, and when you are ready I will bring them."

"Oh, thank yew!"

"Thank *you*. This is a challenging but highly worthy endeavor."

They were floating above Eris's buried palace complex. "There is one more thing I should show you," the Demoness said. "But it requires a violation of the natural order. For this I must kiss you."

"Kiss me?"

Eris brought her close and kissed her on the mouth. And Wenda was seeing pictures from her future.

The first orphan child arrived, a baby boy with a club foot. It was a perfectly formed club, serviceable at need for defense, but ordinary folk did not want him. Wenda picked him up and kissed him, and he smiled for the first time since he had been orphaned.

The second orphan arrived, a blind baby girl. Wenda hugged her and whispered in her ear, and she too smiled for the first time.

The third arrived. She recognized him: Alex, the boy who could not express emotion. She had met him on Planet Comic, but there had been nothing comical about his condition. "Oh, Alex," she said, hugging him. "I am going to make you laugh and cry." And seeing briefly ahead along his timeline, she saw that it was true. She wasn't sure how she did it, but she did it. Love and commitment constantly applied had impact, even in a case like this. For Alex *felt* emotions; he merely had been unable to express them.

Then there was a middling small collection of babies, gazing adoringly at Wenda as she read them a story. She did that at the Social Circle, for which she now had ample use. She brought new children there first thing, and they immediately became sociable because of its magic. The odd thing was that they tended to remain that way after leaving it. All the children generally got along well together.

The Mood Swing, which had started Wenda's adventure, remained next to the Social Circle. The children, knowing its nature, loved it too. Their moods were highly changeable anyway, and this merely added to the fun. Sometimes they tried to trick a newcomer to swing on it, then laughed gleefully as the mood changed. Thereafter the newcomers liked it too. The children were such good sports.

Prince Charming, at first diffident, began to get into it. He told a story of adventure and derring-do that pleased the boys and one or two of the girls. Encouraged by that success, he told more stories, and soon it was a regular thing.

As the children grew older, Charming held classes in martial arts and dragon slaying for the boys and a few of the bolder girls. They loved it. One never knew when one might have to slay a dragon.

As time continued, Charming filled out emotionally and became the man that Wenda had hoped for. He still liked her front- and backside, but now they could talk about more than bodies or children. "Thank you, Wenda, for fulfilling my life," he said. "I never knew what I was missing, until you brought the children. You are twice the woman I took you for, and twice what I ever deserved."

She just smiled and gave him twice the attention he had ever hoped for. She knew he was not referring merely to her sides.

As more time passed, the children grew into impressive little princes and princesses. Charming took them on state visits to other kingdoms, and so did Wenda. Sometimes Jumper and Eris's son visited, and sometimes Hilarion and Ida's daughter. Sometimes Anima, the daughter of the rejuvenated Bink and Chameleon, whose talent was animating the inanimate. The only apparent difference between them was that Charming and Wenda's adopted children were more varied and sensitive to the concerns of others. Everybody remarked on it; these children were special, and they did not mean their physical or mental handicaps.

At last the first orphan, now tall, handsome, and dashing despite his club foot, had to depart to marry his princess. "I owe it all to you, Mother Wenda," he said. "We all do. You saved us from oblivion. You have the kindest heart we ever knew. We will never forget." Then he kissed her.

The kiss ended as Eris drew away. "But you must not tell," the Demoness said. "Lest I be charged with a Violation. Keep it to yourself, and live your life fulfilled."

"I will," Wenda agreed, dizzy with the revelation of her wonderful future. "Thank yew so much."

"It is what a friend is for."

They were back at the wedding. "I do," Princess Ida said. Then King Emeritus Trent made a pronouncement, and Ida kissed Prince Hilarion. This time it did not coruscate, but it was a fine effort regardless. For that moment, Ida's moon orbited both their heads, seeming satisfied to do so.

No one had missed Wenda, if she had even been gone, physically.

There was another brief confusion as the folk organized for the next stage, which involved a giant wedding cake. Ida approached Wenda. "Thank you so much for your support," she said breathlessly. "I would have been so nervous without you."

"Yew are welcome," Wenda said, blushing, for she knew her support had been more apparent than real. She was glad that Hilarion and Ida had finally found each other, but also glad that she had found herself. Those needy children—she could hardly wait. She knew she would not be lonely anymore.

But you will visit me often, and I will visit you, Eris thought.

Yes, of course. Her secret memory verified it. Friendship counted.

AUTHOR'S NOTE

I have written many novels in my day, more than 135. The Xanth series alone now is thirty-four novels, with some corollary games, choose-your-own-ending books by others, a sadly out-of-date *Visual Guide to Xanth*, and possibly a Xanth movie. In fact this novel is well into the second magic trilogy of three cubed, though it is uncertain whether a trilogy of magic trilogies will ever be completed. That would be eighty-one novels. If I continued to write one novel a year, that would take me until age 121. I rather doubt that's feasible in Mundania. But there are only four to go to complete the alphabet in Xanth novels, and that might happen.

I was writing this novel, using the open source Xandros distribution with the OpenOffice word processor, and it was going well, though my time is more limited than it was because my wife's illness—she had what amounted to heart surgery, and is also being treated for polyneuropathy, which is a deadening of the limbs—caused me to take over many of the household chores, like making meals. Then I was tested for bone density, and to my surprise it indicated that I had lost calcium in my bones and was in danger of a hip fracture. I have lived clean, stayed lean, and exercised vigorously most of my life, but it seems this is a complication of the underactive thyroid gland I do have. So I had the expensive medication Reclast to restore calcium to my bones. I'm on Medicare, and Medicare covers Reclast, but the marvel of bureaucratic obscurities refused to cover it for me unless I first fractured a hip or suffered similarly unpleasant complications. This I was for some reason unwilling to do, so I paid for it myself.

Some medications have side effects. This one might bring flu-like symptoms. You know about understatements, like "Some assembly required"? Well, I would rather have had the flu. At least it would have been over in a week or so. Those side-effect symptoms wiped me out. I got violent shivers, my sweat soaked my pajamas at night, I lost my strength so that just getting to my feet was a chore, and a tortoise could have kept pace with my walking velocity. My skin got sensitive so that just combing my hair made me react. The best I could do was sleep much of the day. My fever lasted eighteen days, gradually fading.

While there is not supposed to be much magic in Mundania—the real world—sometimes there is a suspicion, because my malaise of the time was reflected in the stock market, which had its worst descent since 1929. Some of you may have noticed. When I started to mend, the DOW rose over 900 points in a day. But my illness was not yet done, and neither was the stock market, which remained shaky. Many experts were baffled; those of you who believe in magic now know the cause of the mischief.

My exercise routine faded to a halt; I just didn't have the energy. My wife had to take back some of the chores I had taken over from her, like washing the dishes and shopping. And this novel halted in place, 77,000 words along. Reluctantly the symptoms eased, and I started doing things again. But it wasn't easy. For example, I normally ran three times a week at dawn to fetch the newspapers, as our drive on our tree farm is over three quarters of a mile long, with spot chores along the way, like opening our gate. The last day before the treatment I ran it in just under seventeen minutes. When I resumed three weeks later, it took just over twenty-four minutes, alternating slow jogging with walking. Another exercise is archery; I would loose twelve arrows at the target right handed, then twelve more left handed. My aim was never great, but that wasn't the point. When I resumed, I loosed one arrow each side, but lacked the strength to do a second. Obviously I had a way to go, physically.

And the novel: I managed to resume writing, between naps, starting Chapter 12, and my pace picked up as I recovered, so that in two weeks I was near the end of the first draft. If the novel seems to drag in the latter stages, blame the faux flu. I don't think my imagination was washed out, but how would I know?

So that was the carefree life of the author of a funny fantasy novel. I hope not to do it again. I mean the side effects; I do want to continue writing. In the past things like computer crashes have hampered my writing. While I don't like such crashes, they may be less complicated to handle than medicinal side effects. Of course it's all ultimately a complication of age. If you want to avoid similar complications, don't get old.

And of course there is half a slew of credits to list. Readers constantly send ideas, and I try to select and use the best ones. Some readers will send one. Others will send hundreds. As a general policy, I try to use the ideas of one-shot contributors before using additional ideas by repeaters. This means some good ideas have to wait for future novels, while some marginal ones get used immediately. Naturally I want to write the best novel I can, with the best ideas, but fair is fair. So it's a compromise, as is the case with so much of life. Here is the list, roughly in order of use in the novel, with multiple contributions grouped. I don't always have the full name of a contributor, in which case I use what I have.

Mood Swing—Alexandra Campbell; also the "Bizarro" comic for January 28, 2008. Social Circle—Judah from West Hempstead. Woman who freaks out men by dressing normally—Christopher Borriello. Gene Gnome, who changes living things—Ryan Park. Hare net, R Dent, R Cade, R Tillery, R Senic robots, an-gel for Heavenly hair conditioning, steam roll, club sandwich, Banditree, Robust, firehouse with associated puns, summer salt, ad-Dress—Tim Bruening. A gremlin could fix a robot with a screw loose, hay fever causes a robot to go haywire, flees, Bare Village, robot speaks Morse code, cereal killers, Wenda's pet wood chuck, rowbot, Slippery Elm, Pussy Willow, Whispering Pine, Naughty Pine, not taking the Knot for granite, fire ants with death matches, single- and double-yolked eggplant eggs, chilly peppers, bell pepper, wry grass, coral snake guards brain coral, lemon and lime stones for flavoring drinks, soapstone, pet peeve given crackers to shut it up—Robert of Beaverton, Oregon.

Girls literally made of sugar and spice, boys of slugs and snails; Beast of Burden makes folk heavy hearted—Zack Smitherman. Mistletoe—Casey Vitorino. Pollyanna Polecat—Ann Dragera Dragonclawz. Talent of ease—John Smith. GenEric, GenErica—Kari Lambert. Rose of Roogna's rose quartz and pintz necklace—Pat Schuessler. Winged Mermaid (Meryl)—Jennifer Waller. Hero returns to tell the Good Magician the service is too hard—Thomas Richardson. Humidor—Cliff Liles. Sidewalks, straws that break camels' backs—Kyle Cuthbert. Peppermint—Ame Raine. Mountain Ear—Seth

Klinehoffer. Child Hood—Christa Elise. Mist E, Miss T—Misty J. K. Zaebst. Silent Knight—Albert. Barrel of Laughs, cough-fee, to-fee—Cindy Tremblay. Prince Hilarion—borrowed from the operetta *Princess Ida*. Story of the troll and the doll-fin—Kerry. Talent of banishing memories—Alex Asper. Angela Angel—inspired by angels made by Susan Lee of the Ferret & Dove Sanctuary. That is a marvelous organization that specializes in keeping unwanted ferrets and doves, and adopting them out to good homes. Check their Web site at ferretanddovesanctuary.petfinder.org. Susan Lee also explained the angel's bead sash made of seed pearls. No, I don't think the sanctuary rescues and places fallen angels.

Angel food cake, A Gile, A Bull, talent of finding a question for any answer—Eric C. Daniel. Crone's Disease—Deneen Jardstam. Epi Nephrine, Prof Philactic—Deb Murray. Pundit Tree, Tree Sonus (treasonous), candid dates (candidates)—Lou Nelson. Nara Crossbreed—Morgan. Big Band—Alex. Chris Cross—searches and catalogs everything—Wing Chiu Li. The Tractors: Pro, Con, Dis, Sub—Michael Lovvo. Elbow grease—Russell Styles. Knowing the question to evoke a specific answer—Timothy Williams. There's a story here: Timothy made this suggestion years ago, and I lost it in my files. So now it is credited, along with the similar one suggested by Eric Daniel.

Belchin' Waffles—Jon Conyers. Alexythemia—Brian D. Bray.

Sun flours—Logan Addotta. Lilax and Truthlax, wanna-bee—John Gillis. Holding down the fort—Jim Logterman. Five forms of reverse wood—Levi Cromer. Reverse-wood swords or arrows—Eric Gardner, Skeloric. Man's ears ringing—Erica Brauer. Talent of summoning and banishing Demoness Metria—Anthony (no known relation to the author). Harberian Barbarian—J. Spyder

Isaacson. Twins who sense a person's deepest fear, and bring it to life—Thomas Pharrer. Steven Wolf, with the talent of attracting women who forget him—Pamela Wolf.

Dye-a-Log, Diet Tribe—Joshua Klingbeil. Ogres using prune juice to prune—Lissa McGrath. Bee lever—Norm. Flu-Z sickening men—Yisroel Charloff. Story of man attacked by hot tomato, who now can heal with his hands—Michael Lindsay. Toilet tree—Daniel Mayoss. Shenita Life Guard, warning of trouble next day—Sharon Ellis. Metro Gnome, time-oriented—John Atterberry. Care, with whom nothing bad happens—Wayne Schick. Renovation of the old Storm King's Castle—Melissa Huneke. The origin and detailed history of the Maidens Taiwan, Mexico, Japan—Andrew Fine.

Hearing colors—Lucki Melander Wilder. The story of someone who doesn't make it through the Good Magician's Challenges—Elizabeth Koerber. Fragments of souls with baby teeth collected by Save-a-Tooth Tiger—Len Golding. Bink and Chameleon's daughter with the talent of animating the inanimate—Mary Chapin.

As usual, there are more notions I didn't use, for various reasons. Some relate to characters not in this novel. Some deserve more play than was available here. They should get their turns in a future novel. Apart from that, I used ideas through OctOgre 2008, when I completed the novel.

Those who wish to follow my bimonthly blog-type column, my ongoing survey of electronic publishers and related services, or simply get information on my books and series or character list of Xanth, can check my Web site at www.hipiers.com.

Turn the page for a preview of

WELL-TEMPERED CLAVICLE

Piers Anthony

Now available from
Tom Doherty Associates

TOR® A TOR BOOK

understood human speech, but could not speak it. Many animals were like that.

Now they heard a faint "Woof!" Something was in there!

Picka braced himself, got his bone fingers on the stone, and heaved it up and to the side. Walking skeletons had no muscles but were stronger than they looked, being magically animated. The portal was open.

A big dark mongrel mundane dog came out, tail wagging, glad to be freed. He joined the other two. The three were evidently friends, odd as such an association might be.

"You wanted to rescue a dog?" Picka asked the cat, surprised again.

"I think we deserve an explanation," Joy'nt said.

The three animals just looked at her. Maybe they were having trouble with the idea of an explanation, when they couldn't speak human.

"Let's trade," Picka said. "We'll tell you about us if you tell us about you."

The bird, cat, and dog exchanged glances. Then the bird nodded.

"First we need a better way to communicate," Joy'nt said. "I know just the thing." She fished in her hollow skull and brought out a roll of bone-colored paper. She spread this on the ground. "This is a magic marker made from dragon bone," she explained. "I got it from a man I met named Cody, who could decipher any code or language. It works only for living creatures, so I never had use for it before. Whoever wants to talk can put a hand, claw, or paw on it, focus, and it will print your thought. Try it."

The cat touched the paper with a paw. Words formed. I AM MIDRANGE CAT.

The dog tried it. I AM WOOFER DOG.

Finally the bird flew down and landed on it with both feet. II AAMM TTWWEEEETTEERR BBIIRRDD.

Midrange made a mewl of impatience. He touched the paper. JUST ONE FOOT, BIRDBRAIN!

Tweeter hauled up a foot. OOPS.

Woofer touched the marker. HA HA HA!

Joy'nt glanced at Picka. She had no eyes, of course, but her squared-off eyeholes could be expressive. "Now give our history, briefly."

"I am Picka Bone, son of Marrow Bones and Grace'l Ossein," Picka said. "This is my sister, Joy'nt. Our kind, the walking skeletons, originated in the dream realm of the gourd, but Esk Ogre found me on the Lost Path and brought me out to Xanth proper. So Marrow and Grace'l are no longer scary dream figures, but regular Xanth denizens. Marrow once accompanied Prince Dolph on an adventure. That was when he met Electra, and later married her, and they got the twin sisters Sorceresses Dawn and Eve. Later Marrow got half a soul, which he shared, so we have eighth souls. So we feel obliged to do some good in Xanth. We have wandered all around, but living humans tend to avoid our company, so we have been unable to do them much good. We agreed to watch this graveyard for a month so the zombies could take a break. This is our last day; we don't know what we'll do tomorrow, but hope it isn't too boring. Our hollow heads get easily bored." He made a little screwing motion with a bone finger, as if boring into his skull.

Woofer looked blank. Midrange looked disgusted. Tweeter fell over with melodic laughter.

Picka had given them his personal history. Did they really understand any of it? Did they care? How would they respond?

The cat touched the marker. A column of print appeared. Digested, it was this:

"We are three pets brought from Mundania by the

Baldwin family fifteen years ago. Our names are Woofer, Tweeter, and Midrange, as specified above. It seems the Baldwins liked music, so they named us after their speakers. We liked our family, but pets don't live forever in drear Mundania, so when we got old we migrated here, thanks to a dispensation from the Demon Xanth, for whom I once did a favor. Now we are back in our primes of life, but even a magic land can get dull, so we are looking for adventure. Woofer has a nose for that sort of thing, and he led us to this cemetery, and to this crypt. There is something interesting in there. But when Woofer went in, the stone fell down, trapping him. So we came to you to beg for help. You helped us, so we owe you a favor. What favor do you want, that we can do?"

Picka exchanged another eyeless glance with his sister. "We'd like to find something interesting to do tomorrow," she said.

"So would we," Midrange spelled out in the sand. "Maybe we all should share a great adventure."

"Agreed," Joy'nt said. "What adventure?"

"We hoped you would know," Midrange printed.

Picka tapped his skull with a knuckle. "Our empty heads are not great on ideas. In fact I'm not great on anything much. Joy'nt has the usual skeleton talent of disassembly and reformulation; she can form her bones into different configurations if she gets a good starting kick in the—" He caught his sister's warning glare. "Pelvis. But it doesn't work for me. I'm a defective skeleton. A complete nonentity, even among my own kind, which are not exactly live wires. So I'm not sure I'm even worthy of an adventure. But still I wish I could have one."

Tweeter flew across and landed on his shoulder bone. "Tweet!" he tweeted sympathetically.

"Thanks," Picka said. He was beginning to like the little bird.

Woofer woofed.

That reminded Picka. "What were you looking for in the crypt?"

Woofer wagged his tail and trotted back to the crypt. The others followed, Joy'nt lingering only long enough to recover her marker paper. The crypt was a large one, with room for them all. It had attracted the dog, who had the nose for adventure. There had to be something.

But Picka hung back. "We can't be sure what we'll find in there," he said. "Maybe the way that stone fell, sealing Woofer in, was a warning."

That made the others pause. "Yet it was open," Joy'nt said. "Whatever was inside could have escaped."

"Woof!"

"Woofer says no," Picka said. He was coming to understand these animals even without the marker paper.

"There should be a plaque on the entry stone," Joy'nt said. She looked around. "That must be it, fallen to the side. Maybe an ogre slapped at it in passing."

Picka went to look down at the flat stone. "Danger: Think Tank," he read.

"Think what?" Joy'nt asked.

"The stone is weathered," Picka said, "but that's what I read. Maybe it's an old storage tank."

"Then why bury it in a crypt in a graveyard?"

Picka shrugged with both his clavicles. "Maybe there's something dangerous in the tank, like a nest of nickel-pedes."

Even the animals dismissed that. Picka's hollow head sometimes produced empty notions.

Woofer tired of the dialogue. He went into the crypt, sniffing for the tank. The others had no choice but to follow, after making sure nothing else could collapse to trap them inside.

There in the back was a large machine with caterpillar treads and a gun barrel. Picka recognized it from descriptions of bad machines in the dream realm.

"I thought those monsters were imaginary," Joy'nt murmured, awed. "No wonder they buried it."

"I understand such things actually exist in Mundania," Picka said. "Maybe this one escaped, got into Xanth, and someone put it away so it couldn't tear up our landscape."

"Well, now we know enough about it," Joy'nt said. "It is indeed dangerous. We'd better bury it again."

But Woofer was sniffing the tank. He found something on its back. It looked like an on-off switch.

"Don't touch that!" Picka cried, alarmed.

Too late. Woofer was already nosing the switch. It changed position with a brisk click.

The tank animated. A muted light came on somewhere inside. There was the sound of a motor running.

"I think we'd better get out of here," Joy'nt said, alarmed.

They scrambled out. The tank revved up its gears and followed.

"Maybe we should turn it off again," Picka said. "If we can."

"I'll do it," Joy'nt said. She ran toward the emerging tank.

Its turret turned. Its cannon oriented on her.

"Watch out!" Picka cried.

Joy'nt threw herself to the ground just as the cannon fired. An oddly shaped ball of light zapped toward her, touching the back of her skull as she dropped.

Tweeter flew toward the tank, going for the switch. The cannon oriented on him and fired again. The bulb-shaped ball caught the tip of a wing, and Tweeter spun out of control.

By the time they got reorganized, the tank was crashing out of the graveyard and into the surrounding forest. It was too late to stop it.

They compared notes. Neither Joy'nt nor Tweeter

seemed to have been hurt, just disconcerted by the strikes. "Those light balls the tank fired," Picka said. "They looked like bulbs." Then he realized what it meant. "For ideas! It's a *think* tank. It makes people think of ideas."

This time Midrange and Woofer exchanged glances. Midrange went to Joy'nt. She brought out the marker and set it down for him.

He touched it with a paw. "What's your idea, Tweeter?"

Tweeter flew down and put one foot on it. "Picka Bone must have a talent."

Midrange touched it again. "And yours, Joy'nt?"

"That we should visit Princess Eve, who knows all about anything that isn't alive, to ask her what Picka's talent is."

"They are friends of ours," Picka agreed. "We knew them as children; they were three years younger than us. But two years ago Princess Eve married the Dwarf Demon Pluto, and became the Mistress of Hades. She may not be in Xanth now."

"But her twin sister Dawn would know," Joy'nt said. "We can go to Castle Roogna and ask her where Eve is now."

Picka was intrigued. "Let's do it. It may not be much of an adventure, but I'd really like to know about my talent, if I have one."

"We'll go too," Midrange printed.

"Of course," Joy'nt agreed. She was an agreeable person. So was Picka, actually; he was very even tempered, and could get along with anyone who wasn't spooked by his appearance.

"Is there anything to eat? We're hungry."

"We skeletons don't need to eat; we're magical spooks," Picka said. "There's not much around the grave-yard. Just a few palm trees holding coco-nuts containing hot nut-flavored cocoa, and some mints. Pepper, astonish, fig—"

"We'll forage for ourselves," Midrange printed.

Next morning when the zombies returned they set out as a party of five. Picka knew that all of them were glad to be doing something, even if it wasn't much. It gave them the illusion of purpose.

The graveyard was off the beaten path—in fact, there wasn't even an *un*beaten path. This did not bother the skeletons or animals, but they were wary, because there were many dangers in backwoods Xanth.

Not that the walking skeletons had much to fear. Dragons tended to leave them alone because they weren't very edible; even the marrow in their bones was dry and tasteless. Most living creatures spooked at the very sight of them.

The three living animals were protected by an amicability spell put on them by Nimby, the donkey-headed dragon form of the Demon Xanth, so that other creatures meant them no harm. They could still get in trouble on their own, as Woofer had, but that was his own fault.

Still, Xanth could come up with surprises, so they were careful. They made their way toward the nearest enchanted path, not hurrying, because hurrying could attract more attention than they cared for. This was a bit circuitous, because none of them knew exactly where the nearest enchanted path was.

Woofer, always sniffing things ahead, woofed. He was good at woofing. That meant he had found something halfway interesting. They went in that direction.

They came across a standing woman facing away from them. "Hello," Picka called. It was better that a stranger hear his voice first, so she wouldn't be as startled by his form.

The woman did not answer or move.

Joy'nt tried. "Hello. Can you tell us where the nearest enchanted path is?"

Still no answer. Then they caught up and saw the woman's front side. She was a metal statue!

"Woof," Woofer repeated in an I-told-you-so tone.

They inspected the statue at close range. It was solid iron, a marvelous image of a bare young human woman. Picka was not into bare human women, but did understand that this one was extremely well formed. He reached out to brush a fallen leaf from her conic left breast.

"Eeeee!" she squealed.

Picka fell back, startled. "You're alive?" he asked.

"I'm animated, like you," she said. "I'll thank you not to paw me."

"I can't paw you," he protested. "I have no paws."

She turned her head with a certain squeakiness. "You make no bones about it," she agreed.

"Who are you, and what are you doing here?" Joy'nt asked.

"I am the Iron Maiden, a statue animated by an ancient Magician King."

"He animated a statue?" Picka asked, amazed. "Why?"

"I never was quite clear on that. He simply said I was statuesque. But he was good to me; he had me sleep every night in his bed while he cuddled me. I told him the stork would never deliver to a statue, but he kept trying. I suppose he didn't want to be unkind to me, so he pretended it didn't matter. He was a very generous man."

It occurred to Picka that the old king might not actually have wanted the stork to pay attention, but he decided not to argue the case. "What happened then?"

"Finally he died, and his wife kicked me out and banished me from the castle. I don't know why she was so mean. I have been wandering in the wilderness ever since. It gets dull, so sometimes I pause and sleep."

"We wish you well," he said. "Do you know where the nearest enchanted path is?"

"What's an enchanted path?"

It occurred to Picka that the Iron Maiden was a bit out of touch, but again he decided to let it be. She might have napped for a long time; there was rust on her joints. "Never mind. Thank you for your time."

"You are welcome," she said. "If you happen to encounter any other man who would like someone to share his bed, I have experience."

"We'll do that," Joy'nt said briskly. For some reason she seemed impatient.

"Woof!"

"Woofer found a path!" Picka said.

They hurried to catch up to the dog. Sure enough, there was a crazy-looking path. It looped around trees, twisted across fallen logs, and seemed to be aimless. But it was a path, and surely went somewhere, so they decided to follow it.

Yet when Picka tried to put his foot on it, it writhed away from him. He tried again, and it retreated again. Joy'nt tried, and it avoided her also. This was a really odd path!

Then they saw a man walking along the path without difficulty. "How do you do that?" Picka called to him. "We can't touch the path."

The man looked at him. "I think I'm getting crazier by the minute," he remarked. "You look exactly like a walking skeleton."

"I *am* a walking skeleton."

"Now even my hallucinations are talking back. Well,

I'll treat you just as if you are real. This is the Psycho Path. Only crazy folk can use it. You may not be real, but neither are you crazy, so you're out of luck."

Now it was making crazy sense. A crazy path for crazy people. No wonder they couldn't use it. "Thank you," Picka called as the man wandered away.

It was getting dark. "We'll never find our way in the night," Joy'nt complained. "We'd better make camp, and find something for our friends to eat."

That was right: the animals needed food and rest, even if skeletons didn't. They located a glade with a blanket tree, and fashioned several blankets into a warm nest. Then they scouted for a pie plant. But when they returned with slices of pizza and quiche, the blankets were gone. The animals hadn't done it; they were out scouting for water.

There were some drag marks indicating the direction the blankets had gone. Someone had taken them. They went in that direction, and soon discovered a man sleeping on the pile of blankets.

"You took our blankets!" Picka said indignantly.

The man opened an eye. "What?"

"Those are our blankets!"

"I don't know what you're talking about. I found these here."

"You dragged them here. See the drag marks."

"Maybe someone dragged them here before I came. People are always accusing me of stealing. I don't know why."

Again, there was something odd. "Let's introduce ourselves. I am Picka Bone, and this is my sister Joy'nt."

"I am Rob."

Joy'nt angled her head in the way she had when she got an idea. "What is your magic talent, Rob?"

"I have no idea."

"Could it relate to your name? Rob?"

"I don't know what you're talking about," Rob repeated. "All I know is neither men nor women seem to like me much. I don't care about the men, but I'd really like to meet a friendly woman."

They let him be. Apparently Rob robbed people without knowing it.

Then Picka got an idea. "The Iron Maiden has nothing to lose," he murmured. "She's bare."

"And lonely," Joy'nt agreed. She faced Rob. "Follow that crazy path," she said. "I'm sure you can use it. It will lead you to a lovely maiden in need of company."

"That sounds great," Rob agreed. He got off the pile of blankets and went to the nearest twist of the path. He stepped on it. Sure enough, it worked for him. Soon he was walking purposefully toward the spot where they had left the Maiden.

"I think we just did a couple of lonely people a good deed," Picka said.

"And we got our blankets back," she agreed.

They hauled their blankets back to the original spot. Then Joy'nt dislocated her bones and formed them into a roughly block-shaped framework. Picka heaved the largest blanket over the top, forming a tent. Joy'nt caught hold of the edges with her fingers and pulled them taut. Picka folded the other blankets and placed them on the ground inside the tent. It was ready.

The three animals returned, their foraging finished. They paused at the sight of the tent.

"The tent is for you," Picka said. "So you can sleep comfortably for the night. Joy'nt made the framework and I put the blankets on. We thought you'd prefer a bit of shelter, after being out in the forest so long. It's safe; we skeletons don't sleep, so I'll be keeping watch for any mischief."

Surprised, the three checked it. Then Woofer and Mid-range settled down beside each other on the blanket, and Tweeter perched comfortably on Joy'nt's skull. "Tweet!" he tweeted appreciatively.

Darkness closed in. Picka could see well enough without light, as most nightmare spooks could. He and his sister were not in the bad-dream business, despite their ancestry, but their nature remained.

In fact being a walking skeleton was a rather lonely business. There were no others of their kind in Xanth proper, as far as they knew, apart from their parents, which meant that he and Joy'nt were doomed to remain single and have no families. They hated that, but had no choice. They were technically monsters, not wanted around living folk. They made do, but at quiet times like this Picka had occasion to be bothered by it, and he knew Joy'nt felt much the same.

He heard a rumble. It was from the sky. He knew what that meant: Cumulo Fracto Nimbus, Xanth's meanest cloud, had somehow spied the tent and intended to ruin it with a good soaking.

Picka scrambled into motion. He had seen a tarpaulin tree near the blanket tree. He ran to it, harvested a waterproof tarp, and ran back to fling it over the tent. "Better get under cover," he warned Tweeter. The bird quickly fluttered down into the tent.

Fracto arrived and was furious at being balked. He loosed a drenchpour that instantly soaked the tent and formed a puddle around it. Picka hastily fetched a stick and dug a trench around and away from the tent so that the water could not swamp it. They had pitched the tent on a small rise, so that helped. Fracto sent fierce gusts of wind, but Joy'nt kept firm hold on the edges of the tarp.

Fracto raged, but couldn't take out the tent. Finally he stormed off, defeated.

In the morning the three pets emerged, dry and rested.

Picka pulled off tarp and blanket, and Joy'nt disjointed and reformed in her normal shape.

Tweeter flew to her shoulder and tweeted. She brought out the marker, and Tweeter touched it. "We are getting to like you."

"We like you too," she said.

They gave the animals time to forage and take care of whatever natural functions were necessary for living forms. Then they set off again. This time they came across an enchanted path. That made the rest of their journey easy.

They encountered a man walking the opposite way. He was juggling three balls of light. They paused to watch.

After a moment he noticed. The light balls vanished. "Are my eyes deceiving me, or are you walking skeletons?" he inquired. "We don't see many like you on the enchanted path, but I know you don't mean any harm."

"We are skeletons," Picka agreed. "I am Picka Bone, and this is my sister Joy'nt. Plus Woofer, Midrange, and Tweeter. We are going to Castle Roogna."

"It's not far," the man agreed. "I am Aaron. My talent is to make balls of light." He smiled. "They are easy to juggle, because they weigh very little."

"We noticed," Joy'nt said.

"Good luck in your visit," Aaron said. A light ball appeared in his hand. He tossed it up, and another appeared. He tossed that, and a third appeared. He resumed walking, juggling the three.

"Which is the thing about the enchanted paths," Joy'nt said. "No harmful creature can get on one, so travelers know they are safe, and don't freak out at the sight of us."

"That does make it easier," Picka agreed.

Soon they met another traveler. Like the other, he seemed slightly taken aback by their appearance, but not really concerned. "Hello. I am Champion. It is my talent to lend strength of body, substance, or character. But you folk don't look as if you need any of that."

"We don't," Picka agreed, and introduced the members of their party. "I hope I have a talent, and that I can find out what it is."

"I regret I can't help you there," Champion said.

"Do you know something?" Picka said as they moved on. "Normal human beings seem like nice folk."

"We just never got to know many," Joy'nt said. "They were too busy screaming."

"Even though we have left the bad-dream business behind," he agreed. "In fact we never indulged in it. I wish I could somehow have a normal relationship with regular people. But that seems unlikely."

"We are what we are," she agreed somewhat sadly.

When they approached Castle Roogna, three animals intercepted them: a dog, a bird, and a cat.

But Picka had seen such tricks before. "Hello, Princesses," he said. "We are looking for Princess Dawn."

The animals formed into three blossoming fifteen-year-old girls, almost identical triplets. They all wore little gold crowns. "We knew that," Melody said. She wore a green dress, and had greenish-blond hair and blue eyes.

"We told her you were coming," Harmony said. She had a brown dress, hair, and eyes.

"She's already packed and ready to travel," Rhythm concluded. She had a red dress, red hair, and green eyes.

"But all we wanted was to ask her where—"

Princess Dawn arrived. She was twenty and as lovely as a morning sunrise. She hugged Joy'nt, then Picka, not at all put off by their form. They were, after all, friends from childhood. "It can't be told," she said. "My sister values her privacy. I'll show you the way." She glanced around, then dropped to her knees to pet Woofer, stroke

Midrange, and lift a finger for Tweeter to perch on. They had evidently met before.

Then Dawn walked purposefully into the orchard. They followed. So simply, they were on their way again.

TOR

Voted

#1 Science Fiction Publisher
20 Years in a Row

by the *Locus* Readers' Poll

———•———

Please join us at the website below
for more information about this
author and other science fiction,
fantasy, and horror selections, and to
sign up for our monthly newsletter!

www.tor-forge.com